THE WILD
IS ALWAYS THERE

THE
WILD IS
ALWAYS
THERE

Canada Through the Eyes of Foreign Writers

Edited by Greg Gatenby

VINTAGE BOOKS

A Division of Random House of Canada

VINTAGE BOOKS CANADA EDITION, 1994

Copyright © by Greg Gatenby 1993

Canadian Cataloguing in Publication Data

Main entry under title:
The Wild is always there   :   Canada through
the eyes of foreign writers

Includes bibliographical references and index.
ISBN 0-394-28049-0

1. Canada — Description and travel.   I. Gatenby, Greg.

FC75.W55 1994   917.104'647   C93-095173-5
F1017.W55 1994

Printed and bound in Canada
10 9 8 7 6 5 4 3 2 1

Toronto, New York, London, Sydney, Auckland

For

F. V. and B.G.

It is this variety of landscape, weather and occupation in Canada that is to me her greatest charm. It is possible to live an urban and civilized life in one of her great cities and to forget how near the wild country is to your home. I remember that we once went to a skiing camp, and, as we walked through the trees onto the snow, I heard someone say, "there are no houses between us and the North Pole," and then someone else remarked that a bear had come down from the woods and devoured part of the contents of the camp store cupboard. We were not many miles from the governmental and diplomatic capital of Ottawa. The wild is always there, somewhere near....

"My Canada"
Susan Buchan, novelist and wife
of author John Buchan,
Governor General of Canada 1935-1940

Jack London, circa 1897–98. This is the only known photograph of the author in the Klondike. Courtesy of the Bancroft Library, University of California, Berkeley.

CONTENTS

INTRODUCTION

N OT LIKE Saint Paul on the road to Tarsus, but certainly with ferocity, I was struck by an epiphany on the nature and creation of literary history—who writes it, who are its makers, who decides its constituents—while having a tête-à-tête dinner with Morley Callaghan in 1978. The flash of insight was to change my life.

Morley was a Canadian novelist who had been an intimate of Ernest Hemingway, Scott Fitzgerald, Robert McAlmon, and many of the other English-language literary lights of Paris in the 1920s. He was already in his seventies when I first met him in 1975. At the dinner in 1978, Morley had been telling me about the places in Toronto he and Hemingway had haunted while both were reporters at the *Toronto Star*. From there, the conversation drifted to regaling talk of Edmund Wilson's difficulties with the American tax authorities and his week-long escapes to Morley's Toronto home for respite from the auditors. For some reason, this led to discussion of Morley's re-encounter with William Butler Yeats at the home of a grande dame of Toronto society. The memory egged on, no doubt, by a second helping of advocaat, Morley recalled for me his final meeting with John Dos Passos at a legendary Toronto bar.

From almost anyone else's mouth, such name-dropping at one sitting would have been silly, but Morley actually knew these authors well and was always willing to answer my questions about writers who had visited the city. As the Artistic Director of the Harbourfront Reading Series, I was—and am—responsible for bringing hundreds of creative writers to Toronto every year, so I had a keen professional interest in knowing which literary guests had been here earlier. But it was only at this particular dinner with Callaghan that I was sufficiently startled to realize that I must move, in my addresses with the city, from the passive to the active voice: rather than depend upon others to inform me of my city's literary history (a wait, I now realized, that could take decades), I would need to start researching and writing that history. A craving to rectify my ignorance, indeed to discover the reasons for my ignorance of my own city's literary history, coalesced as an epiphany: for the first time, I understood that I did not know that I did not know.

I suddenly discerned that when Morley Callaghan died, the details of his escapades in Toronto with Hemingway and many other authors would die with him. Because the literary recollections of Callaghan (and too many of our other senior writers) were not written down, within two generations those incidents would be irretrievably forgotten. It would be as if they had never happened. And I fathomed that the subsequent conviction that nothing of import had happened, that a vacuum existed—a Sahara of data—would lead to the coast-to-coast assumption among Canadians that they lacked an engaging history, certainly a fascinating literary history.

Alas, the conviction was usually uttered with that fervour unique to the ignorant; denied documentary evidence to the contrary, Canadians believed that they lived in a country which few foreign authors had ever visited. Even erudite Canadians thought that when such authors had visited, they had written nothing about Canada because nothing of interest was to be found here.

This absence of information perhaps explains in part why Canadians feel awkward in the face of internationally applauded excellence created by their fellow citizens: the act of excellence seems so singular, so rare, because it is not—and lacking texts to the contrary, cannot be—seen as part of a continuum.

Cultural history, for the English-speaking world at least, had been written and in some senses continues to be written in the powerful imperial centres of London and New York. The historians working in those centres, naturally enough, look for documents and records on which to base their assessments, but if a culture beyond their borders has been unable to record (or has been foolish enough to ignore) much of its literary history, then those historians will retreat to what they know: the literary history of England and America. Their history books are then sent to the colonies, and the contrast between the seeming richness of the foreign metropolis and the apparent poverty of their own history merely reinforces the colonials' assumption regarding the gross (indeed, for them, shameful) inadequacy of their cultural legacy.

Full of rage at unseen powers denying my compatriots their past, I determined at that dinner, with just a touch of righteousness, and a *soupçon* of good intention, to write the literary history of my city. Being young, I presumed the task would take but a few months. A decade and a half later, my research still continues, with the knowledge that I have much literary ore yet to mine.

I soon discovered that there were many eminent novelists, playwrights, and poets from abroad, beyond those cited by Callaghan, who had visited the city. Initially, I ignored their comments on places other than Toronto, but eventually their observations on all regions of Canada came to interest me as much as (and in many cases were more penetrating than) their comments on the country's biggest city. After some hesitation, I decided to put the literary history of Toronto in abeyance, in order to first produce what seemed far more pressing: a history and anthology of writing by foreign authors about the entire nation of Canada.

From the beginning of my labour, I chose to seek only the commentary of authors traditionally referred to as "creative writers," that is, authors of at least one book of fiction, poetry, or drama written for adults. I did this not because I wished to denigrate the literary accomplishments of those who write what we clumsily call in English "non-fiction." Rather, I circumscribed my research, first, because by professional training I know the world of creative writing best; secondly, because I soon sensed that, even with such restrictions, the pool of authors from whom I could draw would be huge; and thirdly, because I believe it is the work of creative writers which ages best, and is what most people would want to read.

At last count, I have discovered more than 1,200 creative writers who have written about Canada in diaries, journals, journalism, correspondence, plays, poems, stories, and novels. The discovery was rarely easy. Canada has produced few literary biographers, while British and American biographers are lax, to put the matter generously, in citing Canadian items in their indexes—even when the country has been seminal to their subjects.

This embarrassment of riches presents for the anthologist the problem of selection, of course. In this volume I have included authors whose lives were dramatically changed by visits to Canada; for the sake of pacing and bemusement, these are contrasted with the comments of writers for whom Canada was but a stopover. I have tried to give the reader a sense of the large time frame over which literary comments on Canada have been spread, and the inclusion of French authors will remind us that not all literary visitors were native speakers of English. Sober texts have been interspersed with the humorous. Many of these texts are here published for the first time, or for the first time in book form, or for the first time in more than a century.

I debated the merits and demerits of various methods for organizing the excerpts: chronological, geographical, alphabetical. None seemed satisfactory. Finally, it was decided that the best method would be to organize the material in such a way that someone reading the text from cover to cover would encounter a range of opinions on all parts of the country, but that the organization, while patterned, would not be linear. Rather, one would read the book as one sees a constellation in the night sky, or as one "reads" a painting: the gaze moves from an initial comprehensive impression to a viewing of smaller sections, the perusal settling from time to time on specific points, before departure is taken with an overall look. It is also my hope that such organization of material will induce Canadians to read the comments of foreigners on parts of the country other than the one in which they reside.

The very number of authors and the multiplicity of their comments prohibit me from extracting many generalizations regarding what they say about Canada. However, a few observations are pervasive.

The most unexpected discovery was that the preponderance of literary visitors did not like Canada. They loved Canada. They were overwhelmed by its spectacular uniqueness. Having been taught that I lived in a cultural desert uninteresting to sophisticated foreign folk, this was the biggest, and most pleasant surprise of my research.

Common to almost all the writing—sometimes it is an intimation, sometimes it is overt—is a befogged sense of the immensity of the nation. Every Canadian has had the experience of meeting a foreign tourist who has failed to adjust his or her sense of distance to the Canadian calibration, and in these pages one smiles to see authors slowly gleaning that the word "beyond" in Canada can mean thousands of miles. But unlike the average tourist, these literary visitors strive to see both the foreground and the horizon. In looking "beyond" the Canadian town where duty or travel has taken them, they are ever alert to a looming wilderness of a savage purity and Promethean scale which, until they had come to this country, they had not imagined possible.

Certainly for many foreign writers it is the colossal wilderness surrounding the little bastions of human habitation which most compels them to record their thoughts. People born in this country know that our wilderness is not sylvan; rather it can kill. As Northrop Frye has perspicaciously argued, our literature is replete with images reflecting a garrison mentality—we enter the wilderness in search of riches, yes, but at once build palisades behind which to hide, to seek shelter, to keep Nature at bay. Foreign literary visitors, by contrast, have but the merest inkling of the power of our wilderness, and partly because of this miscalculation, and partly because they know their stay is short, they find the danger of our wilderness tantalizing. For them, travelling from lecture to lecture or from urban site to tailored tourist attraction, a consciousness that the wild is always there exists, certainly, but actual experience of Canadian Nature with all its terror is, for most of these writers, rare. So, unaware of its true force, they take a delight in our wilderness that is like ours in a roller-coaster: the danger is piquant, even attractive, because we don't really believe it can hurt.

An optimism about the future of Canada marbles many of these extracts; generally, the optimism is for our material improvement. In the most blatant cases, there is chin-dropping awe at the stupendousness of our natural resources: minerals, wood, water. The Victorian and Edwardian authors in particular were more generous than their Canadian counterparts in predicting great accomplishments by the people and the nation. While they can be galling in their imperial assumptions, these same writers reckoned as easily dismissed phantoms the matters (for example, language disputes, huge geographical distances) which less secure Canadians saw as impediments to national harmony.

British authors were apt, more than American, to explore more widely in Canada. Perhaps they wished to see as much as possible because they had travelled so far, and subsequent visits could be managed only with difficulty. In contrast, American visitors, usually with a better grasp of our geography, saw Canada less as a single nation to be explored and more as a mosaic of regions.

The Canadian bristle at being confused with Americans has little justification within these pages (or the many still to be published). No matter what the national origin of the author, there is the proper realization that, the land being different, the people will be different. Some authors take longer than others to understand this, but that almost all do is a refreshing surprise. Indeed, the number of Americans who cherished Canada's separateness is, for today's reader, unexpected: Harriet Beecher Stowe, Henry Wadsworth Longfellow, and Willa Cather, for example, viewed Canada in near edenic terms, and even Henry James allowed that pause should be given to the loss of the quiddity that makes Canada unique.

Anyone who reads voluminously in the correspondence and

diaries of literary authors active before the Second World War will come to an awareness that attitudes to the use of racial epithets have gone through a sea-change. Only facile reasoners wish to ban such literature today, but it would be wrong not to point out the prevalent use of disparaging nomenclature and racist attitudes common to a disturbing amount of the writing about Canada—by the Edwardians and Victorians especially. Natives and blacks suffer this fate in particular and are casually described by several eminent writers as "savages" and "niggers." I have chosen to leave the terms as they appear in the original because they are part of the record, and their omission, while placating some sensibilities, would be a distortion of the true picture of how others have seen us. The offence is not limited to name-calling; distastefully frequently, the epithets are clarions of actual racialist beliefs. In some cases, this usage is uttered without overt malice, as the common coinage of the day. In other cases, their employment is more sinister and portentous. The excerpts of Charles Dickens and Arthur Conan Doyle are especially unsettling because they are revealing in this way.

Even when Canadian natives are described in heroic terms, a contemporary reader may be nagged by the feeling that one is encountering little more than the intellectual residue of Rousseau's Noble Savage. For other authors, Canada was a *tabula rasa* on which a new European culture could be written; the aboriginal inhabitants were merely unfortunate primitives impeding progress. This self-serving image was as useful to the imperialist cause in Canada as it was in India, South America, Africa and other industrially undeveloped lands.

That these images had wide currency in the imperial capitals is beyond question. The perceptions were given voice by respected authors, and with those *imprimaturs* did much to shape the paternalistic views held of natives (and concomitant government policies) whose consequences linger with us still. Canadians themselves, instructed by pedagogues enthralled by the authority of these noted authors, became conditioned to the falsehoods of what foreigners taught them rather than to the truths beheld by their own eyes.

As for the excerpts in this particular volume, I have strived to reflect in miniature what is available overall. Readers will observe that most of the material is written by men, a reflection both of the history of publishing, and the history of our culture: it was generally easier for men to travel, especially to rugged places, and economics certainly made it easier for men to write about their travels and publish the results. The book contains work by people who are famous still, and others who had a critical respectability in their time which, depending upon academic fashion, may have flagged or waxed. The mélange of fiction and poetry with diaries and letters reflects the variety of means by which authors chose to write about Canada. More authors wrote about the eastern half of the nation than the western, mirroring the history of the country's conquest by Europeans, as well as the relative ease with which a literary tourist could visit an eastern city rather than, for instance, a prairie town.

Some excerpts are short because the authors were brief but trenchant. Some are longer because the writing, while superb, is generally unknown, or the authors are widely known but their writing about Canada is not.

Regardless of length, each excerpt had to be genuinely Canadian, that is, no matter how mistaken in fact, genuinely about Canada. Just as *Hamlet* has little content peculiar to Denmark, and could have been set by Shakespeare in any other land, so too have some authors used Canada merely as a cipher; such writing has not been included in this volume.

It is not my aim to make inflated boasts like a provincial booster, or to make grandiose claims for the influence of Canada beyond what the evidence indicates. However, if the book forces other literary historians and biographers, Canadian and foreign, to re-evaluate their neglect of Canada and its relative importance to their subjects, then an overdue plateau in the international study of our history will have been attained.

What follows is an awesome and frequently scintillating series of perceptions of Canada and her peoples by some of the most famous writers of the Western world. Defenders of Canadian culture will be intrigued, for example, by Mark Twain's calumny of our publishers (whose piracy was so severe that Twain came within a hair of never publishing *Tom Sawyer!*) Many readers, I hope, will be touched by the authors whose lives were transformed by Canada: Algernon Blackwood's metamorphosis, for instance, from remittance man to mature adult is fetchingly, sometimes achingly recounted below, while Willa Cather's discovery of French Canada reads almost like a religious conversion. The connections between Canada and Sherlock Holmes are noted in this book but I suspect that it is Arthur Conan Doyle's belief in the superior ether of Winnipeg and its ability to convey the table-knockings from the spirit world which will strike the reader as more "elementary." Winnipeg, rather than the Yukon, is also featured in one of the funniest sections of this anthology: Jack London's interrogation by the "bulls" of Manitoba. That two of the Victorian world's most famous authors, Charles Dickens and Wilkie Collins, collaborated on a work set almost entirely in Canada remains one of the shocks of my research; the melodrama moved men to tears, and had consequences for Dickens' personal life which were devastating. It is a pleasure to remind readers of Mark Strand's and Elizabeth Bishop's connections to Canada; certainly this country has inspired both authors to some of their best work. That a Canadian features in grand opera astonishes many of my compatriots; that the composer is Rossini and that the work has never before been translated into English compounds the amazement. Everyone seems to know that Ernest Hemingway lived in Canada. But the details of his residence are not well known; indeed, distortions of the facts have much wider distribution than the truth, although the latter, given here, is far more compelling, and flattering to Canadians. I have found that my countrymen are staggered to discover that William Faulkner lived in Toronto for half a year. They are even more stunned to learn, true though it be, that his time in Canada was probably the most important of his life. The evidence stems from Faulkner's own pen, and is included in these pages.

Just as these authors have discovered their own Canada, then have left with their perceptions and prejudices modified or even overturned, I invite the reader to discover authors of old acquaintance in a new land, invite the reader to be prepared to have feelings bumped, perceptions retailored, and strange vistas, literary and geographical, exhilaratingly divulged. Like a dull night sky suddenly made startlingly alive when seen through a telescope, these authors offer Canadians unusual, even amazing prospects, sometimes silly, sometimes brilliant, and always challenging.

Greg Gatenby
August, 1993

WILLIAM
FAULKNER

WHILE William Faulkner's time (1897–1962) in Canada was relatively brief—he lived in Toronto for half a year in 1918—his Canadian stay was to prove galvanizingly alchemical: from the very spelling of his name to the subject matter of much of his fiction, his stay in Canada witnessed—indeed begat—a metamorphosis so transfiguring, the six months in Canada are generally regarded as the most important days of his life.

Like most young men entering adulthood during the First World War, Faulkner believed that the military pilot's life was the most glamorous, sexy, and devoutly to be craved. In Oxford, Mississippi, his hometown, the crudities of war were too far away to be real, the miseries and squalor excised by distance. To Faulker and his contemporaries, even the battle-death of a war ace seemed cleaner, better, more noble, than that of an infantryman or sailor. But like an airplane slowing, circling before it lands, Faulkner took a roundabout route before settling to his goal.

A school dropout, spending his days drinking, writing poems, drifting from idleness to idleness, William Faulkner in 1918 finally found an inspiration to action. His childhood sweetheart, whom he had hoped to marry, had chosen for a husband someone with far better prospects. Hurt by this rejection and anxious to be away when the nuptials proceeded, Faulkner applied for service in the United

States Air Corps, but was rejected owing to his small height and weight. As the dreaded April wedding of his sweetheart quickly approached, he leapt at an invitation to visit an old friend, Phil Stone, at Yale University in Connecticut.

Here the presence of war was palpable: most of the students were enrolled in various officer militias, and the university had its own small artillery unit, the commanding officer of which was aided by two captains who were wounded veterans of the Canadian service. Faulkner met yet another Canadian at Yale, a recruiting officer named Lieutenant Todd who encouraged the boy from Mississippi to join up. Several of Phil Stone's other friends had seen action overseas; some had been wounded. These friends, on learning of Faulkner's desire to fly and to fight, urged Faulkner and Stone to forgo the American services and try for the most beguiling force of all, the Royal Flying Corps (or, as it was known as of April 1, 1918, the Royal Air Force). Stone chose the artillery, but Faulkner, his head already full of tales of dawn raids and daring flights by such legendary aces as the Canadian Billy Bishop, resolved to enlist with the most famous fighters of the day, the knights-errants of the air, the RAF.

Having already been rejected by his own country's military, Faulkner wanted to avoid any snafu escorting his entry into the military service of the British Empire. Therefore, according to more than one biographer, he planned his attack on the RAF recruiters as though it were an espionage campaign. Perhaps because he came from a small town, perhaps because he was young, perhaps because he was just badly informed, Faulkner believed (wrongly) that he had to be British to be eligible for the RAF. So, with coaching from an English friend of Stone's, Faulkner set about to lose his southern drawl and acquire the King's accent. This linguistic experiment lasted, hard as it is to believe, for two full months, until mid-June 1918, when Faulkner travelled to New York City convinced he was ready to deceive the officers at the recruiting depot. Or perhaps not quite convinced. No doubt his writer's ear, even at this early stage of his career, told him that this Pygmalian experiment might be fraught with danger, so to augment his authenticity as an Englishman he carried with him forged papers allegedly penned by a non-existent English vicar, the Reverend Twimberly-Thorndyke, stating that this chap Faulkner was a proper gentleman and the right sort for the RAF.

One can only imagine the response of the recruiting officer upon encountering this hybrid of nationalities and accents, but the officer must have had a generous disposition for he allowed Faulkner's application to stand. The young American was given three weeks to put his affairs in order before reporting to Toronto on July 9, 1918.

Upon arrival in Canada, Faulkner took the first conscious steps in his long-desired self-transformation. He would now create fictions and illusions—with himself as principal subject. Most telling of these early transmogrifications (and, no doubt in order to appear more British) was the change in the spelling of his name: before Canada, he was as his parents had named him, Billy Falkner; in Canada, and for the rest of his life, he adopted the traditional Canadian spelling of his last name; henceforth he would be known only as William Faulkner.

On the day of his arrival in Toronto he wrote breathlessly to his mother:

Toronto
Tuesday, 9 July [1918]

Mother darling—

This certainly is an English place—London "Bobbies" with their capes and high conical hats and no one here is in a hurry as are cities in the states. These people are wonderful to me. There was a Canadian—who has seen three years of war—at the station to meet incipient aviators, the porters and bellboys dont take tips from us. This is a place full of short crooked streets and old houses, and soldiers everywhere—Canadian infantry men some of whom seem to be forty years old with bushy mustaches. No wonder the Huns don't like them. We passed the flying camp on the train this morning. It is Longbranch, on Lake Ontario, which looks like the sea, excepting you can see the

United States across it.... I am sending you and Dad flags. The Canadian service flag has a maple leaf in it—a live leaf, and when it begins to turn crimson, it is very pretty.

Within a week, he was issued a uniform. In itself, this might seem inconsequential, but it brought him, for the first time in his life, into an organization replete with the honour, tradition, and class-consciousness that Faulkner felt was appropriate to his needs and station. These days marked his first and most enduring contact with foreign culture, and the big city of Toronto, the hubbub of war, and the reality of wider, even global, horizons, all combined to impress him powerfully. For the rest of his life, he had an affection for tweeds, pipes, riding to the hounds—the obvious manifestations of the English gentry.

Ten days later, the young cadet, clearly excited by the new world opening before him, had the wit to give a good sense of the Toronto of the day:

Toronto
Friday, 19 June [1918]

Dear Mother and Dad—

They certainly have attractive weather here, its just cool enough to wear a light sweater, and terribly clear. Every where I look I see planes from the flying schools. This is a great fruit growing country, orchards every where. Every thing here is much cheaper. Last night I had leave until Midnight and down town I got some pork, mashed potatoes, macaroni au gratin and peaches and cream and tea for 75¢. This place is about twice as big as Memphis. Some wonderful homes here. The streets are wide and there is no hurry. They have very English signs here—Nichols, Nichols and Nichols; Barristers, they never say lawyer. I went last night and heard Sousa's band. The streets here are full of soldiers and I am kept saluting all the time. They are very strict about this. We must value the uniform. There are wounded of all descriptions here—Scotch in kilts, French, Canadians, English....

The above letter hints at the old army adage Hurry Up And Wait. During the waiting, from the letters he sent and received, it is obvious that Faulkner read an extraordinary amount in Canada.

Following three weeks of drill and tests, Faulkner was transferred to Long Branch, a suburb of Toronto, for full basic training. The squadrons were housed in tents, the flimsiness of which, as winter approached, began to modify Faulkner's high opinion of our climate. Nonetheless, he continued to hold Canadians themselves in high regard. On July 23rd, he wrote again to his mother that "These Canadians are wonderful to me. So easy to get along with. They are very unselfish and good natured." Long Branch agreed with Faulkner. In a letter home, dated July 28th, he described the move:

> They had special cars for us, and so we went through Toronto singing *Pack Up Your Troubles in Your Old Kit Bag* and *Where Do We Go From Here*. We got to Long Branch, loaded down like pack mules and were inspected again.
>
> This camp is on the bank of Lake Ontario and so we go swimming in the lake every day. It's very pretty to see the big lake steamers going up and down. I have a tent with two other cadets and a bed—BED—to sleep on. I've been sleeping on a board so much I couldn't sleep at all the first night....

That Faulkner was very much a Southerner and not an Englishman is borne out by his declarations in correspondence that he was cold and wore sweaters in the middle of a Toronto August! While wearing his uniform over his sweater, he told his mother, he would let his mind wander, his imagination formulating tales:

> I wish you could see the lake. I sit and look out over it and imagine I see Indian canoes going up and down, and deer and moose coming down and swimming out into the sunset, or fleets of

bateaux filled with the soldiers of the Marquis de Montcalm going down to Champlain, with the French and Huron scouts flashing back and forth. In the morning at sunrise, the lake is pink. It's easy then to imagine you see thin spirals of smoke from wigwams in front of which some befeathered warrior is making his prayers to the sun.

The nights here are wonderful. There are lots of trees, that look like poured ink, with stiff, sharp pine trees, as though they had been cut from paper and stuck upon the sky. We see wild geese nearly every sunset. It's queer to be here and think of what this old lake has carried upon it. The Hurons and Iroquois fought all about here. I am acquiring the prettiest mahogany color you ever saw. I'll look like a pair of fashionable shoes soon.

In late September, Faulkner was transferred to the School of Aeronautics at Wycliffe College, the dormitory of which had been seconded by the University of Toronto to the Air Force as a barracks for officer cadets. Faulkner was scheduled to spend six weeks at the school, learning gunnery, bombing, flight theory, aircraft construction, and the myriad other matters vital to a pilot's training on the ground. Up to this point in his letters, there had been no hint of impatience with the speed of his military education, although it would have been only after his arrival in Canada that he realized the immensity of the schooling needed to be a pilot—indeed, anxious as he was to shoot down the Hun, he quickly came to see that he would have to complete a full year of classroom studies before he would even fly in an airplane.

In addition to his studies at the main campus of the University of Toronto, Faulkner and his fellow cadets were sometimes sent to study engines at the aerodrome in a nearby suburb called Leaside. It was here that his itch to fly would have been most tantalized, for he could watch students only a few months further along in their studies than he soaring into the air under the tutelage of instructors, or could watch students, even more privileged, flying solo. The itch would lead to the composition of his first published prose, excerpted below.

Despite what must have been deep frustration at the aeon it was taking for him to get into the air, he found time to write to his mother almost every second day. Descriptions of Toronto sites pepper almost every missive. On August 18th he wrote, "It is perfect weather up here, crisp and clear and cold as time at night. The summer is over, and last night we could see the Aurora Borealis. It certainly looked queer, like a search light. It didn't flicker at all, and about half-way up the sky we could see the shadow of the flat end of the earth at the pole." On October 3rd, he continued, "Dad would be crazy about this country, everything is so pretty now, almost as colorful as our falls, and it lasts so much longer."

It is about this time that Faulkner's first fiction was written—not in the sense that that word is usually used, but in the sense that he was trying to tell truths by augmenting realities. In his autumn letters to his family, he makes veiled but certain reference to sharing rides with unnamed pilots ("I am watching for better weather, so I can get my friend at the flying camp to take me up again,") but according to those with whom he shared rooms at Wycliffe College, it was impossible that a student at their level could have sneaked onto an airplane for an illicit ride. Perhaps Faulkner imagined these flights (literally flights of fancy) as an antidote to the gravity of his terrestrial training in October and November.

Further fiction came in his assessment of his language skills. Given the melange of accents he was affecting, his claims that he was commonly mistaken for a Quebecois stretch credulity. Yet in more than one letter home, he maintained the misconception was frequent: "The people up here all think that I am French, from Montreal, for some reason." On October 14th he wrote:

I have lots of fun with the French Canadians here. They usually think I am French, and I can walk up to any of them with a cigarette and say—"voulez vous la ses allume?" and they take me up at once. I don't last long, however, but it's great sport while it lasts.

The influenza epidemic prevalent throughout the continent that year did not spare Toronto, but to spare the cadets, the authorities ordered the classes in aeronautics suspended and the students quarantined on campus, except for forced marches intended to maintain their vigour. Thus, an already lengthy training period on the ground was now made indefinitely, painfully tedious, this extension itself further exacerbated by the looming (and to Faulkner horrible) possibility that the success of the Allies overseas might lead to a cessation of hostilities before he could earn his wings. And on November 11, 1918, that is exactly what happened. Two days after Armistice, Faulkner, putting on a brave face, continued his falsehoods in a letter to his mother: "Of course we are all glad that the fighting is over, but I am certainly glad it lasted long enough for me to get a pilot's licence which I can do quite easily now."

On December 8, 1918, Faulkner left Canada by train for his hometown of Oxford, Mississippi. Almost every detail of the train's journey would be used in the opening pages of his 1926 novel, *Soldier's Pay*.

Despite his angry, impetuous claim that he had nothing but a weight gain to show for his time in Canada, Faulkner knew in his bones that the period had been seminal. It was while in this country, at first tentatively and then with bravura, that he learned to reshape events so that their narrative was compelling and their insights genuinely fresh. Disappointment at not learning to fly, for example, was transformed by Faulkner into splendour and greatness. While other cadets might be content to return home in civilian clothes as regulations demanded, William Faulkner ordered a full pilot's uniform from the nation's finest military tailor, William Scully of Montreal. The uniform, which it was illegal for him to wear, of course, consisted of a handsome jacket, Sam Browne belt, peaked cap, stylish trench coat, and swagger stick. To these he added wings (purportedly obtained at a pawn shop on Queen Street), a lieutenant's pips, and a shoulder patch indicating he had seen service in the Royal Flying Corps and, by implication, had been active overseas. And, for the balance of his life, he kept, in the manner of the great war aces, a

William Faulkner in full RAF uniform, December 1918. Note the pilot wings (to which he was not entitled) on his left breast, the veteran's jaunty angle to his officer's cap, and the cane to overcome his "war wound." Courtesy of the Canadian War Museum, Ottawa.

good luck charm in his pocket: a Canadian coin. What the King's minions had failed to provide, Faulkner himself would supply. But just as he had felt a last-minute need to augment his credentials when enlisting, he now felt an eleventh-hour necessity to enhance his return: stepping off the train in Mississippi, Faulkner, not content to be merely impressive in the fetching uniform of an RAF officer, also affected a cane and, outlandishly, a limp, the disability the result, he told his immediately worried and sympathetic family, of a daring flight and its unfortunate conclusion, a crash. Later, to his brother Murry Falkner, he embellished the tale:

> "The war quit on us before we could do anything about it. The same day they lined up the whole class, thanked us warmly for whatever it was they figured we had done to deserve it, and announced that we would be discharged the next day, which meant that we had the afternoon to celebrate the Armistice and some planes to use in doing it. I took up a rotary-motored Spad with a crock of bourbon in the cockpit, gave diligent attention to both, and executed some reasonably adroit chandelles, an Immelman or two, and part of what could easily have turned out to be a nearly perfect loop." "What do you mean—part of a loop?" I asked. He chuckled and replied, "That's what it was; a hangar got in the way and I flew through the roof and ended up hanging on the rafters."

To other friends and family, the story of (and the results of) the crash in Toronto varied substantially in details, including a broken nose, and the insertion of a metal plate (later revised to a silver plate) into his skull. The significance of these variant tellings has been noted best by one of Faulkner's principal biographers, Frederick Karl:

> This proliferation of stories, deceptions and outright lies foreshadows what Faulkner would be as a novelist. He was continuous in his methods. This overlapping of stories, some of them

close to the truth, some outrageous, link with his strategies of relaying information in his major novels. A tale which is told is retold in manifold ways, until the original story has vanished, and what remains is an elaboration which may or may not be close to the truth. That "elaboration" was for Faulkner in his fiction an impression, the closest we can get to truth. This was, in many respects, the strategy he devised for his own life, once he decided to re-create himself. Once he activated his imagination, he discovered both a life and a fictional method which held for much of his career.

What is unusual about Faulkner's lifelong descriptions of his Canadian experience is the degree to which he appeared to believe his own fictions after his return to the United States. He had himself photographed in his uniform and wore it on every public occasion imaginable (partly accounted for by the fact, according to a sibling, that the uniform made him immensely popular with the belles of Mississippi) and he even wore his tunic while playing golf. He affected his limp well into the 1920s, and made little or no effort to correct the increasingly flattering tales of his war record. He wore his officer's trench coat until it practically fell from his shoulders, then ordered another, and another, and another, long after they went out of style, such was his desire to appear to be what time and the Armistice had denied. The distortion of truth reached an apex of sorts when he was interviewed for *The New Yorker* in 1931; he told the august periodical that he had joined the Canadian Air Force in 1915, had been sent to France, had crashed behind his own lines, and was suspended in his plane upside down with two broken legs before an ambulance reached him. Faulkner maintained that one of the ambulance men said, "He's dead all right," at which point Faulkner was able to, albeit meekly, contradict him. He then, piling untruth upon falsehood, told *The New Yorker* that following this crash he had regained his health, and had decided to resign his commission with the Canadians in order to join the air force of the United States.

Faulkner had gleaned enough vocabulary from his aeronautics

classwork, and had gathered enough knowledge of the essentials of flying from the RAF ether enveloping Toronto, that he was able to write convincingly in fiction (and probably bluff his landlubber friends) of the perils of being airborne. But as for actually being able to pilot a plane, he was now nothing but the great impostor. In the months immediately following his return from Canada, he had no need to prove himself. But as opportunities to take the controls of aircraft presented themselves, he was forced to rely increasingly on yet more fictions to explain his inability to take the controls. Eventually, he settled on the legend that the crash in Toronto had caused him to lose his nerve, and this condition (along with the alleged plate in his head and his allegedly gimpy leg) no doubt abetted the sympathy which accompanied his increasingly excessive drinking. William Faulkner was not to fly solo, in fact, until 1933. Even then he convinced his pilot-instructor that he had needed the fifteen-year interval (since his return from Canada) to regain his nerve. Such an explanation had the additional merit of explaining his faulty acquaintanceship with the cockpit controls. Having finally learned to fly, Faulkner soon boasted to at least one friend that he was flying bootleg whisky from Canada into the United States—highly unlikely, and more probably just another half-credible claim to the *élan* of being an aviator.

The Canadian experience, however, did more than feed the quirks of his personal habits. Much more. He was to call upon his time in Toronto over and over in his published fiction. Although he might change the venue of a war scene or a pilot's daring (as he did in stories such as "Death Drag," "All the Dead Pilots," "Ad Astra," "Turnabout," "With Caution and "Dispatch," and "Thrift," and in novels such as *Soldier's Pay*, *Flags in the Dust*, *A Fable*), it was from his time in Canada that he derived those details which gave the stories their verisimilitude. As one noted critic has remarked, "The war turned Billy into a storyteller, a fictionist, which may have been the decisive turnabout of his life."

Faulkner's time in Canada had a different impact on two of his best novels, *The Sound and the Fury* and *Absalom, Absalom!* Both books have overlapping characters, and one of them, Shreve, appears briefly in the first and substantially in the second. That Shreve is Canadian may seem, at first glance, relatively inconsequential, of no more import than the author declaring him to be, let us say, left-handed. But on reflection, it is aesthetically absolutely vital that Shreve be Canadian, for he proves to be the neutral chorus to the Sutpen tragedy related in both books. Shreve, the Canadian, being an outsider, is untainted by the Sutpen pollution and so is an ideal person to whom the sordid tale can be told without fear that it will contaminate him. It may even be that Shreve, coming from Canada, appears to be metaphorically, geographically, above the morass of the American Civil War, the war whose fact and legacy, Faulkner maintained, contributed to the decline of the Sutpens, indeed, of the whole South. Regardless of the veracity of this interpretation, it seems that the campus and buildings in the two novels, ostensibly Harvard, are much more likely to have been modelled on those of the University of Toronto, a campus with which Faulkner was far more intimate.

Some idea of the endurance of Faulkner's affection for his days in Canada can be had by realizing he gave serious consideration to rejoining his old squadron in the Second World War. In fact, had he been "called up," it is likely that he would have returned to Canada to do his duty. Later in his life, as he made vain attempts to correct the war fictions in his biography, he was still able to say with evident pride to a correspondent in 1950: "Am proud to have belonged to RAF even obscurely."

William Faulkner began his literary career as a poet, but he won the Nobel Prize in 1950, of course, for his fiction. But as we have seen, it was not until he came to Canada that Faulkner appears to have created fiction. In fact, the very first story he ever published appeared in *The Mississippian*, the newspaper of the University of Mississippi, on November 26, 1919, less than a year after his return from Canada. The story is set at the Leaside Aerodrome in Toronto and is a marvellous ur-example of Faulkner's blend of fact with wishful thinking. The tail section of the story even contains an endearing bit of self-mockery. While the story deals more with Faulkner's alter ego than it deals with Canadians (the reference to Borden in the tale is a reference to what was then the nearest aerodrome to Toronto), it fully addresses the immensity of what his days in Canada taught him—lessons too often unheralded even in the country which changed his life.

LANDING IN LUCK

The machine levelled off and settled on the aerodrome. It turned and taxied back and stopped, headed into the wind again, its engine running idle. The instructor in the forward cockpit faced about and raised his goggles.

"Fairish," he said, "not so bad. How many hours have you had?"

Cadet Thompson, a "barracks ace," who had just made a fairly creditable landing, assumed an expression of assured confidence.

"Seven hours and nine minutes, sir."

"Think you can—hold that stick back, will you?—think you can take her round alone?"

"Yes, sir," he answered as he had answered at least four times a day for the last three days, with the small remaining part of his unconquered optimism in his voice. The instructor climbed slowly out onto the lower wing, then to the ground, stretching his legs. He got a cigarette from his clothes after a fashion resembling sleight-of-hand.

"You've got to solo some day. The C.O. gave us all a raggin' last night. It's chaps like you that give this stage such a name for inefficiency. Here you have had seven hours, and yet you never know if you are goin' to land on this aerodrome or down at Borden. And then you always pick a house or another machine to land on. What ever brought you to think you could fly? Swear I don't know what to do with you. Let you try it and break your neck, or recommend you for discharge. Get rid of you either way, and a devilish good thing, too."

A silence hung heavily about Thompson's unhappy head. The instructor, sucking his cigarette, stared off across the aerodrome, where other wild and hardy amateurs took off, landed and crashed. A machine descended tail high, levelled off too soon and landed in a series of bumps like an inferior tennis ball.

"See that chap there? He's probably had half your time but he makes landings alone. But you, you cut your gun and sit up there like a blind idiot and when you condescend to dive the bus, you try your best to break our necks, yours and mine too; and I'll say right now, that's somethin' none of you rockin' chair aviators is goin' to do. Well, it's your neck or my reputation, now. Take her off, and what ever you do, keep your nose down."

Thompson pulled down his goggles. He had been angry enough to kill his officer for the better part of a week, so added indignities rested but lightly upon him. He was a strange mixture of fear and pride as he opened the throttle wide and pushed the stick forward—fear that he would wreck the machine landing, and pride that he was on his own at last. He was no physical coward, his fear was that he would show himself up before his less fortunate friends to whom he had talked largely of spins and side slips and gliding angles.

All-in-all, he was in no particularly safe frame of mind for his solo flight. He gained speed down the field. The tail was off the ground now and Thompson, more or less nervous, though he had taken the machine off like a veteran with the instructor aboard, pulled the stick back before the machine had gained speed sufficient to rise. It lurched forward and the tail sank heavily, losing more speed. He knew that he had gone too far down the field and should turn back and take off again, so he closed the throttle. When the noise of the engine ceased he heard the instructor shouting at him, and the splutter of a motor cycle. Sending after him, were they?

Cadet Thompson was once more cleanly *sic* angry. He jerked the throttle open.

His subconscious mind had registered a cable across the end of the field, and he had flown enough to know that it was touch and go as to whether he would clear it. He was afraid of rising too soon again and he knew that he would not stop in time were he to close the throttle now. So, his eyes on the speed indicator, he pulled the stick back. The motion at once became easier and he climbed as much as he dared.

A shock; he closed his eyes, expecting to go over and down on his back in the road below. When nothing happened he ventured a frightened hurried glance. Below him was the yellow of a wheat field and the aerodrome far to the rear.

So the cable had broken! Must have, for here he was still going forward. His altimeter showed two hundred feet. Thompson felt like shouting. Now he'd show 'em what flying was. Rotten, was he? He'd pull a perfect landing and walk up to that officer and tell him just what kind of a poor fish he was.

"Blasted Englishman," he said, "thinks he's the only man in this wing who can really fly. Bet if he'd a' hit that cable he'd a' been on his back in that road, right now. Wish t'hell he was."

He made his turn carefully. Below at the edge of the aerodrome stood the ambulance, its crew gaping foolishly at him. "Like fish," he thought, "like poor fish." He leaned out of his cockpit and gestured pleasantly at them, a popular gesture known to all peoples of the civilized world.

Eight hundred feet. "High enough," he decided, and made another circle, losing height. He picked his spot on the field. "Now," he thought, cut the throttle and pushed the stick forward. He found a good gliding angle, wires singing, engine idle and long flames wrapping back from the exhausts. The field was filled with people running about and flapping their arms. Another machine rose to meet him. He opened the throttle and closed it again, a warning. "Why'n the hell don't they get off and lemme land?" he wondered.

The other machine passed him in a long bank, its occupants

shouting at him; one of them carried something to which he gestured and pointed frantically. Thompson came out of his dive. They circled again and he saw that the object was about the size and shape of a wheel? A wheel from the landing gear of a machine. What kind of a joke was this? Why had they brought a wheel up to show him? He'd seen lots of wheels. Had two on his machine—on his machine—wheels? Then Thompson remembered the cable. He had stripped a wheel on that cable, then. There was nothing else it could mean. His brain assimilated this fact calmly. Having lost a wheel, he had nothing to land on. Therefore it were quite pointless to bother about landing, immediately, anyway. So he circled off and climbed, followed cautiously by the other machine, like two strange dogs meeting.

"Sir," said an orderly, entering the mess where the C.O. and three lesser lights were playing bridge, "sir, the Flight Commander, B Flight, reports that a cadet is abaht to crash."

" 'Crash?' " repeated the C.O.

"Out 'ere, sir. Yes, sir, 'e 'assn't got no landing gear."

" 'No landing gear?' What's this? What's this?"

"Yes, sir. 'E wiped it orf a-taking orf, sir. 'E's abaht out of petrol and the Flight Commander says 'e'll be a-coming down soon, sir."

"My word," said the C.O., going to the door and closely followed by the others.

"There 'e is, sir, that's 'im in front."

"My word," said the C.O. again and went off toward the hangars at a very good gait.

"What's this? What's this?" Approaching the group of officers.

"Cadet Thompson, sir," volunteered one, "Mr. Bessing's cadet. Oh, Bessing!"

Bessing came over, lifting his feet nervously.

"What's all this, Mr. Bessing?" The C.O. watched him narrowly. An instructor gets a bad name when his cadet crashes; he is responsible for the cadet's life as well as the machine.

"Rotten take off, sir. He tried to rise too soon, and when he failed, instead of comin' back and tryin' again, he carried right on.

Struck that cable and lost his right wheel and he's been sittin' up there ever since. We sent another chap up to pull him up a bit. He's almost out of petrol and he'll have to come down soon."

"H-m. Didn't send him up too soon, did you, Mr. Bessing?"

"Chap's had seven hours, sir," he protested, and produced Thompson's card.

The C.O. studied it a moment, then returned it.

"Wharton, sir?" He helped the C.O. to a light and lit a cigarette for himself.

"Good lad, good lad," said the C.O., shading his eyes as he stared into the sky. "Something in you people at this wing, though. Cadets and officers both. N.C.O.'s got it, too. G.O.C. gave me a jolly raggin' not a fortnight ago. Do something. Do something, swear I will."

The drone from the engines above suddenly ceased. Thompson was out of petrol at last. The two machines descended in a wide spiral, and they on the earth stood watching him as he descended, as utterly beyond any human aid as though he were on another planet.

"Here they come," Bessing muttered half aloud. "If he only remembers to land on his left wing—the fool, oh, the blind, bounding fool!"

For Thompson's nerve was going as he neared the earth. The temptation was strong to kick his rudder over and close his eyes. The machine descended, barely retaining headway. He watched the approaching ground utterly unable to make any pretence of levelling off, paralyzed; his brain had ceased to function, he was all staring eyes watching the remorseless earth. He did not know his height, the ground rushed past too swiftly to judge, but he expected to crash any second. Thompson's fate was on the laps of the Gods.

The tail touched, bounded, scraped again. The left wing was low and the wing tip crumpled like paper. A tearing of fabric, a strut snapped, and he regained dominion over his limbs, but too late to do anything—were there anything to be done. The machine struck again, solidly, slewed around and stood on its nose.

Bessing was the first to reach him.

"Lord, Lord!" he was near weeping from nervous tension. "Are you all right? Never expected you'd come through, never expected it! Didn't think to see you alive! Don't ever let anyone else say you can't fly. Comin' out of that was a trick many an old flyer couldn't do! I say, are you all right?"

Hanging face downward from the cockpit, Cadet Thompson looked at Bessing, surprised at the words of this cold, short tempered officer. He forgot the days of tribulation and insult in this man's company, and his recent experience, and his eyes filled with utter adoration. Then he became violently ill.

That night Thompson sat gracefully on a table in the writing room of a down town hotel, tapping a boot with his stick and talking to sundry companions.

"—and so, when my petrol gave out, I knew it was up to me. I had already thought of a plan—I thought of several, but this one seemed the best—which was to put my tail down first and then drop my left wing, so the old bus wouldn't turn over and lie down on me. Well, it worked just as I had doped it out, only a ditch those fool A.M.'s had dug right across the field, mind you, tripped her up and she stood on her nose. I had thought of that, too, and pulled my belt up. Bessing said—he's a pretty good scout—"

"Ah-h-h—" they jeered him down profanely.

"Look at the nerve he's got, will you?"

"He'—"

"Ah, we know you! Why, the poor bum crashed on his solo, and listen at the line he's giving us!"

"Well, Bessing said—"

"Bessing said! Bessing said! Go tell the G.O.C. what Bessing said!"

"Dammit, don't I know what Bessing said? Ask him! That's all. You're a bunch of poor hams that think you can fly! Why, I got an hour and a half solo time. You poor fish. Ask Bessing! there's a guy that knows what's what."

He flung out of the room. They watched him with varying expressions.

"Say," spoke one, a cadet but recently enlisted and still in ground school: "D'you think he really did all that? He must be pretty good."

"That guy? That guy fly? He's so rotten they can't discharge him. Every time he goes up they have to get a gun and shoot him down. He's the 'f' out of flying. Biggest liar in the R.A.F."

Thompson passed through again, with Bessing, and his arm was through the officer's. He was deep in discussion evidently, but he looked up in time to give them a cheerfully condescending:

"Hello, you chaps."

ALGERNON BLACKWOOD

ALGERNON BLACKWOOD (1869–1951) is today associated exclusively in the public mind with the macabre and the mysterious. This is understandable, given that he published more than thirty books with titles such as *The Empty House and Other Ghost Stories*, and *Tales of the Uncanny and Supernatural*. But he also published work that dealt overtly with humour, travel, and the more formal aspects of the mystical.

This voluminous output followed his two-year stay in Canada, and while it would be wrong to maintain that his time in Canada was the sole trigger of his literary career, there is no denying that his Canadian tenure made him adult, and clarified what was important for him, as opposed to important to others. Moreover, Canadian imagery haunted Blackwood's writing for the rest of his life, and it was in Canada that he first became aware of the often hostile power of Nature.

Blackwood was the son of a dowager duchess and Sir Arthur Blackwood, the head of the British Post Office. When his son was eighteen and, according to the father, lacking direction, the two set out for a cross-country tour of Canada with a view to finding a place where Algernon could establish himself, or, less benevolently but more accurately, a place where the family could remit the desultory child. Three years later, in September 1890, Algernon returned on his own, theoretically to become a farmer and a beekeeper.

His farming career ended pathetically just a few months after his arrival—specifically because he lacked farming experience. The fiasco cost him half his remittance capital; the other half was guzzled (or possibly swindled) a year later with the bankruptcy of The Hub Wine Company, a small hotel and pub in Toronto in which he had invested the balance of his savings.

Dodging creditors, he and his partner left for an island in the Muskoka Lakes district of Ontario. Following this summer idyll, he moved to New York to work as a journalist, returning only once more to Canada, in April 1893, to participate in a minor gold rush around Kenora and the Lake of the Woods. This third and final trip to Canada yielded no gold of the shiny sort, but the legend of the Wendigo, prevalent among the natives of the region, would later inspire Blackwood to write one of his most famous stories.

The following lesser-known extract from his memoirs illustrates Canada's resonating influence on Blackwood, and evinces the countryside's remedial effect on his outlook, his health, and his maturing.

———————————————

from EPISODES BEFORE THIRTY

The second big and daily astonishment of those awakening years, which also has persisted, if not actually intensified, concerned the blank irresponsiveness to beauty of almost everybody I had to do with. Exceptions, again, were either cranks or useless, unpractical people, failures to a man. Many liked "scenery," either perceiving it for themselves, or on having it pointed out to them; but very few, as with myself, knew their dominant mood of the day influenced— well, by a gleam of light upon the lake at dawn, a faint sound of music in the pines, a sudden strip of blue on a day of storm, the great piled coloured clouds at evening—"such clouds as flit, like splendour-winged moths about a taper, round the red west when the sun dies in it." These things had an effect of intoxication upon me, for it was the wonder and beauty of Nature that touched me most; something like the delight of ecstasy swept over me when I read of sunrise in the Indian Caucasus…. "The point of one white star is quivering still, deep in the orange light of widening morn beyond the purple mountains…" and it was a genuine astonishment to me that so few, so very few, felt the slightest response, or even noticed, a thousand and one details in sky and earth that delighted me with haunting joy for hours at a stretch. With Kay, my late "partner in booze," as I had heard him called, there was sufficient response in these two particulars to make him a sympathetic companion. If these things were not of dominant importance to him, they were at least important. Humour and courage being likewise his, he proved a delightful comrade during our five months of lonely island life. What his view of myself may have been is hard to say; luckily perhaps, Kay was not a scribbler…. He will agree, I think, that we were certainly very happy in our fairyland of peace and loveliness amid the Muskoka Lakes of Northern Ontario.

Our island, one of many in Lake Rosseau, was about ten acres in extent, irregularly shaped, overgrown with pines, its western end running out to a sharp ridge we called Sunset Point, its eastern end facing the dawn in a high rocky bluff. It rose in the centre to perhaps a hundred feet. It had little secret bays, pools of deep water beneath the rocky bluff for high diving, sandy nooks, and a sheltered cove where a boat could ride at anchor in all weathers. Close to the shore, but hidden by the pines, was a one-roomed hut with two camp-beds, a big table, a wide balcony, and a tiny kitchen in a shack adjoining. A canoe and rowing-boat went with the island, a diminutive wharf as well. On the mainland, a mile and a half to the north, was an English settler named Woods who had cleared the forest some twenty-five years before, and turned the wilderness into a more or less productive farm. Milk, eggs and vegetables we obtained from time to time. To the south and east and west lay open water for several miles, dotted by similar islands with summer camps and bungalows on them. The three big lakes—Rosseau, Muskoka and Joseph—form the letter Y, our island being where the three strokes joined.

To me it was paradise, the nearest approach to a dream come true I had yet known. The climate was dry, sunny and bracing, the air clear as crystal, the nights cool. In moonlight the islands seemed to float upon the water, and when there was no moon the reflection of the stars had an effect of phosphorescence in some southern sea. Dawns and sunsets, too, were a constant delight, and before we left in late September we had watched through half the night the strange spectacle of the Northern Lights in all their rather awful splendour.

The day we arrived—May 24th—a Scotch mist veiled all distant views, the island had a lonely and deserted air, a touch of melancholy about its sombre pines; and when the small steamer had deposited us with our luggage on the slippery wharf and vanished into the mist, I remember Kay's disconsolate expression as he remarked gravely: "We shan't stay here long!" Our first supper deepened his conviction, for, though there were lamps, we had forgotten to bring oil, and we devoured bread and porridge quickly before night set in. It was certainly a contrast to the brilliantly lit corner of the Hub dining-room where we had eaten our last dinner.... But the following morning at six o'clock, after a bathe in the cool blue water, while a dazzling sun shone in a cloudless sky, he had already changed his mind. Our immediate past seemed hardly credible now. Jimmy Martin, the "Duke," the Methodist woodcuts, the life insurance offices, to say nothing of the sporting goods emporium, red-bearded bailiffs, Alfred Cooper, and a furious half-intoxicated Irish cook—all faded into the atmosphere of some half-forgotten, ugly dream.

We at once set our house in order. We had saved a small sum in cash from the general wreck; a little went a long way; pickerel were to be caught for the trouble of trolling a spoon-bait round the coast, and we soon discovered where the black bass hid under rocky ledges of certain pools. In a few weeks, too, we had learned to manage a canoe to the point of upsetting it far from shore, shaking it half-empty while treading water, then climbing in again—the point where safety, according to the Canadians, is attained. Even in these big lakes, it was rare that the water was too rough for going out, once the craft was mastered; a "Rice Lake" or "Peterborough," as they were called, could face anything; a turn of the wrist could "lift" them; they answered the paddle like a living thing; a chief secret of control being that the kneeling occupant should feel himself actually a part of his canoe. This trifling knowledge, gained during our idle holiday, came in useful years later when taking a canoe down the Danube, from its source in the Black Forest to Budapest.

Time certainly never hung heavy on our hands. Before July, when the Canadians came up to their summer camps we had explored every bay and inlet of the lakes, had camped out on many an enchanted island, and had made longer expeditions of several days at a time into the great region of backwoods that began due north. These trips, westward to Georgian Bay with its thousand islands, on Lake Huron, or northward beyond French River, where the primeval backwoods begin their unbroken stretch to James Bay and the Arctic, were a source of keen joy. Our cooking was perhaps primitive, but we kept well on it. With books, a fiddle, expeditions, to say nothing of laundry and commissariat work, the days passed rapidly. Kay was very busy, too, "preparing for the stage," as he called it, and Shakespeare was always by his hand or pocket. The eastern end of the island was reserved for these rehearsals, while the Sunset Point end was my especial part, and while I was practising the fiddle or deep in my Eastern books, Kay, at the other point of the island, high on his rocky bluff, could be heard sometimes booming, "The world is out of joint. Oh cursed fate that I was born to set it right," and I was convinced that he wore his Irving wig, no matter what lines he spouted. In the evenings, as we lay after supper at Sunset Point, watching the colours fade and the stars appear, it was the exception if he did not murmur to himself "… the stars came out, over that summer sea," and then declaim in his great voice the whole of "The Revenge," which ends "I, Sir Richard Grenville, die!"—his tall figure silhouetted against the sunset, his voice echoing among the pines behind him. Considerations for the future were deliberately shelved;

we lived in the present, as wise men should; New York, we knew, lay waiting for us, but we agreed to let it wait. My father's suggestion— "your right course is to return to Toronto, find work, and live down your past"—was a counsel of perfection I disregarded. New York, the busy, strenuous, go-ahead United States, offered the irresistible lure of a promised land, and we both meant to try our fortunes there. How we should reach it, or what we would do when we did reach it, were problems whose solution was postponed. On looking back I can only marvel at the patience with which neither tired of the other. Perhaps it was perfect health that made squabbles so impossible. Nor was there any hint of monotony, strange to say. We had many an escape, upsetting in wild weather, losing our way in the trackless forests of the mainland, climbing or felling trees, but some Pan-like deity looked after us.... The spirit of Shelley, of course, haunted me day and night; "Prometheus Unbound," pages of which I knew by heart, lit earth and sky, peopled the forests, turned stream and lake alive, and made every glade and sandy bay a floor of dancing silvery feet: "Oh, follow, follow, through caverns hollow; As the song floats thou pursue, Where the wild bee never flew...." I still hear Kay's heavy voice, a little out of tune, singing to my fiddle the melody I made for it. And how he used to laugh! Always at himself, but also at and with most other things, an infectious, jolly wholesome laughter, inspired by details of our care-free island life, from his beard and Shakespeare rehearsals to my own whiskers and uncut hair, my Shelley moods and my intense Yoga experiments....

Much of the charm of our lonely life vanished when, with high summer, the people came up to their camps and houses on the other islands. The solitude was then disturbed by canoes, sailing-boats, steam-launches; singing and shouting broke the deep silences; camp-fires in a dozen directions blazed at night. Many of these people we had known well in Toronto, but no one called on us. Sometimes we would paddle to some distant camp-fire, lying on the water just outside the circle of light, and recognizing acquaintances, even former customers of Hub and Dairy and the Sporting Goods Emporium, but never letting ourselves be seen. Everybody knew we were living on the island; yet avoidance was mutual. We were in disgrace, it seemed, and chiefly because of the Hub—not because of our conduct with regard to it, but, apparently, because we had left the town suddenly without saying good-bye to all and sundry. This abrupt disappearance had argued something wrong, something we were ashamed of. All manner of wild tales reached us, most of them astonishingly remote from the truth.

This capacity for invention and imaginative detail of most ingenious sort, using the tiniest insignificant item of truth as starting point, suggests that even the dullest people must have high artistic faculties tucked away somewhere in them. Many of these tales we traced to their source—usually a person the world considered devoid of fancy, even dull. Here, evidently, possessing genuine native power, were unpublished novelists with distinct gifts of romance and fantasy who had missed their real vocation. The truth about us was, indeed, far from glorious, but these wild tales made us feel almost supermen. Many years later I met other instances of this power that dull, even stupid people could keep carefully hidden till the right opportunity for production offers—I was credited, to name the best, with superhuman powers of Black Magic, whatever that may be, and of sorcery. It was soon after a book of mine, "John Silence," had appeared. A story reached my ears, the name of its author boldly given, to the effect that, for the purposes of this Black Magic, I had stolen the vases from the communion altar of St. Paul's Cathedral and used their consecrated content in some terrible orgy called the Black Mass. Young children, too, were somehow involved in this ceremony of sacrilegious sorcery, and I was going to be arrested. The author of this novelette was well known to me, connected even by blood ties, a person I had always conceived to be without the faintest of imaginative gifts, though a credulous reader, evidently, of the medieval tales concerning the monstrous Gilles de Rais. Absurd as it sounds, a solicitor's letter was necessary finally to limit the author's prolific output, although pirated editions continued to sell for a considerable time. There is a poet hidden, as Stevenson observed, in most of us!

Meanwhile, summer began to wane; we considered plans for attacking New York; hope rose strongly in us both; disappointments and failures were forgotten. In so big a city we were certain to find work. We had a hundred dollars laid aside for the journey and to tide us over the first few days until employment came. We could not hide for ever in fairyland. Life called to us.... Late in September, just when the lakes were beginning to recover their first solitude again, we packed up to leave. Though the sun was still hot at midday, the mornings and evenings were chill, and cold winds had begun to blow. The famous fall colouring had set fire to the woods; the sumach blazed a gorgeous red, the maples were crimson and gold, half of the mainland seemed in flame. Sorrowfully, yet with eager anticipation in our hearts, we poured water on our camp-fire that had served us for five months without relighting, locked the door of the shanty, handed over to Woods the canoe and boat, and caught the little steamer on one of its last trips to Gravenhurst where the train would take us, via Toronto, to New York.

It had been a delightful experience; I had seen and known at last the primeval woods; I had even seen Red Indians by the dozen in their pathetic Reservations, and if they did not, like the spirit of the Medicine Man in Edinburgh, advise me to "scratch," they certainly made up for the omission by constantly scratching themselves. It seems curious to me now that, during those months of happy leisure, the desire to write never once declared itself. It never occurred to me to write even a description of our picturesque way of living, much less to attempt an essay or a story. Nor did plans for finding work in New York—we discussed them by the score—include in their wonderful variety any suggestion of a pen and paper. At the age of twenty-two, literary ambition did not exist at all.

The Muskoka interlude remained for me a sparkling, radiant memory, alight with the sunshine of unclouded skies, with the gleam of stars in a blue-black heaven, swept by forest winds, and set against a background of primeval forests that stretched without a break for six hundred miles of lonely and untrodden beauty.

ENID BAGNOLD

E NID BAGNOLD (1889–1981), the author of the enduring
National Velvet, lived an exotic childhood worthy of one of her
heroines. This English novelist and playwright spent much of her
girlhood in Jamaica, but, at the age of twelve, returned to Britain to
study at a private school run by Aldous Huxley's mother. Pursuing
art studies until the outbreak of the First World War, she then
turned to nursing, the subject of her first and, as it developed, controversial novel. She was dismissed from her post for her mild criti-
cisms of the ambience of the hospital where she worked; ludicrously,
in retrospect, her faint admonishments were considered a breach of
military discipline. Her greatest commercial success as a writer came
in 1935 with the publication of *National Velvet* (made into the
famous film starring Elizabeth Taylor in 1944).

Although her plays featured some of the most famous actors of
the day, her stagework, while popular, was never as prevailing as her
fiction—with the spectacular exception of one of her final dramas,
The Chalk Garden.

In 1920 she married Sir Roderick Jones, the head of Reuters, the
famed worldwide news agency. Her marriage augmented her social
standing and no doubt helped her to keep a high profile on the
British literary scene. Bagnold married relatively late for a woman of
her time and her husband was eleven years her senior.

People of their maturity should have devised a more compelling honeymoon. As it was, they chose to spend their post-nuptials traversing Canada by train for four weeks while the bridegroom attended to duties as a key participant in the Second Imperial Press Conference (the First had been held in 1909 in England). The renowned Canadian-born novelist Gilbert Parker also travelled in the entourage. The Conference comprised one hundred delegates: sixty representing news- papers from Britain, the balance representing all corners of the Empire. The formal proceedings took place over three days in Ottawa, but the main attraction for the visitors was an all-expense-paid vacation by rail, car, and boat covering 8,600 miles from coast to coast.

Subsequently, from Bagnold's point of view, the decision to travel as a convention widow was—to put it generously—unfortunate. Like a gem in a ring, she was deliberately visible, shown off, admired, but unable to move. Perhaps these factors, combined with her consciousness of her new wealth—and sense that she deserved better—account for her truculence, and dislike of this country. Certainly she seems an unwise traveller. She complained that the train roomette was too small, and regarding Canadian railroad travel in general further remarked, "We don't bathe, we just dab cold water over ourselves.... The great anxiety of each day is the hunt for the aperient. For that reason, we leap out of the train at little stopping places and take hurried, busy exercise."

By the end of her time in Canada, Bagnold admitted to recipients of her letters home that she probably was not doing justice to the country, that she had not, in fact, seen the real Canada: "They hoick us from banquet to banquet and take us over steel plants and round the towns."

Bagnold's Canadian adventures—crabby, spoiled, or amusing, depending upon one's charity—can be sampled in this excerpt from her *Autobiography*, published in 1969. The passage begins in England in 1920 where a nervous, even gauche, Roderick Jones has just proposed marriage to an Enid Bagnold intent upon telling all.

from

ENID BAGNOLD'S AUTOBIOGRAPHY

On this week-end at Dane End we sat in a cornfield. (How could we have? It was in June.)

Roderick didn't sit easily in cornfields but there he was.

So I told him about my lovers. Not with jauntiness, I hope: and not as a confession. He looked away in silence and didn't answer.

At length—"Well?" That came from me.

He turned round and he was laughing. I stared.

"I'm thinking what a mug I've been!"

"Mug…?"

"All those pretty girls I've known—would they have slept with me?"

And that was all. What an extraordinary way for a conventional man (but he wasn't) to take the past of his future wife.

We were married by special licence in Chelsea Old Church before it was bombed. Lord Northcliffe signed the Register. And Ivor Wimborne, looking like a strange, mad goat, signed too. I got my trousseau from Reveille, plus another fur coat. We went on our honeymoon, two extraordinary strangers. But the man who could take the cornfield so easily couldn't take lesser things.

On the morning of our first night he was missing from my bed. I found him in an ante-room, dressed, ready to go to London, writing a letter to me that our marriage was over.

"Of course I shall arrange," he had just written, "that you have an income…"

To this day I am not sure what had happened. He said I had kicked him in bed.

"But I was ASLEEP … *ASLEEP*!" I said, indignant.

(Silence.)

Enid Bagnold with Sir Roderick Jones on their honeymoon in Canada. Exact location unknown. Courtesy of Weidenfeld & Nicholson Archives.

"Did I say anything? Was it anything I *said*!"

He looked at me. He took in the blank innocence of my bewilderment. He undressed and came back to bed. We rang for breakfast.

He has heard me tell this story. He has laughed over it. But he has never explained it. Though it was a kick in a dream it must have confirmed to him his marriage-panic. He had never meant to marry. He was forty-two, ambitious, very hard-worked, and taking on what sort of burden—and for life?

"Was it panic?"

"I suppose it must have been. But I can't recall it: I can't call back the frame of mind. But I only know I was *so* afraid of marriage."

The honeymoon of these two strangers was a journey with a hundred editors to the Imperial Press Conference at Montreal (or perhaps Ottawa). We took ship for Newfoundland and the then Lady Burnham (the Burnhams headed the English contingent) ticked me off for lying in the cabin sick.

"You shouldn't leave him on deck alone. It's your duty to come up." She was right and I struggled up.

When we landed there were two trains waiting to carry us across Canada—two trains—our home. Restaurant cars, shaded lamps, polished brass, polished waiters (oh lost world of wonderful trains). As we travelled we took on the fruits of the countryside, river-trout, game, eggs, butter, cream. Each night we stopped for some vast dinner at some hotel where speeches on Empire were made by us, and to us from the Canadian Press. We dressed for dinner on the train—a hundred men and women—shuffling and passing each other to the luggage van and dragging from piled trunks and suitcases evening dresses, petticoats, stockings, shoes. The speeches went on till nearly midnight and then back to sleep on the train, which would sometimes be stationary or sometimes moving off to the next halt.

I had never in my life done anything like this. Never had a duty. Never had to behave myself. Never heard anything so mockworthy as all this hot air. The only fun was to laugh at it and I never doubted but that Roderick would laugh too.

He didn't laugh. And the first tremendous row blew up, muted, in the little "drawing-room" of the train.

He had no notion of what I was, how much of his relationships I might endanger, how much he dared encourage me. These men at whose speeches I laughed belonged to his difficult daily life, some friends, some enemies. Reuters was not exactly "press," Reuters was stiff and proud, Reuters ran a course alone. Reuters was de Gaulle, if you like. I had no idea of his passion, his love for this other wife, a woman he had courted since he was seventeen. I had to live with him to get to know it. He was reticent then, and it was his soul. He wondered, as he had wondered on the marriage-morning, whether he had married something that bit. (But he hadn't.)

Such a man of forty-two who could take such a woman of thirty on such a journey—looking back I wonder he got away with it. Did he think he could "train" me at that age?—Well he thought it and he did.

Canada, fifty years ago, was naïve, touchy, longing to be praised, young. "What do you think of us?" (said immediately before one had even thought.) I was always so nearly saying, "I think you're a bore." I wouldn't have thought it if I hadn't been so disgruntled by the haste of the question. The Daughters of Empire were always asking it and always taking me aside. I could see what a marvellous country it was but I never could get into it. I was chained to Empire and the train. Yet really and truly I got to love the train. I heard moose call. And some man of imagination had modelled the train's call on the moose. The same hollow echoing sound, loud but minor. And the way the train took us forward and on, always leaving the horrors behind. But always, as trains are, there was a landscape just outside the windows, a denied paradise. The coolness of pools, the glitter of lakes, alleys in forests, birds in swamps, men's faces upturned and left behind. But all known Canada to me was the press and the press' wives.

It was the dry time, alcoholically. But there were wet spots, much sought after. Montreal was one. In Montreal we met a man, very important to Roderick, who was a hard and successful press man but a poet as well. Some special agreement connected with Reuters had to be come to between them. He was the most attractive man I had met in Canada. Clothes careless and elegant. Face a bit architectural, city-white. Elliptical speech, constantly in brackets as it scooped up double-harnessed ideas. In fact a treasure of a man whom we were to meet again next day.

The lunch he arranged to give us was at the best hotel in Montreal.

At the appointed time there was no one in the vestibule. Deep leather chairs, columns, gilt staircases, lobbies, hidden writing-tables with lamps—no man. Then out of one armchair, overlooked till then, rose a rumpled figure, hair on end, face scarlet, unsteady, advancing a hand. He had ordered a luncheon in a private room. The head waiter led. He followed. We behind. He put one hand on the wall to steady himself as he walked.

It began as a nightmare. He was conscious enough for us not to be able to leave, but not conscious enough for talk. First came the soup. His shirt-bulge, as he slouched forward, elbows planted, drew up the soup in a dark patch. The five ordered courses came and went. He ate nothing. He knew he was drunk and now and then said "very ashamed." When he said this we very slightly bowed.

We got used to it and talked to each other while his eyes with curiosity watched our lips. He seemed contented except that now and then he said he was ashamed. The waiter, with no glance of conspiracy (the host was too conscious and too powerful for that) hurried the courses, flashed out the dishes—we were through. We rose. He tipped the waiter accurately, signed his bill with ease, opened the door and took us to the corridor that led back to the hall. Once more, but more clearly, "I am very ashamed." It was odd the things he could do and the things he couldn't.

Roderick had his business meeting with him, very agreeably next day. Nothing was mentioned.

I seemed to be getting used to Roderick, after the amazed storms of the first week. I think he began to be more sure I wouldn't explode in public, to know I was not a fool and not disloyal. We had quite enjoyed together the poor big shot at Montreal. And at Calgary....

It was hot. We were panting hot. On the nineteenth floor of the biggest hotel about 11 at night Roderick was in bed: I not. I put my hand on a radiator and said, "Good God—they've got the heat on!"

"WHAT!" He jumped out of bed and stubbed his toe on the heavy copper spittoon. "HELL!"—he said, picked it up and shot it clean out of the open window. All his life he punished inanimate objects that hurt him.

I rushed to the switch and put the light out. Then back to the window and looked down. A man was walking nineteen floors below on the pavement *alive*.

We got into our beds. The manager came tapping on the door.

"Has anything been thrown?... Out of the window?"

"What's that...? We're asleep."

"I beg your pardon."

Nothing more, not a word. But on the bill was written—"One metal spittoon seven dollars." It was paid in equal silence.

JOHN DOS PASSOS

L IKE HIS FRIEND Ernest Hemingway, John Dos Passos (1896–
1970) used his experiences as an ambulance driver in the First
World War to good effect in his earliest novels. His literary reputation rests, however, on the trilogy of books given the overall title
U.S.A.: The 42nd Parallel, 1919, and *The Big Money.*

His encounters with Canada were several but brief, and only two
seemed memorable enough to merit being written about: a swim in
Newfoundland, and a trip to Toronto. For reasons which remain
unclear, Dos Passos had already visited Toronto by 1917. From Paris,
he wrote to a close friend,

> So you've been to Toronto—don't you think it's a beastly place?
> Toronto on a Sunday morning.... A very dear friend of mine—
> he's just been drafted, poor devil—went to school there—and
> his description of the utter middle-class gracelessness of it has
> perhaps tinged my ideas. But I have been there—and I admit
> that I loathe it.

His first expedition to Canada had taken place a few years earlier
and was paid for by his father. Dos Passos and a friend, in August
1913, before starting their college sophomore years, were sent for rest
and relaxation to Quebec and Newfoundland. More than two years
later, writing to a friend, Dos Passos recalled the trip with obvious

delight. "Why should that make me think of our glorious swim at Ocean Beach, I don't know.... That's one of the two or three red-letter swims of my life. Another one was up in Newfoundland. I'll tell you about it some day."

And a few months later (December 6, 1915), Dos Passos did.

———————————

from THE FOURTEENTH CHRONICLE

Oh, I must tell you about that swim in Newfoundland. There was a wonderful bay, without a house or a town on it, that had a wide white beach backed up by pine forests. We were absolutely the only living things about except white cawing sea gulls. The water was pale-green, and simply stung when you got in—but it was like a bath in champagne! After it we danced about the beach like Greek fauns or nymphs. You can imagine what fun it was. You'd have loved it I know.

ERNEST HEMINGWAY

F EW FOREIGN WRITERS are more associated with Canada than Ernest Hemingway (1899–1961). People who have never read his work—even people who know next to nothing of our literary history—are quick to cite his presence in Canada and recall his employment at the *Toronto Daily Star*. Given the fact that Hemingway's association with Canada has wide currency, it is indeed passing strange (and once again, no compliment to our country's professors of literature) that almost a century after his birth, there is still no book, no comprehensive study, of Hemingway's time in Canada.

In late 1919, in Petoskey, Michigan, Hemingway gave a lecture about his experiences as a soldier in the First World War, and his recovery from his battle wounds. One of the women attending the lecture, impressed by the young Ernest's bearing and words, was Harriet Connable, a friend of his mother. Mrs. Connable was making a brief visit to Petoskey from Toronto, where she was the chatelaine of a large home presided over by her husband, Ralph Connable Sr., the chief executive officer of the Woolworth chain of stores in Canada.

Following the lecture, Mrs. Connable offered the twenty-year-old Hemingway a job as a paid companion to her son, Ralph Jr. The latter had a physical disability (and possibly other problems) which, the parents believed, impeded his growth. Mrs. Connable, sensible

to Hemingway's desire to write, offered him, in addition to a generous stipend, private accommodation at her demesne and plenty of
free time so that he could pursue his avocation. For Hemingway, a
major attraction of the job was an offer by Mr. Connable (Woolworth's was a major newspaper advertiser) to arrange for Hemingway to meet the senior editors of the biggest newspaper in the
country. Restless, hungry for the adventure and the salary, he
accepted the offer immediately, and promised to leave for Toronto
within days.

Apart from a brief fishing trip to Sault Ste. Marie made in 1917,
the job in Toronto was to mark Hemingway's first encounter with
this country. It was an experience which would affect him—in many
ways—for life.

Shortly after Hemingway arrived in Toronto, Mr. Connable
honoured his promise, presenting Ernest to Arthur Donaldson, an
advertising executive with the *Toronto Daily Star*. Following a tour
of the *Star* premises, Donaldson left Hemingway in the company of
Greg Clark, the features editor of the *Star*'s sister publication, *The
Star Weekly*, a Saturday colour magazine.

Clark would later reminisce that he was chary of Hemingway's
boasts of experience (journalistic and military), but the young man's
bravura eventually persuaded Clark to introduce Hemingway to
J.H. Cranston, the managing editor of *The Star Weekly*. Because
Ralph Connable was a major advertiser, and because Hemingway
had worked briefly at the *Kansas City Star*, a newspaper small but
respected throughout the continent, Cranston invited Ernest to
submit some stories "on spec." The results were sufficiently pleasing
to both parties that the business relationship lasted for a full four
years more, or to put it more cogently, for as long as Hemingway
chose to remain a journalist.

In late May of 1920, Hemingway—having spent almost half a
year in Toronto—left the Connable home, in order to spend part of
the summer fishing with friends in Michigan, a diversion he put to
use in an article he subsequently sold to *The Star Weekly*.

The Star Weekly, appealing to a mass audience, had a huge appetite for freelance articles on a wide range of subjects. This omnivorous maw not only allowed Hemingway to supplement his income while resident outside of the city, it allowed—indeed encouraged—him to hone his storytelling skills and widen his character studies. This first Canadian period in his life, so often treated offhandedly by even Canadian critics and historians as a biographical divertissement of little consequence, was of gigantic consequence:

> The Toronto Star Limited, the organization within which the two papers operated, was as appropriately suitable to Hemingway's training requirements at this stage as the Kansas City *Star* had been ideal as a preliminary school. The American and Canadian papers, indeed, were of such diverse natures that had his relationship with them been reversed—had he gone to Toronto in 1917 and to Kansas City in 1920—the entire pattern of his apprenticeship would have been seriously altered and damaged.

In February 1921, the editor of the *Toronto Daily Star*, John Bone, impressed with the young man's writing talent, wrote to Hemingway, urging him to return to Toronto to work as a full-time reporter for the daily paper, rather than as a freelancer for the weekly magazine. Ernest was seriously tempted, but forwent the offer either because he asked for too much salary, or because he wished to spend as much time as possible on his literary work: the correct answer, if there is one, depends upon which source one believes.

However, by the autumn of the same year, the shoe was on the other foot. Now married, but unemployed, Hemingway, still in America, was forced to write to Bone, asking him for regular employment—of a sort. Determined to live in Paris, where he believed any young man of burgeoning literary talent should be, Hemingway with typical bravado offered his services to the *Daily Star* as the European correspondent (with his base of operations, not coincidentally, the capital of France). Bone accepted his offer. Bone's gesture, seemingly trivial at the time, we can now see changed twentieth-century modernism. Without the new *Daily Star* job, yes, Hemingway might still have reached Paris, but he would not have had the funds to buy the leisure time to write as he wanted, would not have been able to rent an office, away from his apartment, where he could write his poems and fictions undisturbed, and incontrovertibly, would not have had the money to promenade over Europe, to ease into the role of widely travelled sage so essential to his persona and his literature.

Though he was only in his early twenties, Hemingway, covering wars, councils of leading politicians, and the titillating world of bohemian Paris, quickly became famous in Canada as one of the pre-eminent correspondents of the Toronto newspaper; concomitantly, in Europe, his affiliation with such a famous newspaper as the *Daily Star* gained him entrée into the elite circles of European journalists which his young age ordinarily would have prevented him from knowing. It was while in Paris working for the *Star* that Hemingway also discovered the singular pleasures of cablese, that telegraphic vocabulary in which much has to be conveyed in so few words. Its influence on his writing continues to divert simple-minded critics from more meaningful scholarly work. Of far larger import is the number of articles which Hemingway wrote for his masters in Toronto which soon became grist for his fiction mill: such transmo-grified articles number in the dozens. Without the *Star* paying his bills, without the *Star* sending him yon and thither, allowing him access to scenes and persons he would never have encountered other-wise, scenes which sear readers of his creative writing, such is their verisimilitude, Hemingway would probably have been just another expatriate in Paris writing a middle-class *Bildungsroman*.

Perhaps the clearest example of how his work for the Canadian journal affected his fiction can be seen in his reportage of the Greek-Turkish War in the autumn of 1922.

Hemingway, at the behest of the *Star*, travelled to the Balkans and wrote a series of articles concentrating on personality profiles rather than political analysis, undoubtedly because he was only twenty-three years old, and woefully ignorant of the nuances of eth-nic conflict. But just because he was twenty-three he was prone to bluff, and his reports were spiced with judgements and asides uttered as if he were an old Middle East hand. Nonetheless, he witnessed sights more horrible than any he had seen in Italy in the First World War, and one of his most famous descriptions, the flight from Adrianople (adumbrating Beckett in its starkness and misery) told of long, pitiful columns of frightened refugees, of battle-weary soldiers marching morosely in ragged file, of carts carrying all that these people possessed. This same scene, only slightly modified, Hemingway later used, to brilliant, chilling effect, in *A Farewell to Arms*. His work for the *Star*, in other words, was essential to his development as a creative writer, not just because he learned the crisp, clean-edged journalistic style for which he is renowned, but crucial because he accrued a worldly maturity far excelling that possessed by others of his generation (Morley Callaghan, for example, arriving in Paris, was stunned to learn that he and Ernest were almost of the same age, for the American had seemed so much older, confident, aware, sophisticated). Working for the *Star*, entire worlds opened to Hemingway which remained for ever closed to so many of his colleagues: the machinations of warring nations; scenes of horror appropriate to Bosch; the insider's view of the thrill of blood sport. For Hemingway, the *Star* was no mere pit stop.

Most books on Hemingway state that he chose to return to Toronto in the fall of 1923 (less than a year after his experience in Turkey) because of his wife, Hadley's, first pregnancy and her desire to have a North American doctor supervise the birth. James Mellow in his 1992 biography has shown, however, that Hemingway had decided to return to Canada long before Hadley became pregnant. The editor of the *Daily Star*, John Bone, had been exhorting him to return to Toronto, apparently to write feature articles and to be a doctor to the *Star*'s ailing cable department. The pending birth and its concurrent responsibilities merely helped Hemingway to fix the date. Ernest honestly believed he would stay in Toronto for two years, to be, for a change, a stay-at-home father with a regular, reliable salary. In fact, his second Toronto tenure lasted less than five months.

Hadley and Ernest arrived by ship in Quebec in late August and travelled by train to Toronto, where they were met by Bone and Greg Clark. They checked into a quiet, residential hotel, the Selby, until they could find a suitable apartment. They soon did: a one-bedroom unit with a sun-room in a new building on Bathurst Street, complete with Murphy bed and a view over the same ravine that Ernest had explored when he had lived with the Connables. His first weeks were busy not only with the unpacking of furniture, but with the disbursement of alleged pornography: Sylvia Beach, knowing that Canada had not banned *Ulysses*, by James Joyce, had arranged for Hemingway to include an unspecified number (dozens, if not hundreds) of copies in his luggage. From Toronto, Ernest arranged for the successful smuggling into the United States of all of "his" copies of *Ulysses*; according to Beach, all of her American subscribers to the first edition of the Joycean masterpiece received their copy from Canada, courtesy of the arch-criminal Ernest Hemingway. Hemingway wrote to Ezra Pound, "Someday someone will live here and be able to appreciate the feeling with which I launched *Ulysses* on the States (not a copy lost) from this city."

While it was John Bone, the editor, who had lured Hemingway back to Toronto, it was a new man, Harry Hindmarsh, the city editor, who was to be Hemingway's boss. Within days, Hemingway hated Hindmarsh.

Hindmarsh was a martinet, and believed that famous reporters such as Hemingway needed quick lessons in humility, obedience, and discipline. So instead of interviewing celebrities in Toronto, Hemingway found himself doing fires, break-ins, puff pieces, and other inanities generally inflicted on cub reporters. Occasionally, he was given meatier fare, but at a cost: though Hindmarsh knew that Hadley was expecting any day, he sent Hemingway out of the city to write articles about the escape of Red Ryan in Kingston, about coal mining in the Sudbury Basin, to New York to report on the arrival of Lloyd George. It was while he was returning from New York that his first child was born a Canadian; Hadley had an easy labour, but Hemingway would never forgive Hindmarsh for keeping him away from the birth.

When the Toronto Newspaper Guild was trying to form a union at the *Star*, Hemingway readily contributed to the drive although he had been long gone from the city. Having originally planned to give a generous $100, he decided, on reflection, to donate a formidable $200 in order, he said, "to beat Hindmarsh." The measure of his antipathy to his former boss, even decades after he had left Canada, can be taken from the following amusing if macabre account related by Greg Clark's nephew, Tom Williams, himself a reporter:

> When Hindmarsh died, I helped write his obit. I phoned Hemingway in Havana. I told him I admired his work, he recalled Uncle Greg with kindness, and I said Hindmarsh was lying in the funeral parlours of McDougal and Brown with a stake through his heart.
>
> There was a long silence and heavy breathing. "Mr. Williams," said Hemingway, "this started out as a shitty day. It is raining and cold and my old wounds are bothering me. I ran into bad rum last night." Pause and more breathing. "He is really dead, you say?" I assured him. More chuckles and then hellish laughter. "That saves me killing him," said Hemingway.

From Bathurst Street, Hemingway carried on an active correspondence with his friends in Europe. One of these, Ezra Pound, mocked Hemingway's new home (and so addressed his letters) as "Tomato, Can." Such an address, while raising a weak smile, would more likely have achingly reminded Hemingway that he was, indeed, sealed away. Having been tricked into returning to Toronto, working for a boss who, even from the perspective of our own time, seems to have been an exceptional fool, it is no wonder that Hemingway would write with compressed anger if not lexical accuracy, that Canada was "the fistulated asshole of the father of seven among Nations."

Yet this rage, while real (and often distorted by self-loathing, colonially minded Canadians as proof of what a nonentity our country really is), is not an accurate reflection of Hemingway's overall impression of Canada.

It is a compliment to Hemingway's ear, and literary acumen, that from his earliest writing in Canada, he was sensitive to, and on occasion sympathetic with, the Canadian voice. In his first story in Toronto to receive a byline, Hemingway astutely appealed to the Canadians' assumption that theirs was a land superior to the nation below them. He filled a slightly later article (published April 10, 1920) with the dialogue of two Canadian war veterans.

Many of his subsequent articles contrasted life in the United States with life in Canada (as he knew it from the cocoon of Toronto), always to the advantage of Canada. This may seem to have been an obvious prejudice to adopt, given that he was writing for a Canadian newspaper, but given the ferocity of American patriotism, the intensity with which Hemingway held opinions, and the brevity of his time in the land, his tack on these cross-border issues is remarkably discriminating and mature. Recall that he was only twenty.

Four years later, though he loathed Harry Hindmarsh and the anal-retentive aspects of Toronto contrasting so unhappily with the *joie de vivre* of Paris, he was able to write two poems meant to be read together: "I Like Americans" and "I Like Canadians." Both were published under the pseudonym of "A Foreigner." For the purposes of this anthology, it is the second poem which deserves quotation:

I like Canadians.
They are so unlike Americans.
They go home at night.
Their cigarets don't smell bad.
Their hats fit.
They really believe that they won the war.
They don't believe in Literature.
They think Art has been exaggerated.
But they are wonderful on ice skates.
A few of them are very rich.
But when they are rich they buy more horses
Than motor cars. Chicago calls Toronto a puritan town.

But both boxing and horse-racing are illegal in Chicago.
Nobody works on Sunday.
Nobody.
That doesn't make me mad.
There is only one Woodbine.
But were you ever at Blue Bonnets?
If you kill somebody with a motor car in Ontario
You are liable to go to jail.
So it isn't done.
There have been over 500 people killed by motor cars
In Chicago
So far this year.
It is hard to get rich in Canada.
But it is easy to make money.
There are too many tea rooms.
But, then, there are no cabarets.
If you tip a waiter a quarter
He says "Thank you."
Instead of calling the bouncer.
They let women stand up in the street cars.
Even if they are good-looking.
They are all in a hurry to get home to supper
And their radio sets.
They are a fine people.
I like them.

Throughout his adult life, Hemingway would continue to long for the open spaces of Canada, where a man could confront the elements and fish and hunt to his heart's satiation. The emptiness of Canada must have seemed, especially during his late-in-life depressions, the perfect place to escape to. Once free from the tyranny of Hindmarsh, Hemingway was able to separate his feelings for the man from those for the city. For example, in his 1938 preface to his noted collection *The Short Stories* he cited Toronto as being among the few places where he had been able to write well. Since in that same preface he says there were other places which were not so good for his writing, we must take him at his word—a word which is in stark contrast to his 1923 remark to Sylvia Beach that Canada was "a dreadful country" or his comment to his fellow reporter at the *Star*, Mary Lowry, that Toronto had destroyed ten years of his literary life. Overall, it would seem his aversion to Hindmarsh coloured all of his 1923 comments on the city and nation, whereas his later perceptions, tempered by perspective, were far more generous. In 1951, for example, he wrote to his first boss, Cranston, "I never enjoyed myself so much as working under you and with Greg Clark and with Jimmy Frise. It was why I was sad to quit newspaper work."

But quit he did. His resignation took effect on January 1, 1924. Because by leaving so early they were breaking their lease, Hadley and Ernest enlisted the aid of their friends to smuggle their belongings out of the apartment. On January 12, 1924, the Connables held a farewell party in their honour, and the next day, at Toronto's Union Station, with Mary Lowry to wave goodbye, they boarded a train for New York, where they would catch a ship bound for France. To their chagrin, the ship stopped in at Halifax, and they were actually afraid they might be arrested for having absconded from Bathurst Street. The Halifax authorities seemed uninterested in the "criminals" briefly in their midst.

Hemingway told various people about two novels he was going to write with Canadian settings and characters. One, to be called *The Son-in-Law*, was to be an eviscerating portrayal of Hindmarsh. It was never begun, because Hemingway soon realized that his hate blinded him to the aesthetic needs of the story. The other novel was begun but abandoned for reasons which remain unclear. Titled *A New Slain Knight*, it was modeled on the life of the famous Canadian gangster Red Ryan, the same man whose escape Hemingway had been sent to Kingston to cover by Hindmarsh. Hemingway wrote:

It will be about Red Ryan and his escape from Kingston Pen. The flight—the hiding in the wood—the bank robbery in

Toronto—the double-crossing by his girl in Minneapolis—the arrest—the double-crossing newspaper men in Minneapolis—the trip back to Toronto and Kingston—or it will be a story of all the tough guys.

While neither of these novels came to fruition, Canada looms large in the Hemingway opus. Most of Hemingway's articles for the *Daily Star* and the *Star Weekly* have been collected in an admirable volume titled *Dateline: Toronto*. In 1992 the *Toronto Star* published a number of articles written by Hemingway whose authorship had been previously unknown. It seems likely that more may yet be discovered.

Toronto was good to Hemingway. It was here that he saw his first professional bout. It was here that he first wrote about bullfighting. It was here that he moved from apprentice to professional.

While many articles by Hemingway describe the topography and individuals he encountered in the country, the following article is unique in its focused ruminations on what makes the two nations of Canada and the United States (and their citizens) different. The article was first published in the *Star Weekly* on October 9, 1920.

CANADIANS: WILD/TAME

Seeing ourselves as others see us is interesting but sometimes appalling. Remember the unexpected glimpse of your profile caught in one of those three-way mirrors at your tailor's?

This refers to men and nations—women see full face, profile and their back hair at least every day and therefore are not appalled.

William Stevens McNutt, in a recent issue of *Collier's Weekly*, told his version of what Canadians think of Americans.

Herein is the opinion and views of that average American, whom cub reporters delight to call the man in the street, on Canadians.

Just as a tip to budding journalists, there is no such thing as the man in the street in either the States or the Dominion. The phrase is French and is applicable enough there where nearly all human intercourse is carried on in or on the streets. But here the only time an American either north or south of the border is in the street is when he is busily going somewhere.

An average citizen should be called the man going hungry from the quick-lunch joint to the man standing in the streetcar or, even, the righteous man afraid of a policeman.

In the States the average unseated male in a public conveyance has a vague idea of Canada.

Canada is, for him, the North-West Mounted Police, winter sports, open snowy places replete with huskie dogs, Canadian whiskey, race reports from Windsor, the Woodbine and Blue Bonnets, and a firm and dominant passion that no one will slip him any Canadian silver.

He remembers that when Taft was president there was a big fuss about reciprocity—but he isn't quite sure how it all came out. He is sure to have heard of Sir Wilfrid Laurier and may have heard of ex-Premier Borden but is apt to confuse him with the milk manufacturer. That covers his knowledge of Canadian politics.

Surprising as it may be to many Canadians, the average American is tremendously proud of Canada's war record. An American who served with the Canadian forces, whether in the A.S.C. or originals, is a hero to his fellow countrymen.

A typical Canadian as pictured by the man in the pressed-while-you-wait shop in the States is of two types, wild and tame.

Wild Canadians mean Mackinaw blanket pants, fur caps, have rough bewhiskered but honest faces and are closely pursued by corporals of the Royal North-West Mounted Police.

Tame Canadians wear spats, small mustaches, are very intelligent looking, all have M.C.'s, and are politely bored.

Both wild and tame Canadians are in contrast with the average

American man munching peanuts in the ballpark's conception of the British.

All inhabitants of Great Britain are divided into three classes, to wit, sanguinary Englishmen, cricket players and lords.

Sanguinary Englishmen are so considered because of their penchant for qualifying all remarks with the term sanguinary. They wear cloth caps and eat raw herrings.

Cricket players stalk in flannels through the best American fiction, and lords are dealt with by the comic supplements.

Then there is a type of Englishman created for American consumption by Mr. William Randolph Hearst, who is a combination of the Emperor Nero, the worst phases of the Corsican, George the Third, and whoever wouldn't give the Bay three grains of corn.

Jesting aside, there is a lamentable lack of sympathetic understanding between Canada and the United States. It is a fact that Canada is a closed book to the average Yank, a book with a highly colored jacket by Robert W. Service.

Americans admire and respect Canadians. There is not the slightest trace of anti-Canadian sentiment anywhere in the States. And among the roughneck element there is a positive love for Canada.

But you know what the average Canadian roughneck thinks of a Yank.

Maybe when Hearst dies and the war is a longer way off and exchange gets back to normal and there is an exchange system between Canadian and American universities and Americans lower their voices and Canadians lower their pride, or say there was a good war and we both went in at the same time, maybe we'd be pals.

ELIZABETH BISHOP

L IKE A COMET returning every few years, the Maritimes revisited the prose and poetry of Elizabeth Bishop (1911–1979), widely regarded as one of the best American writers of the twentieth century. Nova Scotia, in particular, was central to her imaginative life.

A mere eight months after her birth in Massachusetts, her father died of Bright's disease. Her mother's extant mental illness, now exacerbated by widowhood (she wore mourning black for five years), caused child and parent to remove in 1914 to Great Village, Nova Scotia, to live with Elizabeth's maternal grandparents. By 1916 her mother was sufficiently ill to be placed in an institution; only five at the time, Elizabeth Bishop never saw her mother again.

Her paternal grandparents arranged in 1917 for Bishop to live with them in Boston, so that she could "be saved from a life of poverty and provincialism, bare feet, suet puddings, unsanitary school slates, perhaps even from the inverted r's of my mother's family." The shock of the experience, and her early cognizance of Boston Brahmin snobbery versus Maritime humility, are related without mercy in her prose memoir "The Country Mouse."

This paternalistic habitation in Boston was cut short by the onset of asthma, and a bouquet of other lesser afflictions, resulting in her happy transfer to the home of a maternal aunt, also in Boston. Her summers for the next years, however, were always spent with her maternal grandparents in Great Village, and it is these summer vacations in Nova Scotia, as much as her first years in the province, that inspired so much of her best writing. In an interview published in 1966, she said:

> I didn't spend all of my childhood in Nova Scotia. I lived there from 1914 to 1917 during the first World War. After that I spent long summers there until I was thirteen. Since then, I've made only occasional visits. My relatives were not literary in any way. But in my aunt's house we had quite a few books, and I drew heavily on them. In some ways, the little village in Canada where I lived was more cultured than the suburbs of Boston where I lived later.

Recollections of her years in Canada figure slightly more prominently in her prose than in her poetry. In addition to "The Country Mouse," she wrote about fanatical religious conversion in a Maritime village in "The Baptism," her first published story.

In "Primer Class" Bishop affectionately details her earliest education in a one-room schoolhouse in Great Village. Her writing and reading skills were well above those of her classmates, and she recounts how she would eavesdrop on higher grades while they studied geography. It was here that she first became conscious of maps, an icon that was to haunt her writing for the rest of her life:

> Only the third and fourth grades studied geography. On their side of the room, over the blackboard, were two rolled-up maps, one of Canada and one of the whole world... On the world map, all of Canada was pink; on the Canadian, the provinces were different colors. I was so taken with the pull-down maps that I wanted to snap them up, and pull them down again, and touch all the countries and provinces with my own hands. Only dimly did I hear the pupils' recitations of capital cities and islands and bays. But I got the general impression that Canada was the same size as the world, which somehow or other fitted into it, or the

other way around, and that in the world and Canada the sun was always shining, and everything was dry and glittering. At the same time, I knew perfectly well that this was not true.

This same sensual, tactile desire whetted by Canadian cartography is caressingly described in a stanza from her poem "The Map":

The shadow of Newfoundland lies flat and still.
Labrador's yellow, where the moony Eskimo
has oiled it. We can stroke these lovely bays,
under a glass as if they were expected to blossom,
or as if to provide a clean cage for invisible fish.
The names of seashore towns run out to sea,
the names of cities cross the neighbouring mountains
—the printer here experiencing the same excitement
as when emotion too far exceeds its cause.
These peninsulas take the water between thumb and finger
like women feeling for the smoothness of yard-goods.

Elizabeth Bishop's addiction to hymns and their singing had, as Robert Giroux noted, "more to do with the arts of poetry and music than religion." In an interview, Bishop herself explained:

Where I lived in Canada, people used to sing hymns in the evening. They liked to play on the piano and the organ, and they'd sing and sing and sing. My grandfather went to two churches—one Presbyterian, one Baptist—one in the morning, one in the afternoon. So I'm full of hymns.

At the memorial service at Harvard following her death in 1979, the congregation sang "Rock of Ages," "A Mighty Fortress," "We Gather Together," and "There Is a Balm in Gilead." In other words, Elizabeth Bishop's soul was escorted to her final home with the very hymns she had learned as a girl at her first real home in Great Village, Nova Scotia.

The following short story "In the Village" is not only set in Canada, it is also Elizabeth Bishop's most powerful work of fiction.

In the Maritime hamlet of her childhood, a scream lingers like a late-morning fog that will not burn off. The child who narrates the tale unconsciously savours Canadian village life while being only semi-conscious of gathering emotional thunders at home. As an evocation of the complications of childhood, it has little match.

IN THE VILLAGE

A scream, the echo of a scream, hangs over that Nova Scotian village. No one hears it; it hangs there forever, a slight stain in those pure blue skies, skies that travelers compare to those of Switzerland, too dark, too blue, so that they seem to keep on darkening a little more around the horizon—or is it around the rims of the eyes?—the color of the cloud of bloom on the elm trees, the violet on the fields of oats; something darkening over the woods and waters as well as the sky. The scream hangs like that, unheard, in memory—in the past, in the present, and those years between. It was not even loud to begin with, perhaps. It just came there to live, forever—not loud, just alive forever. Its pitch would be the pitch of my village. Flick the lightning rod on top of the church steeple with your fingernail and you will hear it.

She stood in the large front bedroom with sloping walls on either side, papered in wide white and dim-gold stripes. Later, it was she who gave the scream.

The village dressmaker was fitting a new dress. It was her first in almost two years and she had decided to come out of black, so the dress was purple. She was very thin. She wasn't at all sure whether she was going to like the dress or not and she kept lifting the folds of the skirt, still unpinned and dragging on the floor around her, in her thin white hands, and looking down at the cloth.

"Is it a good shade for me? Is it too bright? I don't know. I haven't worn colors for so long now.... How long? Should it be black? Do you think I should keep on wearing black?"

Drummers sometimes came around selling gilded red or green books, unlovely books, filled with bright new illustrations of the Bible stories. The people in the pictures wore clothes like the purple dress, or like the way it looked then.

It was a hot summer afternoon. Her mother and her two sisters were there. The older sister had brought her home, from Boston, not long before, and was staying on, to help. Because in Boston she had not got any better, in months and months—or had it been a year? In spite of the doctors, in spite of the frightening expenses, she had not got any better.

First, she had come home, with her child. Then she had gone away again, alone, and left the child. Then she had come home. Then she had gone away again, with her sister; and now she was home again.

Unaccustomed to having her back, the child stood now in the doorway, watching. The dressmaker was crawling around and around on her knees eating pins as Nebuchadnezzar had crawled eating grass. The wallpaper glinted and the elm trees outside hung heavy and green, and the straw matting smelled like the ghost of hay.

Clang.

Clang.

Oh, beautiful sounds, from the blacksmith's shop at the end of the garden! Its gray roof, with patches of moss, could be seen above the lilac bushes. Nate was there—Nate, wearing a long black leather apron over his trousers and bare chest, sweating hard, a black leather cap on top of dry, thick, black-and-gray curls, a black sooty face; iron filings, whiskers, and gold teeth, all together, and a smell of red-hot metal and horses' hoofs.

Clang.

The pure note: pure and angelic.

The dress was all wrong. She screamed.

The child vanishes.

Later they sit, the mother and the three sisters, in the shade on the back porch, sipping sour, diluted ruby: raspberry vinegar. The dressmaker refuses to join them and leaves, holding the dress to her heart. The child is visiting the blacksmith.

In the blacksmith's shop things hang up in the shadows and shadows hang up in the things, and there are black and glistening piles of dust in each corner. A tub of night-black water stands by the forge. The horseshoes sail through the dark like bloody little moons and follow each other like bloody little moons to drown in the black water, hissing, protesting.

Outside, along the matted eaves, painstakingly, sweetly, wasps go over and over a honeysuckle vine.

Inside, the bellows creak. Nate does wonders with both hands; with one hand. The attendant horse stamps his foot and nods his head as if agreeing to a peace treaty.

Nod.

And nod.

A Newfoundland dog looks up at him and they almost touch noses, but not quite, because at the last moment the horse decides against it and turns away.

Outside in the grass lie scattered big, pale granite discs, like mill-stones, for making wheel rims on. This afternoon they are too hot to touch.

Now it is settling down, the scream.

Now the dressmaker is at home, basting, but in tears. It is the most beautiful material she has worked on in years. It has been sent to the woman from Boston, a present from her mother-in-law, and heaven knows how much it cost.

Before my older aunt had brought her back, I had watched my grandmother and younger aunt unpacking her clothes, her "things." In trunks and barrels and boxes they had finally come, from Boston, where she and I had once lived. So many things in the village came from Boston, and even I had once come from there. But I remembered only being here, with my grandmother.

The clothes were black, or white, or black-and-white.

"Here's a mourning hat," says my grandmother, holding up something large, sheer, and black, with large black roses on it; at least I guess they are roses, even if black.

"There's that mourning coat she got the first winter," says my aunt.

But always I think they are saying "morning." Why, in the morning, did one put on black? How early in the morning did one begin? Before the sun came up?

"Oh, here are some housedresses!"

They are nicer. Clean and starched, stiffly folded. One with black polka dots. One of fine black-and-white stripes with black grosgrain bows. A third with a black velvet bow and on the bow a pin of pearls in a little wreath.

"Look. She forgot to take it off."

A white hat. A white embroidered parasol. Black shoes with buckles glistening like the dust in the blacksmith's shop. A silver mesh bag. A silver calling-card case on a little chain. Another bag of silver mesh, gathered to a tight, round neck of strips of silver that will open out, like the hatrack in the front hall. A silver-framed photograph, quickly turned over. Handkerchiefs with narrow black hems—"morning handkerchiefs." In bright sunlight, over breakfast tables, they flutter.

A bottle of perfume has leaked and made awful brown stains.

Oh, marvelous scent, from somewhere else! It doesn't smell like that here; but there, somewhere, it does, still.

A big bundle of postcards. The curdled elastic around them breaks. I gather them together on the floor.

Some people wrote with pale-blue ink, and some with brown, and some with black, but mostly blue. The stamps have been torn off many of them. Some are plain, or photographs, but some have lines of metallic crystals on them—how beautiful!—silver, gold, red, and green, or all four mixed together, crumbling off, sticking in the lines on my palms. All the cards like this I spread on the floor to study. The crystals outline the buildings on the cards in a way buildings never are outlined but should be—if there were a way of making the crystals stick. But probably not; they would fall to the ground, never to be seen again. Some cards, instead of lines around the buildings, have words written in their skies with the same stuff, crumbling, dazzling and crumbling, raining down a little on little people who sometimes stand about below: pictures of Pentecost? What are the messages? I cannot tell, but they are falling on those specks of hands, on the hats, on the toes of their shoes, in their paths—wherever it is they are.

Postcards come from another world, the world of the grandparents who send things, the world of sad brown perfume, and morning. (The gray postcards of the village for sale in the village store are so unilluminating that they scarcely count. After all, one steps outside and immediately sees the same thing: the village, where we live, full-size, and in color.)

Two barrels of china. White with a gold band. Broken bits. A thick white teacup with a small red-and-blue butterfly on it, painfully desirable. A teacup with little pale-blue windows in it.

"See the grains of rice?" says my grandmother, showing me the cup against the light.

Could you poke the grains out? No, it seems they aren't really there any more. They were put there just for a while and then they left something or other behind. What odd things people do with grains of rice, so innocent and small! My aunt says that she has heard they write the Lord's Prayer on them. And make them make those little pale-blue lights.

More broken china. My grandmother says it breaks her heart. "Why couldn't they have got it packed better? Heaven knows what it cost."

"Where'll we put it all? The china closet isn't nearly big enough."

"It'll just have to stay in the barrels."

"Mother, you might as well use it."

"*No,*" says my grandmother.

"Where's the silver, Mother?"

"In the vault in Boston."

Vault. Awful word. I run the tip of my finger over the rough, jeweled lines on the postcards, over and over. They hold things up to each other and exclaim, and talk, and exclaim, over and over.

"There's that cake basket."

"Mrs. Miles…"

"Mrs. Miles' sponge cake…"

"She was very fond of her."

Another photograph—"Oh, that *Negro* girl! That friend."

"She went to be a medical missionary. She had a letter from her, last winter. From Africa."

"They were great friends."

They show me the picture. She, too, is black-and-white, with glasses on a chain. A morning friend.

And the smell, the wonderful smell of the dark-brown stains. Is it roses?

A tablecloth.

"She did beautiful work," says my grandmother.

"But look—it isn't finished."

Two pale, smooth wooden hoops are pressed together in the linen. There is a case of little ivory embroidery tools.

I abscond with a little ivory stick with a sharp point. To keep it forever I bury it under the bleeding heart by the crab-apple tree, but it is never found again.

Nate sings and pumps the bellows with one hand. I try to help, but he really does it all, from behind me, and laughs when the coals blow red and wild.

"Make me a ring! Make me a ring, Nate!"

Instantly it is made; it is mine.

It is too big and still hot, and blue and shiny. The horseshoe nail has a flat oblong head, pressing hot against my knuckle.

Two men stand watching, chewing or spitting tobacco, matches, horseshoe nails—anything, apparently, but with such presence; they are perfectly at home. The horse is the real guest, however. His harness hangs loose like a man's suspenders; they say pleasant things to him; one of his legs is doubled up in an improbable, affectedly polite way, and the bottom of his hoof is laid bare, but he doesn't seem to mind. Manure piles up behind him, suddenly, neatly. He, too, is very much at home. He is enormous. His rump is like a brown, glossy globe of the whole brown world. His ears are secret entrances to the underworld. His nose is supposed to feel like velvet and does, with ink spots under milk all over its pink. Clear bright-green bits of stiffened froth, like glass, are stuck around his mouth. He wears medals on his chest, too, and one on his forehead, and simpler decorations—red and blue celluloid rings overlapping each other on leather straps. On each temple is a clear glass bulge, like an eyeball, but in them are the heads of two other little horses (his dreams?), brightly colored, real and raised, untouchable, alas, against backgrounds of silver blue. His trophies hang around him, and the cloud of his odor is a chariot in itself.

At the end, all four feet are brushed with tar, and shine, and he expresses his satisfaction, rolling it from his nostrils like noisy smoke, as he backs into the shafts of his wagon.

The purple dress is to be fitted again this afternoon but I take a note to Miss Gurley to say the fitting will have to be postponed. Miss Gurley seems upset.

"Oh dear. And how is—" And she breaks off.

Her house is littered with scraps of cloth and tissue-paper patterns, yellow, pinked, with holes in the shapes of A, B, C, and D in them, and numbers; and threads everywhere like a fine vegetation. She has a bosom full of needles with threads ready to pull out and make nests with. She sleeps in her thimble. A gray kitten once lay on the treadle of her sewing machine, where she rocked it as she sewed, like a baby in a cradle, but it got hanged on the belt. Or did she make that up? But another gray-and-white one lies now by the arm of the machine, in imminent danger of being sewn into a turban.

There is a table covered with laces and braids, embroidery silks, and cards of buttons of all colors—big ones for winter coats, small pearls, little glass ones delicious to suck.

She has made the very dress I have on, "for twenty-five cents." My grandmother said my other grandmother would certainly be surprised at that.

The purple stuff lies on a table; long white threads hang all about it. Oh, look away before it moves by itself, or makes a sound; before it echoes, echoes, what it has heard!

Mysteriously enough, poor Miss Gurley—I know she is poor — gives me a five-cent piece. She leans over and drops it in the pocket of the red-and-white dress that she has made herself. It is very tiny, very shiny. King George's beard is like a little silver flame. Because they look like herring—or maybe salmon-scales, five-cent pieces are called "fish scales." One heard of people's rings being found inside fish, or their long-lost jackknives. What if one could scrape a salmon and find a little picture of King George on every scale?

I put my five-cent piece in my mouth for greater safety on the way home, and swallowed it. Months later, as far as I know, it is still in me, transmuting all its precious metal into my growing teeth and hair.

Back home, I am not allowed to go upstairs. I hear my aunts running back and forth, and something like a tin washbasin falls bump in the carpeted upstairs hall.

My grandmother is sitting in the kitchen stirring potato mash for tomorrow's bread and crying into it. She gives me a spoonful and it tastes wonderful but wrong. In it I think I taste my grandmother's tears; then I kiss her and taste them on her cheek.

She says it is time for her to get fixed up, and I say I want to help her brush her hair. So I do, standing swaying on the lower rung of the back of her rocking chair.

The rocking chair has been painted and repainted so many times that it is as smooth as cream—blue, white, and gray all showing through. My grandmother's hair is silver and in it she keeps a great many celluloid combs, at the back and sides, streaked gray and silver to match. The one at the back has longer teeth than the others and a row of sunken silver dots across the top, beneath a row of little balls. I pretend to play a tune on it; then I pretend to play a tune on each of the others before we stick them in, so my grandmother's hair is full of music. She laughs. I am so pleased with myself that I do not feel obliged to mention the five-cent piece. I drink a rusty, icy drink out of the biggest dipper; still, nothing much happens.

We are waiting for a scream. But it is not screamed again, and the red sun sets in silence.

Every morning I take the cow to the pasture we rent from Mr. Chisolm. She, Nelly, could probably go by herself just as well, but I like marching through the village with a big stick, directing her.

This morning it is brilliant and cool. My grandmother and I are alone again in the kitchen. We are talking. She says it is cool enough to keep the oven going, to bake the bread, to roast a leg of lamb.

"Will you remember to go down to the brook? Take Nelly around by the brook and pick me a big bunch of mint. I thought I'd make some mint sauce."

"For the leg of lamb?"

"You finish your porridge."

"I think I've had enough now…"

"Hurry up and finish that porridge."

There is talking on the stairs.

"No, now wait," my grandmother says to me. "Wait a minute."

My two aunts come into the kitchen. She is with them, wearing the white cotton dress with black polka dots and the flat black velvet bow at the neck. She comes and feeds me the rest of the porridge herself, smiling at me.

"Stand up now and let's see how tall you are," she tells me.

"Almost to your elbow," they say. "See how much she's grown."

"Almost."

"It's her hair."

Hands are on my head, pushing me down; I slide out from under them. Nelly is waiting for me in the yard, holding her nose just under in the watering trough. My stick waits against the door frame, clad in bark.

Nelly looks up at me, drooling glass strings. She starts off around the corner of the house without a flicker of expression.

Switch. Switch. How annoying she is!

But she is a Jersey and we think she is very pretty. "From in front," my aunt sometimes says.

She stops to snatch at the long, untrimmed grass around the gatepost.

"Nelly!"

Whack! I hit her hipbone.

On she goes without even looking around. Flop, flop, down over the dirt sidewalk into the road, across the village green in front of the Presbyterian church. The grass is gray with dew; the church is dazzling. It is high-shouldered and secretive; it leans backwards a little.

Ahead, the road is lined with dark, thin old elms; grass grows long and blue in the ditches. Behind the elms the meadows run along, peacefully, greenly.

We pass Mrs. Peppard's house. We pass Mrs. McNeil's house. We pass Mrs. Geddes house. We pass Hills' store.

The store is high, and a faded gray-blue, with tall windows, built on a long, high stoop of gray-blue cement with an iron hitching rail along it. Today, in one window there are big cardboard easels, shaped like houses—complete houses and houses with the roofs lifted off to show glimpses of the rooms inside, all in different colors—with cans of paint in pyramids in the middle. But they are an old story. In the other window is something new: shoes, single shoes, summer shoes, each sitting on top of its own box with its mate beneath it, inside, in the dark. Surprisingly, some of them appear to be exactly the colors and texture of pink and blue blackboard chalks, but I can't stop to examine them now. In one door, great overalls hang high in the air on hangers. Miss Ruth Hill looks out the other door and waves. We pass Mrs. Captain Mahon's house.

Nelly tenses and starts walking faster, making over to the right. Every morning and evening we go through this. We are approaching Miss Spencer's house. Miss Spencer is the milliner the way Miss Gurley is the dressmaker. She has a very small white house with the doorstep right on the sidewalk. One front window has lace curtains with a pale-yellow window shade pulled all the way down, inside them; the other one has a shelf across it on which are displayed four summer hats. Out of the corner of my eye I can see that there is a yellow chip straw with little wads of flamingo-colored feathers around the crown, but again there is no time to examine anything.

On each side of Miss Spencer's door is a large old lilac bush. Every time we go by, Nelly determines to brush off all her flies on these bushes—brush them off forever, in one fell swoop. Then Miss Spencer is apt to come to the door and stand there, shaking with anger, between the two bushes still shaking from Nelly's careening passage, and yell at me, sometimes waving a hat in my direction as well.

Nelly, leaning to the right, breaks into a cow trot. I run up with my stick.

Whack!

"Nelly!"

Whack!

Just this once she gives in and we rush safely by.

Then begins a long, pleasant stretch beneath the elms. The Presbyterian manse has a black iron fence with openwork foursided pillars, like tall, thin bird cages, bird cages for storks. Dr. Gillespie, the minister, appears just as we come along, and rides slowly toward us on his bicycle.

"Good day." He even tips his hat.

"Good day."

He wears the most interesting hat in the village: a man's regular stiff straw sailor, only it is black. Is there a possibility that he paints it at home, with something like stove polish? Because once I had seen one of my aunts painting a strawcolored hat navy blue.

Nelly, oblivious, makes cow flops. Smack. Smack. Smack. Smack.

It is fascinating. I cannot take my eyes off her. Then I step around them: fine dark-green and lacy and watery at the edges.

We pass the McLeans', whom I know very well. Mr. McLean is just coming out of his new barn with the tin hip roof and with him is Jock, their old shepherd dog, long-haired, black and white and yellow. He runs up barking deep, cracked, soft barks in the quiet morning. I hesitate.

Mr. McLean bellows, "Jock! You! Come back here! Are you trying to frighten her?"

To me he says, "He's twice as old as you are."

Finally I pat the big round warm head.

We talk a little. I ask the exact number of Jock's years but Mr. McLean has forgotten.

"He hasn't hardly a tooth in his head and he's got rheumatism. I hope we'll get him through next winter. He still wants to go to the woods with me and it's hard for him in the snow. We'll be lost without him."

Mr. McLean speaks to me behind one hand, not to hurt Jock's feelings: *"Deaf as a post."*

Like anybody deaf, Jock puts his head to one side.

"He used to be the best dog at finding cows for miles around. People used to come from away down the shore to borrow him to find their cows for them. And he'd always find them. The first year we had to leave him behind when we went up to the mountain to get the cows I thought it would kill him. Well, when his teeth started going he couldn't do much with the cows any more. Effie used to say, 'I don't know how we'd run the farm without him.'"

Loaded down with too much black and yellow and white fur, Jock smiles, showing how few teeth he has. He has yellow caterpillars for eyebrows.

Nelly has gone on ahead. She is almost up the hill to Chisolms' when I catch up with her. We turn in to their steep, long drive, through a steep, bare yard crowded with unhappy apple trees. From the top, though, from the Chisolms' back yard, one always stops to look at the view.

There are the tops of all the elm trees in the village and there, beyond them, the long green marshes, so fresh, so salt. Then the Minas Basin, with the tide halfway in or out, the wet red mud glazed with sky blue until it meets the creeping lavender-red water. In the middle of the view, like one hand of a clock pointing straight up, is the steeple of the Presbyterian church. We are in the "Maritimes" but all that means is that we live by the sea.

Mrs. Chisolm's pale frantic face is watching me out the kitchen window as she washes the breakfast dishes. We wave, but I hurry by because she may come out and ask questions. But her questions are not as bad perhaps as those of her husband, Mr. Chisolm, who wears a beard. One evening he had met me in the pasture and asked me how my soul was. Then he held me firmly by both hands while he said a prayer, with his head bowed, Nelly right beside us chewing her cud all the time. I had felt a soul, heavy in my chest, all the way home.

I let Nelly through the set of bars to the pasture where the brook is, to get the mint. We both take drinks and I pick a big bunch of mint, eating a little, scratchy and powerful. Nelly looks over her shoulder and comes back to try it, thinking, as cows do, it might be something especially for her. Her face is close to mine and I hold her by one horn to admire her eyes again. Her nose is blue and as shiny as something in the rain. At such close quarters my feelings for her are mixed. She gives my bare arm a lick, scratchy and powerful, too, almost upsetting me into the brook; then she goes off to join a black-and-white friend she has here, mooing to her to wait until she catches up.

For a while I entertain the idea of not going home today at all, of staying safely here in the pasture all day, playing in the brook and climbing on the squishy, moss-covered hummocks in the swampy part. But an immense, sibilant, glistening loneliness suddenly faces me, and the cows are moving off to the shade of the fir trees, their bells chiming softly, individually.

On the way home there are the four hats in Miss Spencer's window to study, and the summer shoes in Hills'. There is the same shoe in white, in black patent leather, and in the chalky, sugary, unearthly pinks and blues. It has straps that button around the ankle and above, four of them, about an inch wide and an inch apart, reaching away up.

In those unlovely gilded red and green books, filled with illustrations of the Bible stories, the Roman centurions wear them, too, or something very like them.

Surely they are my size. Surely, this summer, pink or blue, my grandmother will buy me a pair!

Miss Ruth Hill gives me a Moirs chocolate out of the glass case. She talks to me: "How is she? We've always been friends. We played together from the time we were babies. We sat together in school. Right from primer class on. After she went away, she always wrote to me—even after she got sick the first time."

Then she tells a funny story about when they were little.

That afternoon, Miss Gurley comes and we go upstairs to watch the purple dress being fitted again. My grandmother holds me against her knees. My younger aunt is helping Miss Gurley, handing her the scissors when she asks. Miss Gurley is cheerful and talkative today.

The dress is smaller now; there are narrow, even folds down the skirt; the sleeves fit tightly, with little wrinkles over the thin white hands. Everyone is very pleased with it; everyone talks and laughs.

"There. You see? It's so becoming."

"I've never seen you in anything more becoming."

"And it's so nice to see you in color for a change."

And the purple is real, like a flower against the gold-and-white wallpaper.

On the bureau is a present that has just come, from an uncle in Boston whom I do not remember. It is a gleaming little bundle of flat, triangular satin pillows—sachets, tied together with a white satin ribbon, with an imitation rosebud on top of the bow. Each is a different faint color; if you take them apart, each has a different faint scent. But tied together the way they came, they make one confused, powdery odor.

The mirror has been lifted off the bureau and put on the floor against the wall.

She walks slowly up and down and looks at the skirt in it.

"I think that's about right," says Miss Gurley, down on her knees and looking into the mirror, too, but as if the skirt were miles and miles away.

But, twitching the purple skirt with her thin white hands, she says desperately, "I don't know what they're wearing any more. I have no *idea*!" It turns to a sort of wail.

"Now, now," soothes Miss Gurley. "I do think that's about right. Don't you?" She appeals to my grandmother and me.

Light, musical, constant sounds are coming from Nate's shop. It sounds as though he were making a wheel rim.

She sees me in the mirror and turns on me: "Stop sucking your thumb!"

Then in a moment she turns to me again and demands, "Do you know what I want?"

"No."

"I want some humbugs. I'm dying for some humbugs. I don't think I've had any humbugs for years and years and years. If I give you some pennies, will you go to Mealy's and buy me a bag?"

To be sent on an errand! Everything is all right.

Humbugs are a kind of candy, although not a kind I am particularly fond of. They are brown, like brook water, but hard, and shaped like little twisted pillows. They last a long time, but lack the spit-producing brilliance of cherry or strawberry.

Mealy runs a little shop where she sells candy and bananas and oranges and all kinds of things she crochets. At Christmas, she sells toys, but only at Christmas. Her real name is Amelia. She also takes care of the telephone switchboard for the village, in her dining room.

Somebody finds a black pocketbook in the bureau. She counts out five big pennies into my hand, in a column, then one more.

"That one's for you. So you won't eat up all my humbugs on the way home."

Further instructions:

"Don't run all the way."

"Don't stop on the bridge."

I do run, by Nate's shop, glimpsing him inside, pumping away with one hand. We wave. The beautiful big Newfoundland dog is there again and comes out, bounding along with me a ways.

I do not stop on the bridge but slow down long enough to find out the years on the pennies. King George is much bigger than on a five-cent piece, brown as an Indian in copper, but he wears the same clothes; on a penny, one can make out the little ermine trimmings on his coat.

Mealy has a bell that rings when you go in so that she'll hear you if she's at the switchboard. The shop is a step down, dark, with a counter along one side. The ceiling is low and the floor has settled well over to the counter side. Mealy is broad and fat and it looks as though she and the counter and the showcase, stuffed dimly with things every which way, were settling down together out of sight.

Five pennies buys a great many humbugs. I must not take too long to decide what I want for myself. I must get back quickly, quickly, while Miss Gurley is there and everyone is upstairs and the dress is still on. Without taking time to think, quickly I point at the brightest thing. It is a ball, glistening solidly with crystals of pink and yellow sugar, hung, impractically, on an elastic, like a real elastic ball. I know I don't even care for the inside of it, which is soft, but I wind most of the elastic around my arm, to keep the ball off the ground, at least, and start hopefully back.

But one night, in the middle of the night, there is a fire. The church bell wakes me up. It is in the room with me; red flames are burning the wallpaper beside the bed. I suppose I shriek.

The door opens. My younger aunt comes in. There is a lamp lit in the hall and everyone is talking at once.

"Don't cry!" my aunt almost shouts to me. "It's just a fire. Way up the road. It isn't going to hurt you. Don't *cry*!"

"Will! Will!" My grandmother is calling my grandfather. "Do you have to go?"

"No, don't go, Dad!"

"It looks like McLean's place." My grandfather sounds muffled.

"Oh, not their new barn!" My grandmother.

"You can't tell from here." He must have his head out the window.

"*She's* calling for you, Mother." My older aunt: "I'll go."

"No. I'll go." My younger aunt.

"Light that other lamp, girl."

My older aunt comes to my door. "It's way off. It's nowhere near us. The men will take care of it. Now you go to sleep." But she leaves my door open.

"Leave her door open," calls my grandmother just then. "Oh, why do they have to ring the bell like that? It's enough to terrify anybody. Will, be *careful*."

Sitting up in bed, I see my grandfather starting down the stairs, tucking his nightshirt into his trousers as he goes.

"Don't make so much noise!" My older aunt and my grandmother seem to be quarreling.

"Noise! I can't hear myself think, with that bell!"

"I bet Spurgeon's ringing it!" They both laugh.

"It must have been heat lightning," says my grandmother, now apparently in her bedroom, as if it were all over.

"*She's* all right, Mother." My younger aunt comes back. "I don't think she's scared. You can't see the glare so much on that side of the house."

Then my younger aunt comes into my room and gets in bed with me. She says to go to sleep, it's way up the road. The men have to go; my grandfather has gone. It's probably somebody's barn full of hay, from heat lightning. It's been such a hot summer there's been a lot of it. The church bell stops and her voice is suddenly loud in my ear over my shoulder. The last echo of the bell lasts for a long time.

Wagons rattle by.

"Now they're going down to the river to fill the barrels," my aunt is murmuring against my back.

The red flame dies down on the wall, then flares again.

Wagons rattle by in the dark. Men are swearing at the horses.

"Now they're coming back with the water. Go to sleep."

More wagons; men's voices. I suppose I go to sleep.

I wake up and it is the same night, the night of the fire. My aunt is getting out of bed, hurrying away. It is still dark and silent now, after the fire. No, not silent; my grandmother is crying somewhere, not in her room. It is getting gray. I hear one wagon, rumbling far off, perhaps crossing the bridge.

But now I am caught in a skein of voices, my aunts' and my grandmother's, saying the same things over and over, sometimes loudly, sometimes in whispers:

"Hurry. For heaven's sake, *shut the door!*"

"Sh!"

"Oh, we can't go on like this, we…"

"It's too dangerous Remember that…"

"Sh! Don't let her…"

A door slams.

A door opens. The voices begin again.

I am struggling to free myself.

Wait. Wait. No one is going to scream.

Slowly, slowly it gets daylight. A different red reddens the wallpaper. Now the house is silent. I get up and dress by myself and go downstairs. My grandfather is in the kitchen alone, drinking his tea. He has made the oatmeal himself, too. He gives me some and tells me about the fire very cheerfully.

It had not been the McLeans' new barn after all, but someone else's barn, off the road. All the hay was lost but they had managed somehow to save part of the barn.

But neither of us is really listening to what he is saying; we are listening for sounds from upstairs. But everything is quiet.

On the way home from taking Nelly to the pasture I go to see where the barn was. There are people still standing around, some of them the men who got up in the night to go to the river. Everyone seems quite cheerful there, too, but the smell of burned hay is awful, sickening.

Now the front bedroom is empty. My older aunt has gone back to Boston and my other aunt is making plans to go there after a while, too.

There has been a new pig. He was very cute to begin with, and skidded across the kitchen linoleum while everyone laughed. He grew and grew. Perhaps it is all the same summer, because it is unusually hot and something unusual for a pig happens to him: he gets sunburned. He really gets sunburned, bright pink, but the strangest thing of all, the curled-up end of his tail gets so sunburned it is brown and scorched. My grandmother trims it with the scissors and it doesn't hurt him.

Sometime later this pig is butchered. My grandmother, my aunt, and I shut ourselves in the parlor. My aunt plays a piece on the piano called "Out in the Fields." She plays it and plays it; then she switches to Mendelssohn's "War March of the Priests."

The front room is empty. Nobody sleeps there. Clothes are hung there.

Every week my grandmother sends off a package. In it she puts cake and fruit, a jar of preserves, Moirs chocolates.

Monday afternoon every week.

Fruit, cake, Jordan almonds, a handkerchief with a tatted edge.

Fruit. Cake. Wild-strawberry jam. A New Testament.

A little bottle of scent from Hills' store, with a purple silk tassel fastened to the stopper.

Fruit. Cake. "Selections from Tennyson."

A calendar, with a quotation from Longfellow for every day.

Fruit. Cake. Moirs chocolates.

I watch her pack them in the pantry. Sometimes she sends me to the store to get things at the last minute.

The address of the sanatorium is in my grandmother's handwriting, in purple indelible pencil, on smoothed-out wrapping paper. It will never come off.

I take the package to the post office. Going by Nate's, I walk far out in the road and hold the package on the side away from him.

He calls to me. "Come here! I want to show you something."

But I pretend I don't hear him. But at any other time I still go there just the same.

The post office is very small. It sits on the side of the road like a package once delivered by the post office. The government has painted its clapboards tan, with a red trim. The earth in front of it is worn hard. Its face is scarred and scribbled on, carved with initials. In the evening, when the Canadian Pacific mail is due, a row of big boys leans against it, but in the daytime there is nothing to be afraid of. There is no one in front, and inside it is empty. There is no one except the postmaster, Mr. Johnson, to look at my grandmother's purple handwriting.

The post office tilts a little, like Mealy's shop, and inside it looks as chewed as a horse's manger. Mr. Johnson looks out through the little window in the middle of the bank of glassfronted boxes, like an animal looking out over its manger. But he is dignified by the thick, beveled-edged glass boxes with their solemn, upright gold-and-black-shaded numbers.

Ours is 21. Although there is nothing in it, Mr. Johnson automatically cocks his eye at it from behind when he sees me.

21.

"Well, well. Here we are again. Good day, good day," he says.

"Good day, Mr. Johnson."

I have to go outside again to hand him the package through the ordinary window, into his part of the post office, because it is too big for the little official one. He is very old, and nice. He has two fingers missing on his right hand where they were caught in a threshing machine. He wears a navy-blue cap with a black leather visor, like a ship's officer, and a shirt with feathery brown stripes, and a big gold collar button.

"Let me see. Let me see. Let me see. Hm," he says to himself, weighing the package on the scales, jiggling the bar with the two remaining fingers and thumb.

"Yes. Yes. Your grandmother is very faithful."

Every Monday afternoon I go past the blacksmith's shop with the package under my arm, hiding the address of the sanatorium with my arm and my other hand.

Going over the bridge, I stop and stare down into the river. All the little trout that have been too smart to get caught—for how long now?—are there, rushing in flank movements, foolish assaults and retreats, against and away from the old sunken fender of Malcolm McNeil's Ford. It has lain there for ages and is supposed to be a disgrace to us all. So are the tin cans that glint there, brown and gold.

From above, the trout look as transparent as the water, but if one did catch one, it would be opaque enough, with a little slick moon-white belly with a pair of tiny, pleated, rose-pink fins on it. The leaning willows soak their narrow yellowed leaves.

Clang.

Clang.

Nate is shaping a horseshoe.

Oh, beautiful pure sound!

It turns everything else to silence.

But still, once in a while, the river gives an unexpected gurgle. "*Slp,*" it says, out of glassy-ridged brown knots sliding along the surface.

Clang.

And everything except the river holds its breath.

Now there is no scream. Once there was one and it settled slowly down to earth one hot summer afternoon; or did it float up, into that dark, too dark, blue sky? But surely it has gone away, forever.

It sounds like a bell buoy out at sea.

It is the elements speaking: earth, air, fire, water.

All those other things—clothes, crumbling postcards, broken china; things damaged and lost, sickened or destroyed; even the frail almost-lost scream—are they too frail for us to hear their voices long, too mortal?

Nate!

Oh, beautiful sound, strike again!

MARK STRAND

Although born in Summerside, P.E.I., Mark Strand (1934–) emigrated with his parents to the United States at the age of four and a half. He is now one of his country's most respected poets. In 1990, he was made Poet Laureate of the United States of America.

The Strand family moved from Prince Edward Island to Halifax almost immediately after Mark's birth, then moved again to Montreal, where his father toiled at a variety of jobs. By the outbreak of the Second World War, they were resident in Philadelphia, but Mark returned repeatedly to Nova Scotia (French Village, Glen Margaret, Hackett's Cove) to spend summers with relatives.

The pull of the Maritimes lasted into adulthood: in 1963, he lived at Indian Harbour for a summer, and the following summer he resided in Hubbards. His parents returned to live in Halifax in 1955, and they died there in the late 1960s. In the early 1970s, Strand, in partnership with a painter, purchased one whole side of the cove at East Dover, but they eventually sold the property, and since that time Mark Strand's physical contact with Canada has been intermittent and occasioned principally by readings.

While his physical contact with the country has been limited of late, much of his poetry has been profoundly coloured by Canada. Of St. Margaret's Bay, near Halifax, he says, "[it] remains the single steady landscape of my childhood, a place in which I was unequivocally happy," and his Canadian poems are among the most tender and moving he has published. The recollections of emotions evoked by Nova Scotian villages ring throughout his work: in some, the references are direct; in others, implied.

The following poem is dedicated to Elizabeth Bishop, the remarkable American author with whom Strand shared many conversations in adulthood about the happy land of their childhood. While they knew no one in common in Nova Scotia, their poetry of place salutes the province in a manner—and at a level—yet to be surpassed.

THE HOUSE IN FRENCH VILLAGE

for Elizabeth Bishop

It stood by itself
in a sloping field,
it was white
with green
shutters and trim,

and its gambrel roof
gave it the look
of a small
prim barn.
From the porch

when the weather was clear,
I could see Fox Point,
across the bay
where the fishermen,
I was told,

laid out
their catch of tuna
on the pier
and hacked away with axes
at the bellies

of the giant fish.
I would stare
at Wedge Island
where gulls wheeled
in loud broken rings

above their young;
at Albert Hubley's shack
built over water, and sagging;
at Boutelier's wharf
loaded down

with barrels of brine
and nets to be mended.
I would sit
with my grandmother,
my aunt, and my mother,

the four of us rocking
on chairs, watching
the narrow dirt road
for a sign
of the black

baby Austin
my father would drive
to town and back.
But the weather
was not often clear

and all we could see
were sheets of cold rain
sweeping this way and that,
riffling the sea's coat
of deep green,

and the wind
beating the field flat,
sending up to the porch
gusts of salt spray
that carried

the odor of fish
and the rot,
so it seemed,
of the whole bay,
while we kept watch.

DOUGLAS HYDE

COLLEAGUE of W. B. Yeats, confidante of Lady Gregory, Douglas Hyde (1860–1949) remains one of the most widely respected writers and scholars in Ireland, a nation not noted for unanimity in citing its heroes. Until quite recently in the Republic of Ireland, according to the distinguished Irish poet John Montague, Douglas Hyde was as well known as James Joyce. In 1938, when Eire adopted its current constitution, Hyde, aged seventy-eight, even though a Protestant, was elected, unopposed, the first President of the Republic of Ireland. His election was a reflection not so much of his popularity as of the nation's esteem for his pioneering work in restoring the Irish language, for his ground-breaking efforts to save Irish folklore, and for his tenacity in ignoring the English and Irish who jeered at his love of his own culture. His own play, *Twisting of the Rope*, was the first drama ever produced in Irish at the Abbey Theatre. How unusual, then, that for a man so closely linked to Ireland, Canada was to be so important.

By the time he was merely twenty, Hyde had already accumulated a formidable library of Irish literature, some of it in manuscript, at a time when the study of Irish was considered beneath serious scholarly concern. His academic studies at Trinity College, Dublin, in law and divinity placated the scholastic demands of the authorities, but Celtic literary studies increasingly subsumed his life. While he was wary of the overt politicizing of the Nationalist movement, "his collection and translation of Irish oral traditions had a profound effect on Yeats," and other giants of the Celtic renaissance.

But publishing poems and folktales would not pay the rent. So it was with relish that Hyde accepted a friend's offer to teach modern languages for the 1890–91 academic year at the University of New Brunswick in Fredericton. After years of study, it would be his first real job.

Eventually, he settled onto the small campus (eighty-six students were taught by eight faculty) and quickly discovered that most of the students were appallingly ill-prepared for college and seemingly uninterested in learning. The faculty were equally uninspiring. With only a few exceptions, they were as conservative and uninquisitive as the high society of the town.

But the brightness of the weather and the colours of the fall soon induced him outdoors when his teaching duties were done. He frequently fished and hunted, either alone or with one of the two colleagues he found simpatico and intellectually curious. By November he was relishing the cold, and took to skating miles up the Saint John River. Canada seemed to inspire a spartan vigour in him, and he soon made an hour's walk and a daily cold bath essential to his regimen.

By late December, he was ready for longer forays, and the Christmas break gave him time to indulge a season-long desire to hunt caribou. On Boxing Day, he set out with a couple of traders and three "Milicete" Indians (the current spelling is Malecite) on an expedition that, in the words of his biographers, "was to be one of the most memorable trips of his life."

His ignorance of natives to this point is probably accounted for by his adopting, on his arrival, the prejudice of the locals. By the end of the hunting trip, however, his fascination with languages and folklore sufficiently overcame his passive bigotry that he seemed nearly indifferent to not, because of bad weather, having killed any big game. Initially, he was struck by the similarity of some Malecite tales to Gaelic stories. But he later revised a belief (suggested in the following excerpt) that the tales had come to the natives via Scots-Irish factors working for the Hudson's Bay Company, to a more

Douglas Hyde in New Brunswick, late 1890 or early 1891, while professor of Modern Languages at the University of New Brunswick in Fredericton. It was this photo of himself in Canada which Hyde, the first President of Ireland, kept perennially in his den. Courtesy of Douglas Sealy, Dublin.

profound understanding of archetypes in folklore. In this, and in methodology, he was decades—several decades—ahead of more celebrated folklorists of this century, but it was not until he actually experienced alternate tales in Canada that he was able to reach this intellectual position.

Given the current debate in Canada about the propriety of using, even recording, Indian stories, Hyde's respect for the reluctance of the natives to tell one of their tales is perhaps ahead of its time. As noted in Hyde's most recent biography:

> Hyde asked a Milicete whose father was French Canadian if he would recite it ["Glooscap and the Great Turtle"] in English. The man agreed, although he told Hyde that he himself had never heard the story "except in Indian," and there were those who maintained it could not be told properly in any other tongue. Hyde wanted to make notes as he listened, but he was concerned that his storyteller might be discomfited by the idea of having his words written down on paper. His solution was to seat himself behind a caribou skin.

The population decline of the Malecites and their means of preserving their culture were equally compelling to Hyde, for the parallels with the Gaelic became excitingly, sometimes painfully, obvious. As on the west coast of Ireland, he learned it was the Malecite women who did most to conserve the language, the legends, the cultural history. He was fascinated to discover that some of the women refused or were unable to speak English, a situation he had not experienced outside of Ireland, and the contempt of the invading culture for the place names of the indigenous held for him upsetting equivalents with Eire.

For every aspect of life in Fredericton annoying him, there was an aspect to praise. For the duration of his stay, he remained irritated by the prohibition of alcohol, but was charmed by the frequency, accessibility, and opulence of evening parties. Canada's apparent disdain for class was eminently preferable to the snobbery of home, but he remained shocked at the blatancy of political bribery. He was always struck by the generosity of Canadians to strangers, a response, he maintained, untypical of the Irish "sets and cliques [who] think only of themselves." And he clearly enjoyed the relative emancipation of Canadian women to the strictures of those in his hometown. To friends he wrote that he had "danced, talked, laughed, and flirted more in a month than in six months in Dublin."

But Fredericton was not heaven. Shortly after arriving he could still write optimistically to his sister:

> I don't think the spirit of Rationalism has touched them at all. They ... have no thoughts on unpleasant subjects of the soul but follow their good bishop and go to church and sing, oh sing, hymns on all occasions possible.... It is quite refreshing to be among them.

Yet, near the end of his stay, he observed that Frederictonians, *vis-à-vis* their religion, were "grandmotherly stick-in-the-muds who cling to the outside husk, the dry form," while wilfully ignoring the core.

He was enamoured enough of Canada to consider immigration seriously, and weighed the merits of a firm offer from McGill University. The pull of Ireland proved too strong, however. The demise of Parnell had happened in his absence, and inevitably, in Tory Fredericton, Hyde must have felt achingly marginal while believing he had a key role to play in the Irish national debate. At the end of term, on June 3, 1891, he began a brief visit to New England and Niagara, and then returned to Ireland, and a rising fame in his own country that was to lead to the highest honour the country could bestow: its presidency.

Just prior to leaving, he penned a few poems for the University literary society, one of which, "To Canada," probably because it was oozingly sentimental, had wide currency with a myriad of Canadian newspapers. Of more serious import in relation to Canada was the essay "On Some Indian Folk-lore," quoted below. The essay was originally published in the *Providence Sunday Journal* on April 12, 1891. The Malecite natives were never a large tribe in New Brunswick; their population may never have risen above a few thousand members. But they continue to this day in New Brunswick, organized in six bands.

Some measure of the depth of his fondness for the country is gleaned from the fact that (to the ongoing astonishment of his family) for his entire life Douglas Hyde kept, unique among his possessions, arrestingly hung at his home in Ireland, just one image: a photograph taken in Fredericton of himself in fur hat, fur coat, and fur gloves, holding snowshoes. And prominently visible beneath this photograph: artefacts given to him as gifts by the Malecites.

———————

ON SOME INDIAN FOLK-LORE

There are many spots in Canada where, despite repeating Winchesters and growth of population, the big game, moose and caribou, are not yet extinct. Such places are to be found all over the province of New Brunswick, especially in the Northern counties. This province is thinly populated, and about four-fifths, or even more, of it is still covered with forest and jungle, interspersed by "barrens" or pieces of poor, untimbered land, varying from a quarter of a mile to several miles in extent, and forming the feeding ground of the caribou, who live on moss, which they paw up from under the snow, and on a kind of grey lichen, which hangs from the branches of the hackmatack or tamarack (English spruce) trees.

I had long been endeavoring to secure some folk-lore and old stories from the Milicete Indians, who dwell along the St. John and other inland rivers in New Brunswick, but somehow or other the aspect of a stranger in the broad daylight seemed always to have a depressing influence upon them, and they invariably either alleged that they knew no stories, or else that they used to hear them but had now forgotten them. The few Milicete stories, which in the end I succeeded in getting, I must attribute to the caribou, after which I went out hunting with two Indians and two half-breeds. One of these half-breeds was a curious combination of blood, his father having been a Russian Finn and his mother a squaw, yet though the Finns are one of the cleverest races in Europe, it so turned out that he was the stupid one of the party, and could tell no stories outside of a personal adventure or two. The other half-breed was the son of an old Hudson Bay voyageur, who had become so Indianized that he had never spoken anything to his children but Indian, and this man, who had an exuberance of French vivacity in his nature, was, like Mercurius, chief speaker and also chief story teller for the rest of the party. The full bred Indians were more taciturn and did not know English sufficiently well to tell a long story in it, and although I had picked up several hundred words and phrases of Milicete I did not understand it sufficiently to follow a rapidly told story. Accordingly the majority of the stories which I jotted down came from the French half-breed, who, having been born in an English-speaking part of the province of New Brunswick, where his father had settled, spoke Indian and not very fluent English, but strange to say, hardly any French. I may here mention that the northern part of the province contains a large number of French speakers, whose language, far from tending to die out as German is dying in the States seems bent upon holding its place for all time in Canada, and competing with English and Spanish in the linguistic distribution of the new world. Almost two-fifths of Canada is at present French speaking, and as the French population is increasing faster than the English they may soon be equal. The French of the habitants, however, is becoming largely anglicised, and they speak of potatoes for *pommes de terre*, post cartes for *cartes de poste*, and what is more remarkable some families of French origin appear to have a mania for translating their names into English; thus numberless Blancs now call themselves Whites or Wites, even though they continue to speak French.

As to the Indian population of New Brunswick, it is probably under a thousand, and is chiefly composed of two different tribes speaking, as far as I could find out, almost totally distinct languages, the Milicetes, the Micmacs. These Indians pull very well with the whites, and men who will walk out of a lumber camp and refuse to work in it if a negro is taken into employment, make not the slightest objection to working with Indians. The men and squaws are saluted still as brother and sister. The red man is, however, decreasing in numbers here as elsewhere, partly from disease, partly from the increasing scarcity of game, and partly through his inability to adapt himself to the new civilisation, though I must confess that the most of those with whom I came in contact appeared as capable of taking care of themselves as anyone need wish, and more than one who had in time past served as guide or hunter to the officers of the regular army—before it was withdrawn from Canada —had completely acquired the offhand manners of the English officer, and uttered passing oaths and planted themselves with their back to the fire and extended legs with all the charming insouciance and polish of club or mess room. The worst of the red man is his improvidence. He spends money as he gets it, and even after great hunting or "furring" successes and making a coup of several hundred dollars, he always runs through his wealth immediately on getting it in the silliest way, and it seems probable that another generation or two will be necessary to eradicate this failing from the breed.

Of our hunting exploits I am not going to speak; suffice it to say that we pitched our camp in a great thicket, shovelling away the snow, which was about two feet thick, and leaving about three inches of it on the ground; we covered it over with a quantity of fine spruce boughs, and spreading our skins and blankets over them we slept very comfortably, nor did we find it hard to keep the tent warm, although the thermometer stood for several days at 35 below zero. Unfortunately snow had fallen, and changed into a half rain just as we were encamping ourselves, and this, freezing on the top of the snow, made a kind of hard crust, which our snow shoes cracked at every step, so that it became impossible to stalk either caribou or moose, for the noise of the snow crust as it cracked could be distinctly heard for half a mile. We were obliged, accordingly, to remain in camp for about a fortnight, waiting for fresh snow to fall, which would deaden the noise of our snow shoes, and give us an opportunity to creep on the caribou who were in our vicinity. It was during this time that, having nothing better to do, each of us told all the stories he could think of, and I know, for my part, I must have told over thirty. Many of the stories of the half-breed seemed to me to have filtered into Indian from a French Canadian, and some actually from a Scotch Gaelic or Irish source. The most of them he had been told by his father in Indian, others he had picked up round camp fires, but the proportion that seemed to me to be of pure Indian origin was less than half. It was, however, quite natural that his father, having been an old Hudson Bay voyageur, should have picked up Scotch Gaelic stories from his fellow hunters, great numbers of whom were Scotch, and afterwards recited them in Indian to his children. Several, indeed, the majority of his stories, were probably of French origin, and many of them were too gross for repetition. Amongst other stories of European origin which he had picked up through the medium of Indian was that of the *Merchant of Venice*. The story was alleged to have happened in France, no names were given except that the hero was, as usual, Jack, nor was the nationality of the Jew mentioned. Jack wheeled down to his creditor his money in a wheelbarrow, but came later and would have had to pay his pound of flesh, had not the primitive Portia, his wife, not his sweetheart, dressed herself up in an officer's clothes with a sword and threatened to kill the other if he drew blood while taking his pound of flesh. I have not the slightest doubt that this story was derived from an original French source, and would probably have been told to me just the same had Shakespeare never existed. The story itself, which is probably of Eastern origin, is to be found in the great medieval assortment of tales of the Gesta Romanorum, and no doubt some Frenchman carried with him the traditional version which filtered into an Indian and from that into a broken English dress. Another story, undoubtedly of French origin, was that most indecent of all the tales in Boccaccio's *Decameron*, "How They Sent the Devil Back into Hell," the hero of which piece was, as usual, the ubiquitous and mythic "Jack."

The genuine Indian stories, however, were, like the stories of every primitive race, of two kinds; the first of war and hunting and personal adventures, the other, and to me the most interesting, consisted of what I may call folk-lore, pure and simple, in which the supernatural or extravagantly impossible plays the largest part, such folk-lore as I gave a sketch of some months ago, in relation to the Irish Gaels. Of the war and hunting stories, the most noticeable was one which I have since heard corroborated by many Indians, and which has frequently been retold me in nearly the same manner, so that I have little doubt of the essential truth of it. A couple of hundred years ago, more or less, for none of my informants were accurate in matters of time, there arose a great war between the Milicetes on the St. John river and the Mohawks or Iroquois, for they are called by both names, who lived farther north in Canada and nearer to the St. Lawrence. One time 250 Mohawk warriors started and came down the St. John river in flat canoes as far as Little Falls, and when they got there they surprised two Indian women, whose husbands and uncle were out hunting. As the warriors were quite ignorant of the river they took the women prisoners and made them act as guides. In order to keep their band together they lashed their canoes one to the other, so that they made a broad belt of boats almost extending from bank to bank of the stream, which is pretty rapid and about half a mile broad. They questioned the women closely as to the nature of the river, but the women assured them that it was all equally smooth and level until they should come to the Milicete camp. This was not true, for right before them, but many miles away, lay the Grand Falls, a tremendous cataract, which I have heard many overpatriotic New Brunswickers place, in their enthusiasm, on a level with Niagara. However, as night came on, most of the warriors ceased to paddle, and, on the repeated assurances of the women that there was no danger from the river, most of them, including the chiefs, lay down and slept, while the current carried the whole flotilla slowly along. The women, however, who knew the river perfectly, continued to gradually pass over into the end boats, next the shore, and in these they still continued paddling. When the roar of the Grand Falls was at length heard, the few Mohawks who were awake started to their feet, but the women assured them that the noise of the waters came from a great stream which fell into the St. John. By this time the centre canoes were well caught in the treacherous current and drawn in towards their destruction. On seeing this, the women leaped into the water, and, being nearer the shore, where the current was less powerful, they managed to gain the land, but the canoes in the centre drew those at the two wings after them, and before the half-sleeping Mohawks could unlash their canoes or grasp their paddles, they were irresistibly drawn to the cataract, shot over it, and perished to a man. Below the falls many scores of their dead bodies were thrown ashore by the river. The two women scalped all the chiefs and then choosing an enormous pine tree about 100 feet high, they peeled all the greenery off it, leaving on it only a few naked branches, and to these they affixed the chieftains' scalps. They then cut away all the bushes and little trees for about a hundred feet from the trunks, and in this space they danced their war dance round the tree all day and all night. The next day their uncle coming back from hunting heard their cries and following the sound came up with them and seeing the scalps, he joined the dance also. Their husbands came up the next day and they, too, fell to dancing the war dance round the tree, and so those five danced for one fortnight without stopping, the Indians said, but this must be exaggeration. At the end of their wild fortnight's dance they returned home and told the Milicetes how they had been saved by the two women. The tree is standing yet, and the Indians eagerly assured me that if I came with them they could show me the place where not a bush has grown ever since round that grim pine, and where the earth is trodden down in a deep circle all round it by the feet of those savage dancers so long ago.

After this the Mohawks came again with a still greater fleet of canoes to wipe the Milicetes off the face of the earth. After they had come a good way below Grand Falls they encamped, and were espied by three Milicetes, one of whom was sent off to warn the tribe, while the other two paddled their canoe up the river and past the Mohawk camp; then when they had got out of sight of their enemies' encampment they landed on the opposite side of the river, carried their canoes back again on dry land, keeping themselves concealed amongst the trees, and embarking again below their foes they again paddled up river past the camp of the Iroquois, only to land on the other side and do the same thing over again. For three days and three nights they continued to pass by the Iroquois in this fashion and make their enemies believe that canoe after canoe of Milicete warriors had gone up the river to cut off their retreat. This belief induced the Iroquois to come to terms, and when the Milicetes had finally been mustered and encamped opposite to them, both parties remained for several days without any hostilities breaking out. At last a meeting took place between the chiefs on both sides and a treaty of peace was made, and as they did not understand a word of each other's language they solemnly buried their guns and tomahayguns (axes) in each other's presence, and the Mohawks departed again to their homes in Canada. This treaty was renewed every two years, the Milicetes sending at considerable expense and inconvenience a deputation to the Mohawks near the St. Lawrence. About 10 years ago, however, the absurdity of renewing this treaty under the altered conditions of affairs, when the slender remnants of either tribe, enclosed and eaten up by a white population, had nothing to fear from the other dawned upon the Mohawks, and they dissuaded the Milicetes from sending ambassadors any more to renew the treaty by saying "once made, made forever." And so for the last ten years the custom has been left in abeyance, and probably will be for all futurity, and thus snaps another link binding Canada with a poetic past.

ALBERT CAMUS

A WARDED THE NOBEL PRIZE in 1957, Albert Camus (1913–1960) is regarded as one of the seminal thinkers and writers of the mid-twentieth century. His essay *The Myth of Sisyphus* (1942, English translation 1955) had—and has—a profound impact on philosophy, art, and literature.

His contact with Canada was brief. He finally yielded to appeals from organizers in Montreal to give a lecture in that city during a trip he made to New York for the production of his play *Caligula*. With the play's producer, he arrived in Montreal on May 26, 1946, from New York by car. They departed immediately after his talk.

Not surprisingly, given the brevity of his Canadian stopover, his notes on Canada, published posthumously in his *American Journal*, are equally brief. Nevertheless, Quebec clearly left him speechless.

The stupendous Quebec countryside. At the point of Diamond Cape before the immense breach of the Saint Lawrence, air, light, and water interpenetrate in infinite proportions. For the first time on this continent a real impression of beauty and true magnitude. It seems that I would have something to say about Quebec and its history of men who came to struggle in the wilderness, driven by a force that was greater than they were. But to what end? Now there are a lot of things that artistically speaking I know I could make work. But this no longer means anything to me. The only thing that I want to say I have been incapable of saying up to now and I will without a doubt never say it.

GRAHAM GREENE

THE WORK of the illustrious novelist Graham Greene (1904–1991) is generally associated with more humid climes than Calgary, Alberta, but as the following tale confirms, Canada and Christmas became much linked in his mind.

Greene's daughter, Caroline, adventurous by nature, had made the decision to leave Britain and become a rancher in the Canadian west. In 1955, father and daughter made their first exploratory visit to southern Alberta, scouting various sites. Eventually, in 1957, she purchased land about seven miles from Cochrane, Alberta, a village northwest of Calgary, and there, at the age of twenty-one, started her career: farming and raising horses. Greene returned to Alberta in 1957 in order to spend time with Caroline during her first Christmas in the new country. He returned for the next two Christmases as well, staying for a full month one year, writing a large part of *Our Man in Havana* on the ranch. His daughter recalls that he found the area pleasingly quiet, and surprisingly warm; his visits were blessed by chinooks that raised the temperature well into the sixties.

Caroline eventually abandoned farming and moved to Montreal. While she was living in Quebec, Graham Greene spent two more Christmases with his daughter. On one of these encounters, he toured the better bars of Montreal with an up-and-coming novelist whose work he admired greatly: Brian Moore. Although this was the only occasion on which the two men met, the experience, alas, seems not to have yielded literary material. Rather, as the following tale makes clear, it was Calgary, not Montreal, which inspired one of the pre-eminent fiction writers of the twentieth century to gruesomely humorous prose.

DEAR DR. FALKENHEIM

Dear Dr. Falkenheim.

You have asked me to draw up a report—perhaps I ought to say a case history—dealing with a certain traumatic experience belonging to my son's childhood in connection with the Father Christmas myth. I will try to be precise, not disguising my own feelings because I do realize that the analysis of a child must be to some extent an analysis of his parents. How much more closely "one flesh" applies to a man's child than to his wife. I have been spending the whole weekend reading the book you recommended by Dr. Doppeldorf and I was fascinated by much of it, to learn for example of the punning instincts in the unconscious and of the importance of the irrelevant, so you must not be surprised at irrelevance in my report. And here I am already running on (perhaps I ought to write running away) instead of making the short report you expect of me, but do you really expect a short report? After reading Dr. Doppeldorf I suspect not.

I am aware that I am writing flippantly, and I know you will see through the flippancy. What I see is my child coming home every year from school, every December, with his eye blackened or his mouth bleeding, and still with the terrible courage that a child shows alone in a hostile world because he cannot believe that *we* know what life is like. In his eyes I am only concerned about the new price war between Esso and Shell, and my wife is concerned about the Women's Institute, and both of us have to respect his independence and pay no attention. The wound doesn't exist—the bruise came because he walked into a brick wall absent-mindedly.

My son was six years old when the event I am trying to describe occurred. With my wife and son I had left England for Canada only a few months before and we were none of us yet accustomed to the great steely neonlit city which lay on the foothills of the Rockies more than three thousand feet up. The sky seemed higher and larger than our English skies, above the level of the clouds we knew, and the air was cold and fresh like lake water. From our bungalow which was called Kosy Nuick on the outskirts of the city we could see across the rolling beige ranchland to the snowy peaks of the Rockies; they changed colour every hour of the day—sometimes they were a hard glittering white, sometimes a pale rose and even at moments a deep blue like storm clouds.

I only mention these effects to show that we did not feel in the least exiled in the far West. If anything there was a sense of exhilaration, of freedom, and of a new life beginning. Certainly there was nothing to prepare us for the kind of wanton shock which drove us all away after we had only stayed a few months. We have never returned, so what my son now remembers of the place must be the real memories of a six-year-old. They are an odd assortment when he speaks of them: men dressed like cowboys buying Weetabix in the self-help stores, the garage right up on top of the Perkins building where sitting in the car he could see the river and the tops of the houses and the mountains, the roar and stamp of a multitude of beasts in the cattle trucks at the station, the arch of cloud above the Rockies which heralded what they call the chinook, when the temperature suddenly rises in a matter of hours from twenty degrees below zero to thirty-five above, and of course, but he doesn't speak of that, there is the terrible memory which is the subject of your investigation.

In western Canada we had found all our English myths—the Easter eggs were there and not the Easter rabbit, and long before Christmas white-bearded men began to distribute chewing gum and paper hats to the children in the toy basements at both the big stores, Perkins and Browne's. Somehow it seems to be tacitly understood by children that these men are only stand-ins for the genuine character, or is there a confusion with the Christian saints who Catholics believe can appear in more than one place at the same time? Perhaps the idea of a multiple Father Christmas is no more puzzling than all that business of the Trinity which children are expected to accept quite easily at Sunday school. If they are tiresome with their questions, I suppose they are told, as we adults are to this day, that it is an unfathomable mystery.

My son had drawn up early in November his Christmas list. None of the objects on this list could possibly be found in the old men's sacks at Perkins or Browne's, and I don't think he even expected them to be. We were even uncertain—you know how little parents realize about their children—whether he believed in Father Christmas at all. He had been promoted a class at school his first term, coming as he did from England where the standard is higher, and now he was working among the old sceptics of seven and eight. Looking back to my own childhood I seem to remember a period when I kept up the appearance of belief for the sake of my parents: they so obviously enjoyed the ceremony of the stocking, the clandestine appearance in my bedroom in costume in case I had remained wakeful, and certainly one Christmas I *had* been quite wakeful enough to notice that Father Christmas wore size eleven in brown Delta shoes like my father. It's funny how that word Delta has stuck in my mind. You'll probably have a theory about that too, Doctor. The Delta of the Nile perhaps—Moses and the bulrushes—the seven plagues—what a long journey one can make from a pair of fifty shilling shoes.

I said to my wife, "Why don't we this year just say nothing about Father Christmas? We've made a break with England; surely we can make a break with Father Christmas too."

"It's fun for me finding the little objects for his stocking," she said or words to that effect (I am introducing the dialogue as accurately as I can, but after six years...). "Only too soon we'll be buying him silk ties and the Collected Poems of Ezra Pound."

"Well, there's no reason why the stocking shouldn't continue for a while. We'll detach it from the idea of Father Christmas, that's all. We could even convert it into a bran tub."

"Then there'd be no heel for the tangerines."

That year his Christmas list was a little daunting as though it had been drawn up by NATO. It led off with a space gun and a tactical nuclear weapon which he had seen in the window of Perkins. Almost the least harmful thing on his list, if one could forget the purposes of uranium, was a Geiger counter.

"You aren't telling me, with a list like that, that he still believes in Father Christmas," I said.

"I don't see why not. I expect you asked in your time for toy soldiers and an air gun. This is only progress."

"I wonder no one has yet made a toy Hiroshima," I said, "to bombard with the tactical nuclear weapons. I've a good mind to patent the idea ready for next Christmas."

But by next year Father Christmas was as dead as mutton you might say.

We had still not quite definitely made up our minds whether to liquidate the old man this year or next when my wife came home with some excitement from the big self-service stores that looked after the needs of our outer fringe of the city. (It was really unnecessary for any housewife to drive into the city at all, for at this local store you could buy everything from washing machines to paperbacks—and of course Weetabix, and there was a great parking space sufficient for five hundred cars at least.) She said to me, "Father Christmas is arriving on Christmas Eve by air."

"By air? With reindeer?" I asked.

"By helicopter. He's going to touch down in the car park; just before sunset."

"We certainly are in the van of progress here."

"It's Browne's helicopter. They've stolen a march on Perkins. We are the last store on his route. You must admit that if this is to be Colin's last Father Christmas, we've struck a winner." (That was our general attitude. Sympathetic to the child, sympathetic to Father Christmas, just trying to choose the tactful way of—well of breaking reality gently to the child. I don't remember my parents taking so much trouble.)

Well, there it was, all provided by a paternal store—Father Christmas arriving by helicopter. No payment. A completely free show. There's a kind of generosity in American advertising. And this arrival, of course, had the blessing of all the business interests in the city and all the denominations too. Elias went off by air in a chariot, and Father Christmas was going to descend, but of course, the story of Elias was supposed to be for grown-up people like myself, while Father Christmas was for the kids. (I really hate that word kids, perhaps because kid was a favourite dish of mine in Greece during the war—it's rather as though one called one's children *escalopes de veau*.)

But I have to get back to Christmas Eve whether I want to or not, and the parking place outside the glassy self-service store, with a small area no larger than a house roped off for the helicopter, and the three of us waiting for it to arrive from the city and the high sky and the cold air and my wife saying, "This couldn't happen at home. I love Christmas here," and we both talked I'm sure about wide open spaces and little cramped Europe and the soaring imagination of the Admen in this city three thousand feet up in the air. Father O'Connor was waiting there with a bunch of veal cutlets from his congregation, wearing cowboy hats and Davy Crockett caps with fur tails and blue jeans and windbreakers with tartan linings. The sun would be going down soon below the Rockies and we heard the helicopter a long way off in the wide green sky; it rose vertically up from some store in the city, hovered like a vulture, and then came buzzing busily towards us, while the babies screamed and gurgled in the perambulators. When Father Christmas looked down from two hundred feet up, below the knifing rotary blades, he must have seen hundreds of open mouths. The helicopter circled above us, and he untied his sack and the air was full of small bright objects dropping down. They fell into the prams and into the cowboy hats and ricochetted all around beside the high heels and the miniature cowboy boots—just the same things which were distributed every day outside the big stores—chewing gum and paper hats—but of course they had more of a sense of glory about them rained like that out of the sky. Then swaying a little, first this way and then that, the helicopter sank slowly plumb in the centre of the roped-off space with its big rubber buffers, and a loudspeaker warned the parents to keep their children away until the blades stopped turning.

The trouble was, no one bothered to warn Father Christmas. The rotary blades above his head were slowing down and he didn't wait for the steps but jumped to the ground with the big sack slung over his shoulder. The windmill over his head was cutting big swaths in the air and hundreds of children screamed with delight to see him land. Perhaps there was some extra enthusiasm behind the helicopter or perhaps he had the idea that the children there couldn't see him properly and he moved round the plane to show himself off there too. But he had quite forgotten, if he had ever known, that a helicopter has a propeller behind as well as overhead and he stepped right into it. The blades took his body and flung it in a kind of violent dance back the way he had come and his head was sliced right off and spun through the air, white detachable beard and all, and it landed a dozen paces away with open eyes and a look of amazement before the body had time to topple out of its dance.

So it was that the trauma was born—I owe the word to you and Dr. Doppeldorf. My wife wasted a lot of time between the tranquillizers explaining to the child that after all it was only an old man called Jeff Drew who had died and not Father Christmas. The papers did their best to contradict her with all the obvious headlines, "Death of Father Christmas," and the like, and the authorities contributed to the confusion by giving the old man, who would have been on poor relief again in a few weeks' time, a slap-up city funeral with mounted police and wreaths of holly and a Christmas tree stuck up above the grave covered with coloured lights, and there was a procession of school children, though I would not let my son go. I wanted him to forget the affair as quickly as possible, and that is just what he hasn't done. So now it is that at the age of twelve he has become the mock of all his contemporaries; each year when December comes around he suffers from endless practical jokes, and as a result he gets into fights, which he can't win, how can he for he's in a perpetual minority of one, because he believes that Father Christmas really existed. "Of course he's real," he says, a bit like an early Christian, "I saw him die." He's dead, and so he's indestructible. Please do what you can, Doctor....

FLEUR ADCOCK

ALTHOUGH CONSIDERED a New Zealand poet, Fleur Adcock (1934–) has spent most of her life in England. Born near Auckland, she moved to Britain at the age of five, returned to New Zealand as a teenager, then returned to Britain in 1963. She worked as a librarian until 1979, at which time she became a full-time writer.

Her first volume of poetry appeared in 1964, to be followed by several other highly praised collections of verse. As a belle-lettrist, she has translated mediaeval work, and more importantly has edited two seminal anthologies: *The Oxford Book of Contemporary New Zealand Poetry* (1982) and *The Faber Book of Twentieth Century Women's Poetry* (1987).

Adcock's contacts with Canada have been transient but national nonetheless. The following poem was written after her first visit to the country in 1980, while she was on a transcontinental reading tour with the British poets Adrian Henri and Dannie Abse.

The author writes: "The fact that I am a New Zealander by birth (although I don't choose to live there) makes me instinctively sympathetic to a country which has had to fight for its identity in proximity to a more aggressively visible neighbour. Even in the small matter of accents, for example, Canadians abroad suffer from being mistaken for Americans, just as New Zealanders are for Australians. For this kind of reason I was predisposed to like Canada before I

went there; and on the strength of two admittedly brief visits I still
like it."

———————————

COAST TO COAST

for Dannie Abse and Adrian Henri

I. West

"From shore to shining shore."
Or, as we now say, coast to coast:
from coast to bleeding coast and back again
in fourteen days. Three British poets,
jet-lagged already, and it's only Sunday;
and this is Victoria, B.C.

"You'll like Victoria, it's so English,"
English? We can have that at home:
we've just flown over the Rockies,
we want grain-hoppers and grizzly bears.
Lead us to your trackless forests,
your endless prairies under snow,

your lumberjacks and fur-trappers.
When shall we need snowshoes? Give us
clichés!
              The afternoon is mild,

sunny and gentle. We've been driven
along the Summit Trail to a rocky knoll
which could be in the Lake District—

apart from the madrona tree,
its ragged wrapping-paper bark, its
foreign berries. Thank you; and yes,
we liked the little oaks. And of course the view:
enough to make us all light-headed,
which in any case we were already.

"No, it's not English. But it has devices"
to make us feel at home—or to make me,
at least, see in its colonial bungalows
leafed off by trees a recognisable suburb
(of Auckland, I'd say, flicking through comparisons
in the back files on my other country.)

Who's English, anyway? Not you, now, Robin,
ex-Yorkshireman, Canadian citizen,
on your home ground here as I've never seen you:
frail suddenly, thinner, unexpectedly limping
but flourishing that silver-headed cane
like an accessory you'd always wanted—

a foil for your flashy rings. You're undiminished:
the chuckles gurgle through your beard,
the stories flow. It's your island we're
seeing bits of on the way from the airport,
your crew-cut son at the wheel; and now he's brought us
through farmland (kale and cattle) to

the sea. The Sea. "Thalassa!" I want to shout,
silly with salt air. Look, the Pacific!

Cormorants diving into it, great logs
of driftwood, grey-green swell slapping the pebbles.
I shall stand here on the shining shore
and nothing will get me back into the car.

The meal they took us to before the reading was
Japanese (Japan's just over there,
separated from this island by nothing
but ocean and the guillotined edge of
the page in any atlas you consult
where the Pacific's not left whole.)

Hot mounds of threatening crab! Indelicate
delicacy, pronged with claws and shell-shards:
unmanageable. But not to us, who are
learning to manage, disciplined as we are
by schedules and itineraries,
by Arlene's motherly hands (purveyors

of cheques and lists and airline tickets
and hotel reservations) back in Toronto
where it's 3 a.m., the time our stomachs tell—
unless they say it's London, 8 a.m.,
breakfast-time. Here it's midnight now,
and this is the after-the-reading party,
in P.K. Page's house, elegant as
herself and her poems. She's given me
her latest book; and Robin's given me his;
and Dorothy Livesay's given me…
Are they all poets here? Mike's one of them:
we've known each other twenty-seven years,

from Wellington; tonight we squatted on
the stairs together for perhaps ten minutes.

I think he asked me "What's it all about?"
I think I laughed.
                    Back to the party.
A poet admires my necklace: Pacific
pearl-shell, from the Cook Islands,

a gift. And they ask where we go next:
Vancouver tomorrow, Tuesday Edmonton,
Wednesday Saskatoon … P.K.'s made coffee.
Victoria's not Canada, she says: "It's
a nice place, but nothing to do with my country."
I shan't find out what it has to do with mine.

II. East

Saint John, New Brunswick: last, earliest, easternmost
port of our tour, so close-lapped by the narrow
Atlantic that the architecture's been
floated across it from our northern Borders
intact, Victorian bandstand and all,
to settle here with Elliots and Fenwicks.

The Court House could be Tyneside Classical,
and the covered market (1876),
by which the Pocket Guide tells us to be
reminded of an upturned galley hull,
reminds me only of the Grainger Market
at home. Saint John is Newcastle:

Newcastle's where you find it. For the Tyne
plunge downhill and settle for the harbour.
"Discover a part of yourself." I've rediscovered
my knees. They rear and frisk, remembering what

they're for, merry at being of use again:
a city not built on hills is not a city.

*

Dreamy with our dislocating nostalgias
we could easily have missed the 'plane; or should we
blame it on last night's Golden Glow, still
bubbling in our veins from the final party? —
Not wine but cider, the colour of clear honey
and curiously salty: a maritime brew.

It gradually warmed the genteel audience
into a crew of eccentrics and fanatics,
manic in corners or radiant with evangelism.
"It's all to do with Antichrist, you know"
said the blond athlete with the perfect teeth,
talking of Reagan: "I'm obsessed with Antichrist.

I was out driving today—I'd just been reading
Revelation—and there was this great rock
with 666 painted on it:
a house-number, I guess, but wow!" And someone
opened another flagon of Golden Glow—
but wow! And the room sang. We stayed up late.

*

So here we stand on a street with suddenly no
taxis, Adrian and I, the late drinkers,
the late risers (Dannie was out early:
he'll be packed and pacing about the hotel.)
Shall we be stranded here in the Loyalist City,
marooned in our own imaginings, at the mercy

of Golden Glow and a pack of tourist brochures?
But a passing angel dressed in a business suit
asks if he can be of any assistance.
"Wait here: I'm parked in the lot just over there."
And yes, he'd heard of the visiting British poets—
sorry he missed our reading; he loves England;

we love him. He drives us to our hotel,
glowing, and hands us over to our taxi
for the long ride to the airport; which restores
our sense of where we are. This is its own
place, not ours, not mine: a Canadian place,
a low conifered landscape, a long road

strung out past wooden houses, each one different—
prairie-style, or colonial with verandahs,
or Georgian sweetly imitated in wood.
We know our own place: it's on the aircraft
where we shall snuggle into our seats again,
cuddled on Mummy's lap, and wait for take-off.

HENRY JAMES

L ONG BEFORE he achieved renown as a novelist, Henry James (1843–1916) wrote literary travel essays. Indeed, only slightly uncharitably, many of his novels could be described as little more than travel essays in disguise. Sadly, he never wrote fiction set in Canada, but he did pen two essays which continue to be of interest: in September 1871 he published in *The Nation* an account of his visit to Quebec, and later that year in the same journal he published his reactions to Niagara. Both compositions were later revised and then published in James' *Portraits of Places* (London 1883).

Despite the brevity of his encounter with Canada, James was an astute observer. Like many American authors, he saw in Canada a land that must—inevitably—be absorbed by the United States, but in making the observation he allows some regret at this possibility. Time has not been so kind to his predictions for the decline of the French fact, but his prognostications were logically argued and sympathetically uttered. In light of his enchantment with Quebec in 1871, then, his disenchantment with the city upon his only return, in August 1910, would be confusing were it not for our knowledge of his ill health and other disorders that eased him into moroseness.

In 1910, in England, Henry James had written that his languor was deepening into depression. His brother, the famous philosopher William James, despite his own ailing condition, was concerned enough about his brother's health that he went to Britain to provide succour for Henry. Once he arrived, though, their physical conditions reversed, with Henry regaining some of his vigour and William lapsing into serious illness. As William deteriorated, he wished to return to the United States to die at his cottage retreat in New Hampshire. Henry agreed, and the two set out by ship for Quebec, since that port would provide the nearest access to their destination. Henry, still visited by demons and further depressed at his brother's failing, described in his notebooks their voyage and arrival:

> [We] were on board Empress of Britain by 5 ... the voyage in itself a marvel. We passed the Straits of Belle Isle all lucidly and smoothly—wondrous sight at about 10–11 etc. on Tuesday. Wednesday, the sea a great smooth bright river. Entered the St. Lawrence in the p.m.—bad weather (heavy rain only) for the 1st time. Landed Quebec by four o'clock Thursday 18th—six days' voyage. But bad night at horrible vulgar Frontenac Hotel, perched on the eminence as *the* object of interest in the scene. Dismal difficulties over Custom House and luggage, horrible delays and *déceptions*.

William died shortly after their arrival at the New Hampshire retreat. In correspondence with friends, just before and after his brother's death, Henry James further described the journey from Quebec as "trying" and "a dreadful memory," but the circumstances of the journey and his brother's wrack and imminent demise probably did more to foment his negativism than anything the city itself might have purveyed. Poignantly, a more balanced picture of the 1910 trip came from William. In a reminiscence of the occasion, William's son wrote:

> My father was too ill to eat, but he found it easier to breathe while erect than lying down, and accordingly would sit sideways at the table with us to listen to the talk. On one such occasion, Uncle Henry was describing with tremendous adjectives the

dreariness of the part of Canada they had passed through on the Intercolonial Railway: "That flat desert of fir trees broken only here and there by a bit of prehistoric swamp!" I remember Dad's half-smiling rejoinder: "Better than anything in Europe, Henry, better than anything in England."

The following excerpt conflates the two Canadian essays of Henry James, using the revised versions published in 1883.

---

from PORTRAITS OF PLACES

Quebec, 1871

I

A traveller who combines a taste for old towns with a love of letters ought not, I suppose, to pass through "the most picturesque city in America" without making an attempt to commemorate his impressions. His first impression will certainly have been that not America, but Europe, should have the credit of Quebec. I came, some days since, by a dreary night-journey, to Point Levi, opposite the town, and as we rattled toward our goal in the faint raw dawn, and, already attentive to "effects," I began to consult the misty window-panes and descried through the moving glass little but crude, monotonous woods, suggestive of nothing that I had ever heard of in song or story. I felt that the land would have much to do to give itself a romantic air. And, in fact, the feat is achieved with almost magical suddenness. The old world rises in the midst of the new in the manner of a change of scene on the stage. The St. Lawrence shines at your left, large as a harbour-mouth, gray with smoke and masts, and edged on its hither verge by a bustling waterside *faubourg* which looks French or English, or anything, not local that you please; and beyond it, over against you, on its rocky promontory, sits the ancient town, belted with its hoary wall and crowned with its granite citadel. Now that I have been here awhile I find myself wondering how the city would strike one if the imagination had not been bribed beforehand. The place, after all, is of the soil on which it stands; yet it appeals to you so cunningly with its little stock of transatlantic wares that you overlook its flaws and lapses, and swallow it whole. Fancy lent a willing hand the morning I arrived, and zealously retouched the picture. The very sky seemed to have been brushed in like the sky in an English water-colour, the light to filter down through an atmosphere more dense and more conscious. You cross a ferry, disembark at the foot of the rock on unmistakably foreign soil, and then begin to climb into the city proper—the city *intra muros*. These walls, to the American vision, are of course the sovereign fact of Quebec; you take off your hat to them as you clatter through the gate. They are neither very high nor, after all, very hoary. Our clear American air is hostile to those mellow deposits and incrustations which enrich the venerable surfaces of Europe. Still, they are walls; till but a short time ago they quite encircled the town; they are garnish with little slits for musketry and big embrasures for cannon; they offer here and there to the strolling bourgeoisie a stretch of grassy rampart; and they make the whole place definite and personal.... In a place so small as Quebec, the bloom of novelty of course rubs off; but when first I walked abroad I fancied myself again in a French seaside town where I once spent a year, in common with a large number of economically disposed English. The French element offers the groundwork, and the English colony wears, for the most part, that half-genteel and migratory air which stamps the exiled and provincial British. They look as if they were still *en voyage*—still in search of low prices—the men in woollen shirts and Scotch bonnets; the ladies with a certain look of being equipped for dangers and difficulties. Your very first steps will be likely to lead you to the market-place, which is a genuine bit of Europeanism. One side of it is occupied by a huge edifice of yellow plaster, with stone facings painted in blue, and a manner of *porte-cochère*, leading into a veritable court—originally I believe, a college of the early Jesuits, now a place of military-stores. On the other stands the French cathedral, with an ample stone facade, a bulky stone tower, and a high-piled, tin-scaled belfry; not architectural, of course, nor imposing, but with a certain gray maturity, and, as regards the belfry, a quite adequate quaintness. Round about are shops and houses, touching which, I think, it is no mere fancy that they might, as they stand, look down into some dull and rather dirty *place* in France....

Among the other lions of Quebec—notably in the Citadel—you find Protestant England supreme. A robust trooper of her Majesty, with a pair of very tight trousers and a very small cap, takes charge of you at the entrance of the fortifications, and conducts you through all kinds of incomprehensible defences. I cannot speak of the place as an engineer, but only as a tourist, and the tourist is chiefly concerned with the view. This is altogether superb, and if Quebec is not the most picturesque city in America, this is no fault of its incomparable site. Perched on its mountain of rock, washed by a river as free and ample as an ocean-gulf, sweeping from its embattled crest, the view, the forest, the blue undulations of the imperial province of which it is warden—as it has managed from our scanty annals to squeeze out a past, you pray in the name of all that is majestic that it may have a future....

Another opportunity for some such reflections, worthy of a historian or an essayist, as those I have hinted at, is afforded you on the Plains of Abraham, to which you probably adjourn directly from the Citadel—another, but I am bound to say, in my opinion, a less inspiring one. A battlefield remains a battlefield, whatever may be done to it; but the scene of Wolfe's victory has been profaned by the erection of a vulgar prison, and this memento of human infirmities does much to efface the meagre column which, with its neat inscription, "Here died Wolfe, victorious," stands there as a symbol of exceptional virtue.

II

To express the historical interest of the place completely, I should dwell on the light provincial—French provincial—aspect of some of the little residential streets. Some of the houses have the staleness of complexion which Balzac loved to describe. They are chiefly built of stone or brick, with a stoutness and separateness of structure which stands in some degree in stead of architecture. I know not that, externally, they have any greater charm than that they belong to that category of dwellings which in our own cities were long since pulled down to make room for brown-stone fronts. I know not, indeed, that I can express better the picturesque merit of Quebec than by saying that it has no fronts of this luxurious and horrible substance. The greater number of houses are built of rough-hewn squares of some more vulgar mineral, painted with frank chocolate or buff, and adorned with blinds of a cruder green than we admire. As you pass the low windows of these abodes, you perceive the walls to be of extraordinary thickness; the embrasure is of great depth; Quebec was built for winter. Door-plates are frequent, and you observe that the tenants are of the Gallic persuasion. Here and there, before a door, stands a comely private equipage—a fact agreeably suggestive of a low scale of prices; for evidently in Quebec one need not be a millionaire to keep a carriage, and one may make a figure on moderate means. The great number of private carriages visible in the streets is another item, by the way, among the Europeanisms of the place; and not, as I may say, as regards the simple fact that they exist, but as regards the fact that they are considered needful for women, for young persons, for gentility. What does it do with itself, this gentility, keeping a gig or not, you wonder, as you stroll past its little multicoloured mansions. You strive almost vainly to picture the life of this French society, locked up in its small dead capital, isolated on a heedless continent, and gradually consuming its principal, as one may say—its vital stock of memories, traditions, superstitions. Its evenings must be as dull as the evenings described by Balzac in his

Vie de Province; but has it the same ways and means of dullness? Does it play loto and "boston" in the long winter nights, and arrange marriages between its sons and daughters, whose education it has confided to abbés and abbesses? I have met in the streets here little old Frenchmen who looked as if they had stepped out of Balzac— bristling with the habits of a class, wrinkled with old-world expressions. Something assures one that Quebec must be a city of gossip; for evidently it is not a city of culture. A glance at the few booksellers' windows gives evidence of this. A few Catholic statuettes and prints, two or three Catholic publications, a festoon or so of rosaries, a volume of Lamartine, a supply of ink and matches, form the principal stock.

In the lower class of the French population there is a much livelier vitality. They are a genuine peasantry; you very soon observe it, as you drive along the pleasant country-roads. Just what it is that makes a peasantry, it is, perhaps, not easy to determine; but whatever it is, these good people have it—in their simple, unsharpened faces, in their narrow patois, in their ignorance and naïveté, and their evident good terms with the tin-spired parish church, standing there as bright and clean with ungrudged paint and varnish as a Nurnberg toy. One of them spoke to me with righteous contempt of the French of France—"They are worth nothing; they are bad Catholics." These are good Catholics, and I doubt whether anywhere Catholicism wears a brighter face and maintains more docility at the cost of less misery. It is, perhaps, not Longfellow's Evangeline for chapter and verse, but it is a tolerable prose transcript. There is no visible squalor, there are no rags and no curses, but there is a most agreeable tinge of gentleness, thrift, and piety. I am assured that the country-people are in the last degree mild and peaceable; surely, such neatness and thrift, without the irritability of the French genius—it is true the genius too is absent—is a very pleasant type of character. Without being ready to proclaim, with an enthusiastic friend, that the roadside scenery is more French than France, I may say that, in its way, it is quite as picturesque as anything within the city.... Winter here gives a stamp to the year, and seems to leave even through spring and summer a kind of scintillating trail of his presence. To me, I confess it is terrible, and I fancy I see constantly in the brilliant sky the hoary genius of the climate brooding grimly over his dominion.

The falls of Montmorency, which you reach by the pleasant avenue I speak of, are great, I believe, among the falls of the earth. They are certainly very fine, even in the attenuated shape to which they are reduced at the present season. I doubt whether you obtain anywhere in simpler and more powerful form the very essence of a cataract—the wild, fierce, suicidal plunge of a living, sounding flood. A little platform, lodged in the cliff, enables you to contemplate it with almost shameful convenience; here you may stand at your leisure and spin analogies, more or less striking, on the very edge of the white abyss....

The spectacle at Montmorency appears to be the private property of a Negro innkeeper, who "runs" it evidently with great pecuniary profit. A day or two since I went so far as to be glad to leave it behind, and drive some five miles farther along the road, to a village rejoicing in the pretty name of Château-Richer. The village is so pretty that you count on finding there the elderly manor which might have baptized it. But, of course, in such pictorial efforts as this Quebec breaks down; one must not ask too much of it. You enjoy from here, however, a revelation of the noble position of the city. The river, finding room in mid-stream for the long island of Orleans, opens out below you with a peculiar freedom and serenity, and leads the eye far down to where an azure mountain gazes-up the channel and responds to the dark headland of Quebec. I noted, here and there, as I went, an extremely sketchable effect. Between the road and the river stand a succession of ancient peasant-dwellings, with their back-windows looking toward the stream. Glancing, as I passed, into the apertures that face the road, I saw, as through a picture-frame, their dark, rich-toned interiors, played into by the late river light and making an admirable series of mellow *tableaux de genre*. The little curtained alcoves, the big household beds, and presses, and dressers, the black-mouthed chimney-pieces, the crucifixes, the old women at their spinning wheels, the little heads at the supper-table, around the big French loaf, outlined with a rim of light, were all as warmly, as richly composed, as French, as Dutch, as worthy of the brush, as anything in the countries to which artists resort for subjects.

I suppose no patriotic American can look at all these things, however idly, without reflecting on the ultimate possibility of their becoming absorbed into his own huge state. Whenever, sooner or later, the change is wrought, the sentimental tourist will keenly feel that a long stride has been taken, roughshod, from the past to the present. The largest appetite in modern civilisation will have swallowed the largest morsel. What the change may bring of comfort or of grief to the Canadians themselves, will be for them to say; but, in the breast of this sentimental tourist of ours, it will produce little but regret. The foreign elements of eastern Canada, at least, are extremely interesting; and it is of good profit to us Americans to have near us, and of easy access, an ample something which is not our expansive selves. Here we find a hundred mementoes of an older civilization than our own, of different manners, of social forces once mighty, and still glowing with a sort of autumnal warmth. The old-world needs which created the dark-walled cities of France and Italy seem to reverberate faintly in the steep and narrow and Catholic streets of Quebec. The little houses speak to the fancy by rather inexpensive arts; the ramparts are endued with a sort of silvery innocence; but the historic venue, conscious of a general solidarity in the picturesque, ekes out the romance and deepens the colouring.

Niagara, 1871

My journey hitherward by a morning's sail from Toronto across Lake Ontario, seemed to me, as regards a certain dull vacuity in this episode of travel, a kind of calculated preparation for the uproar of Niagara—a pause or hush on the threshold of a great impression; and this, too, in spite of the reverent attention I was mindful to bestow on the first seen, in my experience, of the great lakes. It has the merit, from the shore, of producing a slight ambiguity of vision. It is the sea, and yet just not the sea. The huge expanse, the landless line of the horizon, suggest the ocean; while an indefinable shortness of pulse, a kind of fresh-water gentleness of tone, seem to contradict the idea.

I was occupied, as we crossed, in wondering whether this dull reduction of the main contained that which could properly be termed "scenery" at the mouth of the Niagara River, however, after a sail of three hours, scenery really begins, and very soon crowds upon you in force. The steamer puts into the narrow channel of the stream, and heads upward between high embankments. From this point, I think, you really enter into relations with Niagara....

Onwards from Lewiston, where you are transferred from the boat to the train, you see it from the edge of the American cliff, far beneath you, now superbly unnavigable. You have a lively sense of something happening ahead; the river, as a man near me said, has evidently been in a row. The cliffs here are immense; they form a *vomitorium* worthy of the living floods whose exit they protect. This is the first act of the drama of Niagara for it is, I believe, one of the common-places of description that you instinctively convert it into a series of "situations." At the station pertaining to the railway suspension-bridge, you see in mid-air, beyond an interval of murky confusion produced at once by the farther bridge, the smoke of the trains, and the thickened atmosphere of the peopled bank, a huge far-flashing sheet which glares through the distance as a monstrous absorbent and irradiant of light. And here, in the interest of the picturesque, let me note that this obstructive bridge tends in a way to enhance the first glimpse of the cataract. Its long black span, falling dead along the shining brow of the Falls, seems showered and smitten by their fierce effulgence, and trembles across the field of vision like some enormous mote in a light too brilliant. A moment later, as the train proceeds, you plunge into the village, and the cataract, save as a vague ground-tone to this trivial interlude, is, like so many other goals of aesthetic pilgrimage, temporarily postponed to the hotel.

With this postponement comes, I think, an immediate decline of expectation; for there is every appearance that the spectacle you have come so far to see is to be choked in the horrible vulgar shops and booths and catchpenny artifices which have pushed and elbowed to within the very spray of the Falls, and ply their importunities in shrill competition with its thunder. You see a multitude of hotels and taverns and stores, glaring with white paint, bedizened with placards and advertisements, and decorated by groups of those gentlemen who flourish most rankly on the soil of New York and in the vicinage of hotels; who carry their hands in their pockets, wear their hats always and every way, and, although of a stationary habit, yet spurn the earth with their heels....

Though hereabouts so much is great, distances are small, and a ramble of two or three hours enables you to gaze hither and thither from a dozen standpoints. The one you are likely to choose first is that on the Canada cliff, a little way above the suspension-bridge. The great fall faces you, enshrined in its own surging incense. The common feeling just here, I believe, is one of disappointment at its want of height; the whole thing appears to many people somewhat smaller than its fame. My own sense, I confess, was absolutely gratified from the first; and, indeed, I was not struck with anything being tall or short, but with everything being perfect. You are, moreover, at some distance, and you feel that with the lessening interval you will not be cheated of your chance to be dizzied with mere dimensions. Already you see the world-famous green, baffling painters, baffling poets, shining on the lip of the precipice; the more so, of course, for the clouds of silver and snow into which it speedily resolves itself. The whole picture before you is admirably simple. The Horseshoe glares and boils and smokes from the centre to the right, drumming itself into powder and thunder; in the centre the dark pedestal of Goat Island divides the double flood; to the left booms in vaporous dimness the minor battery of the American fall; while on a level with the eye above the still crest of either cataract, appear the white faces of the hithermost rapids. The circle of weltering froth at the base of the Horseshoe, emerging from the dead white vapours—absolute white, as moonless midnight is absolute black—which muffle impenetrably the crash of the river upon the lower bed, melts slowly into the darker shades of green. It seems in itself a drama of thrilling interest, this blanched survival and recovery of the stream. It stretches away like a tired swimmer, struggling from the snowy scum and the silver drift, and passing slowly from an eddying foam-sheet, touched with green lights, to a cold, verd-antique, streaked and marbled with trails and wild arabesques of foam. This is the beginning of that air of recent distress which marks the river as you meet it at the lake. It shifts along, tremendously conscious, relieved, disengaged, knowing the worst is over, with its dignity injured but its volume undiminished, the most stately, the least turbid of torrents. Its movement, its sweep and stride, are as admirable as its colour, but as little as its colour to be made a matter of words. These things are but part of a spectacle in which nothing is imperfect. As you draw nearer and nearer, on the Canada cliff, to the right arm of the Horseshoe, the mass begins in all conscience to be large enough. You are able at last to stand on the very verge of the shelf from which the leap is taken, bathing your boot-toes, if you like, in the side-ooze of the glassy curve. I may say, in parenthesis, that the importunities one suffers here, amid the central din of the cataract, from hackmen and photographers and vendors of gimcracks, are simply hideous and infamous. The road is lined with little drinking-shops and warehouses, and from these retreats their occupants dart forth upon the hapless traveller with their competitive attractions. You purchase release at last by the fury of your indifference, and stand there gazing your fill at the most beautiful object in the world.

The perfect taste of it is the great characteristic. It is not in the least monstrous; it is thoroughly artistic and, as the phrase is, thought out. In the matter of line it beats Michael Angelo. One may seem at first to say the least, but the careful observer will admit that one says the most, in saying that it *pleases*—pleases even a spectator who was not ashamed to write the other day that he didn't care for cataracts. There are, however, so many more things to say about it—its multitudinous features crowd so upon the vision as one looks—that it seems absurd to begin to analyse. The main feature, perhaps, is the incomparable loveliness of the immense line of the shelf and its lateral abutments. It neither falters, nor breaks, nor stiffens, but maintains from wing to wing the lightness of its semicircle. This perfect curve melts into the sheet that seems at once to drop from it and sustain it. The famous green loses nothing, as you may imagine on a nearer view. A green more vividly cool and pure it is impossible to conceive.... It is to the vulgar greens of earth what the blue of a summer day is to artificial dyes, and is, in fact, as sacred, as remote, as impalpable as that. You can fancy it the parent green, the head-spring of colour to all the verdant water-caves and all the clear, sub-fluvial haunts and rivers of naiads and mermen in all the streams of the earth. The lower half of the watery wall is shrouded in the steam of the boiling gulf—a veil never rent nor lifted. At its heart this eternal cloud seems fixed and still with excess of motion—still and intensely white; but, as it rolls and climbs against its lucent cliff, it tosses little whiffs and fumes and pants of snowy smoke, which betray the convulsions we never behold. In the middle of the curve, the depth of the recess, the converging walls are ground into a dust of foam, which rises in a still column, and fills the upper air with its hovering drift. Its summit far overtops the crest of the cataract, and, as you look down along the rapids above, you see it hanging over the averted gulf like some far-flowing signal of danger. Of these things some vulgar verbal hint may be attempted; but what words can render the rarest charm of all—the clear-cut brow of the Fall, the very act and figure of the leap, the rounded passage of the horizontal to the perpendicular? To say it is simple is to make a phrase about it. Nothing was ever more successfully executed. It is carved as sharp as an emerald, as one must say and say again. It arrives, it pauses, it plunges, it comes and goes for ever; it melts and shifts and changes, all with the sound as of millions of bass-voices; and yet its outline never varies, never moves with a different pulse. It is as gentle as the pouring of wine from a flagon—of melody from the lip of a singer. From the little grove beside the American Fall you catch this extraordinary profile better than you are able to do at the Horseshoe. If the line of beauty had vanished from the earth elsewhere, it would survive on the brow of Niagara. It is impossible to insist too strongly on the grace of the thing as seen from the Canada cliff. The genius who invented it was certainly the first author of the idea that order, proportion and symmetry are the conditions of perfect beauty. He applied his faith among the watching and listening forests, long before the Greeks proclaimed theirs in the measurements of the Parthenon. Even the roll of the white batteries at the base seems fixed and poised and ordered, and in the vague middle zone of difference between the flood as it falls and the mist as it rises you imagine a mystical meaning—the passage of body to soul, of matter to spirit, of human to divine.

GEORGE
WASHINGTON
CABLE

THE AMERICAN NOVELIST and short-story writer George
Washington Cable (1844–1925) remains in print after a century
primarily for the accurate tenderness of his accounts of Creole life.
Although he fought in the Confederate Army during the American
Civil War, he was, paradoxically, morally opposed to slavery. In fact,
his attitudes and especially his published urgings to his neighbours
that they assist in the financial furtherance of blacks caused such
outrage throughout the South that he was forced to move to Massachusetts in 1885. Although always a Son of Dixie at heart, he lived
in the North for the rest of his life, even as he continued to write
about Louisiana and its Creole culture.

It is a measure of Cable's massive popularity that Mark Twain
(known to his friends by his real name, Samuel Clemens), while organizing his own first continent-wide reading tour, anxious about his
prospects, insisted on having Cable share the bill to guarantee the
financial success of the tour. The duo were generally in vogue wherever they spoke and lectured, thanks also in part to the marketing and
publicity acumen of their lecture agent, Major J.B. Pond, legendary
for his promotional savvy and his Falstaffian girth. Their Canadian
stops were few: London, Toronto, Kingston, Ottawa, Montreal; their

Toronto appearance, however, was such a hit that they returned to the city at the end of the scheduled tour—one of only half a dozen stops with audiences sufficient to justify such an encore.

It was during his second appearance in Toronto that Cable wrote to his wife about his singular escapades in Canada.

Toronto, Canada
February 15, 1885

As we were leaving the hall on Friday evening, in London, we encountered a large group of young seminary girls in charge of a lady teacher who introduced herself & invited us to visit the school a little way out of town. A moment later the principal, a Mr. English, repeated the invitation urgently and proposed to call for us next morning at 8:45 with a sleigh. We accepted.

The morning drive was one of the most delightful I have ever had in my whole life. The thermometer had been 21 below zero in the night & was still below. The sun shone bright and clear over dazzling hills and still, white valleys. The distances were half-veiled in a tender opaline haze. The deep snowdrifts lay in long, graceful curling billows like foamless breakers turned to white marble. The tinkle of sleigh-bells was everywhere. The snow creaked under the flying runners, the frost hung from the horses' muzzles, breasts and flanks, men's beards hung hard & heavy and white with ice, and the still air was pure, cold and sweet like the waters of a crystal spring.

The school—Helmuth Female College—stood upon a high hill with its grounds undulating away on every hand in spotless white. Soon we were out of the sleigh robes, and free of our wraps and over-wear, seated among a group of teachers, male & female, sipping good coffee from blue china.

Presently we went down a stair and into the drawing-rooms. Mark and I are certainly a pair of hardened old tramps, but it as surely taxed our power of face to the utmost to enter & stand in silence before that ranged battery of seventy-odd pairs of young girls' eyes. I can only say we did not run or crawl under the furniture.

Then the presentation began. The girls were brought forward by twos and introduced by the Principal first to me and then to Clemens, that happening to be the order in which we had entered and were standing. At length this pleasant labor was done. Then came the autograph books and every girl in the school, and the teachers, too, asked an autograph.

This over, the cry was for the toboggans. Away went the girls for furs and like belongings and out we sallied with them, walking, laughing, skipping along the beaten path and some of them, trying to make short cuts over the snow-crust, breaking through and tumbling headlong, but up again and on with rosy cheeks and snow-dusted robes and laughter and shouts and every boisterous innocence. So to the crest of a precipitous hill that ran off below into a broad level field whose snow-crust was unbroken.

A moment of preparation, a piling on of girls and then away we went! The toboggan that I was on went, on its second trip down, far beyond any other. When it finally came to a stand and we got off to toil back it was through snow more than knee-deep. We were long recovering the top of the hill and as, with laugh & shout, we did so it was to find it deserted & to be told that a telephone message had been received stating that a change had been made in the movement of trains and that the train for Toronto was at the moment being held for us at the London station.

Clemens was already gone. I saw him in a pretty sleigh behind a tandem team whistling through the distant gate of the grounds and those seventy girls waving and hurrahing and he swinging his hat and tossing kisses right and left; and the scene repeated again as he swept around the slope of a hill & came in sight again a few hundred yards further on.

In a moment I was in another sleigh drawn by two horses abreast, a young lady, one of the teachers, was in beside me, the huge furs were bundled around and off we flew, down through the cheering, waving line of pretty maids, out into the road, into view again, waving, throwing kisses, laughing, cheering, the horses clattering at full gallop and the snowy road gliding under us.

We missed the train by a few minutes; its conductor could get no telephonic reply that we were coming, and after waiting 25 minutes, departed. We arrived here by a later train, after dark.

Montreal
February 19, 1885

Put Montreal down as one of the brightest, liveliest and most charming cities—at least in winter—that can be. We got here something after noon of yesterday. I can't tell you of all the pretty sights. There is much quaint old, and not a little good new, architecture. The snow is wonderful to see, for quantity and for beauty. The remains of the Carnival, i.e., the statuary of ice and the ice-palace (it should be ice-castle) are extremely fine.

The dress of the Canadian people is picturesque beyond anything else in America. The furs, in endless quantity, and variety of kind and color, are enough to give most striking character to them without anything further; but to this feature is added the frequent costumes of the snowshoers & tobogganers (or tobogganists, if that is it) white, red, blue, brown and other flannels in solid colors and tasteful bands & facings of one color on another, and the sashes & belts & hoods and moccasins. It is a charming sight. And the superb sleighs with their wealth of fur robes, and their elegant teams and tinkling bells; and the rosy cheeks & hurried steps. One cannot describe these things. The people have simply turned the bitter months of the year into days so full of exhilaration that there is hardly left time for sleep.

We dined at one & went to bed. Slept till 4:30 and then went into the hotel's three large drawing-rooms thrown into one, where the Atheneum Club were to give us a grand reception. It lasted till six and was the most elaborate affair I have ever had part in. I don't think I could have shaken less than two hundred and fifty hands.

In the evening we read to a huge audience full of enthusiasm and yet critical; a peculiar and specially pleasing audience—something like Toronto's & something like Boston's.

After the reading we went, by starlight, at headlong speed, bundled in furs to the eyes, in a sleigh, through & out of the town up, up, over the hills looking down upon the twinkling city as upon a brooch of innumerable topazes and diamonds, on and on with the Great Bear directly overhead and the creaking, groaning snow under-foot, the new moon not long set and the horses' bells jingling in our front, until we drew up at last at a door by the wayside where a large man in a snowshoer's uniform bade us welcome and helped us to alight. Up a stair and into a room blue with the smoke of innumerable pipes & cigars, our ears deafened with the wild cheers of uniformed snowshoers—the "Toute Bleue" club, huzzaing at our— I doubt not I should say Mark Twain's—entrance. So we were walked down the middle of the room to the platform at the bottom; but just as we set foot on its lowest step, the master of ceremonies called for silence and formally announced our arrival & presence, and proposed that as Mark Twain was already a member of the club though never seen by them before, he should be initiated. Instantly, with a roaring cheer, he was laid hold of and walked out into the middle of the floor. Then at the word, "Bounce um!" he was lifted from his feet in the midst of a tightly huddled mass of young athletes, laid out at full length on their hands and then—what think you?—thrown bodily into the air almost to the ceiling, caught upon their hands as he came down, thrown up again, caught again, thrown again—so four, five times amid resounding cheers.

Then the cry was for me. It was my turn. The sensation, you may imagine, was something tremendous. To know that one is falling horizontally back downward, through the impalpable air, depending on a lot of young snowshoers to catch him & throw him up

Letter from George Washington Cable to his wife written hastily on the back of the programme for his and Mark Twain's 1884 readings in Toronto.

Courtesy of the George Washington Cable Collection, Manuscript Department, Howard-Tilton Memorial Library, Tulane University, New Orleans, Louisiana.

again, is something that must be experienced to be—enjoyed.

Well, then Mark was walked up upon the platform for a speech which he made with great effect. Then I.

Then, if you'll believe me, they "bounced" the gigantic Major Pond. It was a sight to see that huge black bundle of wraps go up to the ceiling & back & up again & back again.

After our speeches a song was sung. At every point where a speech or song was to be given, the word was first, "sit down," and it was a bright—a charming sight, to see that great hall full of jolly fellows in their white & blue flannel uniforms with tasseled hoods falling down the back, sink to floor and sit cross-legged upon their buckskin & moccasins. Then I was hauled out for a song & gave them Zizi, they taking up the chorus. Then an anecdote—one of his inimitable "yarns"—from Clemens, a little speech of one sentence—but good—from Pond, a jolly snowshoe song & chorus, really very pretty; and then those superb young stalwarts sang—it was a grand sight—sang "God Save the Queen."

Came back to the hotel, slept—for these experiences make great drafts on the nerves & at 3 o'clock waked & received Dr. Louis Frechette, whose name you may remember—the Canadian poet. He has translated some of my stories into French.

Tomorrow we leave Canada and read tomorrow night in Saratoga.

MARK TWAIN

B UCCANEERS, PIRATES, VILLAINS, AND THIEVES were just
a few of the more printable terms Mark Twain (1835–1910) used
to describe Canadian publishers for most of his professional life.
Long before his first documented visit to the country, he was aware
of Canada and the unsavoury habit of its publishing houses of steal-
ing his work and robbing him of tens of thousands of dollars.

In 1870, shortly after Confederation, the practice of copyright,
indeed, even its legal definition, was still in its embryonic development. Until then, British law had sufficed for the Empire, but with
the establishment of the first independent nation of the realm, confusion set in as to whether Canadian or British law would prevail in
the Canadian courts. Excited by their status as citizens of a young
country, a few aggressive businessmen chose to exploit that confusion, wrapping their theft of foreign (read American) intellectual
property in the cloak of nationalism. The more specious among
them even justified their piracy on the grounds that they were literary Robin Hoods, providing great literature to the masses who could
otherwise not afford it. While doubt may have existed concerning
the legality of book piracy, no one in Canada, except its practition-
ers, doubted its immorality.

The Bluebeard among these pirates was Alexander Belford, an
immigrant from Ireland who had settled at the age of three with his
parents in Toronto in 1857. By the age of fourteen, he had "published"

his first pirated book, the start of a remarkable career of pedantic looting so severe that he and his brothers were soon the objects of unparalleled calumny from American authors. The Belford brothers were undeterred.

From early 1869 until March 1871, Mark Twain lived in Buffalo, New York, but apart from visits to Niagara Falls, there is no record that he crossed into Canada. If he had done so, he would have noticed that illegal reprints of his first and second books, *The Celebrated Jumping Frog of Calaveras County* (1867) and *The Innocents Abroad* (1869) had appeared under a Toronto imprint by 1870. The following year, two other titles, recently published in the United States, appeared throughout Canada at prices far below what was charged to Americans.

Initially, Twain was much more concerned with pirated editions of his work in England, where the population was larger than in Canada, and the distribution of books more efficient. But even as he was taking steps to ensure his financial safety on British soil, he was aware of the danger posed by the back-door printing shenanigans of Belford and ilk. By June 1871 there is already a tone of resignation in his assessment of his plight; to his American publisher, he wrote, "There seems to be no convenient way to beat those Canadian re-publishers anyway—though I can go over the line and get out a copyright if you wish it and think it would hold water."

Because the United States had not signed the Berne Treaty, an international agreement on copyright, American authors were generally unprotected in England, and authors of the United Kingdom had no copyright protection in the U.S.A. Various decisions of the British courts had clarified matters somewhat, so that by the late 1870s it appeared there might be reciprocity regarding the protection of each other's authors. Many Canadian publishers continued to argue, in the newspapers, in the courts, and by their actions, that Canadians should not—and would not—be bound by the decisions of British courts or the British Parliament. The vigour of their piracy increased. So brazen did they become, they bribed employees of

American printing firms (where the works of bestselling writers were known to be typeset) to steal proofs of forthcoming novels. The proofs were raced to Toronto and, to the outrage of the Americans, were used to print Canadian editions which would be shipped to the United States, often long before the legitimate American edition could be published. Worse, the Canadian pirates advertised their wares in American periodicals, inviting American readers to order the Canadian editions by mail, editions which sold for as little as ten per cent of the American cover price. Of course, the pirates paid nothing to Twain.

With each year, Twain realized more and more how much the Canadians were costing him in lost income. Exasperated, he wrote to his English agent in November 1876:

> Belford Bros., Canadian thieves, are flooding America with a cheap pirated edition of "Tom Sawyer." I have just telegraphed Chatto to assign Canadian copyright to me, but I suppose it is too late to do any good. We cannot issue for 6 weeks yet, and by that time, Belford will have sold 100,000 over the frontier and killed my book dead. This piracy will cost me $10,000, and I will spend as much more to choke off those pirates, if the thing can be done....

As he had believed that he would make more money from *Tom Sawyer* than any of his previous titles, Twain's rage and depression at the actions of Belford reached new depths. In December of 1876, he wrote again to his British publisher:

> It's a mistake, I am not writing any new book. Belford has taken the profits all out of "Tom Sawyer." We find our copyright law here to be nearly worthless, and if I can make a living out of plays, I shall never write another book.... The Canadian "Tom Sawyer" has actually taken the market away from us in every village in the Union.

Incensed by the Canadians, Twain was writing to friends that he could not "get down to work again" unless the issue was resolved once and for all. In 1881, he consulted with various lawyers and members of the book trade to ascertain the best means by which, as he phrased it, "to go north to kill a pirate." The consultations yielded a complex plan calling, among other tactics and documents, for him to reside in Canada at the time of publication of his next book, so as to obtain both Imperial and Canadian copyright. In late November 1881, he arrived in Montreal, intending to stay for approximately a fortnight, to establish that he was domiciled in the country at the hour of publication, a legal fiction necessary to have proprietary rights in Canada over his literary fiction. Sadly, it was under these unsavoury conditions that he arrived in Canada for the very first time.

Graciously, Mark Twain appears, during each of his five visits to this land, to have distinguished between the general populace and the pirates. Indeed, letters to his family, especially his wife Livy, during his first visit, are warm with endearment:

Montreal
November 27, 1881

I can not only look out upon the beautiful snowstorm, past the vigorous blaze of my fire; and upon the snow-veiled buildings which I have sketched; and upon the churchward drifting umbrellas; and upon the buffalo-clad cabmen stamping their feet and thrashing their arms on the corner yonder: but I also look out upon the spot where the first white men stood, in the neighborhood of four hundred years ago, admiring the mighty stretch of leafy solitudes, and being admired and marveled at by an eager multitude of naked savages. The discoverer of this region, and namer of it, Jacques Cartier, has a square named for him in the city. I wish you were here; you would enjoy your birthday, I think.

Montreal
November 29, 1881

Well, sweetheart, I have walked a few miles this morning with the same gentleman who took me to the mountain-top (Mr. Iles) & inspected a lot of Catholic churches, French markets, shop windows, &c. But for the shame of it, the indignity to my pride, I would like to be a Catholic priest's slave, & glide in with my basket or my bundle, & duck my head & crook my knee at a painted image, & glide out again with my immortal part refreshed & strengthened for my day's burdens. But—I am not a priest's slave, & so it hurts me, hurts me all through, to recognize, by these exhibitions, what poor animals we are, what children, how easily fooled, beguiled, & by what cheap & trivial devices, by what thin & paltry lies. Which reminds me—you must read about the early Jesuit missionaries in Canada. Talk about self-abnegation! heroism! fidelity to a cause! It was sublime, it was stupendous. Why what these men did & suffered, in trying to rescue the insulting & atrocious savages from the doom of hell, makes one adore & glorify human nature as exemplified in those priests—yes, & despise it at the very same time. In endurance & performance they were gods; in credulity, & in obedience to their ecclesiastical chiefs, they were swine.

One is so carried out of his mind with enthusiasm over these marvelous labors & sufferings & sacrifices, that for a moment he is deceived into imagining that nothing but a religion can make men do these things, (& he is helped toward that delusion by his life-long pulpit-and-tract-teaching.) But no—all that these men did & suffered, the love of money, hatred of an enemy, affection for a child, a wife, a betrothed, can make men do & suffer—yes, infatuation for a filthy prostitute can make a man rival the Jesuit missionaries at their grandest & finest.

But a friend waits to take me to luncheon—so I break off my sermon.

Presumably to sightsee, Twain and his American publisher, Osgood, travelled to Quebec City at the start of December 1881, an unfortunate choice: "Thus far, I don't like Quebec. The hotel is infernal. You couldn't endure these beds. Everything in the hotel is of the date of Champlain, or even of Cartier & thoroughly worn out."

It was in Montreal on this excursion that he probably met the eminent Canadian poet Louis Fréchette who was to remain a lifelong correspondent and friend.

> Livy darling, I received a letter from Monsieur Fréchette this morning, in which certain citizens of Montreal tendered me a public dinner next Thursday, and by Osgood's advice I accepted it....
>
> We drove about the steep hills and narrow, crooked streets of this old town during three hours, yesterday, in a sleigh, in a driving snow-storm. The people here don't mind snow; they were all out, plodding around on their affairs—especially the children, who were wallowing around everywhere, like snow images, and having a mighty good time. I wish I could describe the winter costume of the young-girls, but I can't. It is grave and simple, but graceful and pretty—the top of it is a brimless fur cap. Maybe it is the costume that makes pretty girls seem so monotonously plenty here. It was a kind of relief to strike a homely face occasionally.
>
> You descend into some of the streets by long, deep stairways; and in the strong moonlight, last night, these were very picturesque. I did wish you were here to see these things. You couldn't by any possibility sleep in these beds, though, or enjoy the food.

Fortunately, it was not until after he had left Montreal in 1881 for home that Twain learned he had been denied Canadian copyright because of a legal technicality; otherwise, his letters to his wife might not have been so kind about Canada. The refusal of the Canadian Government to grant copyright to Twain became news on both sides of the border. Distortions of fact proliferated, including a suggestion that Twain might move to Canada. If permanent residence in Canada as a solution to his copyright problems struck him as abhorrent, temporary residence continued to hold out the best means of wrestling from the earth the Antaeus of Canadian pirating.

Twain's temporary abode in Ottawa in May 1883 rivalled the pleasures he had enjoyed at Montreal two years earlier. He had chosen the capital because the Governor General of the day, the Marquis of Lorne, had learned of his pending visit, and had invited him to be his guest at Rideau Hall. At times in his letters home Twain squeaks with the innocent pleasure of a child, such is his enjoyment mingling with royalty:

> Government House
> Ottawa,
> May 24, 1883

> Livy darling, I must not attempt a scenery letter, it would seduce me into spinning out too long; & I must reserve my strength for the duties of these stirring times. I've had rattling good luck, as to blunders. True, the valet didn't ask for my shoes yesterday afternoon (had to remind him myself)—all was explained, in the evening when I observed that I was the only male creature in the drawing room who hadn't patent leathers on. Yes, that omission was a blunder, but I scored a great success to make up for it: to-wit, although I had a burning desire to speak to her royal highness about those unlucky shoes, I resisted it & didn't do it. And I had another lucky accident. Sitting at her right at dinner, I fell to delivering [illegible] free but appreciative & admiring comments upon an oil portrait on the wall, & it so happened that God had allowed her to have painted it. As I hadn't suspected that, wasn't it a lucky stroke? I was saying I supposed it was a portrait, but that maybe it wasn't, because there was a grace & ease in the attitude & a deep & gracious something in the expression that suggested that it must be a composition. She called that a fine compliment; & when I asked "to the picture, or to the artist?" she said to the artist, which was herself. God was

very good to me in this instance. But I was less fortunate earlier; when I had finished writing you, yesterday evening, I went down into the long corridor, & she was just entering a door. It was dim; I could not be sure it was she, but I thought I had better speak, for I was *nearly* sure; so I drew back respectfully, & said inquiringly, "Your royal highness?" Now you see, I should have been all right if I hadn't had the letter in my hand; but that, & my inquiring inflection, made her think I had been looking around the house for her, to ask how I was to mail my letter. So she said she would show me; & she led the way down the corridor, & I was very sorry it proved so far. But I couldn't know it would be so far. It would have been further, but a soldier happened to cross our path & she gave the letter to him. So I was all right, again....

Mark Twain's third trip to Canada was occasioned by his first international reading tour, conducted with George Washington Cable in 1884–5. However, despite the seeming success of his Canadian copyright obtained a year before in Ottawa (one wonders whether his public affiliation with the Governor General may have quelled the pirates as much as any legal strategy employed), Twain remained doubtful that the pirates could be perpetually suppressed.

Fortunately, given the extraordinary response of the Toronto audiences, the return to Canada "4 or 5 weeks later" made financial as well as legal sense. The only Canadian stop in 1884 was in Toronto for two nights of readings at the Horticultural Pavilion in Allan Gardens on December 8 and 9. After visiting several American centres, the duo returned to Canada, stopping in London on February 13, 1885, Toronto for the 14th and 15th, Brockville on the 16th, Ottawa on the 17th, and Montreal on the 18th and 19th. It was during these latter dates that Twain and Cable especially enjoyed the peculiarly Canadian aspects of the trip. From Toronto, Twain wrote to his wife about a visit to a girls' school (which included tobogganing, also described by Cable in a letter of the same date quoted above) in London, Ontario. Twain enjoyed the experience so much that he bought

Mark Twain and George Washington Cable, 1884. Publicity photograph for their 1884–85 Canadian-American lecture tour. This photo was used in newspapers throughout Canada in advertisements for the readings as well as news coverage of their Canadian visits. Courtesy of the New York Historical Society, New York, New York.

a toboggan before returning home as a gift for his own children.

His penultimate visit to Canada occurred a decade later when financial reverses forced him, yet again, to take to the lecture stage. On this occasion, he was to make a round-the-world trip, reading and talking in most of the English-speaking nations. The trip began in the late summer of 1895 with a trip across the northern United States, and from internal evidence in his papers, it appears he may have made one, or even two, visits to Winnipeg. The initial destination was Vancouver, for it was from that city that he was to take a cruise to Australia and points east. The global voyage was described in typical Twain style in his book *Following the Equator*. There are brief references to Victoria, and Vancouver, and short descriptions of some Canadian remittance men, but all in all, Canada does not figure in the tome. His final journey to Canada took him to the opposite end of the nation: in August 1901, he sailed with friends on a yacht for a fortnight in the Bay of Fundy, stopping occasionally for supplies, local colour, and brief adventures (in towns such as Yarmouth) along the Nova Scotia and New Brunswick coasts.

While Canada and its book pirates constantly figured in Twain's thinking, it was his native United States which preoccupied him aesthetically. Apart from a minor short story, "The Esquimeau Maiden's Romance," no creative writing by Mark Twain features Canada.

However, when he visited Montreal for the first time, he spoke, as noted above, at the Windsor Hotel on December 8, 1881, at the dinner held in his honour. The Montreal *Gazette* described the packed banquet room as "thoroughly representative of the intellectual and commercial greatness of Canada." Stephen Leacock, Canada's most famous humorist, wrote an affectionate account of America's most famous humorist in the spring 1935 issue of *Queen's Quarterly*. In the paean, he cites every guest who was present, as well as the entire text of Twain's remarks. He implies that the audience found Twain amusing and moving. The speech remains so today.

That a banquet should be given to me in this ostensibly foreign land and in this great city, and that my ears should be greeted by such complimentary words from such distinguished lips, are eminent surprises to me; and I will not conceal the fact that they are also deeply gratifying. I thank you, one and all, gentlemen, for these marks of favor and friendliness; and even if I have not really or sufficiently deserved them, I assure you that I do not any the less keenly enjoy and esteem them on that account.

When a stranger appears abruptly in a country, without any apparent business there, and at an unusual season of the year, the judicious thing for him to do is to explain. This seems peculiarly necessary in my case, on account of a series of unfortunate happenings here, which followed my arrival, and which I suppose the public have felt compelled to connect with that circumstance. I would most gladly explain if I could; but I have nothing for my defense but my bare word; so I simply declare, in all sincerity, and with my hand on my heart, that I never heard of that diamond robbery till I saw it in the morning paper; and I can say with perfect truth that I never saw that box of dynamite till the police came to inquire of me if I had any more of it. These are mere assertions, I grant you, but they come from the lips of one who was never known to utter an untruth, except for practice, and who certainly would not so stultify the traditions of an upright life as to utter one now, in a strange land, and in such a presence as this, when there is nothing to be gained by it and he does not need any practice. I brought with me to this city a friend—a Boston publisher—but, alas, even this does not sufficiently explain these sinister mysteries; if I had brought a Toronto publisher along the case would have been different. But no, possibly not; the burglar took the diamond studs but left the shirt; only a reformed Toronto publisher would have left the shirt.

To continue my explanation, I did not come to Canada to commit crime—this time—but to prevent it. I came here to place myself under the protection of the Canadian law and secure a copyright. I have complied with the requirements of the law; I have followed the instructions of some of the best legal minds in the city, including my

own, and so my errand is accomplished, at least so far as any assertions of mine can aid that accomplishment. This is rather a cumber-
some way to fence and fortify one's property against the literary
buccaneer, it is true; still, if it is effective, it is a great advance upon
past conditions, and one to be correspondingly welcomed.

It makes one hope and believe that a day will come when, in the
eye of the law, literary property will be as sacred as whiskey, or any
other of the necessaries of life. In this age of ours, if you steal another
man's label to advertise your own brand of whiskey with, you will be
heavily fined and otherwise punished for violating that trademark; if
you steal the whiskey without the trademark, you go to jail; but if
you could prove that the whiskey was literature, you can steal them
both, and the law wouldn't say a word. It grieves me to think how far
more profound and reverent a respect the law would have for literature if a body could only get drunk on it. Still the world moves; the
interests of literature upon our continent are improving, let us be
content and wait.

We have with us here a fellow craftsman [Fréchette], born on our
own side of the Atlantic, who has created an epoch in this continent's literary history—an author who has earned and worthily
earned and received the vast distinction of being crowned by the
Academy of France. This is honor and achievement enough for the
cause and the craft for one decade, assuredly.

If one may have the privilege of throwing in a personal impression or two, I may remark that my stay in Montreal and Quebec has
been exceedingly pleasant, but the weather has been a good deal of a
disappointment. Canada has a reputation for magnificent winter
weather, and has a prophet who is bound by every sentiment of
honor and duty to furnish it; but the result this time has been a mess
of characterless weather, which all right-feeling Canadians are probably ashamed of. Still, only the country is to blame; nobody has a
right to blame the prophet, for this wasn't the kind of weather he
promised.

Well, never mind, what you lack in weather you make up in the
means of grace. This is the first time I was ever in a city where you

couldn't throw a brick without breaking a church window. Yet I was told that you were going to build one more; I said the scheme is good, but where are you going to find room? They said, we will build it on top of another church and use an elevator. This shows that the gift of lying is not yet dead in the land.

I suppose one must come in the summer to get the advantages of the Canadian scenery. A cabman drove me two miles up a perpendicular hill in a sleigh and showed me an admirable snowstorm from the heights of Quebec. The man was an ass; I could have seen the snowstorm as well from the hotel window and saved my money. Still, I may have been the ass myself; there is no telling; the thing is all mixed up in my mind; but anyway there was an ass in the party; and I do suppose that wherever a mercenary cabman and a gifted literary character are gathered together for business, there is bound to be an ass in the combination somewhere. It has always been so in my experience; and I have usually been elected, too. But it is no matter; I would rather be an ass than a cabman, any time, except in summertime; then, with my advantages, I could be both.

I saw the Plains of Abraham, and the spot where the lamented Wolfe stood when he made the memorable remark that he would rather be the author of Gray's "Elegy" than take Quebec. But why did he say so rash a thing? It was because he supposed there was going to be international copyright. Otherwise there would be no money in it. I was also shown the spot where Sir William Phipps stood when he said he would rather take a walk than take two Quebecs. And he took the walk. I have looked with emotion, here in your city, upon the monument which makes forever memorable the spot where Horatio Nelson did not stand when he fell. I have seen the cab which Champlain employed when he arrived overland at Quebec; I have seen the horse which Jacques Cartier rode when he discovered Montreal. I have used them both; I will never do it again. Yes, I have seen all the historical places; the localities have been pointed out to me where the scenery is warehoused for the season. My sojourn has been to my moral and intellectual profit; I have behaved with propriety and discretion; I have meddled nowhere but in the election. But I am used to voting, for I live in a town where, if you may judge by local prints, there are only two conspicuous industries—committing burglaries and holding elections—and I like to keep my hand in, so I voted a good deal here.

Where so many of the guests are French, the propriety will be recognized of my making a portion of my speech in the beautiful language in order that I may be partly understood. I speak French with timidity, and not flowingly—except when excited. When using that language I have often noticed that I have hardly ever been mistaken for a Frenchman, except, perhaps, by horses; never, I believe, by people. I had hoped that mere French construction—with English words—would answer, but this is not the case. I tried it at a gentleman's house in Quebec, and it would not work. The maid servant asked, "What would Monsieur?" I said, "Monsieur So-and-So, is he with himself?" She did not understand that either. I said, "He will desolate himself when be learns that his friend American has arrived and he not with himself to shake him at the hand." She did not even understand that; I don't know why, but she didn't and she lost her temper besides. Somebody in the rear called out, "*Qui est donc là?*" or words to that effect. She said, "*C'est un fou,*" and shut the door on me. Perhaps she was right; but how did she ever find that out? for she had never seen me before till that moment.

But, as I have already intimated, I will close this oration with a few sentiments in the French language. I have not ornamented them, I have not burdened them with flowers or rhetoric, for, to my mind, that literature is best and most enduring which is characterized by a noble simplicity: *J'ai belle bouton d'or de mon oncle, mais je n'ai pas celui du charpentier. Si vous avez le fromage du brave menuisier, c'est bon; mais si vous ne l'avez pas, ne se désolé pas, prenez le chapeau de drap noir de son beau frère malade. Tout à l'heure! Savoir faire! Qu'est ce que vous dit! Pâté de fois gras! Revenons à nos moutons! Pardon, messieurs, pardonnez moi; essayant à parler la belle langue d'Ollendorf* strains me more than you can possibly imagine. But I mean well, and I've done the best I could.

MATTHEW ARNOLD

I N HIS OWN CENTURY, Matthew Arnold (1822–1888) was one of Europe's foremost men of letters. Today, he is an author more respected than read, although "Dover Beach" is a poem which remains compulsory reading on most freshman English courses. He was Professor of Poetry at Oxford for ten years. His commentaries on literature specifically, culture generally, and the nascent split between the sciences and humanities appealed strongly to the Romantic pessimism of the day and neared the status of dogma for many.

Matthew Arnold visited Canada on only one occasion, as part of an 1884 lecture tour throughout North America. Throughout his tour, which commenced in the United States, Arnold was looking forward to the Canadian visit. On January 30, 1884, from St. Louis, he wrote to his old friend from Oxford, Goldwin Smith, the publisher of the periodical *Grip*, and a liberal social critic and journalist who had settled in Toronto in 1870:

My Dear Goldwin Smith,

It was a great pleasure to be met on my first arrival in this country by your kind invitation, and all through the *tota discimina rerum* which I have had to encounter, I have looked forward to a visit to you as a consolation. Would it suit you if Mrs. Arnold and I came to you on Tuesday, the 12th of February? We can stay only two nights, I fear; but that will be better than nothing....

From Chicago, he closed a letter to his younger daughter, Nelly, with "We hope to get some furs for you in Canada." And to his older daughter he wrote from St. Louis, "When I think of England, the desire to be back rises sometimes into a passion; but we are in February, and our berths taken for the 5th of March. And I shall like to see Canada ... Lucy is in bliss at New York, but she is a goose to prefer it to Canada."

He did arrive in Toronto on February 12, 1884, both to lecture, and to relax and recuperate with Goldwin Smith. Because of indiscreet remarks he had made in the United States regarding philistinism in America, the newspapers in that country, ever sensitive to slights—perceived or real—repeatedly castigated Arnold for being a too-proud, snobbish Briton. The Canadian press responded far more warmly and concentrated on the man's philosophy rather than his off-the-cuff remarks. On February 16 Arnold was in Ottawa, a guest of the Governor General, Lord Lansdowne. On February 18 he spoke in Quebec City, then retraced his steps to lecture in Montreal over the following two days.

Regrettably, most of the correspondence Matthew Arnold presumably wrote while in Canada seems to have vanished. Fortunately, the archives of "The Grange," the Goldwin Smith residence in Toronto, have preserved this perceptive letter which Arnold sent to Smith following his visit.

Athenaeum Club
Pall Mall S.W.
May 2, 1884

My dear Goldwin Smith,

Ever since our very pleasant visit to you I have had it in my mind to write to you, and now that I have just finished reading your article in last month's "Contemporary," I seize a pen and fulfil my intention. I agree with almost every word of your article; I think I had a sort of anticipation of the truths there uttered before I visited Canada, but to be in a country, even for a week or ten days only, is a wonderful aid to one's perceptions. Perhaps I do not think so favourably of the States as you do; "the restless craving for the notice and patronage of England," shows, you say, "a lack of English self-reliance and self-respect" in Canadians, which is due to their dependence; but do you not find among the Americans, independent, powerful, and boastful as they are, at the same time "a restless craving for the notice and patronage of England"? Perhaps you have seen notices of the "Chicago hoax" by which I have recently suffered; surely one cannot imagine a like supposed deliverance of Holmes or Howells about London or Edinburgh society causing a similar storm, or causing anything but the very faintest of ripples. Your friend Mr. Geo. Stewart was most hospitable, but we had the feeling we were over-crowding him though he would not admit it. Quebec is the most interesting place we saw in America, and the French population there seemed amiable and moderate; at Montreal, on the other hand, Ultramontanism was in the ascendant and took much offence at my saying that with high Ultramontane pretensions on the one side, and Orangism on the other, there could be no real fusion of the people.

We often talk of our stay with you and Mrs. Goldwin Smith in that delightful old house at Toronto; we found nothing so pleasant and so like home in all our travels. I should tell you that Lord Lansdowne spoke with strong admiration of you as a writer, and said that when at Toronto he did not like to seek you out because it might have looked like making up to a powerful political opponent—or something to that effect. I tell you this confidentially for your guidance: you on your part were probably averse to seem to be making up to a Governor General. But he is an able and unaffected man though an "aristocrat" probably at bottom; you ought to come together.

Have you a new editor for the "Week"? If you have, and you are satisfied with him, and continue to write in it yourself, I must get them to take it on here.

I write in London, but if I were at home Mrs. Arnold would desire to unite with me in kindest and most cordial remembrances to your wife (the most perfect of hostesses) and yourself. I shall send you shortly a little book meant to facilitate the reading of that admirable publicist, Isaiah—and meanwhile, I remain, my dear Goldwin Smith,

Very Sincerely Yours

Matthew Arnold

JACK LONDON

ALTHOUGH HE PUBLISHED more than four hundred articles in periodicals, more than two hundred short stories, and more than fifty books, few of which had anything to do with Canada, no foreign author of the twentieth century has been more associated with this country than has Jack London (1876–1916). To merely mention the Klondike is to conjure up his name and his stories of virile heros courageous in their duels with Arctic Nature. Paradoxically, while his time actually lived in the land was relatively brief, Canada was ore that he would mine profitably, at will, until his death by suicide at age forty.

Born a bastard in San Francisco, Jack London's childhood was laden with crushing poverty, frequent moves of domicile, and inordinate loneliness relieved only by books. As a teenager, he took a series of jobs notable for being either illegal or brain-numbing in their monotony. Escape and adventure seemed to offer themselves when a worker's protest march, known as Coxey's Army, set out in April 1894 from San Francisco for Washington D.C. to plead with Congress for aid. Thousands of men began the march, but long before their efforts dilapidated into tragi-comedy (by the time Coxey, with a few remnants of his "army," reached Washington, he was arrested for walking on the grass) Jack London had abandoned them in order to tramp on his own across the United States. He was to spend seven months on the road, and every commentator on Jack

London's life has remarked that these experiences riding the rods were as lasting as a searing brand held to the flesh and made this "the most eventful and politically formative year of his life." While it would seem that when he left Coxey's Army he had no forethought of visiting Canada, his subsequent month-long stay north of the border was to prove literarily lucrative.

London deserted Coxey in May 1894 in Missouri and tramped throughout the northeastern United States. He was unlawfully arrested for vagrancy in Niagara, New York, and imprisoned for thirty days in hellish conditions. Witness on his travels to brutalities surpassing any he had seen in San Francisco, London came slowly to comprehend the economic forces which made refuse of so many humans and riches for a few. He bummed in the major cities of New England, but as autumn loomed, he decided to return to his home in California, for reasons he never explained, via the railroads of Canada. Despite his new vocation, London waited until many years had elapsed, waited until late 1906, before writing his hobo recollections. The ensuing book, as close as he ever came to a formal autobiography, appeared originally as unrelated essays in *Cosmopolitan* magazine in 1907, later between hardcovers as *The Road*.

By mid-September 1894, Jack London had arrived in Montreal from Boston. The novelist Irving Stone, in his biography of London, maintains that Jack often went hungry in Canada because he could not speak French. Presumably such conditions would have been true only in the Montreal area, which may account for his promptness in deciding to leave that city for Ottawa. Neither town, as he wrote in *The Road*, proved hospitable:

> The distance between Montreal and Ottawa is one hundred and twenty miles. I ought to know, for I had just come over it and it had taken me six days. By mistake I had missed the main line and had come over a small "jerk" with only two locals a day on it. And during these six days I had lived on dry crusts, and not enough of them, begged from the French peasants.
>
> Furthermore, my disgust had been heightened by the one

day I had spent in Ottawa trying to get an outfit of clothing for my long journey. Let me put it on record right here that Ottawa, with one exception, is the hardest town in the United States and Canada to beg clothes in; the one exception is Washington, D.C.... At eight sharp in the morning I started out after clothes. I worked energetically all day. I swear I walked forty miles. I interviewed the housewives of a thousand homes. I did not even knock off work for dinner. And at six in the afternoon, after ten hours of unremitting and depressing toil, I was still shy one shirt, while the pair of trousers I had managed to acquire was tight and, moreover, was showing all the signs of an early disintegration.

At six I quit work and headed for the railroad yards, expecting to pick up something to eat on the way. But my hard luck was still with me. I was refused food at house after house. Then I got a "hand-out." My spirits soared, for it was the largest hand-out I had ever seen in a long and varied experience. It was a parcel wrapped in newspapers and as big as a mature suit-case. I hurried to a vacant lot and opened it. First, I saw cake, then more cake, all kinds and makes of cake, and then some. It was all cake. No bread and butter with thick firm slices of meat between—nothing but cake; and I who of all things abhorred cake most! In another age and clime they sat down by the water of Babylon and wept. And in a vacant lot in Canada's proud capital, I, too, sat down and wept.

Jack London later admitted that his life on the road forced him to hone his talents as a teller of yarns; if he couldn't relate a tale tall enough to win a housewife's sympathy, he probably didn't eat: "I have often thought that to this training of my tramp days is due much of my success as a storywriter." Such polished spinning also kept him out of jail in Canada, as the following amusing encounter with the Winnipeg constabulary attests:

I remember lying in a police station at Winnipeg, Manitoba. I was bound west over the Canadian Pacific. Of course, the police wanted my story, and I gave it to them—on the spur of the moment. They were landlubbers, in the heart of the continent, and what better story for them than a sea story? They could never trip me up on that. And so I told a fearful tale of my life on the hell-ship *Glenmore*. (I had once seen the *Glenmore* lying at anchor in San Francisco Bay.)

I was an English apprentice, I said. And they said that I didn't talk like an English boy. It was up to me to create on the instant. I had been born and reared in the United States. On the death of my parents, I had been sent to England to my grandparents. It was they who had apprenticed me on the *Glenmore*. I hope the captain of the *Glenmore* will forgive me, for I gave him a character that night in the Winnipeg police station. Such cruelty! Such brutality! Such diabolical ingenuity of torture! It explained why I had deserted the *Glenmore* at Montreal.

But why was I in the middle of Canada going west, when my grandparents lived in England? Promptly I created a married sister who lived in California. She would take care of me. I developed at length her loving nature. But they were not done with me, those hard-hearted policemen. I had joined the *Glenmore* in England; in the two years that had elapsed before my desertion at Montreal, what had the *Glenmore* done and where had she been? And thereat I took those landlubbers around the world with me. Buffeted by pounding seas and stung with flying spray, they fought a typhoon with me off the coast of Japan. They loaded and unloaded cargo with me in all the ports of the Seven Seas. I took them to India, and Rangoon, and China, and had them hammer ice with me around the Horn and at last come to moorings at Montreal.

And then they said to wait a moment, and one policeman went forth into the night while I warmed myself at the stove, all the while racking my brains for the trap they were going to spring on me.

I groaned to myself when I saw him come in the door at the

heels of the policeman. No gypsy prank had thrust those tiny hoops of gold through the ears; no prairie winds had beaten that skin into wrinkled leather; nor had snowdrift and mountain-slope put in his walk that reminiscent roll. And in those eyes, when they looked at me, I saw the unmistakable sunwash of the sea. Here was a theme, alas! with half a dozen policemen to watch me read—I who had never sailed the China seas, nor been around the Horn, nor looked with my eyes upon India and Rangoon.

I was desperate. Disaster stalked before me incarnate in the form of that gold-ear-ringed, weather-beaten son of the sea. Who was he? What was he? I must solve him ere he solved me. I must take a new orientation, or else those wicked policemen would orientate me to a cell, a police court, and more cells. If he questioned me first, before I knew how much he knew, I was lost.

But did I betray my desperate plight to those lynx-eyed guardians of the public welfare of Winnipeg? Not I. I met that aged sailorman glad-eyed and beaming, with all the simulated relief at deliverance that a drowning man would display on finding a life-preserver in his last despairing clutch. Here was a man who understood and who would verify my true story to the faces of those sleuth-hounds who did not understand, or, at least, such was what I endeavoured to play-act. I seized upon him; I volleyed him with questions about himself. Before my judges I would prove the character of my saviour before he saved me.

He was a kindly sailorman—an "easy mark." The policemen grew impatient while I questioned him. At last one of them told me to shut up. I shut up; but while I remained shut up, I was busy creating, busy sketching the scenario of the next act. I had learned enough to go on with. He was a Frenchman. He had sailed always on French merchant vessels, with one exception of a voyage on a "lime-juicer." And last of all—blessed fact!—he had not been on the sea for twenty years.

The policeman urged him on to examine me.

"You called in at Rangoon?" he queried.

I nodded. "We put our third mate ashore there. Fever."

If he had asked me what kind of fever, I should have answered, "Enteric," though for the life of me I didn't know what enteric was. But he didn't ask me. Instead, his next question was—

"And how is Rangoon?"

"All right. It rained a whole lot when we were there."

"Did you get shore-leave?"

"Sure," I answered. "Three of us apprentices went ashore together."

"Do you remember the temple?"

"Which temple?" I parried.

"The big one, at the top of the stairway."

If I remembered that temple, I knew I'd have to describe it. The gulf yawned for me.

I shook my head.

"You can see it from all over the harbour," he informed me. "You don't need shore-leave to see that temple."

I never loathed a temple so in my life. But I fixed that particular temple at Rangoon.

"You can't see it from the harbour," I contradicted. "You can't see it from the town. You can't see it from the top of the stairway. Because—" I paused for the effect. "Because there isn't any temple there."

"But I saw it with my own eyes!" he cried.

"That was in—?" I queried.

"Seventy-one."

"It was destroyed in the great earthquake of 1887," I explained. "It was very old."

There was a pause. He was busy reconstructing in his old eyes the youthful vision of that fair temple by the sea.

"The stairway is still there," I aided him. "You can see it from all over the harbour. And you remember that little island on the right-hand side coming into the harbour?" I guess there must have been one there (I was prepared to shift it over to the left-hand side), for he nodded. "Gone," I said. "Seven fathoms of water there now."

I had gained a moment for breath. While he pondered on time's changes, I prepared the finishing touches of my story.

"You remember the custom-house at Bombay?"

He remembered it.

"Burned to the ground," I announced.

"Do you remember Jim Wan?" he came back at me.

"Dead," I said; but who the devil Jim Wan was I hadn't the slightest idea.

I was on thin ice again.

"Do you remember Billy Harper, at Shanghai?" I queried back at him quickly.

That aged sailorman worked hard to recollect, but the Billy Harper of my imagination was beyond his faded memory.

"Of course you remember Billy Harper," I insisted. "Everybody knows him. He's been there forty years. Well, he's still there, that's all."

And then the miracle happened. The sailorman remembered Billy Harper. Perhaps there was a Billy Harper, and perhaps he had been in Shanghai for forty years and was still there; but it was news to me.

For fully half an hour longer, the sailorman and I talked on in similar fashion. In the end he told the policemen that I was what I represented myself to be, and after a night's lodging and a breakfast I was released to wander on westward to my married sister in San Francisco.

Once he reached British Columbia, Jack London chose to linger in southern B.C. rather than return to California at once. With a Canadian hobo named George Smith, he spent a fortnight visiting Kamloops, North Bend, and finally Mission, before the two split, Smith heading due south, London continuing west to Vancouver, a city that also exerted its charms.

I always liked Vancouver. I was never given a handout there in all the time I slammed the gates—always was "set down" to tables. I was only refused twice, and both times because I came out of meals hours. And, further, at each of said places I was given a quarter of a dollar to make up for the refusal. Fine town! Eh? What do you think? Though I suppose the tramps have worked it out pretty well.

At an unspecified date, but apparently in the first half of October, Jack London left Vancouver, bound for Oakland, as a deckhand on the steamer *Umatilla*—ironically, the same ship which a few years hence would take him to the Klondike.

Gold in record amounts was discovered in tributary streams of the Klondike River, Yukon Territory, in the autumn of 1896. News of the discovery did not reach the big cities of North America, however, until July of the following year—it took that long for the ice to melt and ships to sail south with the news.

Fever is, perhaps, too slight a term to describe the ferocity of the gold infection which swept the United States in particular. It is impossible today to grasp completely the continent-wide lunacy, the immensity of the craving for the Klondike, the greed for instant wealth, and the mass stupidity which gripped so many otherwise intelligent people. With no knowledge of the geography, topography, or climate of where they were heading, tens of thousands mortgaged their futures for what they ludicrously believed would be easy money.

Jack London, recently graduated, caught Klondike fever, but not so fully that he lost all reason. He purchased books about Alaska to determine what to wear and where to go. With his brother-in-law as partner, as financier of the junket, he left San Francisco on July 25, 1897, hungry for Klondike riches.

For the student of Canadian-American relations, the Klondike Gold Rush presents a terrific microcosm. Whether it be the manner in which the authorities aided the gold-seekers, or the policing of the Rush, or even the population demographics, the differences between national attitudes were apparent and remain deep. As Pierre Berton noted in his book *Klondike*:

> The differing behaviour of the two military forces during the stampede—the American infantry companies and the Canadian Mounted Police—gives a further insight into Canadian and American attitudes to law, order, freedom, and anarchy. The American style was to stand aside and let the civilians work out matters for themselves, even at the risk of inefficiency, chaos and bloodshed. The Canadian style was to interfere at every step of the way in the interests of order, harmony, and the protection of life and property.

The Mounties, who were to figure repeatedly in Jack London's stories as "the good guys," were established in the Yukon prior to the arrival of the madding crowds. To the chagrin of the Americans, the Mounties manned every border crossing, charging duties payable in cash on any items being imported, and insisting that each immigrant have food on hand sufficient to last a year. The insistence on the food supply was especially galling to people who had just carried a hundred pounds or more on their backs—through blizzards and unspeakable squalor—up the side of a steep mountain. The Mounties refused to yield, though, with the result that most of those arriving exhausted at the Chilkoot or the White passes (the border between Canada and the States) had to leave their burdens at the summit, descend to Dyea for supplies sufficient to placate the Mounties, and reclimb the mountain perhaps as many as fifteen times. Such behaviour might seem obscenely punctilious in retrospect but, in fact, it saved thousands of lives, for had they not been strict, those same thousands, arriving in Dawson (a town inadequately victualled for so many persons, and one cut off from supplies for eight months a year), would have certainly starved to death.

In the summer of 1898, at the height of the Rush, eighty per cent of Dawson's population was American, a fact reflected in the population of Jack London's tales where most of the characters are emigrés from the United States. That there should be any Americans at all was not, as some might suspect, a tribute to their larger aggression or superior gold-seeking skills over Canadians. Rather, the numbers reflected the laxness of the Canadian Government—*plus ça change, plus c'est la même chose*—in protecting our natural resources from exploitation and export by foreigners. In Alaska, only Americans were permitted to goldmine, but in Canada, anyone could take the resource out of the country.

Just as he had craved to be considered a "profesh" as a tramp, Jack London was determined to be, instantly, the best trail-blazer on the Klondike. As a back-packer, he boasted of setting a new standard for carrying weight, a boast that did double duty, for it not only arrogantly displayed his virility, it succoured his nascent theories of the supremacy of the Anglo-Saxon peoples.

Further bravura was inevitable when London, with his new partners, whom he had met on the Trail (his brother-in-law had returned to California almost as soon as their ship had landed at Skagway), became the first men in years to conquer by boat the rapids of the White Horse River.

With the wisdom of hindsight, it could be argued that for Jack London, in any enterprise, the journey was all, or nearly all. Having vanquished the natural forces which slowed other men, he prospected for gold desultorily in the few weeks left before freeze-up. He panned on Henderson Creek for just a few days, found sufficient grains of gold dust to register his claim in Dawson, stayed in Dawson doing no one knows what, then returned to a deserted log cabin upriver to wait for spring and presumably more prospecting. The absence of vitamin C was to intervene.

By May of 1898, London's scurvy was so advanced he knew he had to get medical help. With the breakup of river-ice, he rafted to Dawson, only to discover he was too sick for the medical facilities available. So he floated down the hundreds of miles of the Yukon River, through the Yukon Territory and Alaska, arriving at the town of St. Michael on the Bering Sea at the end of June, and soon thereafter set sail for California and home. He had spent less than a year in the Canadian North, yet was to mine the experience for a lifetime.

Jack London would later state: "It was in the Klondike that I found myself. There nobody talks. Everybody thinks. You get your true perspective. I got mine." He dreamed of returning. He wrote in 1900, in a letter to a friend, "There must be some charm about the North which draws men back again and again. I can hardly contain myself, so strongly do I desire to go back. And I shall soon, probably next year—I mean a year from now."

When he returned to Oakland, he sputtered, then roared into creative activity, transmuting the weeks of frozen time in the Klondike into story after story for a periodical market hot for his talent. His first tale appeared in January 1899; not twelve months later he was published in *Atlantic Monthly*; and less than a year after that his first book rolled off the press: *The Son of the Wolf: Tales of the Far North* (Houghton Mifflin, 1900).

The public reaction to his Klondike stories was national and gigantic. Scholars have speculated that the public was famished for tales that featured realistic responses, rough justice, and virile, full-blooded men, having been offered for too long, apart from those of Kipling, stories whose strong points were bathos and unctuous characters. Jack London throughout his life acknowledged Kipling as a mentor. In a letter to a friend as late as 1914, he could write, "I should dearly have loved to have had Kipling in the Klondyke so that he might have done for the Klondyke what he did for India. Nobody else could have done it a tithe as well."

Of Jack London's opus, the Klondike was featured in an overwhelming seventy-eight stories, much journalism, a play, and four novels. While the newspaper book reviewers were generally lavish in their encomia of his Northern lore, others were less so. Academic critics have always had trouble treating with Jack London—perhaps because of his commercial popularity. Some Canadians were bothered by what they regarded as inaccuracies in his tales, the most notorious criticism coming from Arthur Stringer, himself a novelist popular in both Canada and the United States. In reading the complaints of Canadians, though, one cannot help but wonder whether the subtext is a resentment of the depictions of hardship and rugged-ness, or even animosity that others would dare to see us in anything less than godly terms.

With the publication of *The Call of the Wild* in 1903, Jack Lon-don's place in American letters was secured. It was further cemented with the arrival in 1906 of *White Fang* and with the publication in 1910 of the collection *Lost Face*, which contains his most famous short story, "To Build a Fire." One other of his works is tangentially Canadian: *The Sea-Wolf* (1904) is based in part on the life of Alexan-der MacLean, a pirate from Cape Breton, Nova Scotia, who plied his trade on the Pacific shore of America.

Choosing a representative story from the myriad of Jack London Klondike tales is like trying to differentiate one nugget from another in a poke full of gold: it cannot be done. But the following story, "In a Far Country," contains many of the themes and subjects prevalent in his shorter and longer Canadian works. Perhaps more forthrightly than any other tale he penned, "In a Far Country" articulates Lon-don's Code of the North, those rules by which honest men must live to survive in the Arctic.

The confinement for months to a small space reflects London's own bout with cabin fever in the winter of 1897–8, and the symp-toms of scurvy he knew as well as the back of his hand. Begging for winter to cease, and the sun's warmth to return, are prayers uttered frequently in London's Klondike fiction, but never more pathetically than here. Unlike the characters depicted in most of his Klondike tales, the protagonists of this account try to reach Dawson by the all-Canadian approach from Edmonton, the longest, most dangerous and illogical of all the then available trails. The story may have been based on a legend (involving the deaths of two tenderfeet) having some currency in the Arctic at the end of the century. "In a Far Country" was first published in the magazine *Overland Monthly* in June 1899, and first appeared in book form in *The Son of the Wolf.*

IN A FAR COUNTRY

When a man journeys into a far country, he must be prepared to forget many of the things he has learned, and to acquire such customs as are inherent with existence in the new land; he must abandon the old ideals and the old gods, and oftentimes he must reverse the very codes by which his conduct has hitherto been shaped. To those who have the protean faculty of adaptability, the novelty of such change may even be a source of pleasure; but to those who happen to be hardened to the ruts in which they were created, the pressure of the altered environment is unbearable, and they chafe in body and in spirit under the new restrictions which they do not understand. This chafing is bound to act and react, producing divers evils and leading to various misfortunes. It were better for the man who cannot fit himself to the new groove to return to his own country; if he delay too long, he will surely die.

The man who turns his back upon the comforts of an elder civilization, to face the savage youth, the primordial simplicity of the North, may estimate success at an inverse ratio to the quantity and quality of his hopelessly fixed habits. He will soon discover, if he be a fit candidate, that the material habits are the less important. The exchange of such things as a dainty menu for rough fare, of the stiff leather shoe for the soft, shapeless moccasin, of the feather bed for a couch in the snow, is after all a very easy matter. But his pinch will come in learning properly to shape his mind's attitude toward all things, and especially toward his fellow man. For the courtesies of ordinary life, he must substitute unselfishness, forbearance, and tolerance. Thus, and thus only, can he gain that pearl of great price,—true comradeship. He must not say "Thank you"; he must mean it without opening his mouth, and prove it by responding in kind. In short, he must substitute the deed for the word, the spirit for the letter.

When the world rang with the tale of Arctic gold, and the lure of the North gripped the heartstrings of men, Carter Weatherbee threw up his snug clerkship, turned the half of his savings over to his wife, and with the remainder bought an outfit. There was no romance in his nature,—the bondage of commerce had crushed all that; he was simply tired of the ceaseless grind, and wished to risk great hazards in view of corresponding returns. Like many another fool, disdaining the old trails used by the Northland pioneers for a score of years, he hurried to Edmonton in the spring of the year; and there, unluckily for his soul's welfare, he allied himself with a party of men.

There was nothing unusual about this party, except its plans. Even its goal, like that of all other parties, was the Klondike. But the route it had mapped out to attain that goal took away the breath of the hardiest native, born and bred to the vicissitudes of the Northwest. Even Jacques Baptiste, born of a Chippewa woman and a renegade voyageur (having raised his first whimpers in a deerskin lodge north of the sixty-fifth parallel, and had the same hushed by blissful sucks of raw tallow), was surprised. Though he sold his services to them and agreed to travel even to the never-opening ice, he shook his head ominously whenever his advice was asked.

Percy Cuthfert's evil star must have been in the ascendant, for he, too, joined this company of Argonauts. He was an ordinary man, with a bank account as deep as his culture, which is saying a good deal. He had no reason to embark on such a venture,—no reason in the world, save that he suffered from an abnormal development of sentimentality. He mistook this for the true spirit of romance and adventure. Many another man has done the like, and made as fatal a mistake.

The first break-up of spring found the party following the ice-run of Elk River. It was an imposing fleet, for the outfit was large, and they were accompanied by a disreputable contingent of half-breed *voyageurs* with their women and children. Day in and day out, they labored with the bateaux and canoes, fought mosquitoes and other kindred pests, or sweated and swore at the portages. Severe toil like this lays a man naked to the very roots of his soul, and ere Lake

Athabasca was lost in the south, each member of the party had hoisted his true colors.

The two shirks and chronic grumblers were Carter Weatherbee and Percy Cuthfert. The whole party complained less of its aches and pains than did either of them. Not once did they volunteer for the thousand and one petty duties of the camp. A bucket of water to be brought, an extra armful of wood to be chopped, the dishes to be washed and wiped, a search to be made through the outfit for some suddenly indispensable article,—and these two effete scions of civilization discovered sprains or blisters requiring instant attention. They were the first to turn in at night, with a score of tasks yet undone; the last to turn out in the morning, when the start should be in readiness before the breakfast was begun. They were the first to fall to at meal-time, the last to have a hand in the cooking; the first to dive for a slim delicacy, the last to discover they had added to their own another man's share. If they toiled at the oars, they slyly cut the water at each stroke and allowed the boat's momentum to float up the blade. They thought nobody noticed; but their comrades swore under their breaths and grew to hate them, while Jacques Baptiste sneered openly and damned them from morning till night. But Jacques Baptiste was no gentleman.

At the Great Slave, Hudson Bay dogs were purchased, and the fleet sank to the guards with its added burden of dried fish and pemmican. Then canoe and bateau answered to the swift current of the Mackenzie, and they plunged into the Great Barren Ground. Every likely-looking "feeder" was prospected, but the elusive "pay-dirt" danced ever to the north. At the Great Bear, overcome by the common dread of the Unknown Lands, their voyageurs began to desert, and Fort of Good Hope saw the last and bravest bending to the tow-lines as they bucked the current down which they had so treacherously glided. Jacques Baptiste alone remained. Had he not sworn to travel even to the never-opening ice?

The lying charts, compiled in main from hearsay, were now constantly consulted. And they felt the need of hurry, for the sun had already passed its northern solstice and was leading the winter south again. Skirting the shores of the bay, where the Mackenzie disembogues into the Arctic Ocean, they entered the mouth of the Little Peel River. Then began the arduous up-stream toil, and the two Incapables fared worse than ever. Tow-line and pole, paddle and tump-line, rapids and portages,—such tortures served to give the one a deep disgust for great hazards, and printed for the other a fiery text on the true romance of adventure. One day they waxed mutinous, and being vilely cursed by Jacques Baptiste, turned, as worms sometimes will. But the half-breed thrashed the twain, and sent them, bruised and bleeding, about their work. It was the first time either had been man-handled.

Abandoning their river craft at the head-waters of the Little Peel, they consumed the rest of the summer in the great portage over the Mackenzie watershed to the West Rat. This little stream fed the Porcupine, which in turn joined the Yukon where that mighty highway of the North countermarches on the Arctic Circle. But they had lost in the race with winter, and one day they tied their rafts to the thick eddy-ice and hurried their goods ashore. That night the river jammed and broke several times; the following morning it had fallen asleep for good.

"We can't be more 'n four hundred miles from the Yukon," concluded Sloper, multiplying his thumb nails by the scale of the map. The council, in which the two Incapables had whined to excellent disadvantage, was drawing to a close.

"Hudson Bay Post, long time ago. No use um now." Jacques Baptiste's father had made the trip for the Fur Company in the old days, incidentally marking the trail with a couple of frozen toes.

"Sufferin' cracky!" cried another of the party. "No whites?"

"Nary white," Sloper sententiously affirmed; "but it's only five hundred more up the Yukon to Dawson. Call it a rough thousand from here."

Weatherbee and Cuthfert groaned in chorus.

"How long'll that take, Baptiste?"

The half-breed figured for a moment. "Workum like hell, no

man play out, ten—twenty—forty—fifty days. Um babies come" (designating the Incapables), "no can tell. Mebbe when hell freeze over; mebbe not then."

The manufacture of snowshoes and moccasins ceased. Somebody called the name of an absent member, who came out of an ancient cabin at the edge of the camp-fire and joined them. The cabin was one of the many mysteries which lurk in the vast recesses of the North. Built when and by whom, no man could tell. Two graves in the open, piled high with stones, perhaps contained the secret of those early wanderers. But whose hand had piled the stones?

The moment had come. Jacques Baptiste paused in the fitting of a harness and pinned the struggling dog in the snow. The cook made mute protest for delay, threw a handful of bacon into a noisy pot of beans, then came to attention. Sloper rose to his feet. His body was a ludicrous contrast to the healthy physiques of the Incapables. Yellow and weak, fleeing from a South American fever-hole, he had not broken his flight across the zones, and was still able to toil with men. His weight was probably ninety pounds, with the heavy hunting-knife thrown in, and his grizzled hair told of a prime which had ceased to be. The fresh young muscles of either Weatherbee or Cuthfert were equal to ten times the endeavor of his; yet he could walk them into the earth in a day's journey. And all this day he had whipped his stronger comrades into venturing a thousand miles of the stiffest hardship man can conceive. He was the incarnation of the unrest of his race, and the old Teutonic stubbornness, dashed with the quick grasp and action of the Yankee, held the flesh in the bondage of the spirit.

"All those in favor of going on with the dogs as soon as the ice sets, say ay."

"Ay!" rang out eight voices,—voices destined to string a trail of oaths along many a hundred miles of pain.

"Contrary minded?"

"No!" For the first time the Incapables were united without some compromise of personal interests.

"And what are you going to do about it?" Weatherbee added belligerently.

"Majority rule! Majority rule!" clamored the rest of the party.

"I know the expedition is liable to fall through if you don't come," Sloper replied sweetly; "but I guess, if we try real hard, we can manage to do without you. What do you say, boys?"

The sentiment was cheered to the echo.

"But I say, you know," Cuthfert ventured apprehensively; "what's a chap like me to do?"

"Ain't you coming with us?"

"No-o."

"Then do as you damn well please. We won't have nothing to say."

"Kind o' calkilate yuh might settle it with that canoodlin' pardner of yourn," suggested a heavy-going westerner from the Dakotas, at the same time pointing out Weatherbee. "He'll be shore to ask yuh what yur a-goin' to do when it comes to cookin' an' gatherin' the wood."

"Then we'll consider it all arranged," concluded Sloper. "We'll pull out to-morrow, if we camp within five miles,—just to get everything in running order and remember if we've forgotten anything."

The sleds groaned by on their steel-shod runners, and the dogs strained low in the harnesses in which they were born to die. Jacques Baptiste paused by the side of Sloper to get a last glimpse of the cabin. The smoke curled up pathetically from the Yukon stove-pipe. The two Incapables were watching them from the doorway.

Sloper laid his hand on the other's shoulder.

"Jacques Baptiste, did you ever hear of the Kilkenny cats?"

The half-breed shook his head.

"Well, my friend and good comrade, the Kilkenny cats fought till neither hide, nor hair, nor yowl, was left. You understand?—till nothing was left. Very good. Now, these two men don't like work. They won't work. We know that. They'll be all alone in that cabin all winter,—a mighty long, dark winter. Kilkenny cats,—well?"

The Frenchman in Baptiste shrugged his shoulders, but the Indian in him was silent. Nevertheless, it was an eloquent shrug, pregnant with prophecy.

Things prospered in the little cabin at first. The rough badinage of their comrades had made Weatherbee and Cuthfert conscious of the mutual responsibility which had devolved upon them; besides, there was not so much work after all for two healthy men. And the removal of the cruel whip-hand, or in other words the bulldozing half-breed, had brought with it a joyous reaction. At first, each strove to outdo the other, and they performed petty tasks with an unction which would have opened the eyes of their comrades who were now wearing out bodies and souls on the Long Trail.

All care was banished. The forest, which shouldered in upon them from three sides, was an inexhaustible woodyard. A few yards from their door slept the Porcupine, and a hole through its winter robe formed a bubbling spring of water, crystal clear and painfully cold. But they soon grew to find fault with even that. The hole would persist in freezing up, and thus gave them many a miserable hour of ice-chopping. The unknown builders of the cabin had extended the sidelogs so as to support a cache at the rear. In this was stored the bulk of the party's provisions. Food there was, without stint, for three times the men who were fated to live upon it. But the most of it was of the kind which built up brawn and sinew, but did not tickle the palate. True, there was sugar in plenty for two ordinary men; but these two were little else than children. They early discovered the virtues of hot water judiciously saturated with sugar, and they prodigally swam their flapjacks and soaked their crusts in the rich, white syrup. Then coffee and tea, and especially the dried fruits, made disastrous inroads upon it. The first words they had were over the sugar question. And it is a really serious thing when two men, wholly dependent upon each other for company, begin to quarrel.

Weatherbee loved to discourse blatantly on politics, while Cuthfert, who had been prone to clip his coupons and let the commonwealth jog on as best it might, either ignored the subject or delivered himself of startling epigrams. But the clerk was too obtuse to appreciate the clever shaping of thought, and this waste of ammunition irritated Cuthfert. He had been used to blinding people by his brilliancy, and it worked him quite a hardship, this loss of an audience. He felt personally aggrieved and unconsciously held his mutton-head companion responsible for it.

Save existence, they had nothing in common,—came in touch on no single point. Weatherbee was a clerk who had known naught but clerking all his life; Cuthfert was a master of arts, a dabbler in oils, and had written not a little. The one was a lower-class man who considered himself a gentleman, and the other was a gentleman who knew himself to be such. From this it may be remarked that a man can be a gentleman without possessing the first instinct of true comradeship. The clerk was as sensuous as the other was aesthetic, and his love adventures, told at great length and chiefly coined from his imagination, affected the supersensitive master of arts in the same way as so many whiffs of sewer gas. He deemed the clerk a filthy, uncultured brute, whose place was in the muck with the swine, and told him so; and he was reciprocally informed that he was a milk-and-water sissy and a cad. Weatherbee could not have defined "cad" for his life; but it satisfied its purpose, which after all seems the main point in life.

Weatherbee flatted every third note and sang such songs as "The Boston Burglar" and "The Handsome Cabin Boy," for hours at a time, while Cuthfert wept with rage, till he could stand it no longer and fled into the outer cold. But there was no escape. The intense frost could not be endured for long at a time, and the little cabin crowded them—beds, stove, table, and all—into a space of ten by twelve. The very presence of either became a personal affront to the other, and they lapsed into sullen silences which increased in length and strength as the days went by. Occasionally, the flash of an eye or the curl of a lip got the better of them, though they strove to wholly ignore each other during these mute periods. And a great wonder sprang up in the breast of each, as to how God had ever come to create the other.

With little to do, time became an intolerable burden to them.

This naturally made them still lazier. They sank into a physical lethargy which there was no escaping, and which made them rebel at the performance of the smallest chore. One morning when it was his turn to cook the common breakfast, Weatherbee rolled out of his blankets, and to the snoring of his companion, lighted first the slush-lamp and then the fire. The kettles were frozen hard, and there was no water in the cabin with which to wash. But he did not mind that. Waiting for it to thaw, he sliced the bacon and plunged into the hateful task of bread-making. Cuthfert had been slyly watching through his half-closed lids. Consequently there was a scene, in which they fervently blessed each other, and agreed, thenceforth, that each do his own cooking. A week later, Cuthfert neglected his morning ablutions, but none the less complacently ate the meal which he had cooked. Weatherbee grinned. After that the foolish custom of washing passed out of their lives.

As the sugar-pile and other little luxuries dwindled, they began to be afraid they were not getting their proper shares, and in order that they might not be robbed, they fell to gorging themselves. The luxuries suffered in this gluttonous contest, as did also the men. In the absence of fresh vegetables and exercise, their blood became impoverished, and a loathsome, purplish rash crept over their bodies. Yet they refused to heed the warning. Next, their muscles and joints began to swell, the flesh turning black, while their mouths, gums, and lips took on the color of rich cream. Instead of being drawn together by their misery, each gloated over the other's symptoms as the scurvy took its course.

They lost all regard for personal appearance, and for that matter, common decency. The cabin became a pigpen, and never once were the beds made or fresh pine boughs laid underneath. Yet they could not keep to their blankets, as they would have wished; for the frost was inexorable, and the fire box consumed much fuel. The hair of their heads and faces grew long and shaggy, while their garments would have disgusted a ragpicker. But they did not care. They were sick, and there was no one to see; besides, it was very painful to move about.

To all this was added a new trouble,—the Fear of the North. This Fear was the joint child of the Great Cold and the Great Silence, and was born in the darkness of December when the sun dipped below the southern horizon for good. It affected them according to their natures. Weatherbee fell prey to the grosser superstitions, and did his best to resurrect the spirits which slept in the forgotten graves. It was a fascinating thing, and in his dreams they came to him from out of the cold, and snuggled into his blankets, and told him of their toils and troubles ere they died. He shrank away from the clammy contact as they drew closer and twined their frozen limbs about him, and when they whispered in his ear of things to come, the cabin rang with his frightened shrieks. Cuthfert did not understand,—for they no longer spoke,—and when thus awakened he invariably grabbed for his revolver. Then he would sit up in bed, shivering nervously, with the weapon trained on the unconscious dreamer. Cuthfert deemed the man going mad, and so came to fear for his life.

His own malady assumed a less concrete form. The mysterious artisan who had laid the cabin, log by log, had pegged a wind-vane to the ridge-pole. Cuthfert noticed it always pointed south, and one day, irritated by its steadfastness of purpose, he turned it toward the east. He watched eagerly, but never a breath came by to disturb it. Then he turned the vane to the north, swearing never again to touch it till the wind did blow. But the air frightened him with its unearthly calm, and he often rose in the middle of the night to see if the vane had veered,—ten degrees would have satisfied him. But no, it poised above him as unchangeable as fate. His imagination ran riot, till it became to him a fetish. Sometimes he followed the path it pointed across the dismal dominions, and allowed his soul to become saturated with the Fear. He dwelt upon the unseen and the unknown till the burden of eternity appeared to be crushing him. Everything in the Northland had that crushing effect,—the absence of life and motion; the darkness; the infinite peace of the brooding land; the ghastly silence, which made the echo of each heart-beat a sacrilege; the solemn forest which seemed to guard an awful, inexpressible something, which neither word nor thought could compass.

The world he had so recently left, with its busy nations and great enterprises, seemed very far away. Recollections occasionally obtruded,—recollections of marts and galleries and crowded thoroughfares, of evening dress and social functions, of good men and dear women he had known,—but they were dim memories of a life he had lived long centuries agone, on some other planet. This phantasm was the Reality. Standing beneath the wind-vane, his eyes fixed on the polar skies, he could not bring himself to realize that the Southland really existed, that at that very moment it was a-roar with life and action. There was no Southland, no men being born of women, no giving and taking in marriage. Beyond his bleak sky-line there stretched vast solitudes, and beyond these still vaster solitudes. There were no lands of sunshine, heavy with the perfume of flowers. Such things were only old dreams of paradise. The sunlands of the West and the spicelands of the East, the smiling Arcadias and blissful Islands of the Blest,—ha! ha! His laughter split the void and shocked him with its unwonted sound. There was no sun. This was the Universe, dead and cold and dark, and he its only citizen. Weatherbee? At such moments Weatherbee did not count. He was a Caliban, a monstrous phantom, fettered to him for untold ages, the penalty of some forgotten crime.

He lived with Death among the dead, emasculated by the sense of his own insignificance, crushed by the passive mastery of the slumbering ages. The magnitude of all things appalled him. Everything partook of the superlative save himself,—the perfect cessation of wind and motion, the immensity of the snow-covered wilderness, the height of the sky and the depth of the silence. That wind-vane,—if it would only move. If a thunderbolt would fall, or the forest flare up in flame. The rolling up of the heavens as a scroll, the crash of Doom— anything, anything! But no, nothing moved; the Silence crowded in, and the Fear of the North laid icy fingers on his heart.

Once, like another Crusoe, by the edge of the river he came upon a track,—the faint tracery of a snowshoe rabbit on the delicate snow-crust. It was a revelation. There was life in the Northland. He would follow it, look upon it, gloat over it. He forgot his swollen muscles, plunging through the deep snow in an ecstasy of anticipation. The forest swallowed him up, and the brief midday twilight vanished; but he pursued his quest till exhausted nature asserted itself and laid him helpless in the snow. There he groaned and cursed his folly, and knew the track to be the fancy of his brain; and late that night he dragged himself into the cabin on hands and knees, his cheeks frozen and a strange numbness about his feet. Weatherbee grinned malevolently, but made no offer to help him. He thrust needles into his toes and thawed them out by the stove. A week later mortification set in.

But the clerk had his own troubles. The dead men came out of their graves more frequently now, and rarely left him, waking or sleeping. He grew to wait and dread their coming, never passing the twin cairns without a shudder. One night they came to him in his sleep and led him forth to an appointed task. Frightened into inarticulate horror, he awoke between the heaps of stones and fled wildly to the cabin. But he had lain there for some time, for his feet and cheeks were also frozen.

Sometimes he became frantic at their insistent presence, and danced about the cabin, cutting the empty air with an axe, and smashing everything within reach. During these ghostly encounters, Cuthfert huddled into his blankets and followed the madman about with a cocked revolver, ready to shoot him if he came too near. But, recovering from one of these spells, the clerk noticed the weapon trained upon him. His suspicions were aroused, and thenceforth he, too, lived in fear of his life. They watched each other closely after that, and faced about in startled fright whenever either passed behind the other's back. This apprehensiveness became a mania which controlled them even in their sleep. Through mutual fear they tacitly let the slush-lamp burn all night, and saw to a plentiful supply of bacon-grease before retiring. The slightest movement on the part of one was sufficient to arouse the other, and many a still watch their gazes countered as they shook beneath their blankets with fingers on the triggerguards.

What with the Fear of the North, the mental strain, and the ravages of the disease, they lost all semblance of humanity, taking on the appearance of wild beasts, hunted and desperate. Their cheeks and noses, as an aftermath of the freezing, had turned black. Their frozen toes had begun to drop away at the first and second joints. Every movement brought pain, but the fire box was insatiable, wringing a ransom of torture from their miserable bodies. Day in, day out, it demanded its food,—a veritable pound of flesh,—and they dragged themselves into the forest to chop wood on their knees. Once, crawling thus in search of dry sticks, unknown to each other they entered a thicket from opposite sides. Suddenly, without warning, two peering death's-heads confronted each other. Suffering had so transformed them that recognition was impossible. They sprang to their feet, shrieking with terror, and dashed away on their mangled stumps; and falling at the cabin door, they clawed and scratched like demons till they discovered their mistake.

Occasionally they lapsed normal, and during one of these sane intervals, the chief bone of contention, the sugar, had been divided equally between them. They guarded their separate sacks, stored up in the cache, with jealous eyes; for there were but a few cupfuls left, and they were totally devoid of faith in each other. But one day Cuthfert made a mistake. Hardly able to move, sick with pain, with his head swimming and eyes blinded, he crept into the cache, sugar canister in hand, and mistook Weatherbee's sack for his own.

January had been born but a few days when this occurred. The sun had some time since passed its lowest southern declination, and at meridian now threw flaunting streaks of yellow light upon the northern sky. On the day following his mistake with the sugar-bag, Cuthfert found himself feeling better, both in body and in spirit. As noontime drew near and the day brightened, he dragged himself outside to feast on the evanescent glow, which was to him an earnest of the sun's future intentions. Weatherbee was also feeling somewhat better, and crawled out beside him. They propped themselves in the snow beneath the moveless wind-vane, and waited.

The stillness of death was about them. In other climes, when nature falls into such moods, there is a subdued air of expectancy, a waiting for some small voice to take up the broken strain. Not so in the North. The two men had lived seeming eons in this ghostly peace. They could remember no song of the past; they could conjure no song of the future. This unearthly calm had always been,—the tranquil silence of eternity.

Their eyes were fixed upon the north. Unseen, behind their backs, behind the towering mountains to the south, the sun swept toward the zenith of another sky than theirs. Sole spectators of the mighty canvas, they watched the false dawn slowly grow. A faint flame began to glow and smoulder. It deepened in intensity, ringing the changes of reddish-yellow, purple, and saffron. So bright did it become that Cuthfert thought the sun must surely be behind it,—a miracle, the sun rising in the north! Suddenly, without warning and without fading, the canvas was swept clean. There was no color in the sky. The light had gone out of the day. They caught their breaths in half-sobs. But lo! the air was a-glint with particles of scintillating frost, and there, to the north, the wind-vane lay in vague outline on the snow. A shadow! A shadow! It was exactly midday. They jerked their heads hurriedly to the south. A golden rim peeped over the mountain's snowy shoulder, smiled upon them an instant, then dipped from sight again.

There were tears in their eyes as they sought each other. A strange softening came over them. They felt irresistibly drawn toward each other. The sun was coming back again. It would be with them to-morrow, and the next day, and the next. And it would stay longer every visit, and a time would come when it would ride their heaven day and night, never once dropping below the sky-line. There would be no night. The icelocked winter would be broken; the winds would blow and the forests answer; the land would bathe in the blessed sunshine, and life renew. Hand in hand, they would quit this horrid dream and journey back to the Southland. They lurched blindly forward, and their hands met,—their poor maimed hands, swollen and distorted beneath their mittens.

But the promise was destined to remain unfulfilled. The Northland is the Northland, and men work out their souls by strange rules, which other men, who have not journeyed into far countries, cannot come to understand.

An hour later, Cuthfert put a pan of bread into the oven, and fell to speculating on what the surgeons could do with his feet when he got back. Home did not seem so very far away now. Weatherbee was rummaging in the cache. Of a sudden, he raised a whirlwind of blasphemy, which in turn ceased with startling abruptness. The other man had robbed his sugar-sack. Still, things might have happened differently, had not the two dead men come out from under the stones and hushed the hot words in his throat. They led him quite gently from the cache, which he forgot to close. That consummation was reached; that something they had whispered to him in his dreams was about to happen. They guided him gently, very gently, to the woodpile, where they put the axe in his hands. Then they helped him shove open the cabin door, and he felt sure they shut it after him,—at least he heard it slam and the latch fall sharply into place. And he knew they were waiting just without, waiting for him to do his task.

"Carter! I say, Carter!"

Percy Cuthfert was frightened at the look on the clerk's face, and he made haste to put the table between them.

Carter Weatherbee followed, without haste and without enthusiasm. There was neither pity nor passion in his face, but rather the patient, stolid look of one who has certain work to do and goes about it methodically.

"I say, what's the matter?"

The clerk dodged back, cutting off his retreat to the door, but never opening his mouth.

"I say, Carter, I say; let's talk. There's a good chap."

The master of arts was thinking rapidly, now, shaping a skillful flank movement on the bed where his Smith & Wesson lay. Keeping his eyes on the madman, he rolled backward on the bunk, at the same time clutching the pistol.

"Carter!"

The powder flashed full in Weatherbee's face, but he swung his weapon and leaped forward. The axe bit deeply at the base of the spine, and Percy Cuthfert felt all consciousness of his lower limbs leave him. Then the clerk fell heavily upon him, clutching him by the throat with feeble fingers. The sharp bite of the axe had caused Cuthfert to drop the pistol, and as his lungs panted for release, he fumbled aimlessly for it among the blankets. Then he remembered. He slid a hand up the clerk's belt to the sheath-knife; and they drew very close to each other in that last clinch.

Percy Cuthfert felt his strength leave him. The lower portion of his body was useless. The inert weight of Weatherbee crushed him,—crushed him and pinned him there like a bear under a trap. The cabin became filled with a familiar odor, and he knew the bread to be burning. Yet what did it matter? He would never need it. And there were all of six cupfuls of sugar in the cache,—if he had foreseen this he would not have been so saving the last several days. Would the wind-vane ever move? It might even be veering now. Why not? Had he not seen the sun to-day? He would go and see. No; it was impossible to move. He had not thought the clerk so heavy a man.

How quickly the cabin cooled! The fire must be out. The cold was forcing in. It must be below zero already, and the ice creeping up the inside of the door. He could not see it, but his past experience enabled him to gauge its progress by the cabin's temperature. The lower hinge must be white ere now. Would the tale of this ever reach the world? How would his friends take it? They would read it over their coffee, most likely, and talk it over at the clubs. He could see them very clearly. "Poor Old Cuthfert," they murmured; "not such a bad sort of a chap, after all." He smiled at their eulogies, and passed on in search of a Turkish bath. It was the same old crowd upon the streets. Strange, they did not notice his moosehide moccasins and tattered German socks! He would take a cab. And after the bath a shave would not be bad. No; he would eat first. Steak, and potatoes, and green things,—how fresh it all was! And what was that? Squares of honey, streaming liquid amber! But why did they bring so much? Ha! ha! he could never eat it all. Shine! Why certainly. He put his foot on the box. The bootblack looked curiously up at him, and he remembered his moosehide moccasins and went away hastily.

Hark! The wind-vane must be surely spinning. No; a mere singing in his ears. That was all,—a mere singing. The ice must have passed the latch by now. More likely the upper hinge was covered. Between the moss-chinked roof-poles, little points of frost began to appear. How slowly they grew! No; not so slowly. There was a new one, and there another. Two—three—four; they were coming too fast to count.

There were two growing together. And there, a third had joined them. Why, there were no more spots. They had run together and formed a sheet.

Well, he would have company. If Gabriel ever broke the silence of the North, they would stand together, hand in hand, before the great White Throne. And God would judge them, God would judge them!

Then Percy Cuthfert closed his eyes and dropped off to sleep.

VOLTAIRE

I N A C O U N T R Y where abnegation of the culture has long been
the guiding spirit of the Establishment, it should not be surprising that Voltaire's allegedly most negative comment on Canada is
widely quoted, whereas his far more flattering and substantial work,
L'Ingénu—featuring a Canadian hero—is largely unknown. Yes, certainly, in his novel *Candide* (1759), Voltaire (1694–1778) wrote with
contempt of the battles between France and England for the territory of New France: "You realize that these two countries have been
fighting over a few acres of snow near Canada, and they are spending
on this splendid struggle more than Canada itself is worth." Without doubt, if one believes he is speaking about Canada, the remark is
a palpable hit. Note however that he speaks of land "near Canada,"
not Canada itself, at a time when Acadia and Canada were perceived
by Europeans as two very different places.

But it is silly for Canadians to continue to quote this remark without knowing that Voltaire also held powerful opinions about the
virtues of our then uncomplicated land. The erroneous observation is
made as well that his "few acres of snow" remark remains his only commentary on Canada. In reality, it is but one of several comments, some
negative, some positive, peppering his correspondence; more than fifty
references to Canada occur in his letters, and in many of them, he
expresses keen regret at the loss of Canada by France. Further, when
told that Montcalm had died, he was sincerely moved, even distressed.

With the possible exception of the famous *Candide*, Voltaire's *The Ingenu* is the most impressive of the French master's "philosophical tales." In fact, Voltaire himself held it in higher regard; in a letter to a friend in July 1767, he wrote quite seriously, "*L'Ingénu* surpasses *Candide*, in that it is infinitely more true to life."

To date, in English, *The Ingenu* has not received, as literature, the critical attention that it deserves. What criticism does exist is generally distracted by the change of tone and mood that splits the work into nearly equal halves. The first half of the novel is comic and satirical, but once the Canadian hero arrives in Paris and prison, the disposition of the story becomes pessimistic. Whether the ending is happy or sad probably depends upon one's politics and belief in the essential goodness of humanity.

It was at his residence, Ferney, in 1767, about a decade after the writing of *Candide*, that *L'Ingénu* was composed. Scholars have wrestled with much about the novel, including Voltaire's specific reasons for writing it. He did not share Rousseau's belief in the essential goodness of mankind, did not believe in the nobility of an aboriginal existence untainted by the pollution of civilization. So, it is possible that one of the motives for *L'Ingénu* was to rebut what he regarded as the idiocy of Rousseau's argument. But rebuttal, if at all, must be only one of the motives, and a digestion of the full text leaves the mature reader with the impression that Voltaire himself was equivocal on the matter of the Noble Savage.

The story of *L'Ingénu* begins when a young man (a child of French colonists but orphaned in infancy, raised by the Hurons in the area north of Lake Ontario) lands on the shores of Brittany. He receives an amicable welcome, and causes delight and consternation among his French hosts with the innocence of his questions. Voltaire, the social critic, in the first half of his novel, has great fun using his Huron to expose the hypocrisies and derisory habits of his compatriots.

After helping his hosts defeat an English invasion, the ingenue travels to Paris to obtain the rewards he has been assured are his due. Alas, he is betrayed, and is incarcerated for a year in the Bastille. The fiancé of the ingenue, worried at his failure to return, travels to Paris. There she discovers his unjust imprisonment, and subsequently learns to which grand personage she must appeal for his release. To her horror, only her provision of sexual favours will inspire the judge to release the man she loves. Torn, she finally yields to her oppressor. Her fiancé, the ingenue, is released, but before they can consummate their love, the bride dies of shame at her dishonour. The novel ends most ambiguously: the obnoxious but powerful judge seems to recant and regret his horrible deeds, and to make recompense, offers sinecures to the living, including the ingenue. His offers are accepted, apparently with relish.

A question to be asked is how savage, in Rousseau's sense of the word, is our noble ingenue? Although raised a Huron, he is, the novel makes clear, not an Indian by parentage but rather an Ontario-born child of French colonists. This is an early instance of the nature versus nurture debate: are a person's behaviour and character determined more by upbringing or by genes? Voltaire (but perhaps few of his readers) would have been aware of this nuance, but the subtlety challenges the thesis that the book was written primarily as rebuttal to Rousseau. If rebuttal of Rousseau were the principle motive in writing the novel, one presumes that Voltaire would have left his hero unambiguously native. More confusion is sown by trying to harvest Voltaire's intent in having the ingenue travel from the free forests of Canada to the prison of Paris. Clearly, for much of the novel, the hero was happier in Canada. And it was only in Canada that the Huron could rely solely on his own exertions to survive; in France, by contrast, he must rely on patronage or starve. Yet, later, Voltaire has the same hero, in deep depression in prison, discover relief, even contentment, from the sublime joys of written philosophy—by implication, such exalted pleasure would not be available to natives because they lacked books.

Throughout the novel, the ingenue's intellect is first-class, and his sense of equality (he thinks nothing of trying to meet with the Pope or the King) disarms his new confrères in France; these are attributes which Voltaire admires, yet he seems uncertain in the book that they deserve unstinting praise. The ambiguity is reinforced by the vocabulary: oxymorons and puns abound.

Voltaire went to more trouble in *L'Ingénu* to establish historical verisimilitude than he did in any other work. The book is replete with references to Canada: the hero is raised near what is now Toronto, the English-French wars for New France are cited; there are allusions to well-known Indian inter-tribal battles; Voltaire uses genuine native words throughout the text, and quotes from an actual Huron grammar; there are ominous hints to the Treaty of Paris (resulting in France's permanent loss of Canada); cumulatively, such details would have had large resonance with his contemporary readers. Voltaire, who never visited North America, by agglomerating this historical data, left no one in doubt regarding from which country his protagonist hailed. Did he do this simply to regale the reader with the vaguely possible, a colonial infant the victim of frontier happenstance? Or was Voltaire, by having the hero hail from Canada, hoping for something more, something peculiar to the North American sensibility which, when confronted with the French sensibility, would prove a compelling social experiment? Though no one knows, the latter possibility seems more likely, and more in keeping with his other work.

L'Ingénu was finished in July 1767 and published anonymously shortly thereafter. A month after publication the censors banned the book, but by that time Voltaire was known to be the author; the banning, of course, only heightened the demand.

The following excerpt is taken from the opening pages of the novel.

from THE INGENU

In the year 1689, on the evening of 15 July, the Abbé de Kerkabon, Prior of Our Lady of the Mountain, was strolling along the seashore with Mlle de Kerkabon, his sister, taking the air. The Prior, who was already getting on a bit in years, was a most excellent cleric, beloved by his neighbours as once he had been by his neighbours' wives. What had led him above all to be held in high regard was that he was the only local incumbent who did not have to be carried to bed when he had supped with his colleagues. He had a reasonable grasp of theology, and when he was tired of reading St. Augustine, he would read Rabelais for fun. Consequently everyone had a good word to say for him.

Mlle de Kerkabon had never married, though she much wanted to, and was well preserved for someone of forty-five. She was of good and sensible character: she liked enjoying herself, and she went to church.

"Alas!" the Prior was saying to his sister, as he gazed out to sea, "this is the very spot where our poor brother took ship on the frigate *Swallow* in 1669 with Mme de Kerkabon, his wife and our dear sister-in-law, to go and serve in Canada. Had he not been killed, we might be looking forward to seeing him again."

"Do you think," Mme de Kerkabon replied, "that our sister-in-law really was eaten by the Iroquois, as we were told she was? Certainly, had she not been eaten, she would have come back home. I shall mourn her to the end of my days. She was a charming woman. And our brother was very clever. He would surely have made a large fortune."

Just as their hearts were growing fonder at the memory of this, they saw a small ship entering the Bay of Rance on the tide. It was Englishmen coming to sell some of their country's wares. They sprang ashore without so much as a glance at the Prior or his good sister, who was most shocked at the lack of consideration shown to her.

Such was not the case when it came to a very handsome young man who leapt right over the heads of his companions in a single bound and landed straight in front of Mademoiselle. Unaccustomed as he was to bowing, he gave her a nod. His physical appearance and manner of dress drew the gaze of brother and sister alike. He was hatless, and hoseless, and wore little sandals; his head was graced with long plaits of hair; and a short doublet clung to a trim and supple figure. He had a look about him that was at once martial and gentle. In one hand he held a small bottle of Barbados water and, in the other, a sort of pouch containing a goblet and some very fine ship's biscuit. He spoke French most intelligibly. He offered some of his Barbados water to Mlle de Kerkabon and her good brother, drank some with them, and pressed them to have some more, all with such a simple, natural air that brother and sister both were charmed. They put themselves at his service and asked him who he was and where he was going. The young man replied that he had no idea, that he was curious, that he had wanted to see what the French coast was like, that he had come, and that he would be going back.

The good Prior, guessing by his accent that he was not English, took the liberty of asking him what country he was from.

"I am a Huron," the young man replied.

Mlle de Kerkabon, amazed and delighted to have seen a Huron show her such civility, asked the young man to supper. He did not wait to be asked a second time, and all three went off together to the Priory of Our Lady of the Mountain.

The diminutive and rotund good lady could not take her little eyes off him, and would periodically say to the Prior: "What a complexion he has, this big lad! Like lilies and roses! And what beautiful skin he's got for a Huron!"

"Yes, dear," said the Prior.

She asked hundreds of questions, one after another, and each time the traveller's answer would be very much to the point. Word soon spread that there was a Huron at the priory. Local society hastened to sup there. The Abbé de Saint-Yves came with Mademoiselle his sister, a young girl of Lower Breton pedigree, who was extremely pretty and very well bred. The magistrate and the tax-collector, and their wives, were also among the guests. The visitor was placed between Mlle de Kerkabon and Mlle de Saint-Yves. Everyone looked at him in astonishment, and they all spoke and questioned him at once. The Huron did not turn a hair. It was as if he had taken Lord Bolingbroke's motto for his own: "nihil admirari."

But eventually, worn out by so much noise, he said to them quite gently but firmly:

"Gentlemen, where I come from, people take it in turns to speak. How do you expect me to reply when you won't let me hear what you say?"

The voice of reason always gives people pause for a moment or two. There was a long silence.

His Honour the magistrate, who always buttonholed strangers no matter whose house he was in, and who was the greatest interrogator in the province, opened his mouth some six inches wide and said:

"What is your name, sir?"

"I always used to be called 'the Ingenu,'" replied the Huron, "and I was confirmed in the name when I was in England because I always ingenuously say what I think, just as I always do exactly as I please."

"How, sir, if you were born a Huron, were you able to come to England?"

"Because someone took me there. I was captured in battle by the English, after putting up rather a good fight, and the English, who like bravery—because they are brave too and just as honourable as we are—offered me the choice between being sent back to my family or coming to England. And I chose the latter because I am by nature passionately fond of travel."

"But, sir," said the magistrate in his important voice, "how could you possibly abandon your father and mother like that?"

"Because I never knew my father and mother," said the visitor.

This moved the company, and they all kept repeating: "Never knew his father and mother!"

"We'll be his father and mother," said the lady of the house to her brother the Prior. "What an interesting person this Huron gentleman is!"

The Ingenu thanked her with proud and noble cordiality and gave her to understand that he lacked for nothing.

"I perceive, Mr. Ingenu," said the solemn magistrate, "that you speak French better than a Huron ought."

"There was this Frenchman we captured," he said, "back in Huronia when I was a young boy. We became good friends, and he taught me his language. I'm very quick at learning what I want to learn. When I arrived in Plymouth, I came across one of those French refugees of yours, the ones you call "Huguenots" for some reason. He helped me to get to know your language better, and as soon as I could make myself understood, I came to have a look at your country, because I quite like the French—when they don't ask too many questions."

The Abbé de Saint-Yves, despite this little admonishment, asked him which of the three languages he liked best: Huron, English, or French.

"Huron, without question," replied the Ingenu.

"Well, would you believe it?" exclaimed Mlle de Kerkabon. "I'd always thought that, after Lower Breton, French was the most beautiful language."

Whereupon it was a matter of who could get in first to ask the Ingenu the Huron for "tobacco," and he answered "taya," and the Huron for "to eat," and he answered "essenten." Mlle de Kerkabon simply had to know the Huron for "to make love." He told her it was "trovander" and maintained, not unreasonably on the face of it, that these words were just as good as their French and English equivalents. "Trovander" struck all the guests as being particularly pretty.

The good Prior, who had in his library the Huron grammar given to him by the Reverend Father Sagard Théodat, the famous Recollect missionary, left the table for a moment to go and consult it. He returned quite breathless with fond emotion and delight. He recognized the Ingenu as a true Huron. There was a brief discussion about the multiplicity of tongues, and it was agreed that, but for that business with the Tower of Babel, the whole world would have spoken French.

The interrogating magistrate, who until then had been somewhat wary of this personage, was filled with new and deep respect. He now spoke to him with more civility than before, a fact which quite escaped the Ingenu's notice.

Mlle de Saint-Yves was most curious to know how they made love in the land of the Hurons.

"By doing good deeds," he replied, "to please people like you."

All the guests applauded in amazement. Mlle de Saint-Yves flushed, and was most obliged. Mlle de Kerkabon flushed too, but she was rather less obliged. She was a little piqued that this compliment had not been paid to her, but she was such a good soul that her affection for the Huron was not in the least diminished. She asked him, in a very well-meaning way, how many sweethearts he had had in Huronia.

"I have only ever had the one," said the Ingenu. "That was Mlle Abacaba, the good friend of my dear wet-nurse. Rushes are not straighter, and ermine is not whiter, sheep are less gentle, eagles less proud, and deer less nimble, than Abacaba. One day she was out hunting a hare near where we lived, about fifty leagues away. An ill-mannered Algonquin, who lived a hundred leagues beyond that, came and stole her hare. I got to hear of it, rushed off, laid the Algonquin out with a single blow of my club and brought him to the feet of my sweetheart bound hand and foot. Abacaba's family wanted to eat him, but I was never much of a one for that sort of feast, so I set him free, and we became friends. Abacaba was so touched by what I had done that she preferred me to all her other lovers. She would love me still if she hadn't been eaten by a bear. I punished the bear and wore its skin for ages, but it was no consolation."

Mlle de Saint-Yves, on hearing this tale, felt secretly pleased to learn that the Ingenu had had only one sweetheart, and that Abacaba was no longer alive, but she did not understand quite why she was pleased. All eyes were on the Ingenu, and he was much praised for having prevented his friends from eating an Algonquin.

The relentless magistrate, who could not control his mania for asking questions, eventually indulged his curiosity to the point of enquiring what the Huron gentleman's religion was, and whether he had chosen the Anglican religion, the Gallican, or the Huguenot.

"I have my own religion," he said, "as you have yours."

"Oh, dear!" cried la Kerkabon. "Clearly it didn't even occur to those wretched English to baptize him."

"But my God," said Mlle de Saint-Yves, "how can it be that the Hurons are not Catholic? Haven't the Jesuit fathers converted them all?"

The Ingenu assured her that no converting went on in his country, that no true Huron had ever changed his mind, and that his language did not even have a word for "inconstancy."

This last remark pleased Mlle de Saint-Yves exceedingly.

"We will baptize him, we will baptize him," Mlle la Kerkabon was saying to the good Prior. "The honour will be yours, my dear brother. I absolutely insist on being his godmother, and the good Abbé de Saint-Yves can be his godfather, and we shall have a jolly splendid service, and it will be the talk of Lower Brittany and do us immense credit."

The whole company supported the lady of the house, and they were all shouting: "We will baptize him!"

The Ingenu replied that in England they let people live as they pleased. He indicated that their proposal was not at all to his liking, and that the religious laws of the Hurons were at least as good as those of Lower Brittany. He ended by saying that he would be leaving the next day. They finished off the bottle of Barbados water, and everyone went to bed.

When the Ingenu had been shown to his room, Mlle de Kerkabon and her friend, Mlle de Saint-Yves, could not refrain from looking through a large keyhole to see how a Huron slept. They saw that he had spread the bedcover on the floor and was lying there in the most beautiful posture one could imagine.

The Ingenu, as was his wont, awoke with the sun at cockcrow, which in England and Huronia is called the "crack of dawn." He was not like society people who languish in an idle bed until the sun has run half its course, who can neither sleep nor rise, and who lose so many precious hours in this intermediate state between life and death and then complain that life is too short.

He had already covered two or three leagues and bagged thirty head of game in as many shots, when he returned to find the good Prior of Our Lady of the Mountain and that soul of discretion, his sister, taking a stroll round their little garden still in their nightcaps. He presented them with his entire bag and, taking from inside his shirt a sort of small talisman which he always wore around his neck, begged them to accept it as a token of his gratitude for their kind hospitality.

"It is the most precious thing I have," he informed them. "I was told I would always be happy as long as I wore this little trinket about me, and I am giving it to you so that you shall always be happy."

The Prior and Mademoiselle smiled fondly at the naïvety of the Ingenu. The present consisted of two rather poorly drawn little portraits tied together with an extremely greasy strap.

Mlle de Kerkabon asked him if there were any painters in Huronia.

"No," said the Ingenu, "this rarity came from my wet-nurse. Her husband acquired it as part of the spoils of war when he was stripping the bodies of some Frenchmen from Canada who had attacked us. That's all I know about it."

The Prior looked carefully at the portraits. His colour changed. He was overcome by emotion, and his hands began to tremble.

"By Our Lady of the Mountain," he exclaimed, "I do believe that these are the faces of my brother, the captain, and his wife!"

Mademoiselle, having inspected them with the same emotion,

came to the same conclusion. Both were filled with astonishment, and with a joy tinged with sorrow. They became agitated: they wept, their hearts pounded, they cried out, they tore the portraits from each other's hands, they grabbed them and handed them back twenty times a second. They scrutinized the portraits intently, and the Huron too. They asked him, each in turn and both at once, where, when, and how these miniatures had fallen into the hands of his wet-nurse. They compared dates. They counted the days since the captain's departure. They remembered receiving word that he had got as far as the land of the Hurons and how they had heard nothing more since then.

The Ingenu had told them that he had known neither father nor mother. The Prior, who was a man of sense, noticed that the Huron had the beginnings of a beard. He was well aware that Hurons cannot grow one.

"There is fluff on his chin, so he must be the son of a European. My brother and sister-in-law were never seen again after the expedition against the Hurons in 1669. My nephew must then have been at the breast. The Huron wet-nurse saved his life and became a mother to him."

Eventually, after hundreds of questions and answers, the Prior and his sister concluded that the Huron was their own nephew. They embraced him in tears, and the Huron laughed, finding it inconceivable that a Huron could be the nephew of a Prior in Lower Brittany.

The rest of the company arrived downstairs. M. de Saint-Yves, who was a great student of physiognomy, compared the two portraits with the Ingenu's face. He pointed out most expertly that the Ingenu had his mother's eyes, the forehead and nose of the late Captain de Kerkabon, and the cheeks of both.

Mlle de Saint-Yves, who had never seen the father or the mother, was firmly of the opinion that the Ingenu looked just like them. They all marvelled at Providence and at the way things turn out in this world. In the end they were all so persuaded, so convinced, of the Ingenu's parentage that he himself consented to be the good

Prior's nephew, saying that he was just as happy to have him for an uncle as anyone else.

They all went to give thanks to God in the church of Our Lady of the Mountain, while the Huron, with unconcerned expression, remained behind and was content to drink.

The Englishmen who had brought him, and who were ready to set sail, came to tell him that it was time to leave.

"It is quite evident that you," he said, "have not just been reunited with your uncles and aunts. I'm staying here. Off you go back to Plymouth. You can have my old clothes. I don't need anything any more, now I'm the nephew of a prior."

The English set sail, caring very little whether the Ingenu had family in Lower Brittany or not.

Once the uncle and aunt and their guests had sung the *Te Deum*, once the magistrate had again badgered the Ingenu with questions, and once they had all exhausted everything that amazement, joy, and warmth of feeling can prompt one to say, the Prior of the Mountain and the Abbé de Saint-Yves decided to have the Ingenu baptized at the earliest opportunity. But a grown Huron of twenty-two was a bit different from a baby being spiritually reborn without knowing a thing about it. He would have to be prepared, and that seemed a tall order, for the Abbé de Saint-Yves supposed that someone who had not been born in France would be quite devoid of common sense.

The Prior pointed out to the company that even though Mr. Ingenu, his nephew, had not had the good fortune to be raised in Lower Brittany, that did not make him any the less intelligent; that this was evident from all the answers he had given; and that nature had most definitely smiled on him, as much on the paternal side as on the maternal.

First they asked him if he had ever read a book. He said he had read an English translation of Rabelais and a few passages from Shakespeare, which he knew by heart; that he had found these books in the captain's cabin on the ship which had brought him from America to Plymouth, and that he was very pleased he had. The magistrate did not fail to question him about these books.

"I must confess," said the Ingenu, "that while I think I understood some of it, the rest was beyond me."

The Abbé de Saint-Yves, on hearing this, reflected that this was just how he had always read, and that most people read in much the same way.

"No doubt you have read the Bible?" he said to the Huron.

"Not a word of it, sir. It was not one of my captain's books. I've never heard of it."

"There you are, that's typical of the damned English," cried Mlle de Kerkabon. "They care more about Shakespeare's plays, and plum puddings, and bottles of rum, than they do about the Pentateuch. Which is why they have never converted a soul in America. They really are God's accursed race. And we'll have Jamaica and Virginia off them before too long."

Be that as it may, the most skilful tailor in Saint-Malo was summoned to come and dress the Ingenu from head to foot. The company took their leave: the magistrate took his questions elsewhere. Mlle de Saint-Yves turned round several times as she was departing to look at the Ingenu, and he bowed lower to her than he had ever bowed to anyone in his life before.

The magistrate, before taking his leave, introduced Mlle de Saint-Yves to his great booby of a son who was just out of college, but she scarcely glanced at him, so absorbed was she by the good manners of the Huron.

The good Prior, in view of the fact that he was getting on in years and that here was God sending him a nephew to comfort him in his old age, took it into his head that he could resign his living in this nephew's favour if he succeeded in baptizing him and getting him to enter holy orders.

The Ingenu had an excellent memory. The soundness of Lower Breton organs, further fortified by the Canadian climate, had given him a head so strong that when it got banged, he hardly felt it, and when something registered within it, not a trace would fade. He had never forgotten a thing. His understanding was all the quicker and sharper for the fact that his childhood had not been burdened with all the useless nonsense that encumbers ours, and things entered his brain as clear as daylight. The Prior resolved at length to make him read the New Testament. The Ingenu devoured it with much enjoyment but, not knowing when or where all the adventures related in the book had taken place, did not for a moment doubt that the scene of the action was Lower Brittany; and he swore that he would cut Caiaphas' and Pilate's ears and noses off for them if he ever came across those scoundrels. His uncle, delighted that he should be so well disposed, explained the position. He praised his zeal but told him that the zeal was misplaced, given that these particular individuals had died approximately sixteen hundred and ninety years earlier.

Soon the Ingenu knew almost the entire book by heart. Sometimes he raised one or two difficulties which considerably embarrassed the Prior. Often he had to go and consult the Abbé de Saint-Yves who, at a loss for a reply, called in a Lower Breton Jesuit to complete the Huron's conversion.

At last grace wrought its effect: the Ingenu promised to become a Christian. He was in no doubt that he should begin by being circumcised.

"For," he said, "I cannot think of one person in that book you made me read who wasn't. It is therefore evident that I must sacrifice my foreskin. The sooner the better."

He did not think twice. He sent for the village surgeon and asked him to perform the operation, thinking to delight Mlle de Kerkabon and the whole company exceedingly with the news once the deed was done. The barber, who had not performed this type of operation before, notified the family, and they kicked up a terrible fuss. Good Kerkabon was afraid that her nephew, who seemed a determined, no-nonsense son, might perform the operation on himself, and clumsily at that, and that this might have sorry consequences of the kind in which the ladies, out of the goodness of their hearts, always take such an interest.

The Prior set the Huron straight. He pointed out that circumcision was no longer the done thing, that baptism was altogether gentler and better for one's health, and that the law of grace was not the same as the law of self-denial. The Ingenu, who had a lot of common sense and decency, argued his case but recognized his error, which is rather a rare thing in Europe among people who debate. In the end he promised to be baptized whenever they wished.

First he would have to say confession, and this was the most difficult part. The Ingenu always carried with him in his pocket the book which his uncle had given him. In it he could find not one single apostle who had said confession, and that made him very uncooperative. The Prior silenced him by showing him the words from the Epistle of Saint James the Less which are such a problem for heretics: "Confess your faults one to another." The Huron held his peace and said his confession to a Recollect. When he had finished, he hauled the Recollect out of the confessional and, with a firm hold on his man, took his place and made him kneel down before him.

"Now then, my friend. It says: 'Confess your faults one to another.' I've told you my sins, and you're not getting out of here till you've told me yours."

So saying, he kept his ample knee pressed against the chest of the opposing party. The Recollect screamed and howled, and the whole church echoed. People came running at the noise to find the catechumen now laying into the monk in the name of Saint James the Less.

The joy at baptizing a Lower Breton Anglo-Huron was so great that they were prepared to overlook this strange behaviour. There was even quite a number of theologians who thought that confession was not necessary, since baptism took the place of everything else. A date was fixed with the Bishop of Saint-Malo, and he, flattered, as well he might be, at having a Huron to baptize, arrived with much pomp and circumstance and a retinue of clergy. Mlle de Saint-Yves, thanking God, put on her best frock and had a hairdresser come from Saint-Malo that she might be the belle of the baptism. The magistrate with all the questions came, as did the whole of local society. The church was magnificently decorated. But when the moment arrived to lead the Huron to the baptismal font, he was nowhere to be found.

Uncle and aunt looked for him everywhere. They thought he might be out hunting, as was his wont. All the guests scoured the nearby woods and villages: not a trace of the Huron.

They began to worry that he might have gone back to England. They remembered hearing him say how much he liked that country. The good Prior and his sister were convinced that no one was ever baptized over there and feared for their nephew's soul. The Bishop was nonplussed and all set to go home, the Prior and the Abbé the Saint-Yves were in despair, and the magistrate interrogated every passer-by with his usual gravity. Mlle de Kerkabon was crying. Mlle de Saint Yves was not crying, but she was heaving deep sighs which seemed to suggest a certain fondness for the sacraments. They were walking disconsolately beside the willows and reeds which grow along the banks of the little river Rance when, in the middle of the river, they caught sight of a tall, rather white figure, with its two hands crossed over its chest. They shrieked and turned away. But, with curiosity soon overcoming all other considerations, they slipped quietly in amongst the reeds and, when they were quite sure they could not be seen, determined to find out what all this was about.

The Prior and the Abbé came running up and asked the Ingenu what he was doing there.

"For goodness sake, gentlemen, I'm waiting to be baptized. I've been standing up to my neck in this water for an hour now. It's just not right leaving me to freeze to death like this."

"My dear nephew," said the Prior affectionately, "this isn't the way we baptize people in Lower Brittany. Put your clothes back on and come with us."

Mlle de Saint-Yves, on hearing this, whispered to her companion:

"Mademoiselle, do you think he's going to put his clothes back on this minute?"

The Huron, however, answered the Prior back.

"You're not going to pull the wool over my eyes this time the way you did the last. I've gone into things a lot since then, and I am quite certain that there is no otherway of being baptized. Queen Candace's eunuch was baptized in a stream. I defy you to show me in that book you gave me any other way of going about it. I will be baptized in a river or not at all."

It was no use telling him that customs had changed. The Ingenu was stubborn, for he was a Breton and a Huron. He kept coming back to Queen Candace's eunuch, and although his maiden aunt and Mlle de Saint-Yves, who had observed him through the willows, had just cause to tell him that he was in no position to quote a man of that water, they nevertheless did no such thing, so great was their discretion. The Bishop himself came to speak to him, which was quite something, but he had no success. The Huron argued his case with the Bishop.

"Show me," he said, "in that book my uncle gave me, one single person who was not baptized in a river and I will do anything you want."

Aunt, now desperate, had noticed that the first time her nephew had bowed, he had made a deeper bow to Mlle de Saint-Yves than to anyone else in the company, and that he had greeted not even the Bishop with the same mixture of respect and cordiality that he had shown the beautiful young lady. She decided to turn to her at this very ticklish moment. She asked her to use her influence to get the Huron to agree to be baptized the Breton way, not believing that her nephew could ever become a Christian if he persisted in wanting to be baptized in running water.

Mlle de Saint-Yves blushed with secret pleasure at being charged with such an important commission. She approached the Huron modestly and, shaking his hand in a thoroughly noble fashion, said to him:

"Would you do something for me?"

And as she uttered these words, she lowered her eyes and lifted them again with a grace that warmed the heart.

"Oh, anything you wish, mademoiselle, anything you command: baptism by water, by fire, by blood. There is nothing I would not do for you."

Mlle de Saint-Yves had the honour and glory of effecting in a few words what neither the entreaties of the Prior nor the repeated questioning of the magistrate nor the arguments even of the Bishop had been able to achieve. She was sensible of her triumph: but she was not yet sensible of its extent.

The baptism was administered and received with all possible decency, magnificence, and enjoyment. Uncle and aunt ceded to M. l'Abbé de Saint-Yves and his sister the honour of holding the Ingenu over the font. Mlle de Saint-Yves beamed with joy to find herself a godmother. She was ignorant of what obligations this great title laid her under, and she accepted the honour without knowing its fatal consequences.

As there never was ceremony that was not followed by a grand dinner, they all sat down to eat after the baptism. The wags of Lower Brittany said how one should never baptize one's wine. The Prior was saying that, according to Solomon, wine rejoices the heart of man. The Lord Bishop added that Judah the Patriarch had had to bind his ass' colt unto the vine and wash his coat in the blood of grapes, and that he personally was very sad one couldn't do the same in Lower Britanny, to which God had denied the vine. Everyone tried to produce some witticism about the Ingenu's baptism and some compliments for the godmother. The magistrate, ever full of questions, asked the Huron if he would be faithful to his promises.

"How could I possibly break my promises," replied the Huron, "since Mademoiselle de Saint-Yves was holding me when I made them?"

The Huron warmed to the occasion. He drank a great deal to the health of his godmother.

"If I had been baptized by your hand," he said, "I feel as though the cold water poured upon the nape of my neck would have scalded me."

The magistrate found this all far too poetical, not knowing how common allegory is in Canada. But godmother was extremely happy about it.

They had given the baptized the name of Hercules. The Bishop of Saint-Malo kept asking who this patron saint was of whom he had never heard. The Jesuit, who was most learned, told him that he was a saint who had worked twelve miracles. There was a thirteenth which was worth more than the other twelve put together, but which it ill became a Jesuit to mention. That was the one of changing fifty maidens into women in the course of a single night. One of those present, who was something of a humorist, energetically elaborated on the merits of this miracle. The ladies all lowered their gaze and considered that, to judge by his face, the Ingenu was worthy of the saint whose name he bore.

RUPERT BROOKE

R UPERT BROOKE (1887–1915) was handsome to the point of
beauty, thirsty for adventure, charming in society, and a
formidably talented prodigy as a poet. It is difficult, indeed, to recall
that during his lifetime, he published but one book of verse.

Opinions are varied as to which English poet conceived the term
"Georgian Poetry" to describe the rustic, sylvan mood common to
the work of John Masefield, W. H. Davies, and A. E. Housman,
among others. Some credit Rupert Brooke with the coinage.
Regardless, he was instrumental in the founding of the biennial
anthology simply titled *Georgian Poetry* (published 1912–1922),
although his friend Edward Marsh was the chief guardian of the
movement.

In 1912 Rupert Brooke received a fellowship to King's College,
Cambridge. Soon after he suffered what is termed today a nervous
breakdown. Medical counsel suggested that he travel, and from
March to September 1913, he perambulated the United States and
Canada, then sailed to Tahiti. Thanks to the Canadian poet
Duncan Campbell Scott, a senior employee of the Department of
Indian Affairs, Brooke was armed with letters of introduction to
department agents across western Canada, in contrast to his failure
to obtain introductions to other Canadians before he arrived in the
country. In the year following his global travel, Brooke volunteered
for service in the First World War, and in 1915 became another

Rupert Brooke (right) with Duncan Campbell Scott during Brooke's visit to Ottawa in July, 1913. Brooke wrote "I'm just off to dine with the only poet in Canada, Duncan Campbell Scott—a very nice fellow." From the Duncan Campbell Scott Papers in the Pelham Edgar Collection. Courtesy of the Pratt Library, Victoria University, Toronto.

casualty of that conflict. He was buried by torchlight on the Greek island of Skyros.

At the age of twenty-five, prior to his departure for North America, Brooke had arranged for the English weekly *The Westminster Gazette* to publish, as a series of public letters, his observations on Canadian life and landscape. The letters—today we would call them "articles"—were also posthumously published in a single volume (with a preface by Henry James) called *Letters from America*. Despite the book's title, much of the contents deal with this country, and as Henry James noted, "the pages from Canada, where as an impressionist, he increasingly finds his feet, and even finds to the same increase a certain comfort of association, are better than those from the States." The further west Brooke moved, the more sympathetic he became to the country and its people.

Reading his private letters, it is difficult to determine Brooke's final response to the country. On the one hand, his supposed rightness, his assumed superiority of English manners and living (a snobbery induced in him, no doubt, in part, by the school system), ran, again and again, into the attractiveness of Canadian informality. On the other hand, his obvious relish of the wilderness ("All the woods around us are full of bears, which is frightfully exciting") is occasionally counterpointed by his encounters with brash pioneer Philistines, stunningly proud of their own ignorance. Even the very newness of the country, while exhilarating to an Old World writer trying to establish a literary reputation back home, comes to grate on his nerves with the force of railcar wheels screeching at tight corners, and drives him to sporadic, impolite sarcasm.

Young, brash, still occasionally immature, purveying many of the prejudices of his day, still savouring collegiate humour, Brooke in these letters can also display a touching self-honesty and a bent for humour for which he has been insufficiently acclaimed. The recipients of the Canadian letters include Edward Marsh, the literary impresario; Wilfrid Gibson, a fellow "Georgian poet"; A.F. Scholfield, a school chum; Edmund Gosse, the influential literary biographer; Cathleen Nesbitt, a young actress with whom Brooke had a platonic (aching to be otherwise) love affair; Sybil Pye, a friend; and Russell Loines, an attorney he had encountered in New York.

TO EDWARD MARSH

Ottawa
9 July [1913]

Mein lieber Eddie,

I picked up a letter of June 23rd or so from you here this morning: which brightened my grey life a moment or two. I got on well in New York and got to know a lot of folks: but here I'm rather astray. With my usual improvidence I omitted to get any introductions for Canada. One to Sir Wilfrid Laurier is all. And he isn't here for a day or two. So I've been—in Montreal and Quebec for the last ten days—rather dull. The Canadians are a churlish race. I find that when I'm alone and don't see my friends, I don't get very miserable or go to pieces (save for occasional bouts of home-sickness just before meals): but my whole level of life descends to an incredible muddy flatness. I do no reading, no thinking, and no writing. And very often I don't see many things. The real hell of it is that I get so numb that my brain and senses don't record fine or clear impressions. So the time is nearly all waste. I'm very much ashamed of it all. For I've always beforehand a picture of myself dancing through foreign cities, drinking in novelty, hurling off letters to the *W[estminster] G[azette]*, breaking into song and sonnet, dashing off plays and novels, Lord—I've not really given the Canadians much chance yet. But my impression *is* that they have all the faults of the Americans, and not their one lovely and redeeming virtue, "hospitality." That "hospitality" is often sneered at in the Americans: but it merely means that with the nice ones, you can be at once on happy and intimate terms…. However I fancy the West may be better. And I'm gradually becoming convinced I must get across there very swiftly. I'm going to stay to see what can be got out of Laurier. After that, I guess I shall shoot through my other places. Especially as I hear there's unemployment in the Middle West; so I couldn't get a job on a farm….

TO MRS. BROOKE

King Edward Hotel
Toronto
21 July [1913]

Dear Mother,

I hope you got my postcard, saying my next mail was to go to me at Vancouver. At least I forget if I did say that. But that's the next thing.... I may get to Vancouver by August 15, or any time up to the end of August. (My birthday I'll probably spend on the train between Winnipeg and Edmonton!) The uncertain parts are my tours off the line.... Laurier was a nice old man—a bit of a "politician," playing the party game, but not so much as the others. I don't trust his policy, because I don't believe he *really* wants to pay anything in any form towards the Navy. He's very French in sympathies. I saw Perley, the acting-Premier on the other side. Borden was away. I had been told by Masefield that he knew (by correspondence) the Canadian poet Duncan Campbell Scott.... I haven't been writing much out here—Rather bad letters to the *Westminster*. Perhaps they'll refuse to print them.

TO EDWARD MARSH

Toronto
22 July [1913]

Oh Eddie ...

I've found here an Arts & Letters Club of poets painters journalists etc., where they'd heard of me, & read G.P.[*Georgian Poetry*], &, oh Eddie, one fellow actually possessed my "Poems." Awful Triumph. Every now & then one comes up & presses my hand & says "Wal, Sir, you cannot know how memorable a Day in my life this is."

Then I do my pet boyish-modesty stunt & go pink all over: & everyone thinks it *too* delightful. One man said to me "Mr. Brooks (my Canadian name) Sir, I may tell you that in my opinion you have Mr. Noyes skinned." That means I'm better than him: I gathered a great compliment here. But they're really quite an up-to-date lot: & very cheery & pleasant. I go on, tomorrow, to the desert & the wilds. My next letters will take a week longer on the way so they won't reach England for a long while after you get this.

Niagara
24 July

Were you ever here? It's very queer. The things are very very low & broad & gloomy. I write with the sound of them monstrous in my ears; one is across the river opposite, one to the right. A dizzying affair. Funny to think that this noise has been continually sounding, & that I'm hearing the same noise as Washington & Poe & Goldie Dickinson, only a little later on.

P.S. The most unpopular person in Canada is Winston. Ever since his lecture-tour. They *do* hate him.

TO WILFRID GIBSON

King Edward Hotel
Toronto
23 July [1913]

My dear Wilfrid,

The only poet in Canada was very nice to me in Ottawa—Duncan Campbell Scott, aetat. 50, married, an authority on Indians. Poor devil, he's so lonely and dried there: no one to talk to. They had a child—daughter—who died in 1908 or so. And it knocked them out. She, a violinist, never played since: he hasn't written, till the last few months. Their house was queerly desolate. It rather went to my heart. Canada's a *bloody* place for a sensitive—in a way 2nd rate— real, slight poet like that to live all his life. Nobody cares if he writes or doesn't. He took me out to a Club in the country near, and we drank whisky and soda, and he said "Well, here's to your youth!" and drank its health, and I nearly burst into tears. He's a very nice chap (especially away from his wife, who's nice enough): and he's *thirsty* to talk literature; and he's very keen on all our work. He saw a little of the 1890–1905 men he's caricatured in Archer's book—and he finds *us far* better! So he's obviously to be encouraged. He's probably visiting England Sept–Oct for a week or two. I gave him letters to Eddie [Marsh] and [Harold] Monro, and told him you'd insist on talking to him and giving him tea in your attic. So get hold of him and cheer him. He'd love it. And, if there's not much on, make Monro (or Eddie) get up a little dinner or lunch of the quietest nature with de la Mare and you and whoever of the immortals is about. It'd be a nice thing to do. Reserve a chair and a plate of soup or blood for me: and you'll see a faint shade lapping at the plate and hear the dimmest of American accents wishing you all well.

I must go out to lunch at the Toronto Arts & Letters. It's a club Wilfrid, where they have HEARD of US! And one or two little men possess our Works—not G.P. but our own—Canada's looking up!

TO A.F. SCHOLFIELD

Toronto
July-August [1913]

I have been on this continent for two months and shall be six more, perhaps.... I can only excuse myself by the fact that I'm writing near Niagara, the spray of which is wafted gently over my paper. There is romance for you! A letter dewy with Niagara read by a corpulent turbaned rajah of a librarian under the deodar of Taj Mahal. (Local

Colour.) But it shows you what the British Empire is! (I am become (1) a strong Imperialist, (2) a rabid anti-Canadian, (3) a *violent* Englander). But, o Scho. I'm so impressed by Niagara. I hoped not to be. But I horribly am. The colour of the water, the strength of it, and the clouds of spray—I'm afraid I'm a Victorian at heart, after all. Please don't breathe a word of it: I want to keep such shreds of reputation as I have left. Yet it's true. For I sit and stare at the thing and have the purest Nineteenth Century grandiose thoughts, about the Destiny of Man, the Irresistibility of Fate, the Doom of Nations, the fact that Death awaits us All, and so forth. Wordsworth Redivivus. Oh dear! oh dear!

I complete this scrawl in the wilderness, eighty miles N. E. of Winnipeg, by a lonely lake where I'm living wild and fishing with an old Rugbeian I found in Winnipeg. And it is August 3 and I am twenty-six years old today. "So little done, so much to do!" as I wittily and originally observed to a chipmunk this morning. I swear, I will have written two plays, a novel, and a long poem by this time next year....

TO EDMUND GOSSE

Lake Superior
27 July [1913]

Dear Edmund Gosse,

... The Americans just now seem almost entirely subsistent on England for serious literature, just as this soulless "Dominion" is on the United States for *all* literature....

I'm writing on Lake Superior. We're steaming along in a little low fog, which just doesn't come up to the top deck, but completely hides the surface of the sea. Occasionally little cones and peaks of the mist float by, and the sun catches them. It is slightly uncanny; like everything in these great lakes. I have a perpetual feeling that a lake ought not to be this size. A river and a little lake and an ocean are natural; but not these creatures. They are too big, and too smooth, and too sunny; like an American business man.

But this is garrulity. I hope you're well; and that England (of which we hear little over here) is still healthy. I become more passionately English, the more I'm absent from England.

I go to Winnipeg, the Rockies, Vancouver, and, I hope, the South Seas. And I'm not writing anything.

TO CATHLEEN NESBITT

Lake George
August [1913]

My dear,

You'll excuse me if this letter is smeared with dirt or mud or blood. I've all of them on my hands. The blood may be mine or may be a caribou's. A caribou is a sort of stag—at least, the male is. I'm writing in bed, by a lake forty or fifty miles from the nearest town, N.E. of Winnipeg, at midnight. The way it happened is this. I found a man, an old Rugbeian, in Winnipeg. He had been working very hard for a long time. And Winnipeg was *very* hot. So we decided to take a holiday. So, first by rail, and then by a truck on some lines to a Power Station by a lake, and then on foot and then in a canoe and then on foot, we got here. It is the "Club House" of a Winnipeg Hunting and Fishing Club. There's no one here now, except the man and his wife who keep it, for it's not the good fishing season. It's just a wooden low house, built on a granite cliff, over a little lake, 2 miles by 5, amidst great woods. There's a family in a shack across the lake, and an Indian and his son on the river two miles away; no other neighbors. Beyond the lake there are low hills all wooded, and other lakes, and hills, and woods, for hundreds and hundreds of miles; all wild; filled with caribou, and moose, and red deer, and BEARS, and timber wolves, and minks, and all sorts of things. All the woods around us are full of bears, which is frightfully exciting. My friend and I bathe all day—diving off rock into the clearest and sweetest of blue water—and row and fish, and try to sail a canoe and get tipped up, and light great fires at evening, and listen to stories and sleep and eat. The man here is a trapper; a fine fellow with a handsome face and a shock of curly black hair, who has hunted and trapped over the whole of North America, and can find his way anywhere, shoot anything, and do anything. He found a little Liverpool scullery-maid who'd emigrated and was working in a town out West, and married her. She is just blossoming into a primitive in-touch-with-Nature squaw woman—very funny. Tonight the trapper and an Indian who lives near here set out in a canoe after "supper"—about 5:45 p.m., to hunt. About 10:30 p.m., after our bonfire had died down, came a hail from the landing stage in the darkness below. The woman went out on to the rock we stand on to answer it, and came back with the news that "the boys were to come down." (It's very nice to be addressed "Say, boys,—.") We went down the steep path, I ahead. By the boat-house in the darkness was Bryan (the trapper) wading ashore, tugging the canoe with two dark forms in it—the Indian, and, as I peered through the dark, something crouching with a vast head of horns. The woman said "Ave ye shot anything?" Bryan replied "Yaw. A rat." (His form of humour.) The canoe came right up, and we distinguished an immense deer, the size of a small pony, dead, strapped into the bottom of the canoe. It weighed 500 lbs.: and they had paddled the canoe six miles, all round by the shore, the water up within half an inch of the gunwales, from the place where they'd shot him. They emptied him out into the muddy edge of the water; we lit a great fire of birch, spruce, and tamarack wood to see what was going on; and we all set to work to string him up for the night (he had been disembowelled.) For two hours we pulled and hauled at this creature, tugging at a rope over the branch of a birch. Then the trapper got an axe and hacked the beast's head off: with the great antlers it weighs some hundred pounds. At length we got the carcass hanging up and supported it with sticks. I got cut and scratched and smeared with the creature's inside. It was a queer sight, lit up by the leaping flames of the fire, which the woman fed—the black water of the lake, muddy with trampling at the edge, and streaked with blood, the trapper in the tree, this great carcass hanging at one end of the rope, my friend and an Indian and I pulling our arms out at the other, the head gazing reproachfully at us from the ground, everybody using the most frightful language, and the rather ironical and very dispassionate stars above. Rather savage. Bryan said, once "Brought it all the way home so as *you* could see it, kid," to his wife; so she was in an ecstasy of delight all evening.

3 August

Today, o my heart, I am twenty-six years old. And I've done so little. I'm very much ashamed. By God, I'm going to make things hum, though.

But that's all so far away. I'm lying quite naked on a beach of golden sand, six miles away from the hunting-lodge, the other man near by, a gun between us in case bears appear, the boat pulled up on the shore, the lake very blue and ripply, and the sun rather strong. We "trolled" for fish coming, which means, you may know, putting out a piece of bright twisting metal with hooks and letting it drag after the boat. It rotates, and flashes, and large fish think it a little one, and swallow it. So! we caught two pike on the way out, which lie picturesquely in the bows of the boat. Along the red-gold beach are the tracks of various wild animals, mostly jumping deer and caribou. One red deer we saw as we came round the corner, lolloping along the beach, stopping and snuffing the wind, and going on again. Very lovely. And the meat wasn't needed, so we didn't shoot at it (I'm glad—I'm no "sportsman"). We bathed off the beach, and then lit a fire of birch and spruce, and fried eggs and ate cold caribou heart, and made tea, and had (oh!) blueberry pie. Cooking and eating a meal naked is the most solemnly primitive thing one can do.

And—and this is the one thing which will make you realize, that I'm living far the most wonderfully, and incredibly romantic life you ever heard of, and *infinitely* superior to your miserable crawling London existence—the place we landed at is an Indian Camp. Indians when they go away from a camping-ground take the strips of birch-bark which answer to canvas in our tents, but leave the poles standing for the next visit—just like Pictures and this birch-grove has six or seven of these, with litter inside, temporarily uninhabited—oh but only temporarily! Any moment a flotilla of birch-bark canoes may sweep round the corner crowded with Indians—braves and squaws and papooses—and not these lonely half-breeds and stray Indians, who speak English, mind you, but the Real Thing. Shades of Fenimore Cooper! But if you don't like Beer or Kenneth Grahame, perhaps you also dislike or don't know Fenimore Cooper. What a woman! My dear one, I'll write you a shaky letter from the train while I'm hurrying across the boundless prairie. But God knows when it'll get to you....

TO EDWARD MARSH

Calgary
16 August [1913]

My dear,

My progress is degenerating into a mere farce. The West insists on taking me seriously as a politician & thinker. Toronto, which is in the East, started in on me as a Poet, with an Interview which I'll send you if I get a spare copy. It's only fairly funny, though it gets better when it's copied into *The Saskatoon Sentinel* & the rest, in fragments, as it does. Every little paper in western Canada has started its Society Column with "Dust" sometime in the last three weeks. Solemn thought. But in most of these towns they know me chiefly as a Political Expert. I average two reporters a day, who ask me my opinion on every subject under the sun. My opinions on the financial situation in Europe are good reading. And there are literally columns of them in the papers. I sit for an hour a day & laugh in my room. When I come back, though, I shall demand a knighthood from Winston. I've been delivering immense speeches in favour of his naval policy. What's really wrong with these damned Canadians is that at bottom they believe it's all play, & that war is impossible, & that there ain't no such place as the continent of Europe. They all live a thousand miles from the sea, and make an iniquitous living by gambling in real estate....

I have been lying in bed for half an hour practising to become American; the spittoon on the floor beside me. It is a lonely sort of game, & I'm not very good at it. I'm becoming the most expert of travellers, though. I've even started washing my own clothes. On Tuesday I get out of this plain up into the Rockies. There I shall rest awhile & try to write. It's so long since I've written anything, except a little painstaking dreariness for the *Westminster*....

England—I dreamt, last night, that at Vancouver I got sick of the trip & came back to England, & landed at Grantchester (you should have seen how we drew up at the Boat-house), & wired to you that I was going to stay a night with you in London, & caught the 4:55— &, oh, woke. Would you have been there? I've a sort of idea you'll go to Venice or some lovely place in September. I envy you. You can't think how sick one's heart gets for something *old*. For weeks I have not seen or touched a town so old as myself. Horrible! Horrible! They gather round me & say, "In 1901 Calgary had 139 inhabitants, now it has 75,000": & so forth. I reply, "My village is also growing. At the time of Julius Caesar it was a bare 300. Domesday Book gives it 347 and it is now close on 390." Which is ill-mannered of me.

Oh, but I have adventures—had I only anybody to tell them to! For a day I travelled with a Scotch Whisky manufacturer, a Radical. At Euston he had got into the carriage with a woman who had turned out to have nursed the late Duke of Sutherland up to the last. "And she gave me most interesting particulars about the Duke's passing away." Isn't it extraordinary what things complete strangers will say to each other?...

TO CATHLEEN NESBITT

Chateau Lake Louise
Laggan, Alta. Canada
2 September [1913]

Liebes Kind (that's German for dear child),

... I've *nothing* to tell you, except that the mountains are ... and the lake is ... and the snow and the trees are ... but it would take me weeks to get out what they are, and I haven't time, for I want this letter to go today or tomorrow. Suffice it that they are wonderful. Did I tell you that I spent a day in an Indian reservation when I was coming through here! I had a letter to the agent—they always have an agent, a white man, to look after the Indians. The reservation is about 15 miles by 8, and contains 600 Indians. The agent was a queer restless fellow called Waddy, who had been all over the world, served in South Africa, etc. When he was talking to the Indians—he had to do it through one of them who knew English, for most didn't—he said "Ask him, did he buy that yesterday".... So I shouted, "You're Irish:" and he was. "Ask him did he"... funny nation the Irish. This one was typical of you all, restless, lively and without humour, and nice.

Oh, but the Indians. They were so fine looking, and so jolly. They kept coming into the store-office to ask for things—the agents are father mother aunt priest doctor lawyer M.P. housemaid and God to the Indians in their charge. An Indian in a blanket and fur and gaudy trimmings would sidle into the room. Then for ten minutes he would stand silent. You must never hurry an Indian. Then he takes the pipe out of his mouth, says "Um" and puts it back again. Five minutes pass. Then he looks at the ceiling, and says: "... Um ... Salt. Um."

The Agent. "Is it more Epsom's Fruit Salts y'r wanting?"
Indian. *(nods)*.
Agent. "But ye had som th'ither day—"
Indian. *(blank)*.
Agent. "Is y'r stomach onaisy?"

Indian. *(nods).*

Agent. *(getting up, taking jar, pouring out some salts into paper, and wrapping them up).* "There you are."

Indian. *(secretes them in some pouch, without a word).*

Agent sits down again.

Indian stands for ten minutes silent and immobile.

Indian. *(suddenly)* "... Um ..."

Exit slowly.

Enter 2nd Indian, cautiously.

(da capo)

But they're far nicer than the other inhabitants of this continent.

This is a stupid letter.... Anyway, from Vancouver (which I'm nearing) I'll write again, better.

For the present, my lovely child, God be with you.

TO MRS. BROOKE

Vancouver Hotel, Vancouver
— and the boat to Victoria
8 September 1913

Dear Mother,

A whole heap of stuff awaited me in Vancouver, and another letter has come since. Somehow, I only seem to be eleven or twelve days from you. I'm very glad you like the *W.G.* articles. They're not always very well written, but I think they're the sort of stuff that ought to interest an intelligent *W.G.* reader more than the ordinary travel stuff one sees. I hope they won't annoy people over this side. Canadians and Americans are so touchy. But it's absurd to ladle out indiscriminate praise, as most people do.

I had several introductions in Vancouver, and only four days. It's a great place, rather different from the rest of Canada. More oriental. The country and harbour are rather beautiful with great violet mountains all round, snow-peaks in the distance. They interviewed me and put (as usual) a quite inaccurate report of it in the paper, saying I'd come here to investigate the Japanese question. In consequence about five people rang me up every morning at 8 o'clock (British Columbians get up an hour earlier than I) to say they wanted to wait on me and give me their views. Out here they always have telephones in the bedrooms. One old sea captain came miles to tell me that the Japanese—and every other—trouble was due to the fact that British Columbia had neglected the teaching of the Gospels on the land question. He wasn't so far out in some respects.

B. Columbia returns 39 Conservatives and 2 Socialists to a local house of 41 members. The Conservative majority was got by turning the population of every doubtful constituency out to build roads for high wages at the public expense for six months before the elections. McBride, who's now in England, the premier of B.C., had practically no money when he entered politics a few years ago; and now he is a millionaire. People have done the same all over Canada.

I'm going on to Victoria, on Vancouver Island, for two days, then to Seattle by water, then to San Francisco by train down along by the American Rockies.

I'll be about there for some time. I gather there's a lot to be learnt in California. Vancouver is full of Chinese and Japanese and Hindus. The Hindus wear their turbans. There is a lot of feeling against all the Orientals. They come in and underbid the white labour, and get rich and buy land. Some trades they've taken over altogether. When British Columbia, California, and Australia get working together against Japan, there'll be trouble out here. They have anti-yellow riots occasionally.

I shall be rather glad to get down into the States again. Canada is a most horribly individualistic place, with no one thinking of anything except the amount of money they can make, by any means, in the shortest time. The States are pretty bad: but they do have a few people trying to do some good, or to do good work or follow ideas for their own sake. The University'll be meeting again when I get down to 'Frisco: and I believe they are rather an interesting lot.

TO SYBIL PYE

[Postcard]
Postmark: Victoria, B.C
12 September [1913]

You think B.C. means before Christ. But it doesn't.

I'm sitting, wildly surmising, on the edge of the Pacific, gazing at mountains which are changing colour every two minutes in the most surprising way. Nature here is half Japanese....

TO RUSSELL LOINES

14 September [1913]

'Shasta Limited'
(Southern Pacific Ogden & Shasta Routes)

Dear Loines,

Your letter to Winnipeg finally reached me in Vancouver. Thence I've started South, & am now rushing in the utmost luxury through Washington (a dry State, on Sundays anyhow, damn it)—*en route* for 'Frisco.

I'm glad, in a way, to be out of Canada. Theoretically, I hold that Life is more important than Art, that intellectual snobbery is the worst kind, etc. etc. But in practice I do like occasionally seeing people who have heard of, say, Shakespeare before, even though we don't discuss it. And the U.S., even where they're ghastly vulgar (as often), are apt to show some—not very healthy—vitality & liveliness. The Canadian is *sehr steif* [very stiff], as my German friends say of me....

WILLA CATHER

F EW EMINENT WRITERS have been as deeply affected by Canada as the American author Willa Cather (1873–1947). Her youth was spent in Nebraska, but upon graduation from the state university, she moved first to Pittsburgh, then to New York to work as a journalist. In 1912, with the publication of her second book, she committed herself full time to creative writing.

She increasingly came to believe that the cultural values and spiritual verities important to her were disappearing from American life. In fact, she was disgusted by the uncouth materialism she believed to be inherent in the rise of American capitalism. Her fiction turned, therefore, from the ugliness of the contemporary to what she perceived as the sublime historical. It was while undergoing this change that she encountered, transformingly, Canada.

Prior to this epiphany Cather had been shocked by the marriage of one of her best friends, Isabelle McClung, and further astounded by her friend's eventual move to Toronto with her husband. Because of the modesty of the era and the distance of time, the exact nature of Cather's relationship with McClung is unclear; perhaps "passionate" is the appropriate adjective to describe the intensity of Cather's feelings for her chum. Initially hurt by what she perceived as rejection, Cather mollified her feelings, and the two women soon restored their bond.

Indeed, Cather's first trip to Canada was a ten-day stay to see

Isabelle in 1917, but even before that date, events in Canada had affected her fiction. Her second novel, *Alexander's Bridge*, arose from the collapse of a bridge near Quebec City in 1907. The disaster had been widely reported in the North American press, and the parallels between the real incident and the fiction are too close for coincidence—or doubt as to the inspiration.

Cather also spent June and July of 1919 in Toronto as Isabelle's guest, and again returned to the city in April 1921 to stay for five months. She had hoped to pass her days in Toronto in anonymity, but Sinclair Lewis, believing he was paying her homage, announced from the Massey Hall stage at his reading that he was honoured to be speaking in the city that was home to Willa Cather. The Canadian reporters descended like locusts on her McClung hideaway and devoured her privacy.

Her whereabouts immediately after this period are unclear, but it seems she ventured to Grand Manan Island in New Brunswick at approximately this time. Why, no one knows, but the attraction the island held for her was magnetic. She revisited Grand Manan during the summers of 1922 and 1924, and in the summer of 1926 she purchased land on the island and arranged for local carpenters to build her a cottage in the Cape Cod style. She estivated there, with rare exceptions, until 1940.

By the late 1920s Cather was more convinced than ever that European values, particularly French values, were the headwaters of civilization. Unlike her compatriots, she did not worship the gods of material progress, and she abhorred the American fiction that encounters with Nature were purifying and ennobling. Rather, she embraced the belief that gentility as she felt it had existed in the past—or existed in Europe—should be fully part of American culture.

In 1928, Cather, ill and depressed, chose to travel to Grand Manan from her home in the United States via Quebec for the first time. On this trip, she was struck with full force like a tympanum *fortissimo*. Her companion, Edith Lewis, recorded Cather's shock of recognition:

From the first moment that she looked down from the windows of the Frontenac on the pointed roofs and Norman outlines of the town of Quebec, Willa Cather was not merely stirred and charmed—she was overwhelmed by the flood of memory, recognition, surmise it called up; by the sense of its extraordinarily French character, isolated and kept intact through hundreds of years as if by miracle, on this great un-French continent.... Willa Cather went roaming alone about the town during most of the ten days we spent there. She visited the Ursuline Convent, the Cathedral, the great Laval Seminary, the Church of Our Lady of Victory, the market-place in the Lower Town; and brought back, I remember, thrilling accounts of them all.

The encounter with Quebec was to be repeated many times. The city fired her imagination; she devoured books on Canadian history, especially religious and Quebec history: the Jesuit *Relations*, the story of Mother Marie de l'Incarnation, Francis Parkman on the death of Montcalm. Out of this diet of reading came what most critics regard as one of her two finest works, *Shadows on the Rock*. The scholar Benjamin George has even argued persuasively that because of this book Cather should be seen as a Canadian writer, rather than American, in sensibility:

In Quebec then, Cather found a society built upon a rock which came as close to any she ever found to meeting her fictive notions of the City Built upon a Rock, for there she found a world which cherished the past, which maintained its traditions, which represented the preservation of European civilization in the New World, and whose roots were those of her most admired country, France.... In doing so, Cather revealed her sympathy with Canadian ideals as opposed to the American counterparts. While a number of her compatriots also expressed one or another of these views in their response to the twenties or more particularly to the Depression, it is Cather's treatment of a constellation of views, similar to a constellation of those characteristic of Canadian literature, which is so striking.

The immensity of the impact of Canada on Cather's writing has not been fully appreciated by Canadians. As is too often the case, it is foreigners who have to point out to us the obvious. For example, Cather's friend Elizabeth Shepley Sergeant in her memoir of Willa Cather explains how essential Canada became to Cather: "The driving force of *Shadows on the Rock* as of *Death Comes for the Archbishop* seemed to me the author's scarcely conscious pioneer longing to press on to a new frontier. New Mexico, New Brunswick and Quebec were not places where fate had situated Willa Cather, or where professional interests had taken her. They were psychic homelands that her love and adventure had eagerly sought and embraced— almost fragments of her soul."

Such an observation reminds us that Canada has been perceived or portrayed by many foreign writers as a Shangri-la, a sanctuary of refuge for those who are noble at heart. This attitude has endured from the seventeenth-century writings of John Dennis and his "noble savages," through the nineteenth century and Harriet Beecher Stowe's Uncle Tom, through Willa Cather's rose-tinted vision of our history, to our own day when draft resisters find spiritual asylum and reinvigorating happiness in the true north strong and free.

Cather guarded her privacy jealously; prior to her death she burned hundreds of her letters, and her will stipulates that nothing may be quoted from her correspondence. For that reason, sadly, most of the rich trove of Cather material dealing with Canada is unknown to the public simply because of an annoying legal stricture.

One facet of her feeling for Canada can be found in her relatively unknown and penultimate short story, "Before Breakfast." It is, strangely, her only work set on Grand Manan. Written less than three years before her death, it is far more affirmative in tone than her correspondence from the same period, and, from the accounts of

Edith Lewis and other friends, we know the story to be largely auto-biographical in mood and feeling.

BEFORE BREAKFAST

Henry Grenfell, of Grenfell & Saunders, got resentfully out of bed after a bad night. The first sleepless night he had ever spent in his own cabin, on his own island, where nobody knew that he was senior partner of Grenfell & Saunders, and where the business correspondence was never forwarded to him. He slipped on a blanket dressing-gown over his pyjamas (island mornings in the North Atlantic are chill before dawn), went to the front windows of his bedroom, and ran up the heavy blue shades which shut out the shameless blaze of the sunrise if one wanted to sleep late—and he usually did on the first morning after arriving. (The trip up from Boston was long and hard, by trains made up of the castoff coaches of liquidated railroads, and then by the two worst boats in the world.) The cabin modestly squatted on a tiny clearing between a tall spruce wood and the sea—sat about fifty yards back from the edge of the red sandstone cliff which dropped some two hundred feet to a narrow beach—so narrow that it was covered at high tide. The cliffs rose sheer on this side of the island, were undercut in places, and faced the east.

The east was already lightening; a deep red streak burnt over the sky-line water, and the water itself was thick and dark, indigo blue—occasionally a silver streak, where the tide was going out very quietly. While Grenfell stood at his window, a big snowshoe hare ran downhill from the spruce wood, bounded into the grass plot at the front door, and began nervously nibbling the clover.

He was puzzled and furtive; his jaws quivered, and his protrud-
ing eyes kept watch behind him as well as before. Grenfell was sure it
was the hare that used to come every morning two summers ago and
had become quite friendly. But now he seemed ill at ease; presently
he started, sat still for an instant, then scampered up the grassy hillside and disappeared into the dark spruce wood. Silly thing! Still, it
was a kind of greeting.

Grenfell left the window and went to his walnut washstand (no
plumbing) and mechanically prepared to take a shower in the shed
room behind his sleeping-chamber. He began his morning routine,
still thinking about the hare.

First came the eye-drops. Tilting his head back, thus staring into
the eastern horizon, he raised the glass dropper, but he didn't press
the bulb. He saw something up there. While he was watching the
rabbit the sky had changed. Above the red streak on the water line
the sky had lightened to faint blue, and across the horizon a drift of
fleecy rose cloud was floating. And through it a white-bright, gold-
bright planet was shining. The morning star, of course. At this hour,
and so near the sun, it would be Venus.

Behind her rose-coloured veils, quite alone in the sky already
blue, she seemed to wait. She had come in on her beat, taken her
place in the figure. Serene, impersonal splendour. Merciless perfection, ageless sovereignty. The poor hare and his clover, poor Grenfell
and his eye-drops!

He braced himself against his washstand and still stared up at her.
Something roused his temper so hot that he began to mutter aloud:

"And what's a hundred and thirty-six million years to you,
Madam? That Professor needn't blow. You were winking and blinking up there maybe a hundred and thirty-six million times before
that date they are so proud of. The rocks can't tell any tales on you.
You were doing your stunt up there long before there was anything
down here but—God knows what! Let's leave that to the professors,
Madam, you and me!"

This childish bitterness toward "millions" and professors was the
result of several things. Two of Grenfell's sons were "professors";

Harrison a distinguished physicist at thirty. This morning, however, Harrison had not popped up in his father's mind. Grenfell was still thinking of a pleasant and courtly scientist whom he had met on the boat yesterday—a delightful man who had, temporarily at least, wrecked Grenfell's life with civilities and information.

It was natural, indeed inevitable, that two clean, closeshaven gentlemen in tailored woods clothes, passengers on the worst tub owned by the Canadian Steamships Company and both bound for a little island off the Nova Scotia coast, should get into conversation. It was all the more natural since the scientist was accompanied by a lovely girl—his daughter.

It was a pleasure to look at her, just as it is a pleasure to look at any comely creature who shows breeding, delicate preferences. She had lovely eyes, lovely skin, lovely manners. She listened closely when Grenfell and her father talked, but she didn't bark up with her opinions. When he asked her about their life on the island last summer, he liked everything she said about the place and the people. She answered him lightly, as if her impressions could matter only to herself, but, having an opinion, it was only good manners to admit it. "Sweet, but decided," was his rough estimate.

Since they were both going to an island which wasn't even on the map, supposed to be known only to the motor launches that called after a catch of herring, it was natural that the two gentlemen should talk about that bit of wooded rock in the sea. Grenfell always liked to talk about it to the right person. At first he thought Professor Fairweather was a right person. He had felt alarm when Fairweather mentioned that last summer he had put up a portable house on the shore about two miles from Grenfell's cabin. But he added that it would soon vanish as quietly as it had come. His geological work would be over this autumn, and his portable house would be taken to pieces and shipped to an island in the South Pacific. Having thus reassured him, Fairweather carelessly, in quite the tone of weather-comment small talk, proceeded to wreck one of Grenfell's happiest illusions, the escape-avenue he kept in the back of his mind when he was at his desk at Grenfell & Saunders, Bonds. The Professor certainly meant no harm. He was a man of the world, urbane, not self-important. He merely remarked that the island was interesting geologically because the two ends of the island belonged to different periods, yet the ice seemed to have brought them both down together.

"And about how old would our end be, Professor?" Grenfell meant simply to express polite interest, but he gave himself away, parted with his only defence—indifference.

"We call it a hundred and thirty-six million years," was the answer he got.

"Really? That's getting it down pretty fine, isn't it? I'm just a blank where science is concerned. I went to work when I was thirteen—didn't have any education. Of course some business men read up on science. But I have to struggle with reports and figures a good deal. When I do read I like something human—the old fellows: Scott and Dickens and Fielding. I get a great kick out of them."

The Professor was a perfect gentleman, but he couldn't resist the appeal of ignorance. He had sensed in half an hour that this man loved the island. (His daughter had sensed it a year ago, as soon as she arrived there with her father. Something about his cabin, the little patch of lawn in front, and the hedge of wild roses that fenced it in, told her that.) In their talk Professor Fairweather had come to realize that this man had quite an unusual feeling for the island, therefore he would certainly like to know more about it—all he could tell him!

The sun leaped out of the sea—the planet vanished. Grenfell rejected his eye-drops. Why patchup? What was the use ... of anything? Why tear a man loose from his little rock and shoot him out into the eternities? All that stuff was inhuman. A man had his little hour, with heat and cold and a time-sense suited to his endurance. If you took that away from him you left him spineless, accidental, unrelated to anything. He himself was, he realized, sitting in his bathrobe by his washstand, limp! No wonder: what a night! What a dreadful night! The speeds which machinists had worked up in the last fifty years were mere babytalk to what can go through a man's head between dusk and daybreak. In the last ten hours poor Grenfell had travelled over seas and continents, gone through boyhood and youth, rounded a business, made a great deal of money, and brought up an expensive family. (There were three sons, to whom he had given every advantage and who had turned out well, two of them brilliantly.) And all this meant nothing to him except negatively—"to avoid worse rape," he quoted Milton to himself.

Last night had been one of those nights of revelation, revaluation, when everything seems to come clear ... only to fade out again in the morning. In a low cabin on a high red cliff overhanging the sea, everything that was shut up in him, under lock and bolt and pressure, simply broke jail, spread out into the spaciousness of the night, undraped, unashamed.

When his father died, Henry had got a job as messenger boy with the Western Union. He always remembered those years with a certain pride. His mother took in sewing. There were two little girls, younger than he. When he looked back on that time, there was nothing in it to be ashamed of. Those are the years, he often told the reformers, that make character, make proficiency. A business man should have early training, like a pianist, at the instrument. The sense of responsibility makes a little boy a citizen: for him there is no "dangerous age." From his first winter with the telegraph company he knew he could get on if he tried hard, since most lads emphatically did not try hard. He read law at night, and when he was twenty was confidential clerk with one of the most conservative legal firms in Colorado.

Everything went well until he took his first long vacation—bicycling in the mountains above Colorado Springs. One morning he was pedalling hard uphill when another bicycle came round a curve and collided with him; a girl coasting. Both riders were thrown. She got her foot caught in her wheel; sprain and lacerations. Henry ran two miles down to her hotel and her family. New York people; the father's name was a legend in Henry's credulous Western world. And they liked him, Henry, these cultivated, clever, experienced people! The mother was the ruling power—remarkable woman. What she planned, she put through relentless determination. He ought to know, for he married that only daughter one year after she coasted into him. A warning unheeded, that first meeting. It was his own intoxicated vanity that sealed his fate. He had never been "made much over" before.

It had worked out as well as most marriages, he supposed. Better than many. The intelligent girl had been no discredit to him, certainly. She had given him two remarkable sons, any man would be proud of them....

Here Grenfell had flopped over in bed and suddenly sat up, muttering aloud. "But God, they're as cold as ice: I can't see through it. They've never lived at all, those two fellows. They've never run after the ball—they're so damned clever they don't have to. They just reach out and take the ball. Yes, fine hands, like their grandmother's; long ... white ... beautiful nails. The way Harrison picked up that book! I'm glad my paws are red and stubby."

For a moment he recalled sharply a little scene. Three days ago he was packing for his escape to this island. Harrison, the eldest son, the physicist, after knocking, had entered to his father's "Come in!" He came to ask who should take care of his personal mail (that which came to the house) if Miss O'Doyle should go on her vacation before he returned. He put the question rather grimly. The family seemed to resent the fact that, though he worked like a steam shovel while he was in town, when he went on a vacation he never told them how long he would be away or where he was going.

"Oh, I meant to tell you, Harrison, before I leave. But it was nice of you to think of it. Miss O'Doyle has decided to put off her vacation until the middle of October, and then she'll take a long one." He was sure he spoke amiably as he stood looking at his son. He was always proud of Harrison's fine presence, his poise and easy reserve. The little travelling bag (made to his order) which on a journey he always carried himself, never trusted to a porter, lay open on his writing table. On top of his pyjamas and razor case lay two little books bound in red leather. Harrison picked up one and glanced at the lettering on the back. King Henry IV, Part I.

"Light reading?" he remarked. Grenfell was stung by such impertinence. He resented any intrusion on his private, personal, non-family life.

"Light or heavy," he remarked dryly, "they're good company. And they're mighty human."

"They have that reputation," his son admitted.

A spark flashed into Grenfell's eye. Was the fellow sarcastic, or merely patronizing?

"Reputation, hell!" he broke out. "I don't carry books around with my toothbrushes and razors on account of their reputation."

"No, I wouldn't accuse you of that." The young man spoke quietly, not warmly, but as if he meant it. He hesitated and left the room.

Sitting up in his bed in the small hours of the morning, Grenfell wondered if he hadn't flared up too soon. Maybe the fellow hadn't meant to be sarcastic. All the same he had no business to touch anything in his father's bag. That bag was like his coat pocket. Grenfell never bothered his family with his personal diversions, and he never intruded upon theirs. Harrison and his mother were a team—a close corporation! Grenfell respected it absolutely. No questions, no explanations demanded by him. The bills came in; Miss O'Doyle wrote the checks and he signed them. He hadn't the curiosity, the vulgarity to look at them. Of course, he admitted, there were times when he got back at the corporation just a little. That usually occurred when his dyspepsia had kept him on very light food all day and, the dinner at home happening to be "rich," he confined himself to graham crackers and milk. He remembered such a little dinner scene last month. Harrison and his mother came downstairs dressed to go out for the evening. Soon after the soup was served, Harrison wondered whether Koussevitzky would take the slow movement in the Brahms Second as he did last winter. His mother said she still remembered Muck's reading, and preferred it.

The theoretical head of the house spoke up. "I take it that this is Symphony night, and that my family are going. You have ordered the car? Well, I am going to hear John McCormack sing *Kathleen Mavourneen.*"

His wife rescued him as she often did (in an innocent, well-bred way) by refusing to recognize his rudeness. "Dear me! I haven't heard

McCormack since he first came out in Italy years and years ago. His success was sensational. He was singing Mozart then."

Yes, when he was irritable and the domestic line-up got the better of him, Margaret, by being faultlessly polite, often saved the situation.

When he thought everything over, here in this great quiet, in this great darkness, he admitted that his shipwreck had not been on the family rock. The bitter truth was that his worst enemy was closer even than the wife of his bosom—was his bosom itself!

Grenfell had what he called a hair-trigger stomach. When he was in his New York office he worked like a whirlwind; and to do it he had to live on a diet that would have tried the leanest anchorite. The doctors said he did everything too hard. He knew that—he always had done things hard, from the day he first went to work for the Western Union. Mother and two little sisters, no schooling—the only capital he had was the ginger to care hard and work hard. Apparently it was not the brain that desired and achieved. At least, the expense account came out of a very other part of one. Perhaps he was a throw-back to the Year One, when in the stomach was the only constant, never sleeping, never quite satisfied desire.

The humiliation of being "delicate" was worse than the actual hardship. He had found the one way in which he could make it up to himself, could feel like a whole man, not like a miserable dyspeptic. That way was by living rough, not by living soft. There wasn't a big-game country in North America where he hadn't hunted, mountain sheep in the wild Rockies, moose in darkest Canada, caribou in Newfoundland. Long before he could really afford it, he took four months out of every year to go shooting. His greatest triumph was a white bear in Labrador. His guide and packmen and canoe men never guessed that he was a frail man. Out there, up there, he wasn't! Out there he was just a "city man" who paid well; eccentric, but a fairly good shot. That was what he had got out of hard work and very good luck. He had got ahead wonderfully ... but, somehow, ahead on the wrong road. At this point in his audit Grenfell had felt his knees getting cold, so he got out of bed, opened a clothes closet, and found his eiderdown bathrobe hanging on the hook where he had left it two summers ago. That was a satisfaction. (He liked to be orderly, and it made this cabin seem more his own to find things, year after year, just as he had left them.) Feeling comfortably warm, he ran up the dark window blinds which last night he had pulled down to shut out the disturbing sight of the stars. He bethought him of his eye-drops, tilted back his head, and there was that planet, serene, terrible and splendid, looking in at him … immortal beauty … yes, but only when somebody saw it, he fiercely answered back! He thought about it until his head went round. He would get out of this room and get out quick. He began to dress—wool stockings, moccasins, flannel shirt, leather coat. He would get out and find his island. After all, it still existed. The Professor hadn't put it in his pocket, he guessed! He scrawled a line for William, his man Friday: "BREAK-FAST WHEN I RETURN," and stuck it on a hook in his dining-car kitchen. William was "boarded out" in a fisherman's family. (Grenfell wouldn't stand anyone in the cabin with him. He wanted all this glorious loneliness for himself. He had paid dearly for it.)

He hurried out of the kitchen door and up the grassy hillside to the spruce wood. The spruces stood tall and still as ever in the morning air; the same dazzling spears of sunlight shot through their darkness. The path underneath had the dampness, the magical softness which his feet remembered. On either side of the trail yellow toadstools and white mushrooms lifted the heavy thatch of brown spruce needles and made little damp tents. Everything was still in the wood.

There was not a breath of wind; deep shadow and new-born light, yellow as gold, a little unsteady like other new-born things. It was blinking, too, as if its own reflection on the dewdrops was too bright. Or maybe the light had been asleep down under the sea and was just waking up.

"Hello, Grandfather!" Grenfell cried as he turned a curve in the path. The grandfather was a giant spruce tree that had been struck by lightning (must have been about a hundred years ago, the islanders said). It still lay on a slant along a steep hillside, its shallow roots in the air, all its great branches bleached grayish white, like an animal skeleton long exposed to the weather. Grenfell put out his hand to twitch off a twig as he passed, but it snapped back at him like a metal spring. He stopped in astonishment, his hand smarted, actually.

"Well, Grandfather! Lasting pretty well, I should say. Compliments! You get good drainage on this hillside, don't you?"

Ten minutes more on the winding uphill path brought him to the edge of the spruce wood and out on a bald headland that topped a cliff two hundred feet above the sea. He sat down on a rock and grinned. Like Christian of old, he thought, he had left his burden at the bottom of the hill. Now why had he let Doctor Fairweather's perfectly unessential information give him a miserable night? He had always known this island existed long before he discovered it, and that it must once have been a naked rock. The soil-surface was very thin. Almost anywhere on the open downs you could cut with a spade through the dry turf and roll it back from the rock as you roll a rug back from the floor. One knew that the rock itself, since it rested on the bottom of the ocean, must be very ancient.

But that fact had nothing to do with the green surface where men lived and trees lived and blue flags and buttercups and daisies and meadow-sweet and steeplebush and goldenrod crowded one another in all the clearings. Grenfell shook himself and hurried along up the cliff trail. He crossed the first brook on stepping-stones. Must have been recent rain, for the water was rushing down the deep-cut channel with sound and fury till it leaped hundreds of feet over the face of the cliff and fell into the sea: a white waterfall that never rested.

The trail led on through a long jungle of black alder then through a lazy, rooty, brown swamp ... and then out on another breezy, grassy headland which jutted far out into the air in a horseshoe curve. There one could stand beside a bushy rowan tree and see four waterfalls, white as silver, pouring down the perpendicular cliff walls.

Nothing had changed. Everything was the same, and he, Henry Grenfell, was the same: the relationship was unchanged. Not even a tree blown down; the stunted beeches (precious because so few) were still holding out against a climate unkind to them. The old white birches that grew on the edge of the cliff had been so long beaten and tormented by east wind and north wind that they grew more down than up, and hugged the earth that was kinder than the stormy air. Their growth was all one-sided, away from the sea, and their land-side branches actually lay along the ground and crept up the hillside through the underbrush, persistent, nearly naked, like great creeping vines, and at last, when they got into the sunshine, burst into tender leafage.

This knob of grassy headland with the bushy rowan tree had been his vague objective when he left the cabin. From this elbow he could look back on the cliff wall, both north and south, and see the four silver waterfalls in the morning light. A splendid sight, Grenfell was thinking, and all his own. Not even a gull they had gone screaming down the coast toward the herring weirs when he first left his cabin. Not a living creature—but wait a minute: there was something moving down there, on the shingle by the water's edge. A human figure, in a long white bathrobe—and a rubber cap! Then it must be a woman? Queer. No island woman would go bathing at this hour, not even in the warm inland ponds. Yes, it was a woman! A girl, and he knew what girl! In the miseries of the night he had forgotten her. The geologist's daughter.

How had she got down there without breaking her neck? She picked her way along the rough shingle; presently stopped and seemed to be meditating, seemed to be looking out at an old sliver of rock that was almost submerged at high tide. She opened her robe, a grey thing lined with white. Her bathing-suit was pink. If a clam stood upright and graciously opened its shell, it would look like that. After a moment she drew her shell together again—felt the chill of the morning air, probably. People are really themselves only when they believe they are absolutely alone and unobserved, he was thinking. With a quick motion she shed her robe, kicked off her sandals, and took to the water.

At the same moment Grenfell kicked off his moccasins. "Crazy kid! What does she think she's doing? This is the North Atlantic, girl, you can't treat it like that!" As he muttered, he was getting off his fox-lined jacket and loosening his braces. Just how he would get down to the shingle he didn't know, but he guessed he'd have to. He was getting ready while, so far, she was doing nicely. Nothing is more embarrassing than to rescue people who don't want to be rescued. The tide was out, slack—she evidently knew its schedule.

She reached the rock, put up her arms and rested for a moment, then began to weave her way back. The distance wasn't much, but Lord the cold,—in the early morning! When he saw her come out dripping and get into her shell, he began to shuffle on his fur jacket and his moccasins. He kept on scolding. "Silly creature! Why couldn't she wait till afternoon, when the death-chill is off the water?"

He scolded her ghost all the way home, but he thought he knew just how she felt. Probably she used to take her swim at that hour last summer, and she had forgot how cold the water was. When she first opened her long coat the nip of the air had startled her a little. There was no one watching her, she didn't have to keep face—except to herself. That she had to do and no fuss about it. She hadn't dodged. She had gone out, and she had come back. She would have a happy day. He knew just how she felt. She surely did look like a little pink clam in her white shell!

He was walking fast down the winding trails. Everything since he left the cabin had been reassuring, delightful—everything was the same, and so was he! The air, or the smell of fir trees—something had sharpened his appetite. He was hungry. As he passed the grandfather tree he waved his hand, but didn't stop. Plucky youth is more bracing than enduring age. He crossed the sharp line from the deep shade to the sunny hillside behind his cabin and saw the wood smoke rising from the chimney. The door of the dining-car kitchen stood open, and the smell of coffee drowned the spruce smell and sea smell. William hadn't waited; he was wisely breakfasting.

As he came down the hill Grenfell was chuckling to himself: "Anyhow, when that first amphibious frog-toad found his waterhole dried up behind him, and jumped out to hop along till he could find another—well, he started on a long hop."

MICHEL TOURNIER

F EW, IF ANY, contemporary imaginative writers from France have written as extensively about Canada as has Michel Tournier (1924–). Some of his compatriots have written with nuanced understanding of Quebec, but none has embraced the breadth of Canada with such singular excitement and expectation.

In the fall of 1972, Tournier arrived by plane in Montreal, and over the next four weeks visited that city, Ottawa, Charlottetown, and the Magdalen Islands, then travelled by plane to Vancouver, subsequently taking the famous domed CPR train, "The Canadian," through the Rockies to Calgary, then catching a plane back to Montreal for his return flight to France.

Tournier was trained as a philosopher, but worked in the electronic media and publishing houses of France before becoming a full-time author. His works have been translated into more than seventeen languages, but the technical originality and linguistic daring of his fiction mean that he remains a respected but controversial figure in his home country, a status unchanged since he won the Prix Goncourt for his first novel.

The trip to Canada yielded two books: a travel memoir titled *Canada: Journal de Voyage* (1977; yet to be translated into English, alas) and *Gemini* (1975), a novel, in which much of the protagonist's wandering reflects, in reverse, Tournier's own Canadian travel. In fact, phrases and paragraphs describing the Canadian landscape appear word for word in either book.

In his preface to the travelogue, Tournier described his gleeful anticipation of encountering the immensity of the land. But the Canadian section of the novel, while reporting this *frisson* which accompanies thoughts of Canada's huge scale, documents how this anticipation, this glee, is diminished, changed, or enhanced by encounters with Canadian reality. The novel, not surprisingly, yields the more studied response to the country.

The plot of *Gemini* centres on identical twins, Jean and Paul. Growing up, they are inseparable, but in young adulthood Jean rebels, and flees. Pained by his brother's absence, Paul travels the globe to find him, encountering lands and cultures (divided Berlin, bilingual Canada) reflecting the halves of his being. On its publication, *Gemini* was described by Jean Genet as "an exceptional, incomparable novel." Canadians will be surprised by several aspects of Tournier's description of the country. In the following passages from *Gemini* (in which the protagonist Paul meets the mysterious Urs Kraus), Tournier's preference for our bicycles and our coffee will strike many readers as a case of the weed outgrowing the corn. And his affection for English Canada, without a single reference to its relationship to Quebec, is, among francophone authors, atypical and refreshingly endearing.

---

from GEMENI

First sight of the suburbs of Vancouver is through the narrow window of the monstrous metal bus, built like a tank, which brought us from the airport. A livelier, more colorful and heterogeneous city than Tokyo. Sex films, shady bars, furtive figures, sodden refuse on the pavements, all that residue of people and things which is the greatest charm of travel in some people's eyes. And, lest you should forget the nearness of the sea, here and there a gull, motionless upon a post, bollard or rooftop.

The uniform yellow of Japan is diversified here into at least four varieties, although it probably takes a little experience to distinguish them at a glance. The largest group consists of the population of Chinatown, who rarely venture beyond their own districts. Then there are the Japanese—mostly in transit and recognizable by an indefinably foreign and temporary air. You can tell the Indians, like wizened young mummies in clothes that are too big and floating on them and with little bright black eyes gleaming from below their broad-brimmed hats. But most easily recognizable are the Eskimos, with their characteristic long heads, coarse hair growing low on their foreheads and especially their broad, plump cheeks. Obesity is widespread in this country, but the fat of the Eskimos is different from the whites'. The latter is made of pastries and ice cream. The Eskimo's has an aroma of fish and smoked meat.

A salmon thrusting powerfully upstream, leaping dams and breasting rapids.... That was how I saw myself landing in Vancouver. Because I have never felt so distinctly the sense of approaching a country back to front. Vancouver is the natural terminus of the long east-west migration that starts from Europe and crosses the Atlantic Ocean and the North American continent. It is a city not of beginnings but of endings. Paris, London, New York are all cities of beginnings. The newcomer to them is given a kind of baptism and is prepared for a new life, full of strange discoveries. The same may be true of Vancouver as far as the Japanese arriving in a Western country are concerned. That point of view is wholly alien to me. The movement of the sun from east to west drew the barbarian adventurers out of Poland, England and France and ever onward, across Quebec, Ontario, Manitoba, Saskatchewan, Alberta and British Columbia. When they reached this shore with its stagnant waters shaded by pines and maples, the long westward march was over. There was nothing more for them to do but sit down and admire the sunset. For the sea at Vancouver is shut in. These shores extend no invitation to take ship and sail out to explore the Pacific. The view is blocked by Vancouver Island, as though by a stopper. No revivifying breath from the high seas is ever going to come to fill their lungs and swell their sails. There is no going on. But I, no, I am arriving....

"This is my kind of city!" Urs Kraus sighs, stopping to gaze up at the sky.

It rained all night and then at dawn the curtain of black clouds began to break up. Now they are splitting into ragged piles with cracks of blue opening between them where the sun is bursting through. The tall wet trees in Stanley Park are shaking themselves in the wind, like dogs after a swim, and their woody smell which already has autumn in it clashes with the reek of mud and seaweed rising from the beach. Nowhere else have I encountered this strange marriage of sea and forest.

"Just look at it," he says, waving his arm. "You'd have to be mad to leave that. Yet I'm going away! I'm always going away!" Walking along the beach strewn with old tree stumps polished like pebbles, we are halted by a little group of strollers pointing field glasses and telephoto lenses out to sea. On a rock about two hundred yards away, a seal stares back at us....

The sky is all one luminous devastation now, vapory castles toppling and snow-white squadrons charging furiously. Against this dramatic backdrop, families are sitting down to picnic, baby carriages bouncing on their high wheels, and bicycles are silhouetted as they pass.

"Have you noticed the endless variety of Canadian bicycles? Handlebars, saddles, wheels, frames, every part is capable of infinite variations. I'm still a draftsman at heart and I find it enchanting. Canadian bicycles are bought to order. You go to the dealer and build up your own machine by choosing its components from the wonderful collection in the shop...."

"Urs, I find your ideas very exciting, but tell me, where is Jean?"

He gestured vaguely toward the horizon.

"We arrived here together. And we fell out at once. Jean sniffed the wind. He invented what he called 'the Canadian method.' If I understood it rightly, the method consisted of *walking*. Yes, walking!

Eastward, if you see what I mean. Crossing the American continent, in short, from one side to the other. But I had fallen in love with Vancouver instantly, this city where it rains all day long and then produces the most sublime sunsets. It's impossible to paint here! The intoxication of impotence! The canvas stays blank while you feast your eyes! It was a drug and I wanted to test its powers to the full before moving on. We parted."...

"What am I to do? You know that if Jean has gone off on foot, I can't take the plane to Montreal. I must follow in his footsteps."

"Walk, then! Vancouver to Montreal is only about three thousand miles."

"You must be joking."

"There is a middle way. The train! It leaves every day from Vancouver and winds its way through the Rocky Mountains and the lakes in the middle and the east like a great big, rather lazy red dragon. It stops everywhere. Perhaps when Jean has worn his shoes out he'll get into your carriage somewhere or other...."

And so the great journey is about to start again. At least I shan't have the same agonizing feeling of turning my back on France as I did when leaving Tokyo, going east. From now on, every step is taking me nearer to the Pierres Sonnantes. I hug the comforting thought to myself as I wander alone along the waterfront of Coal Harbour, newly polished by a fierce downpour. The Royal Vancouver Yacht Club and its next-door neighbor, the Burrard Yacht Club—scarcely less smart—are a brilliant shopwindow of dainty yachts, of every possible design and rig, all streaming with lights. But as you draw nearer the docks the lights grow sparser and the boats more workmanlike, until at last the black tormented shapes of the old trawlers, still rotting away here after they have fished their last, loom up in a sinister halflight. Nothing could be more desolate than those slimy decks, littered with ends of rope, sagging ladders and warped tiller bars, those rusted plates, choked winches and lengths of broken chain. They are so many floating deathtraps, each one surmounted by a torture chamber open to the winds. One is surprised not to see dislocated and dismembered bodies there, contorted in agony. Some black-and-white birds—something between crows and gulls—seem to be expecting them too. Nor is it pure imagination, for the horror of these boats reminds one of the wretched fate of the men, the fishermen who spent their lives in them.

I retreat into a seaman's bar and drink a large cup of coffee, watching the rain which has begun to fall again. The coffee is the light, plentiful kind of the New World, fragrant and thirst-quenching, bearing no relation to the nasty, thick greasy, tarry-tasting syrup they distill for you a drip at a time in France and Italy and which poisons your palate for the rest of the day. This time tomorrow I shall be in the big, lazy red dragon Kraus has told me of.

As always on the eve of a journey, I am seized with alarm, inveterate sedentary that I am, and searching for a saint to commend myself to. In the end, the person I appeal to for protection is Phileas Fogg. Yes, it's not St. Christopher, patron saint of wanderers and migrants, I turn to in my traveler's terrors but Jules Verne's rich Englishman, inured to all the malignity of fate and armed with an exemplary patience and courage in rising above the vagaries of the railway, the inadequacies of the stagecoach, and the steamer's failings. He it is who is truly the greatest patron of travelers, possessing as he does on a heroic scale that highly specialized knowledge, that craft so long to learn, that rarest of virtues: travel.

Tuesday 1815 hours. So here I am on the famous Canadian Pacific Railway, the great red dragon with the shrieking voice and topped with Plexiglas domes that meanders through the Rocky Mountains and across the great prairie from one ocean to the other. It was not for nothing that I recalled Phileas Fogg. In my minute "single," in which it is hardly possible to move at all once the bed has been let down, I am back again in the old-fashioned luxury of the Orient Express in Grandma's day, a mixture of plush, mahogany, and crystal. Snug in this padded shell, I feel all my fears melt away and indulge in

a bout of childish glee at the idea that I shall be here for more than
three whole days and nights, since we do not get to Montreal until
2005 hours on Friday. Our timetable can be summed up in three sets
of figures: 69 stations spread over 2,879.7 miles to be covered in 74
hours and 35 minutes. We start at 1830 hours.

Tuesday 1902 hours. Milepost 2,882.6 COQUITLAM. I note: (1) That
it is too bumpy to write while the train is in motion. I shall have to
make do with the stations. (2) The distance is recorded on mile-
posts, only starting from Montreal. We set out from 2,879.7 and are
going toward 0. I rather like the idea. After all, on this journey I am
going *back*.

Tuesday 1940 hours. Milepost 2,838 MISSION CITY. The forest
already, the real northern forest, which is to say not the neat, thinly
planted woodland of Stanley Park, where every tree is a landmark in
itself, but an impenetrable tangle of small trees all growing into one
another, a real paradise for game of all kinds, furred and feathered.
Conclusion: the beauty of woods is manmade.

Tuesday 2020 hours. Milepost 2,809.6 AGASSIZ! The sliding door of
my compartment opened suddenly and a black steward slammed a
prepacked meal down on my tabletop. One glance assures me that
the restaurant car is not working. So it is total seclusion then, until
tomorrow morning at least. I shall make the best of it in my tiny cell,
the outside wall of which is a clear window letting in the dense,
black, close-set pine forest with the rays of the setting sun breaking
through it mysteriously from time to time.

Tuesday 2215 hours. Milepost 2,750.7 NORTH BEND. A lengthy halt.
Shouts and people running on the platform. I get the impression
that this is the last station of any importance before the long night's
haul. I have time to ask myself the old question which is bound to
occur to a sedentary like myself on any journey: why not stop here?

There are men, women, and children who look on these passing places as home. They were born here. Probably some of them can't even picture any other land over the horizon. So why not me? What right have I to come here and go away again knowing nothing at all about North Bend, its streets, its houses, and its people? Isn't there something in my nocturnal passing which is worse than contempt, a denial of this country's very existence, an implied consigning of North Bend to oblivion? The same depressing question often comes into my mind when I am dashing through some village, town or stretch of countryside and I catch a lightning glimpse of young men laughing in a square, an old man watering his horses, a woman hanging out her washing with a small child clinging round her legs. Life is there, simple and peaceful, and I am flouting it, slapping it in the face with my idiotic rush....

But this time, also, I am going on. The red train heads wailing into the night and the mountains and the platform slips by, taking with it two girls deep in earnest conversation, and I shall never know anything about them, or about North Bend....

Wednesday 0042 hours. Milepost 2,676.5 ASHCROFT. The heat is stifling and I am lying naked on my bunk. Since this is placed directly under the window—feet foremost—I can see, or guess, or feel the great sleeping country gliding past against my legs, my side, my cheek, the depth and silence of its dark silhouettes, its patches of bright moonlight and signals, red, green and orange, the tracery of a coppice caught in a car's headlights, the thunder of a metal bridge, its X-shaped struts slashing across the window frame, and suddenly a moment's total, impenetrable, bottomless blackness, absolute night.

Wednesday 0205 hours. Milepost 2,629.2 KAMLOOPS. I am cold now, in spite of the blankets I have piled on top of myself. By day, the dispaired twin can put on a good face if he must. But at night ... at two o'clock in the morning ... Oh, twin, why aren't you here? After the cruel glare of the station, the merciful darkness covers my eyes again and they bathe in their own tears like two wounded fishes on the bottom of a brackish sea.

Wednesday 0555 hours. Milepost 2,500 REVELSTOKE. I have had to let two or three stations go by in a kind of doze. I was too tired and too miserable to write. My window is frosted right over.

Wednesday 0905 hours. Milepost 2,410.2 GOLDEN. Aptly named. We are winding our way, at speeds of up to eighty, among precipitous gorges with a boiling green torrent below and larchwoods rising in tiers up the sides. The sky is blue, the snow is white, the train is red. We are trapped in a Technicolor photo out of the *National Geographic* magazine.

Wednesday 1030 hours. Milepost 2,375.2 FIELD. While the Rocky Mountains unroll their grandiloquent scenery above our heads, we are guzzling enthusiastically beneath the Plexiglas domes of the coaches. The staff being unequal to the task, we serve ourselves from the kitchens and then take our trays up the little staircase leading to the view. I am beginning to realize the part that food plays in Canadian life—surely greater than in any other country I know. Even in Vancouver, I noticed the extravagant number of food advertisements on the television screens. The Canadian is first and foremost an eating man and putting on weight is his besetting sin, even as a child, in fact especially then.

Wednesday 1235 hours. Milepost 2,355.2 LAKE LOUISE. It is all over. The grandiose scenery has been packed away to wait for the next train. In its place is a countryside that still owes some unevenness to the foothills of the Rockies. But everything proclaims the plains. Two white pigeons are kissing on the black shingle roof of a house. Next door to them, two blue rock thrushes are billing on the red corrugated-iron roof of another.

Wednesday 1320 hours. Milepost 2,320 BANFF. We are following the course of the Bow River, which goes through Calgary, the capital of Alberta. Some horses are galloping away in a staggered bunch, as though swept aside by the wind of the train.

Wednesday 1610 hours. Milepost 2,238.6 CALGARY. A thirty-five-minute halt enables me to take a quick walk through this one-time Mounted Police post, now a city with a population of 180,000. A scorching, dust-laden wind blows through the streets, which are numbered and laid out on a grid system. The center of this concrete desert is the thirty-six-story International Hotel building, looming over a landscape as flat as your hand.

It has been claimed that skyscrapers are justified because of the shortage of space in American cities, as on the island of Manhattan. This is typical of the kind of limited, utilitarian explanation which dodges the real issue. What it should be saying is the opposite: that skyscrapers are a natural reaction to too much space, to the terror of being surrounded by wide-open spaces, like chasms in a horizontal plane. A tower dominates and commands the plain around it. It is a rallying point, to call men from afar. It is centrifugal for the person who dwells in it and centripetal for the one who sees it from a distance.

Wednesday 1910 hours. Milepost 2,062.8 MEDICINE HAT. The guzzling is in full swing again all along the train. It is nothing but massive portions of ice cream, giant sandwiches, hot dogs, and plates of goulash in every coach. And to go with it we are passing through the vast grain-growing region, with agricultural machines like huge diplodocuses rolling across it and nothing on the horizon but the tall shapes of concrete silos. This is the granary of the whole world, the cornucopia out of which cereals flow to Latin America, China, Russia, the Indies, Africa, to all of starving mankind.

Wednesday 2030 hours. Milepost 1,950.3 GULL LAKE. The little envelopes of granulated sugar have the arms of the Canadian provinces on them, Newfoundland, Ontario, British Columbia, and so on, along with the motto: "Explore a part of Canada and you'll discover a part of yourself." It is, of course, aimed at persuading Canadians to get out of their home province and discover their own country in a spirit of national unity, which it seems they are not much inclined to do. But what far-reaching implications that sentence has for me! In which of Canada's provinces am I going to discover that part of myself?

Wednesday 2212 hours. Milepost 1,915.4 SWIFT CURRENT. Another night. Perhaps because I did my share of guzzling this afternoon I refused the black steward's prepacked dinner, which seemed to upset him considerably. Now that it is dark again, the window no longer exhibits the same grotesque shadows that it did last night. The plains have made it a wide, gray screen, a shore of silence on which nothing happens, except that now and then there is a highway with a stream of cars moving along it, each one pushing its own little sheet of light ahead of it....

Friday 1740 hours. Milepost 109 OTTAWA. I have been on this train for more than seventy hours. My feelings are muddled and contradictory. I can't take any more. I am suffocating with boredom and impatience between these narrow walls which I know in every detail until I am sick of them. And at the same time, I am scared of arriving. The way out, the shock of the unknown seem like terrifying prospects to me. A prisoner seeing the end of his sentence approaching must feel the same twofold anguish.

Friday 1841 hours. Milepost 57.5 VANKLEEK HILL. Since Ottawa, we have been running along the right bank of the Ottawa River. Amazing number of aboveground electrical installations. Enormous pylons loaded down with cables, gigantic floodlit masts and stays, gantries, transformers, circuit breakers ... This aerial forest of metal has replaced the other and must herald the approaches of the great city. We shall be in Montreal this evening, at 2005 precisely.

MONTREAL

This is the very image of Canada as I have seen it gradually taking shape ever since Vancouver. For the emptiness of the prairie is still present in these broad streets, in these groups of smokedglass buildings, this mighty river, these parking lots and shops and restaurants. It has simply taken on a different form, become urbanized. Human warmth, animal contact and the sense of all sorts of people, of many different races, is quite missing from this huge city. Yet life there is, vibrant, explosive and dazzling. Montreal, or the electric city.

The revelation came to me almost before the hotel porter closed the door of my room on me. Outside the big glass bay I could see only the myriad windows of a skyscraper whose top was out of sight. Offices, offices and more offices. At this hour all of them deserted and all as bright as day, so that each one could be seen to contain the same metal desk, the same swivel chair, with the secretary's typewriter under a yellow cover to one side and the metal filing cabinet behind.

A few hours' restless sleep. My body, used to the movement of the train, is completely disrupted by the stillness of this bed. The offices are no longer deserted. Charwomen in gray overalls with white caps on their heads are sweeping, dusting, emptying wastepaper baskets.

The lessons I learned in Japan before I crossed Canada have not been wasted on me. In fact, the two countries throw light on one another, and I am usefully applying the Japanese graph to the Canadian chart.

Like the Japanese, the Canadian suffers from a space problem. But while the first is cramped into a tiny, scattered archipelago, the second is reeling with vertigo in the midst of his vast plains. This contrast, which makes Canada an anti-Japan, is responsible for more than one characteristic feature. The Japanese is not afraid of wind or cold. In his paper house, quite unsuitable to any form of heating, the wind comes and goes as it likes. Here, on the other hand, even in summer, one is constantly reminded that the winters are formidable. The roofs of the houses have no gutters because slides of snow and ice would rip them off. Shops, garages and shopping centers are built underground, suggesting that for eight months of the year the citizens lead molelike lives, going from homes to cars, to shops and places of work without ever putting their noses out of doors. To get into the houses one passes through hall-cloakrooms with four doors, airlocks for the prolonged dressing up before going out and the patient undressing before coming in. And even the morbid hunger which has the Canadian stuffing himself at all hours of the day and night, even that is only a defense mechanism against the surrounding vastness and the icy winds howling across it.

To counter the terrors of the besieged, the Japanese invented the garden, the miniature garden and also *ikebana,* the art of flower arrangement. All are ways of making openings in over-crowded spaces, openings inhabited by structures which are light, witty and detached.

To counter the horizontal abyss, the Canadians dreamed up the Canadian Pacific Railway. What else could they do, indeed, but try to *innervate* their vast territory, to cover it with a network of nerves, at first very loosely woven but drawing tighter and tighter, closer and closer together?

That is why Jean's reaction to this country is perfectly rational, logical and understandable. He has responded to the space of Canada in Canadian fashion. By doing his utmost to *cover* the territory. "Cover" is a splendidly ambiguous word, with its simultaneous meanings of traverse (on foot), protect (with a cloak), be prepared for (an eventuality), defend (with troops), roof over, hide, disguise, excuse, justify, compensate, impregnate and so on. Here, Carder-Jean has turned into Surveyor-Jean. To survey a country is *to clothe it intelligently* with the help of chains, rods, drop arrows and graphometer. Once it has been surveyed, a country ceases to be literally *immense*— that is, measureless. It has been measured and so, contours, gradients and such inaccessible areas as marshes and dense undergrowth notwithstanding, assimilated by the intellect and ready for demarcation and land registration.

A walk about the city. Daylight does not suit the electric city.

The offices, shopwindows and stores are still lit up, of course, but the advertisements, the revolving signs, the wan magic of the neon lights are washed out by the sun. Like those nocturnal predators who wait for dusk before spreading their white wings, the electric city suffers the sun's tyranny in silence, patiently dreaming of the coming night.

Is it an illusion? Touching the wall of a building, I felt a kind of prickle in my fingers. Can it be that this city is so saturated with electricity that it seeps out of the houses, like damp or saltpeter rot in other places? I recall the forests of pylons loaded with cables and catenaries—like stylized Christmas trees festooned with paper chains—planted on the banks of the Ottawa and St. Lawrence rivers....

The surveyor's thick studded boots raise a white dust along the road and sink into the newly turned black earth of the prairie. He stops, sticks in his poles, peers through his sights, kneels down to grasp the handle of his measuring chain and waves to his companion in the red hat standing fifty yards off holding the other end of the chain, who goes down on one knee also. But as he rises, he sees in the sky the gigantic yet delicate structure of the pylons, immense steel candelabra holding from the tips of their white porcelain-ringed insulators bundles of high-tension wires dotted with red balls. They too are linked by chains and they survey the great prairies with giant strides, crossing lakes, bestriding forests, leaping over valleys, and jumping from hill to hill to vanish at last as minute dots on the infinite horizon. The surveyor, who has always longed to lie down on this earth and cover the whole country by extending his arms and legs indefinitely so as to innervate it with his own body, feels a bond of friendship with the great wire-carrying chandeliers striding away, skeletal and enormous, into the darkness, the wind and the snow.

HENRY
WADSWORTH
LONGFELLOW

D ESPITE the gargantuan international popularity of books based
in Canada by authors such as Jack London, it is arguable that
no single tale of Canada has more enduringly affected foreigners'
views of our countryside than has *Evangeline* by Henry Wadsworth
Longfellow (1807–1882).

The narrative of the poem was a gift from Nathaniel Hawthorne,
one of Longfellow's oldest and best friends. In his notebook for
October 24, 1838, Hawthorne registered when he had first ascer-
tained the "facts" of the tale from an acquaintance, Reverend Horatio Lorenzo Conolly:

> H.L.C. heard from a French Canadian a story of a young couple
> in Acadie. On their marriage-day all the men of the province
> were summoned to assemble in the church to hear a proclama-
> tion. When assembled, they were all seized and shipped off to be
> distributed through New England,—among them the new
> bridegroom. His bride set off in search of him—wandered about
> New England all her life-time, and at last, when she was old, she
> found her bridegroom on his death-bed. The shock was so great
> that it killed her likewise.

Hawthorne concluded that the story was not suitable for his approach to fiction. But approximately two years later, he was dining at Longfellow's when Conolly was also present. At dinner, Hawthorne complained that he lacked a suitable subject for his next novel. Conolly asked him why he did not employ the sad Acadian tale he had related some years before. Hawthorne persevered in stating the subject did not befit his style. But Longfellow's curiosity was piqued, and he insisted on having the story related to him then and there. With interruptions and questions, Conolly's recounting took an hour, at the conclusion of which Longfellow said, "It is the best illustration of faithfulness and the constancy of woman that I have ever heard of or read." Thus was the seed planted for one of the most popular poems ever written about Canada.

Hawthorne, that night, graciously yielded his prior claim to the tale, but the gestation of the poem was to endure several years. In fact, in 1841, Hawthorne, apparently cagily, prodded Longfellow into action; he had just published a book titled *Famous Old People* in which he had published a general account of the Acadian diaspora, and at the end of his notation, presumably with Longfellow in mind, he wrote, "Methinks if I were an American poet, I would choose Acadia for the subject of my song."

Longfellow took the bait, and began researching the historical background of Nova Scotia. As he was a professor at Harvard and a prolific writer and editor, other tasks had priority on his time, so that it was not until 1845 that he actually began to pen the first lines. Today, it strikes us as near heresy to learn that for several weeks the name of his heroine, indeed the title of the poem, was not Evangeline but rather "Gabrielle."

Longfellow worked on the poem diligently until February 27, 1847, when he recorded bilingually in his journal: "Aujourd'hui j'ai quarante ans, une femme et deux enfants. *Evangeline* is ended. I wrote the last lines this morning."

Longfellow never set foot in either Acadia or Louisiana, believing that since he was writing poetry, not formal history, he had no need to see these places since he could picture them easily in his imagination.

To those who did not actually live in Acadia, the verisimilitude of ambience was overwhelming and infectious; the poem sold thousands of copies and went into several printings in its first year, gaining currency with the passage of time. Indeed, the poem has spawned statues, plays, imitative novels, operas, and, hardly credible but alas true, a film starring Dolores Del Rio.

The work was translated into French by the Quebec poet Léon-Pamphile Lemay (1837-1918) and was included in his first book of poetry, *Essais poétiques* (Quebec 1865). The impact of the translation was cannonating. For a depressing example of how Canadians learned to prefer, over their own tale-tellers, a foreigner's depiction of their history, one need look no further than this description provided by the eminent Quebec man of letters George Stewart (1848–1906):

> Pamphile Le May, a tender poet himself, and a man of exquisite taste, has done much to encourage a love of Longfellow among his compatriots. We are told that by reading Le May's Evangeline, many persons were induced to learn English, that they might get the gentle story at first hand, and in the exact words of its creator. Some, too, learned English from the book itself and a dictionary; but a very great deal of the poem's present popularity among the French is due to Le May's efforts to crystallize it in the susceptible hearts of his countrymen. For many years the Longfellow version of the story has been implicitly regarded as historically correct, even among the English, who cared to accept no other authority. Among the French, of course, no other account of the expulsion will ever be looked upon as true. This one poem, because of the sympathy of the author, as well as his treatment of the incident, has wound itself around the hearts of French Canada; and Longfellow's name is as reverently treasured and respected and loved by them as any of their own writers, ecclesiastical, historical, or poetical.

Longfellow never wrote about Canada directly again. During his life, he had toyed with two other Canadian subjects. One of these he considered, appropriately enough, on the very day before he completed *Evangeline*. On February 26, 1847, he wrote in his journal, "In the afternoon I drove to Fresh Pond to see the ice-cutting.... [Ice] would be a good subject for a poem,—a dithyrambic on Water. I have long thought so. Various scenes would come in: the icebergs, the frozen seas, Labrador...." And, much earlier in his career, for a book he intended to title *New England Sketches*, and long before he had thought of *Evangeline*, he had conjectured a brief prose narration, "Down East: The Missionary of Acadie." Neither project came to fruition.

Some readers mistakenly believe that *Hiawatha* is set in Canada, but while some of the winds do indeed blow from the north, Longfellow was adamant that the setting of the poem was the south shore of Lake Superior.

Ironically, the author of one of the most famous "Canadian" poems ever written made but one brief trip to Canada, and that solely of a week's duration as a tourist visiting the threesome of Niagara, Toronto, and Montreal.

Niagara Falls had been a lure for many years. In June 1862, he set out with a group of friends and relatives, and, in his journal, sounds as harried and ludicrously short of time to appreciate the wonders as any suburbanite on a package tour today:

> [June] 8th. A bright, beautiful day.... Go up the stone tower in the midst of the English fall. It drives me frantic with excitement. In the afternoon, go over the suspension bridge to Table Rock, on the Canada side. It is the finest view of the English fall. In every other particular the American side is preferable.

Longfellow's final overt connection with Canada was an anthology of poems (first published in 1879) about British North America he collected for publication as part of a multi-volume series (of which he was also the editor) known as *Poems of Places*. The Canadian poems are by foreign as well as Canadian authors, and how and why

Henry Wadsworth Longfellow (right, wearing hat) with friends and family at Niagara Falls, June 1862, en route to Toronto, Kingston, the Thousand Islands, and Montreal. Courtesy of the National Park Service, Longfellow National Historic Site.

Longfellow chose these poems over others remains a mystery. Some of the poems appear to be unique impressions, and while the Canadian content comprises approximately forty per cent of the book's extent, these poems are forced to share space with verses about Greenland, Mexico, and other lands of the western hemisphere; hence the book's simple title: *America*.

The following passage from *Evangeline* was chosen by Longfellow himself for inclusion in the Canadian section of his anthology, *America*.

———

from EVANGELINE

Grand Pré, N.S.

In the Acadian land, on the shores of the Basin of Minas,
Distant, secluded, still, the little village of Grand Pré
Lay in the fruitful valley. Vast meadows stretched to the eastward,
Giving the village its name, and pasture to flocks without number.
Dikes, that the hands of the farmers had raised with labor incessant,
Shut out the turbulent tides, but at stated seasons the flood-gates
Opened, and welcomed the sea to wander at will o'er the meadows.
West and south there were fields of flax, and orchards and
    cornfields
Spreading afar and unfenced o'er the plain; and away to the
    northward
Blomidon rose, and the forests old, and aloft on the mountains
Sea-fogs pitched their tents, and mists from the mighty Atlantic
Looked on the happy valley, but ne'er from their station descended.
There, in the midst of its farms, reposed the Acadian village.
Strongly built were the houses, with frames of oak and of hemlock,
Such as the peasants of Normandy built in the reign of the Henrys.
Thatched were the roofs, with dormer-windows; and gables
    projecting
Over the basement below protected and shaded the doorway.
There in the tranquil evenings of summer, when brightlythe sunset
Lighted the village street, and gilded the vanes on the chimneys,
Matrons and maidens sat in snow white caps and in kirtles
Scarlet and blue and green, with distaffs spilling the golden
Flax for the gossiping looms, whose noisy shuttles within doors
Mingled their sound with the whir of the wheels and the songs of
    the maidens.
Solemnly down the street came the parish priest, and the children

Paused in their play to kiss the hand he extended to bless them.
Reverend walked he among them; and up rose matrons and
    maidens
Hailing his slow approach with words of affectionate welcome.
Then came the laborers home from the field, and serenely the
    sun sank
Down to his rest, and twilight prevailed. Anon from the belfry
Softly the Angelus sounded, and over the roofs of the village
Columns of pale blue smoke, like clouds of incense ascending,
Rose from a hundred hearths, the homes of peace and
    contentment.
Thus dwelt together in love these simple Acadian farmers,—
Dwelt in the love of God and of man. Alike were they free from
Fear, that reigns with the tyrant, and envy, the vice of republics.
Neither locks had they to their doors, nor bars to their windows;
But their dwellings were open as day and the hearts of the owners:
There the richest was poor, and the poorest lived in abundance.

ANDRÉ BRETON

A NDRÉ BRETON was a seminal thinker in French, indeed European aesthetics in the first half of this century. Originally a Dadaist, he was the author, in 1924, of the first Surrealist Manifesto, and is generally regarded as the founder of that still influential movement. His early experiments with automatic writing were followed by more traditional books of poems and fictional narratives, as well as criticism in the visual arts.

Throughout his adult life, Breton was fascinated with and sometimes obsessed by the more recondite aspects of the occult. He became learned in the nuances of hieroglyphics, the Tarot, and the hermetic, and often used vocabulary and metaphors from these worlds in his writing. Indeed, his last book of creative writing—which he and most critics consider his best prose—took its title from the Tarot: *Arcane 17*. Within the iconography of the Tarot deck, the card called "Arcane 17" represents the triumph of goodness over the powers of darkness (the latter represented by the cards Arcane 15 and 16), an appropriate metaphor for a man cut off from his country because of war, yet hopeful that right would triumph over might.

Arcane 17, a masterpiece of French letters, was conceived and written not in France, but in Canada. Breton had been living in the United States for some years, forced to flee his home in Paris because of the German occupation during the Second World War. Deeply depressed by the state of the conflict, the destruction of his country, the absence of friends, and his second divorce, he hoped that a lengthy vacation might improve his spirits. Accompanied by a newly found woman friend, Elisa, he arrived in the village of Ste. Agathe near Percé Rock on the Gaspé Peninsula of Quebec in August 1944.

The vacation proved a magnificent tonic. The progress of the Allies following their successful D-Day landing just weeks before his arrival in Canada continued to enhearten him. Equally, he was revitalized by the presence of Elisa. Like Breton, she had suffered the anguish of divorce, and had perfect empathy with their mutual loss of children: Breton's daughter had been taken away by his second wife; Elisa's daughter had drowned. For the next three months, he awoke with the dawn and wrote until noon, finding in Percé Rock a metaphor for many of the themes he wished to address in what he was sure would be his magnum opus. The Rock itself struck him as a magnificent symbol for the current condition of Europe: for both, their history was long; the geological strata mirrored eras and reigns; and the Rock, though hugely split, remained a monolith single— and singular—in its beauty.

Everywhere he turned in Gaspé, he encountered further images reinforcing his belief that hope emerged from despair, that the greatest human love was that which was constantly resurrected. As France continued to be liberated, as his affection for Elisa grew more profound, all about him he witnessed the same hopeful cycle in Nature: birth, death, and then joyous rebirth.

Like much of Breton's imaginative prose, the writing is dense and the imagery often esoteric. But these excerpts from *Arcane 17* give a sense of how the methodic, recurring lives of the Canadian fishermen, the high-latitude early light, the cleansing fall and rise of the waters, even the mists that would hide, then, ghost-like, dissipate to reveal Percé Rock, all combined to give a Canadian accent to a time in his life when he seems to have been most optimistic, seems never to have been happier.

---

from ARCANE 17

Isolation, on this Gaspé coast, is as unexpected today and as total as can be. This region of Canada lives, in effect, under its own laws and in spite of everything, somewhat at the margins of history, because it is incorporated into an English dominion but has kept of France not only its language, in which diverse anachronisms have taken up residence, but also the deep impression of its customs. Perhaps, dramatic as it is, the current landing of numerous French Canadians on the Normandy coast will help re-establish a vital link, missing for almost two centuries. But those who have remained here indicate with their gestures and their remarks that they have never completely been able to get past the stage where their group identity blurs to merge with another. If, on their part, all rancour has probably disappeared, their integration into the heart of the English community appears altogether illusory. The Catholic church, true to its obscurantist methods, makes use here of its all-powerful influence to prevent the dissemination of any literature which is not edifying (classical theater has practically been reduced to *Esther* and *Polyeucte,* which are available in huge stacks in Quebec bookstores, the eighteenth century seems never to have taken place, Hugo is nowhere to be found). *Wagons,* as they call buses here, rare and wheezy, only regain a bit of confidence when they cross the *covered bridges* of a bygone era. What's more, this season has not been favorable for tourism. With very few exceptions, the Americans have refrained from coming for several years. The recent provincial elections, in which the reins of power passed from the Liberal Party to the Union National, will bring in their wake the redistribution of all public offices and dissuade both those already entrenched and those hoping to succeed them from making any vacation plans. The local newspapers, which relate European news in a gleefully apocalyptic style, moreover abound in information whose very presentation right in the middle of the page creates a dissonant effect ("For twenty-five consecutive nights veritable showers of meteors will light up the August sky"), alternating with recipes of a sibylline quality ("rolls of cornflowers": but these words only disguise a blueberry pie). All this creates, in the admirably limpid air, a very effective shield against the madness of the moment, like the mist which on certain mornings stretches from one end of the horizon to the other ("Alouette, natural smoking tobacco," candidly states this package with a picture of a bird singing in the grass and, at the beginning of the song that it tramples, all of Nerval's old Valois gushes out only to evaporate suddenly: *"Alouette, gentille alouette—Alouette, je te fumerai."*)

Here, under the lightness of your step, is a parapet of such dubious stability that it has to be propped up at night with heavy stones, but no matter how firm it seems, nothing prevents the storm from treating it like a straw plaything, here is the fine sand studded with umbels by the birds' feet. From a few miles away, Bonaventure Island continues to loom: legend has it that it was the den of an ogre who, crossing this body of water in one stride, came to grab the women and maids of the coast, with whom he filled his vast pockets. Once back home with his meal finished, he washed his clothes in the high tide and lay them out to dry on the tall cliffs. There could be no better way for the folk imagination to account for the incriminating and radiant persistence of the maculation of the rock, the superhuman efforts and the prodigious quantity of perpetually gushing soapy lather formed by the white plumage which was powerless to make it disappear. What detergent, no less strong, will succeed in wiping from the human spirit the great collective scars and the throbbing memories of these days of hatred! What sacred refuge will they have to build in their hearts for all ideas which, like the gannets on their nests, will struggle to end this period or, with their sumptuous and free flight, will combine to transform the face of this tragic battlement! What choice place will be reserved for feelings of love, like the niches on the flanks of the rock, key to the whole display, where we were shown birds taking shelter two by two! Love, poetry, art, it's only through their resilience that confidence will return, that human thought will succeed in setting sail again. We will not be able to count on science again until it gets a clear idea of how to remedy the strange curse that has fallen on it and which seems to doom it to accumulate so many more mistakes and calamities than benefits. Without prejudice to the measures of moral disinfection which are being imposed on this sombre eve of twice the year one thousand and which are essentially social acts, for mankind considered by itself there can be no more valuable and far-reaching hope than in the beat of a wing....

Here again, perpendicular to the wave crests, to that barely sinuous stippled water line that the agate hunters return to each day in single file, is Percé Rock itself, as it is cut by our window frames and as I'll take its image with me when I'm long gone from here. Working my way around it a little earlier I regretted not being able, from too close up, to discover its totality, and that new arrangements of its mass gave rise to images different from those I had already formed. One can only retain the last image when it's a question of picturing such complex structures. Besides, it's above all from that angle, that is, seen from the west, that it has caught the eye of photographers. "Percé Rock: 280 feet from the top to the prow, 250 feet at its widest point, 1,420 feet long," a tourist brochure says laconically and if I don't much mind copying these figures it's because I wouldn't be surprised if in the relationship of these dimensions the *golden section* should appear; in its proportions Percé Rock can pass for that good a model of natural precision. It presents two parts to us which, from where I'm accustomed to observe them, seem to lead a separate existence, the first initially suggesting a vessel on which an ancient musical instrument has been superimposed, the second a head with its profile missing a little something, a head with a haughty bearing, with a heavy Louis XIV wig. As the prow of the ship drives its north end towards the beach, a wide opening greets us at its base, at the level of the rear mast. Rising above the sea to a height of sixty feet or so, that opening could, only a few years ago, before some cave-ins created an obstacle, serve as a passage for sailboats. It will always remain essential to the emotional appreciation of the monument, and in it lies its truly unique quality. No matter what its diminutiveness relative to the hull it undermines, in effect the opening gives access to the idea that the so-called boat is also an arc and it is admirable that the currents which break all along the wall find there an outlet to be even more frenetically swallowed up. This breach alone is undoubtedly what dictates the secondary resemblance to a sort of distant pipe organ, more this instrument than any other since the day when, searching to identify the face and the posture of the stone head turned towards it, you thought it might be the head of Handel, quickly correcting yourself with: Handel? no, definitely Bach.

Geologists and paleontologists reach new peaks of pleasure all over the Gaspé peninsula where they calculate the immemorial landslides, of which a pebble dressed as a harlequin, uniformly polished by the sea, sometimes gives solitary testimony. From hand to hand are passed superb fragments found in the area of Grand Grève, on which winged towers of trilobites crisscross in every direction, suggesting the most heavily worked tablets of Benin even while dissociating themselves as far as possible from the play of their beige, silver and lilac lights. In everything one treads on, there is something that comes from so much farther back than mankind and which is also going so much farther....

To describe the geometry of an era that has not yet come full circle requires an appeal to an ideal observer, removed from the contingencies of that era, which implies from the start the need for an ideal observation post and, if everything prevents me from placing myself in the role of this observer, it seems to me equally true that no place fulfills the necessary requirements as well as Percé Rock, as it unfolds to me at certain times of day. It's when, at nightfall or on certain foggy mornings, the details of its structure become cloudy that the image of a sloop, always imperiously commanded, can be refined from it. Aboard, everything points to the infallible glance of the captain, but a captain who could also be a magician. It's as if the vessel, just a short while ago bereft of riggings, seems suddenly to be equipped for the most vertiginous of ocean voyages. In fact it is said that the water which accumulates in autumn in the crevices of the rock freezes there in winter, repeatedly causing the crust to overstretch, producing annually about three hundred tons of scree. The experts in this field have not, of course, done us the favour of making the arithmetical calculation any child could do, which once we've reckoned the total weight of the rock at four million tons, allows us to deduce the aggregate time it will take to disappear, that is, thirteen thousand years. However unofficial this calculation may be, at least it has the virtue of setting the enormous vessel in motion, of providing it with motors whose power is comparable to the very slow and yet very noticeable process of disintegration that it's undergoing. It's beautiful, it's moving that its longevity is not limitless and at the same time that it covers such a succession of human lives. In its depths there is more than enough time to see born and die a city like Paris where gunshots are reverberating right now even inside Notre Dame as the great rose window turns. And now that great rose window whirls and twirls in the rock: without a doubt these shots were the prearranged signal because *the curtain is rising*. It has been claimed that, faced with Percé Rock, the pen and the brush must admit their impotence and it's true that those who are called upon to speak least superficially about it will think they have said it all when they have attested to the magnificence of this curtain, when their voices suddenly deepened to depict its dark radiance, when they have succeeded in creating some order out of the modulation of the mass of air that vibrates in its majestically discordant pipes. But, lacking the knowledge that it's a curtain, how could they suspect that its staggering drapery hides a set with many levels?

ARTHUR
CONAN DOYLE

O NE CANNOT BE in Edmonton without hearing about
wheat." Such an observation lacks the surly pithiness, the elementary perspicacity, of Sherlock Holmes, but it was, nonetheless,
penned by Holmes' creator, Sir Arthur Conan Doyle (1859–1930),
following the latter's 1923 visit across much of Canada. The trip was
to be Doyle's last visit to this country, and perhaps sensing that final-
ity, he wrote of the land with the loving affection and stern exhorta-
tions to good behaviour that one expects from a paterfamilias.
Sagacious doyen was certainly a role into which Doyle fell easily; he
was a shameless imperialist:

> Then there is the alternative of Canada becoming an indepen-
> dent nation. That is not so impossible as a union with the
> States, but it is in the last degree improbable. Why should
> Canada wish her independence? She has it now in every essen-
> tial.... Her dependence upon the Mother-Country for
> emigrants, though not so great as her financial dependence, is
> still the greatest from any single source. Besides all this, she has
> the vast insurance policy, which is called the British Navy,
> presented to her for nothing—though honour demands some
> premium from her in the future.... And everywhere there is a
> consciousness of the glory of the empire, its magnificent future,

and the wonderful possibilities of these great nations all growing up under the same flag with the same language and destinies. This sentiment joins with material advantages, and will prevent Canada from having any aspiration towards independence.

There are parents who praise the talents of their children so liberally one realizes eventually the exercise is largely self-flattery. Similarly, this parental, imperial viewpoint was so strongly held by Doyle that one is never entirely sure when reading his lengthy and generally positive remarks about Canada whether he is objectively praising what he sees, or ultimately, semi-consciously, flattering the wisdom of Britain in conquering the place. His insensitivity to the merit of cultures and people other than his own is, alas, even more pronounced than that of other writers of his time. And it should not be forgotten that he was knighted because of, not in spite of, his propaganda and services on behalf of the Empire.

Sherlock Holmes himself had little to say about Canada, and the country rarely surfaces in the Holmes opus. Its most renowned manifestation occurs in *The Hound of the Baskervilles*, where the legendary sleuth encounters the heir to the estate, Sir Henry Basker-ville. The plot thickens. A lost boot becomes a key clue. "Sir Henry smiled. 'I don't know much of British life yet, for I have spent nearly all my time in the States and in Canada. But I hope that to lose one of your boots is not part of the ordinary routine of life over here.'"

Indeed, it is not. But finding the missing boot becomes an important clue to solving the puzzle, and Sherlock Holmes is up to the task:

From amid a tuft of cotton-grass which bore it up out of the slime some dark thing was projecting. Holmes sank to his waist as he stepped from the path to seize it, and had we not been there to drag him out, he could never have set his foot upon firm land again. He held an old black boot in the air. "Meyers, Toronto," was printed on the leather inside.

From this sole reference to Toronto has sprung The Bootmakers, a coterie of fans of Doyle and more especially Holmes, founded in 1970, whose members have created and donated to the Metropolitan Toronto Library the world's largest collection of Holmesiana.

Being able to read the inside of a boot is no proof that Holmes knew anything about Canada. But some glimmering of the famed detective's intimacy with the land can be gathered from this deduction in "The Adventure of Black Peter":

> Stanley Hopkins drew from his pocket a drab-coloured notebook. The outside was rough and worn, the leaves discoloured. On the first page were written the initials "J.H.N." and the date "1883." Holmes laid it on the table and examined it in his minute way, while Hopkins and I gazed over each shoulder. On the second page were the printed letters "CPR" and then came several sheets of numbers.... "What do you make of these?" asked Holmes. "They appear to be lists of Stock Exchange securities. I thought that "J.H.N." were the initials of a broker, and that "CPR" may have been his client."
> "Try Canadian Pacific Railway," said Holmes.

The creator of Sherlock Holmes was far more effusive about Canada. In 1894, he undertook his first lecture tour of North America, an author already famous for his fictional sleuth. The tour was a commercial venture, so his stops were limited to the big cities of the east: a fast foray into Canada brought him to Toronto for a talk before fifteen hundred people at Massey Hall and to Niagara for sightseeing. Doyle would later tell his second wife, so spectacular were they, that it was not at the Reichenbach Falls but at Niagara that he should have arranged for Moriarty and Holmes to drop so precipitously to their deaths.

The 1914 decision of the Grand Trunk Railway to offer Doyle a cross-Canada tour in a private railway car (as a marketing ploy to attract tourists to Jasper), was fetchingly inventive. Who better to observe and analyse the uniqueness of Canada, and then report on it to the world, than the personification of Holmes? Doyle and his wife set out during June and July in the private carriage of the owner of the railway ("a gloriously comfortable and compact little home consisting of a parlour, a dining room and a bedroom") and his observations about Canada, excerpted below, were written from this privileged if not compromised position. Presumably from Doyle's point of view, he was too wealthy and famous to be bought. Besides, anything which promoted tourism in the colonies had to be good for the Empire.

Doyle's impressions of Canada had fantastically wide currency and influence, for he reported on his 1914 trip for *The Cornhill Magazine*, the popular English periodical which had Thackeray as its first editor, and serially published such novelists as Anthony Trollope, George Eliot, and Thomas Hardy. In the case of Doyle, the popularity, on occasion, was unfortunate, in that he could be outrageously wrong in his historical predictions and his appallingly callous racism. The following passage sadly illustrates both:

I do want to take my hat off once again to the French Canadian. He came of a small people. At the time of the British occupation, I doubt if there were more than a hundred thousand of them, and yet the mark they have left by their bravery and activity upon this Continent is an ineffaceable one.... Keep further north and still their footsteps are always marked deep in the soil before you. Cross the whole vast plain of Central Canada and reach the mountains. What is that called, you ask? That is Mount Miette. And that? That is Tête Jaune. And that lake? It is Lake Brulé. They were more than scouts in front of an army. They were so far ahead that the army will take a century yet before it reaches their outposts. Brave, enduring, lighthearted, romantic, they were and are a fascinating race. The ideals of the British and of the French stock may not be the same, but while the future of the country must surely be upon British lines, the French will leave their mark deeply upon it. Five hundred years hence their blood will be looked upon as the aristocratic and distinctive blood of Canada and even as the Englishman is proud of his Norman ancestor, so the most British Canadian will proudly trace back his pedigree to the point where some ancestor had married with a Tachereau or a De Lotbinière. It seems to me that the British cannot be too delicate in their dealings with such a people. They are not a subject people but partners in empire, and should in all ways be treated so.

The other sight which interested us at Sault Ste. Marie was an Indian or half-breed school. The young ladies who conducted it seemed to be kindness itself, but the children struck me as mutinous little devils. Not that their actions were anything but demure and sedate, but red mutiny smouldered in their eyes. All the wrongs of their people seemed printed upon their cast-iron visages. Their race has little to complain of from the Canadian Government, which has treated them with such humanity that they have really become a special endowed class living at the expense of the community. Still, there is the perennial fact that where they once owned lake and forest, they now are confined to the fixed reserve. That no doubt is the whisper which brings that brooding scowl upon young faces. They are a cruel people, and in the days of torture the children were even more bloodthirsty than the rest. They are a race of caged falcons, and perhaps it is as well that they are not likely to survive the conditions which they loved.

His third confirmed Canadian visit took place in 1922, and would have been a mirror image of his first (sightseeing at Niagara, lecture in Toronto) except that now the Canadian clergy were outspoken from the pulpit, and outraged in their letters to the editor, about Doyle's grand claims for his recently acquired passion: spiritualism and the physical manifestations of the occult.

His fourth visit came the following year, at the peak of his proselytizing for psychic research. After traversing America, he returned east via Canada to Montreal, making candid pronouncements about our cities and culture at nearly every stop in his memoir of the period.

In Vancouver, Doyle lectured before 3,000 people, an astonishing number, but what he most remembered about the city was more recondite and may cause today's reader bemused disbelief: "In accor-

Arthur Conan Doyle (second from left) and family at Jasper Park in 1914 during his cross-country tour. Jasper inspired Doyle to his highest encomia and even to poetry. *Courtesy of the Arthur Conan Doyle Room, Metropolitan Reference Library, Toronto.*

dance with my custom, I endeavoured, in spite of our limited time, to explore the psychic possibilities of the place."

In describing his return to the north of the continent he wrote, "Much as I love America, it always gives one a thrill to be under the Union Jack once more with one's feet on British soil." Victoria he regarded as uncontaminated by industry and "the retired wheat-grower or miner in the evening of his days could find no more pleasant waiting place."

From British Columbia, Doyle left his family in Jasper for a vacation while solo he travelled to lecture in Edmonton. He commented upon that city's warm reception of his remarks, upon the ectoplasm (visible, of course, only to seers) while he was on stage, and wheat—as noted above, a seemingly endless major topic of conversation.

In Calgary, Doyle was, by his own reckoning, hampered by evil spirits who kept the crowds small and the weather wet. But in Winnipeg, Doyle had a delightful time, both as a speaker and as a psychic believer and showed that despite his imperialism he was not always blind to improvements engendered here:

> We came upon it on Dominion Day, when all business was suspended and everyone was in festivity, so we fitted ourselves into the picture and attended the international baseball match between Winnipeg and Minneapolis in the morning. Both sides seemed to me to be surprisingly good and the fielding, catching and throwing-in were far superior to that of good English cricket teams. Of course in catching they are aided by the great glove on the left hand, but every cricketer knows the difficulty of judging a long catch, and when I say that not one was misjudged or dropped by either side out of at least fifty, it will show how high was the standard. I wish more and more that this game could acclimatize in Britain, for it has many points which make it the ideal game both for players and spectators. I have all the prejudices of an old cricketer, and yet I cannot get away from the fact that baseball is the better game.

In Winnipeg, Doyle met with a circle for psychical research in an unintentionally amusing séance. His gullibility, by this time, is thoroughly ludicrous, painful to behold.

> The man who goes upon occult paths does certainly have an extraordinary variety of experience. Let me briefly narrate that which happened on the morning of July 4th [1923], the day after my lecture at Winnipeg, which had been a remarkably successful one to a very crowded house. I had heard of a strange circle and of a very remarkable medium whom I will call Mrs. Bolton. At 9 a.m. one of her devotees, who are absolutely wholehearted in their belief and devotion, was at the hotel door with a car. After a four-mile drive we alighted at a lonely villa on the extreme outskirts of the town, where there were six other men and three women to meet us. The men were all alert, middle-aged or young, evidently keen men of business who might have been

accountants or merchants. Yet here they were from ten o'clock onwards on a working day giving themselves up to what was in their eyes infinitely more important than business.

We sat around the room, and presently Mrs. Bolton entered, a woman of the Blavatsky type of rounded face, but less heavy. She seemed gentle and amiable. She sat down while "Lead, kindly Light" was sung. Then she sank into a trance, from which she quietly emerged with an aspect of very great dignity and benevolence. I have never seen more commanding eyes than those which fixed us each in turn. "It is the Master. It is the High Spirit," whispered my neighbours. Standing up, and greeting each of us in turn with very great dignity, the medium, or the entity controlling her, proceeded to baptize a child nine weeks old belonging to one of the circle. The mother might have stood for a model of reverence and awe. She then handed round bread and wine, as in the Sacrament. The wine, I was assured by all, was simply water drawn from the domestic supply. It had now become faintly red with an aromatic odour and taste. At every meeting this miracle of changing the water into wine was performed, according to the unanimous testimony of these very same workaday men of the world, who declare that they themselves have drawn the water. I could not give a name to the taste and smell, which were very pleasant. It was certainly nonalcoholic.

We then had a long address, which was in the medium's own voice and dialect, but purported to come from the high control. My growing deafness made me miss some of it, but what I heard was dignified and impressive. After speaking for nearly an hour, a second control took possession. He was more smiling and homely but less majestic and dignified than the higher one. The latter, by the way, unbent in a very charming way when he blessed a little boy who was present, saying "I remember when I was a little boy myself once." The second control gave messages relating to worldly things to several of the circle, who received them with deep reverence. They assured me that they never failed to be true. He spoke of conditions at death. "The dark valley on the other side waits for all. I am in the glorious city at the end. Those who are prepared by knowledge, as you are, soon pass the Valley. But some linger very long."

Then after some ceremonies which I may not describe the séance ended, and Mrs. Bolton, the plain, homely, uneducated Lancashire woman, came back into her own body. What is one to say of such a performance? It was against all my prepossessions, for I have a deep distrust of ritual and form and sacraments, and here were all these things; yet they were solemn and moving, and nothing can exceed the absolute faith of these men and women. Their faith is founded, as they assure me, upon long experience in which they have seen miracle after miracle, including materialization of these high personages. I cannot claim that I saw anything evidential with my own eyes, and yet I am convinced that my informant was speaking truth so far as he saw it, when he claimed that he poured water into the chalice and that it had been transformed. It all left me with mixed feelings, but the conviction that I had been on the fringe of something very sacred and solemn was predominant. It is true that these high Spirits occasionally used Lancashire speech, but as one of them said, "We cannot open brain cells which have never been opened. We have to use what is there."

When I considered the wonderful psychical phenomena of the one circle seen with my own eyes and the religious atmosphere of the other, I came away with the conclusion that Winnipeg stands very high among the places we have visited for its psychic possibilities.

Curiously, he makes no mention, when passing through Thunder Bay (then known as Fort William and Port Arthur), of the house he bought there while on his 1914 trip. He had been so taken with the economic potential as well as the physical beauty of the site that he had parted with 3,000 pounds to buy a home on one of the main streets of the Lakehead.

Arriving in Montreal, his feelings were at war. On the one hand, he could write:

It was a joy to feel the glamour of history once more as we entered Montreal. On the first day we ascended the mountain and looked down on what is one of the most wonderful views in the world— and I can speak now with some knowledge. At your feet lies the old grey town, which is spreading fast upon either flank, and which is impressive in its wealth of domes and spires.... It is no mushroom city this. It contains buildings which would be considered venerable and historical even by a European standard.

Yet, ever the believer that colonists must die for the preservation of the motherland, Doyle had to state:

One feels at once in this city that vibrant sense of religious earnestness and fierce self-assertion which the dominant Catholic Church always brings with it. It is logical enough, for if your religion is really and literally true, then it must predominate over everything else. There is a good deal of virtue, however, in the "if." On our first day, there was an assembly of Papal Zouaves, who marched past the hotel, some twelve hundred of them, well-uniformed, well-armed, led by very smart officers, and headed by the flag of France. I was sorry to observe, however, that very few of the breasts of the men were decorated with those medals which would show that when France and Belgium were really at death's door they had made some sacrifice to save them. The France of Canada is the France of Louis XIV and of Madame de Maintenon, of ruffling seigneurs, of intriguing abbés, and of persecuted Huguenots. She has no use for the France of free thought and free institutions.

To his surprise, large crowds attended his two lectures in Montreal, for as he adroitly phrased his apprehension, "... the community is largely Roman Catholic, and of the opinion that psychic phenomena which occur within its own ranks are saintly, while those experienced by others are diabolical."

Near the end of his 1914 trip, Doyle spoke to the Canadian Club in Ottawa, giving his impressions of the nation. His high opinion of

Canadian government and its beneficence to the people would certainly raise eyebrows if not voices today. He spoke less naïvely, however, about the land. "Very much we were struck, in all that country, by the mingling of the modern and the wild, sometimes taking a dramatic, sometimes a comic form, but always interesting."

By 1924, when he published recollections of his time in Canada, Doyle was far more interested in the ectoplasmic hereafter than in Sherlock Holmes. As a result, his account of the Canadian junket deals almost exclusively with his impressions of the west, because it was there that he had the most powerful psychic experiences. The following excerpt, from a chapter in his book *Memories and Adventures*, is more attractively concerned with the land and people of Canada rather than its ether.

---

from TO THE ROCKY MOUNTAINS IN 1914

About evening we crossed the Canadian frontier, the Richelieu River, down which the old Iroquois scalping parties used to creep, gleaming coldly in the twilight. There is nothing to show where you have crossed the border. There is the same sort of country, the same cultivation, the same plain wooden houses. Nothing was changed save that suddenly I saw a little old ensign flying on a gable, and it gives you a thrill when you have not seen it for a time.

It is not until one has reached the Prairie country that the traveller meets with new conditions and new problems. He traverses Ontario with its prosperous mixed farms and its fruit-growing villages, but the general effect is the same as in Eastern America. Then comes the enormous stretch of the Great Lakes, those wonderful inland seas, with great ocean-going steamers....

We stopped at Sault Ste. Marie, the neck of the hour-glass between the two great lakes of Huron and Superior. There were several things there which are worthy of record. The lakes are of a different level, and the lock which avoids the dangerous rapids is on an enormous scale; but, beside it, unnoticed save by those who know where to look and what to look for, there is a little stone-lined cutting no larger than an uncovered drain—it is the detour by which for centuries the voyageurs, trappers, and explorers moved their canoes round the Sault or fall on their journey to the great solitudes beyond. Close by it is one of the old Hudson Bay log forts, with its fireproof roof, its loop-holed walls, and every other device for Indian fighting. Very small and mean these things look by the side of the great locks and the huge steamers within them. But where would locks and steamers have been had these others not taken their lives in their hands to clear the way?...

The true division between the East and West of Canada is not the Great Lakes, which are so valuable as a waterway, but lies in the 500 miles of country between the Lakes and Winnipeg....

And now one reached the west of Winnipeg and on that prairie which means so much both to Canada and to the world. It was wonderfully impressive to travel swiftly all day from the early summer dawn to the latest evening light, and to see always the same little clusters of houses, always the same distant farms, always the same huge expanse stretching to the distant skyline, mottled with cattle, or green with the halfgrown crops. You think these people are lonely. What about the people beyond them and beyond them again, each family in its rude barracks in the midst of the 160 acres which form the minimum farm? No doubt they are lonely, and yet there are alleviations. When men or women are working on their own property and seeing their fortune growing, they have pleasant thoughts to bear them company. It is the women, I am told, who feel it most, and who go prairie-mad. Now they have rigged telephone circles which connect up small groups of farms and enable the women to relieve their lives by a little friendly gossip, when the whole district thrills to the news that Mrs. Jones has been in the cars to Winnipeg and bought a new bonnet. At the worst the loneliness of the prairie can never, one would think, have the soul-killing effect of loneliness in a town. "There is always the wind on the heath, brother." Besides, the wireless has now arrived, and that is the best friend of the lonely man....

So much about farms and farming. I cannot see how one can write about this western part and avoid the subject which is written in green and gold from sky to sky. There is nothing else. Nowhere is there any sign of yesterday—not a cairn, not a monument. Life has passed here, but has left no footstep behind. But stay, the one thing which the old life still leaves is just this one thing—footsteps. Look at them in the little narrow black paths which converge to the water—little dark ruts which wind and twist. Those are the buffalo runs of old. Gone are the Cree and Blackfoot hunters who shot them down. Gone, too, the fur-traders who bought the skins. Chief Factor MacTavish, who entered into the great Company's service as a boy, spent his life in slow promotion from Fort This to Fort That, and made a decent Presbyterian woman of some Indian squaw, finally saw with horror in his old age that the world was crowding his wild beasts out of their pastures. Gone are the great herds upon which both Indian hunter and fur-trader were parasitical. Indian, trader and buffalo all have passed, and here on the great plains are these narrow runways as the last remaining sign of a vanished world.

Edmonton is the capital of the western side of the prairie, even as Winnipeg of the eastern. I do not suppose the average Briton has the least conception of the amenities of Winnipeg. He would probably be surprised to hear that the Fort Garry Hotel there is nearly as modern and luxurious as any hotel in Northumberland Avenue. There were no such luxuries in 1914 in Edmonton. The town was in a strangely half-formed condition, rude and raw, but with a great atmosphere of energy, bustle, and future greatness. With its rail-way connections and waterways it is bound to be a large city. At the time of our visit the streets were full of out-of-works, great husky men, some of them of magnificent physique, who found themselves at a loss, on account of cessations in railroad construction. They told me that they would soon be reabsorbed, but meantime the situation was the rudest object-lesson in economics that I have ever witnessed. Here were these SPLENDID men, ready and willing to work. Here was a new country calling in every direction for labour. How came the two things to be even temporarily disconnected? There could be but one word. It was want of capital. And why was the capital wanting? Why was the world of the railroads held up? Because the money market was tight in London—London which finds, according to the most recent figures, 73 per cent of all the moneys with which Canada is developed. Such was the state of things. What will amend it? How can capital be made to flow into the best channels? By encouragement and security and the hope of good returns. I never heard of any system of socialism which did not seem to defeat the very object which it had at heart. And yet it was surely deplorable that the men should be there, and that the work should be there, and that none could command the link which would unite them.

A line of low distant hills broke the interminable plain which has extended with hardly a rising for 1,500 miles. Above them was, here and there, a peak of snow. Shades of Mayne Reid, they were the Rockies—my old familiar Rockies! Have I been here before? What an absurd question, when I lived here for about ten years of my life in all the hours of dreamland. What deeds have I not done among Redskins and trappers and grizzlies within their wilds! And here they were at last glimmering bright in the rising morning sun. At least, I have seen my dream mountains. Most boys never do.

Jasper Park is one of the great national playgrounds and health resorts which the Canadian Government with great wisdom has laid out for the benefit of the citizens. When Canada has filled up and carries a large population, she will bless the foresight of the administrators who took possession of broad tracts of the most picturesque land and put them for ever out of the power of the speculative dealer. The National Park at Banff has for twenty years been a Mecca for tourists. That at Algonquin gives a great pleasure-ground to those who cannot extend their travels beyond Eastern Canada. But this new Jasper Park is the latest and the wildest of all these reserves. Some years ago it was absolute wilderness, and much of it impenetrable. Now, through the energy of Colonel Rogers, trails have been cut through it in various directions, and a great number of adventurous trips into country which is practically unknown can be carried out with ease and comfort.... The park is not as full of wild creatures as it will be after a few years of preservation. The Indians who lived in this part rounded up everything that they could before moving to their reservation. But even now, the bear lumbers through the brushwood, the eagle soars above the lake, the timber wolf still skulks in the night, and the deer graze in the valleys. Above, near the snow-line, the wild goat is not uncommon, while at a lower altitude are found the mountain sheep. On the last day of our visit the rare cinnamon bear exposed his yellow coat upon a clearing within a few hundred yards of the village. I saw his clumsy good-humoured head looking at me from over a dead trunk, and I thanked the kindly Canadian law which has given him a place of sanctuary. What a bloodthirsty baboon man must appear to the lower animals. If any superhuman demon treated us exactly as we treat the pheasants, we should begin to reconsider our views as to what is sport.

The porcupine is another creature which abounded in the woods. I did not see any, but a friend described an encounter between one and his dog. The creature's quills are detachable when he wishes to be nasty, and at the end of the fight it was not easy to say which was the dog and which the porcupine.

Life in Jasper interested me as an experience of the first stage of a raw Canadian town. It will certainly grow into a considerable place, but at that time, bar Colonel Rogers' house and the station, there were only log-huts and small wooden dwellings. Christianity was apostolic in its simplicity and in its freedom from strife—though one has to go back remarkably early in apostolic times to find those characteristics. Two churches were being built, the pastor in each case acting also as head mason and carpenter. One, the corner-stone of which I had the honour of laying, was to be used in turn by several Nonconformist bodies. To the ceremony came the Anglican parson, grimy from his labours on the opposition building, and prayed for the well-being of his rival. The whole function, with its simplicity and earnestness, carried out by a group of ill-clad men standing bareheaded in a drizzle of rain, seemed to me to have in it the essence of religion. As I ventured to remark to them, Kikuyu and Jasper can give some lessons to London.

We made a day's excursion by rail to the Tête Jaune Caché, which is across the British Columbian border and marks the watershed between East and West. Here we saw the Fraser, already a formidable river, rushing down to the Pacific. At the head of the pass stands the village of the railway workers, exactly like one of the mining townships of Bret Harte, save that the bad man is never allowed to be too bad. There is a worse man in a red serge coat and a Stetson hat, who is told off by the State to look after him, and does his duty in such fashion that the most fire-eating desperado from across the border falls into the line of law. But apart from the gunman, this village presented exactly the same queer cabins, strange signs, and gambling-rooms which the great American master has made so familiar to us.

And now we were homeward bound! Back through Edmonton, back through Winnipeg, back through that young giant, Fort William—but not back across the Great Lakes. Instead of that transit we took train, by the courtesy of the Canadian Pacific, round the northern shore of Superior, a beautiful wooded desolate country, which, without minerals, offers little prospect for the future. Some 200 miles north of it, the Grand Trunk, that enterprising pioneer of empire, has opened up another line which extends for a thousand miles, and should develop a new corn and lumber district. Canada is like an expanding flower; wherever you look you see some fresh petal unrolling.

We spent three days at Algonquin Park. This place is within easy distance of Montreal or Ottawa, and should become a resort of British fishermen and lovers of nature. After all, it is little more than a week from London, and many a river in Finland takes nearly as long to reach. There is good hotel accommodation, and out of the thousand odd lakes in this enormous natural preserve one can find all sorts of fishing, though the best is naturally the most remote. I had no particular luck myself, but my wife caught an eight-pound trout, which Mr. Bartlett, the courteous superintendent of the park, mounted, so as to confound all doubters. Deer abound in the park, and the black bear is not uncommon, while wolves can often be heard howling in the night-time.

What will be the destiny of Canada? Some people talk as if it were in doubt. Personally, I have none upon the point. Canada will remain exactly as she is for two more generations. At the end of that time there must be reconsideration of the subject, especially on the part of Great Britain, who will find herself with a child as large as herself under the same roof....

Yes, it will remain exactly as it is for the remainder of this century. At the end of that time her population and resources will probably considerably exceed those of the Mother Land, and problems will arise which our children's children may find some difficulty in solving. As to the French-Canadian, he will always be a conservative force—let him call himself what he will. His occasional weakness for flying the French flag is not to be resented, but is rather a pathetic and sentimental tribute to a lost cause, like that which adorns every year the pedestal of Charles at Whitehall.

I had some presentiment of coming trouble during the time we were in Canada, though I never imagined that we were so close to the edge of a world-war. One incident which struck me forcibly was the arrival at Vancouver of a ship full of Sikhs who demanded to be admitted to Canada. This demand was resisted on account of the immigration laws. The whole incident seemed to me to be so grotesque—for why should sun-loving Hindoos force themselves upon Canada—that I was convinced some larger purpose lay behind it. That purpose was, as we can now see, to promote discord among the races under the British flag. There can be no doubt that it was German money that chartered that ship.

I had several opportunities of addressing large and influential Canadian audiences, and I never failed to insist upon the sound state of the home population.

CYRANO
DE BERGERAC

I T IS OFTEN FORGOTTEN that the massively nasally endowed hero of Edmond Rostand's Victorian play was based upon a real person, a poet and novelist who adopted the Gascon-sounding "de Bergerac" in order to enhance the legend of his noble birth. Contemporary accounts indicate that Cyrano de Bergerac (1619–1655) did, indeed, have a large nose; whether it was excessively large is, of course, a subjective matter. They also confirm that he was a stupendous swordsman, in an age when every man, it seems, would duel at the drop of an insult, real or imagined. During, for example, one eight-year stretch of the reign of Henri IV (the popular king of France who more than any other encouraged colonization of Quebec, and who reigned just prior to Cyrano's birth), more than two thousand "gentlemen" were slain in duels. Cyrano is known to have fought more than one hundred recorded duels, and probably many more, and he killed at least ten people in such contests.

His first book was published in 1654, just a year before he died, although poems and pamphlets had appeared sporadically before then. His reputation as a writer was larger than such a meagre output would justify, so it is believed that much of his work was circulated in manuscript. This is certainly true of his posthumously published, wickedly satirical novels *L'Autre monde; ou les états et empires de la lune* (1657) and *Les Etats et empires du soleil* (1662) which, along with his other work, was reprinted frequently until the beginning of the eighteenth century. The satirical novels were published as one volume in English in 1923 as *Voyages to the Moon and the Sun*, translated by the British novelist Richard Aldington.

The Age of Reason had little patience with Cyrano's flights of imagination and imaginary flights. Voltaire decried his writing as the work of a madman, and from 1699 to 1855 not a single edition of Cyrano's authorship was published in France. The resurrection of his fame began in 1844 when the famous French poet Théophile Gautier published his *Grotesques*, which contained a loosely researched brief life of de Bergerac. Many of the traits associated with Cyrano's name—his exemplary honour, chivalry, swordsmanship, and pride in his proboscis—were first accentuated by Gautier, were assumed to be true by later writers, and were immortalized by Rostand in his eponymous play in 1897.

The failure of Cyrano to publish in his own lifetime probably had much more to do with censorship than the literary taste of the day. Comparing de Bergerac's satirical intentions with such despotic Utopians as Sir Thomas More, the translator Richard Aldington makes this apposite observation:

> Now, Cyrano de Bergerac had no intention of creating one of these ideally unpleasant tyrannies. His purpose was similar to that of Rabelais and Swift. He wanted to satirise existing institutions, humbugs and prejudices; he wanted to mock at a literal belief in the Old Testament; he wanted to hold up to odium the fundamental villainy of man; and he wanted to convey amusingly a number of quasi-scientific and philosophical ideas which it was highly dangerous then to publish and still more dangerous to try to popularise. Even then Cyrano dared not publish the book in his lifetime; and it was mutilated when it appeared after his death. The censorship of the *ancien régime* was almost exactly the antithesis to the police interference of today; great licence in morals and personalities was allowed; obscenities and even blasphemies were tolerated, but when an author, however

eminent and serious, trenched upon the authority of the Church
or the State, or offered new ideas which seemed likely to prove
subversive, he was certain of persecution and punishment.

According to a noted scholar on Swift, de Bergerac's *Voyages to the
Moon and the Sun* "furnished more material for the composition of
[Jonathan Swift's] *Gulliver's Travels* than did the works of any other
author," and the *Voyage to the Moon* "must have been the model for
the adventures of Gulliver in Brobdingnag." The stopover in Quebec here described, brief but essential to the plot, marks one of the
earliest citations of Canada in enduring literature. It is a Canada
completely of the imagination; Cyrano de Bergerac never visited
North America.

---

from VOYAGES TO THE MOON
AND THE SUN

The moon was full, the sky clear, and the clock had just struck nine
as I was returning with four of my friends from a house near Paris.
Our wit must have been sharpened on the cobbles of the road for it
thrust home whichever way we turned it; distant as the moon was
she could not escape it. The various thoughts provoked in us by the
sight of that globe of saffron diverted us on the road and our eyes
were filled by this great luminary. Now one of us likened her to a
window in Heaven through which the glory of the blessed might be
faintly seen; then another, inspired by ancient fables, imagined that
Bacchus kept a tavern in Heaven and had hung out the full moon
for his sign; then another vowed that it was the block where Diana

set Apollo's ruffs; another exclaimed that it might well be the Sun himself who, having put off his rays at night, was watching through a hole what the world did when he was not there. For my part, said I, I am desirous to add my fancies to yours and without amusing myself with the witty notions you use to tickle time to make it run the faster, I think that the Moon is a world like this and that our world is their Moon. The company gratified me with a great shout of mirth.

"Perhaps in the same way," said I, "at this moment in the Moon they jest at some one who there maintains that this globe is a world."

But though I showed them that Pythagoras, Epicurus, Democritus and, in our own age, Copernicus and Kepler had been of this opinion, I did but cause them to strain their throats the more heartily.

This thought, whose boldness jumped with my humour, was strengthened by contradiction and sank so deep in me that all the rest of the way I was pregnant with a thousand definitions of the Moon of which I could not be delivered. By supporting this fantastic belief with serious reasoning I grew well-nigh persuaded of it. But hearken, reader, the miracle or accident used by Providence or Fortune to convince me of it.

I returned home and scarcely had I entered my room to rest after the journey when I found on my table an open book which I had not put there. I recognised it as mine, which made me ask my servant why he had taken it out of the book-case. I asked him but perfunctorily, for he was a fat Lorrainer, whose soul admitted of no exercise more noble than those of an oyster. He swore to me that either the Devil or I had put it there. For my own part I was sure I had not handled it for more than a year.

I glanced at it again; it was the works of Cardan; and though I had no idea of reading it I fell, as if directed to it, precisely upon a story told by this philosopher. He says that, reading one evening by candle-light, he perceived two tall old men enter through the closed door of his room and after he had asked them many questions they told him they were inhabitants of the Moon; which said, they disappeared. I remained so amazed to see a book brought there by itself as well as at the time and the leaf at which I found it open that I took this whole train of events to be an inspiration of God urging me to make known to men that the Moon is a world.

"What!" quoth I to myself, "after I have talked of a matter this very day, a book, which is perhaps the only one in a world that treats of this subject, flies down from the shelf on to my table, becomes capable of reason to the extent of opening at the very page of so marvellous an adventure and thereby supplies meditations to my fancy and an object to my resolution. Doubtless," I continued, "the two old men who appeared to that great man are the same who have moved my book and opened it at this page to spare themselves the trouble of making me the harangue they made Cardan. "But," I added, "how can I clear up this doubt if I do not go there? And why not?" I answered myself at once, "Prometheus of old went to Heaven to steal fire!"

These feverish outbursts were followed by the hope of making successfully such a voyage.

I shut myself up to achieve my purpose in a rather lonely country-house where, after I had flattered my fancy with several methods which might have borne me up there, I committed myself to the heavens in this manner:

I fastened all about me a number of little bottles filled with dew, and the heat of the Sun drawing them up carried me so high that at last I found myself above the loftiest clouds. But, since this attraction caused me to rise too rapidly and instead of my drawing nearer the Moon, as I desired, she seemed to me further off than when I started, I broke several of my bottles until I felt that my weight overbore the attraction and that I was falling towards the earth. My opinion was not wrong; for I reached ground sometime later when, calculating from the hour at which I had started, it ought to have been midnight. Yet I perceived that the Sun was then at the highest point above the horizon and that it was midday. I leave you to conjecture my surprise; indeed it was so great that not knowing how to explain this miracle I had the insolence to fancy that in compliment to my boldness God had a second time fixed the Sun in Heaven to light so glorious an enterprise. My astonishment increased when I found I did not recognise the country I was in, for it appeared to me that, having risen straight up, I ought to have landed in the place from which I had started. Encumbered as I was I approached a hut where I perceived some smoke and I was barely a pistol-shot from it when I found myself surrounded by a large number of savages. They appeared mightily surprised at meeting me; for I was the first, I think, they had ever seen dressed in bottles. And, to overthrow still more any explanation they might have given of this equipment, they saw that as I walked I scarcely touched the ground. They did not know that, at the least movement I gave my body, the heat of the midday sun-beams lifted me up with my dew; and if my bottles had been more numerous I should very likely have been carried into the air before their eyes. I tried to converse with them; but, as if terror had changed them into birds, in a twinkling they were lost to sight in the neighbouring woods. Nevertheless I caught one whose legs without doubt betrayed his intention. I asked him with much diffi-culty (for I was out of breath) how far it was from there to Paris, since when did people go naked in France and why they fled from me in such terror. This man to whom I spoke was an old man, yel-low as an olive, who cast himself at my knees, joined his hands above his head, opened his mouth and shut his eyes. He muttered for some time but as I could not perceive that he said anything I took his lan-guage for the hoarse babble of a dumb man.

Sometime afterwards I saw coming towards me a band of soldiers with drums beating and I noticed that two left the main body to reconnoitre me. When they were near enough to hear I asked them where I was.

"You are in France," replied they, "but who the Devil put you in this condition? How does it happen that we do not know you? Has the fleet arrived? Are you going to warn the Governor of it? Why have you divided your brandy into so many bottles?"

To all this I replied that the Devil had not put me in that condi-tion; that they did not know me because they could not know all men; that I did not know there were ships on the Seine; that I had no information to give Monsieur de Montbazon and that I was not carrying any brandy.

"Oh! Ho!" said they taking me by the arm, "you are pleased to be merry! The Governor will understand you!"

They carried me towards their main body as they spoke these words and I learned from them that I was indeed in France, but not in Europe, for I was in New France.

I was brought before the Viceroy, Monsieur de Montmagnie. He asked me my country, my name and my rank, and when I had satisfied him by relating the happy success of my voyage, whether he believed it or only feigned to believe it, he had the kindness to allot me a room in his house. I was happy to fall in with a man capable of lofty ideas, who was not scandalised when I said that the earth must have turned while I was above it, seeing that I had begun to rise two leagues from Paris and had fallen by an almost perpendicular line in Canada.

That evening just as I was going to bed he came into my room.

"I should not have interrupted your rest," said he, "had I not believed that a man who travels nine hundred leagues in half a day can easily do so without being weary. But you do not know," added he, "the merry dispute I have just had on your behalf with our Jesuit Fathers? They are convinced that you are a magician and the greatest mercy you can obtain from them is to pass for no more than an impostor. And, after all, this movement you assign to the Earth is surely some neat paradox? The reason I am not of your opinion is that although you may have left Paris yesterday you could still have reached this country to-day without the Earth having turned. For the Sun, which bore you up by means of your bottles, must have drawn you hither since, according to Ptolemy, Tycho Brahe, and modern philosophers it moves in a direction opposite to that in which you say the Earth moves. And then what probability have you for asserting that the Sun is motionless when we see it move, and that the Earth turns about its centre with such rapidity when we feel it firm beneath us?"...

"Why, tell me," said I, "do you understand better the nothing which is beyond it? Not at all. When you think of this nothing you imagine at least something like wind, something like air, and that is something; but if you do not comprehend infinity as a general idea you may conceive it at least in parts, for it is not difficult to imagine beyond the earth, air and fire that we see, more air and more earth. Infinity is simply a texture without bounds. If you ask me how these worlds were made, seeing that Holy Scripture speaks only of one created by God, I reply that it speaks only of ours because this is the only world God took the trouble to make with His own hand and all the others, whether we see them or do not see them, hanging in the azure of the universe, are dross thrown off by the suns. For how could these great fires continue if they were not united with matter to feed them? Well, just as fire casts off the ashes which choke it, just as gold in the crucible severs itself from the marcasite which lessens its purity, and just as our heart frees itself by vomiting from the indigestible humours which attack it; so the suns disgorge every day and purge themselves of the remnants of that matter which feeds their fire. But when these suns have altogether used up the matter which maintains them, you cannot doubt but that they will spread out on all sides to seek new fuel and will fall upon all the worlds they had thrown off before and particularly upon the nearest ones: Then these great fires again burning up all these bodies will again throw them off pell-mell on all sides as before, and being purified little by little they will begin to act as suns to these little worlds which they engender by casting them out of their spheres; doubtless it was this which made the disciples of Pythagoras predict a universal conflagration. This is not a ridiculous fancy; New France, where we are, produces a very convincing proof. This vast continent of America is one half of the Earth, and though our predecessors had sailed the ocean a thousand times they never discovered it. At that time it did not exist, any more than many islands, peninsulas and mountains which rise on our globe, until the rusts of the Sun being cleaned off and cast far away were condensed into balls heavy enough to be attracted towards the centre of our world, either little by little in small parts or perhaps suddenly in one mass. And this is not so unreasonable but that Saint Augustine would have applauded it had this country been discovered in his time, for this great personage whose genius was enlightened by the Holy Ghost asserts that in his time the Earth was as flat as an oven and that it swam upon the water like half of a cut orange; but if ever I have the honour to see you in France I will prove to you, by means of a very excellent perspective glass I have, that certain obscurities which from here seem to be spots are worlds in process of formation." My eyes were closing as I said this, which obliged the Viceroy to bid me good-night. The next and following days we had conversations of the like nature; but since some time afterwards the press of business in the Province interrupted our philosophizing I fell back the more eagerly on my plan of reaching the Moon.

As soon as the Moon rose I went off among the woods meditating on the contrivance and issue of my undertaking. At length on Saint John's Eve when those in the fort were debating whether or no they would aid the savages of the country against the Iroquois, I went off by myself behind our house to the summit of a little hill, where I acted as follows.

With a machine I had constructed, which I thought would lift me as much as I wanted, I cast myself into the air from the top of a rock; but because I had taken my measures badly I was tumbled roughly into the valley. Injured as I was I returned to my room without being discouraged. I took beef-marrow and greased all my body with it, for I was bruised from head to foot; and after I had comforted my heart with a bottle of cordial I returned to look for my machine, which I did not find, seeing that certain soldiers who had been sent into the forest to cut wood for the purpose of building a Saint John's fire to be lighted that evening, had come upon it by chance and carried it to the fort. After several hypotheses of what it might be they discovered the device of the spring, when some said they ought to bind around it a number of rockets because their rapid ascent would lift it high in the air, the spring would move its great wings and everyone would take the machine for a fire-dragon.

I sought it for a long time and at last I found it in the middle of the market-place of Quebec just as they were lighting it. The pain of seeing the work of my hands in such peril affected me so much that I rushed forward to grasp the arm of the soldier who was about to fire it. I seized his slow-match and cast myself furiously into the machine to break off the fireworks which surrounded it; but I came too late, for I had scarcely set my two feet in it when I was carried off into the clouds. The fearful horror that dismayed me did not so thoroughly overwhelm the faculties of my soul but that I could recollect afterwards all that happened to me at this moment. You must know then that the flame had no sooner consumed one line of rockets (for they had placed them in sixes by means of a fuse which ran along each half-dozen), when another set caught fire and then another, so that the blazing powder delayed my peril by increasing it. The rockets at length ceased through the exhaustion of material and, while I was thinking I should leave my head on the summit of a mountain, I felt (without my having stirred) my elevation continue; and my machine, taking lease of me, fell towards the Earth. This extraordinary adventure filled me with a joy so uncommon that in my delight at finding myself delivered from certain danger I was impudent enough to philosophize about it. I sought with my eyes and intelligence the reason for this miracle and I perceived that my flesh was still swollen and greasy with the marrow I had rubbed on it for the bruises caused by my fall. I knew that at the time the Moon was waning and that during this quarter she is wont to suck up the marrow of animals; she drank the marrow I had rubbed on myself with the more eagerness in that her globe was nearer me and that her strength was not weakened by any intervening clouds.

CHARLES DICKENS

I N *American Notes*, his published remarks about his first visit to this continent, Charles Dickens (1812–1870) is most positive and cordial about Canada, clearly more at home here than in America, and generally preferring Canada *vis-à-vis* the United States. However, in his private correspondence he is franker, still managing to praise grandiloquently the Canadians he encounters, but at times clearly showing that he is exhausted by his demanding tour.

He made one month-long excursion with his wife Catherine ("Kate") to Canada in 1842 following his lengthy first tour of the States, and he also made two brief stopovers during his second U.S.A. tour: at Halifax on November 18, 1867, to catch a boat for Boston, and at Niagara Falls on March 15, 1868. His euphoria at the sight of Niagara Falls—especially the Canadian Falls from the Canadian (or, since his visit was before Confederation, English) side—is genuine, as proved by his 1868 detour to see the cataract a second time, and by his dozens of letters to friends and acquaintances about his joy in first beholding them. On his first visit, he stayed for a remarkable ten days:

Tuesday, April 26, 1842.
Niagara Falls!!! (upon the *English* side)

I never in my life was in such a state of excitement as coming from Buffalo here, this morning.... At last when the train stopped, I saw two great white clouds rising up from the depths of the earth—nothing more. They rose up slowly, gently, majestically, into the air. I dragged Kate down a deep and slippery path leading to the ferry boat ... when we were seated in the boat, and crossing at the very foot of the cataract—then I began to feel what it was. Directly I had changed my clothes at the inn, I went out again, taking Kate with me, and hurried to the Horse-shoe fall. I went down alone, into the very basin. It would be hard for a man to stand nearer to God than he does there. There was a bright rainbow at my feet; and from that I looked up—great Heaven! to what a fall of bright green water! The broad, deep, mighty stream seems to die in the act of falling; and, from its unfathomable grave arises that tremendous ghost of spray and mist which is never laid, and has been haunting this place with the same dread solemnity—perhaps from the creation of the world.

April 29, 1842

To say anything about this wonderful place, would be sheer nonsense. It far exceeds my most sanguine expectations— although the impression on my mind has been, from the first, nothing but Beauty and Peace.

May 1, 1842

This is the only place we have had to ourselves since we left home.... Directly I arrived, I yearned to come over to the English side, and ordered the Ferryman out, in a pouring rain for that purpose. It fortunately happens that there really is no point of view to see the Falls from, properly, but this. They are under our windows. But in any case I should have come here.

You cannot conceive with what transports of joy I beheld an English Sentinel—though he didn't look much like one, I confess, with his boots outside his trousers, and a great fur cap on his head. I was taken dreadfully loyal after dinner, and drank the Queen's health in a bumper—in Port, too, and by no means bad Port—the first I had put to my lips since leaving home.

From Niagara, Dickens travelled to Toronto where he was appalled by the rabid Toryism (the bigwigs and fumbling authorities, aping what they thought were the manners of London gentry, dealt with the grievances igniting and lingering from the Rebellion of 1837 by wrapping themselves in patriotism and Empire jingo). Otherwise he was impressed with the hustle and bustle, and by the fact that some of the streets had gas lighting. In Montreal, he participated (on behalf of a charity) in a private theatrical, and then, two days later, acted on a public stage for the first time in his adult life. While from his correspondence it is obvious that he was looking forward to his Montreal thespian debut, it was with the notion of being part of an escapade, a lark. The success of the theatricals, though, obviously surprised him, and fired him to repeat the experience many times when he returned home, including a collaboration with Wilkie Collins in a drama set almost entirely in Canada, *The Frozen Deep*.

To the English writer Martin Tupper, who was planning his own tour of North America, Dickens wrote on March 19, 1850, "When I went to America, I did not take my children ... I cannot think of any place in America where I would like to leave my children, they being strangers to the air and soil.... But if I contemplated such a move, I should almost be inclined to leave mine in Canada—at Kingston or Montreal—surrounded by English...."

The following passage is from *American Notes*, published in 1842, and records Charles Dickens' unique impressions of some Canadian towns of the time. His shock at the Toryism of Toronto aside, he is clearly glad to be on British soil. Especially noteworthy is his contemplation of Canadian immigrants, for it suggests both his respect for the potential of the land, and that high moral tone which can make Dickens, at his worst, so obnoxious.

------

from AMERICAN NOTES

We were running (as we thought) into Halifax Harbour, on the fifteenth night, with little wind and a bright moon—indeed, we had made the Light at its outer entrance, and put the pilot in charge—when suddenly the ship struck upon a bank of mud. An immediate rush on deck took place of course; the sides were crowded in an instant; and for a few minutes we were in as lively a state of confusion as the greatest lover of disorder would desire to see. The passengers, and guns, and water-casks, and other heavy matters, being all huddled together aft, however, to lighten her in the head, she was soon got off; and after some driving on towards an uncomfortable line of objects (whose vicinity had been announced very early in the disaster by a loud cry of "Breakers a-head!") and much backing of paddles, and heaving of the lead into a constantly decreasing depth of water, we dropped anchor in a strange outlandish-looking nook which nobody on board could recognise, although there was land all about us, and so close that we could plainly see the waving branches of the trees.

It was strange enough, in the silence of midnight, and the dead stillness that seemed to be created by the sudden and unexpected stoppage of the engine which had been clanking and blasting in our ears incessantly for so many days, to watch the look of blank astonishment expressed in every face: beginning with the officers, tracing it through all the passengers, and descending to the very stokers and furnacemen, who emerged from below, one by one, and clustered together in a smoky group about the hatchway of the engine-room, comparing notes in whispers. After throwing up a few rockets and firing signal guns in the hope of being hailed from the land, or at least of seeing a light—but without any other sight or sound presenting itself—it was determined to send a boat on shore. It was amusing to observe how very kind some of the passengers were, in volunteering to go ashore in this same boat: for the general good, of course: not by any means because they thought the ship in an unsafe position, or contemplated the possibility of her heeling over in case the tide were running out. Nor was it less amusing to remark how desperately unpopular the poor pilot became in one short minute. He had had his passage out from Liverpool, and during the whole voyage had been quite a notorious character, as a teller of anecdotes and cracker of jokes. Yet here were the very men who had laughed the loudest at his jests, now flourishing their fists in his face, loading him with imprecations, and defying him to his teeth as a villain!

The boat soon shoved off, with a lantern and sundry blue lights on board; and in less than an hour returned; the officer in command bringing with him a tolerably tall young tree, which he had plucked up by the roots, to satisfy certain distrustful passengers whose minds misgave them that they were to be imposed upon and shipwrecked, and who would on no other terms believe that he had been ashore, or had done anything but fraudulently row a little way into the mist, specially to deceive them and compass their deaths. Our captain had foreseen from the first that we must be in a place called the Eastern passage; and so we were. It was about the last place in the world in which we had any business or reason to be, but a sudden fog, and some error on the pilot's part, were the cause. We were surrounded by banks, and rocks, and shoals of all kinds, but had happily drifted, it seemed, upon the only safe speck that was to be found thereabouts. Eased by this report, and by the assurance that the tide was past the ebb, we turned in at three o'clock in the morning.

I was dressing about half-past nine next day, when the noise above hurried me on deck. When I had left it overnight, it was dark, foggy, and damp, and there were bleak hills all round us. Now, we were gliding down a smooth, broad stream, at the rate of eleven miles an hour: our colours flying gaily; our crew rigged out in their smartest clothes; our officers in uniform again; the sun shining as on a brilliant April day in England; the land stretched out on either side, streaked with light patches of snow; white wooden houses; people at their doors; telegraphs working; flags hoisted; wharfs appearing; ships; quays crowded with people; distant noises; shouts; men and boys running down steep places towards the pier: all more bright and gay and fresh to our unused eyes than words can paint them. We came to a wharf, paved with uplifted faces; got alongside, and were made fast, after some shouting and straining of cables; darted, a score of us along the gangway, almost as soon as it was thrust out to meet us, and before it had reached the ship—and leaped upon the firm glad earth again!

I suppose this Halifax would have appeared an Elysium, though it had been a curiosity of ugly dullness. But I carried away with me a most pleasant impression of the town and its inhabitants, and have preserved it to this hour. Nor was it without regret that I came home, without having found an opportunity of returning thither, and once more shaking hands with the friends I made that day.

It happened to be the opening of the Legislative Council and General Assembly, at which ceremonial the forms observed on the commencement of a new Session of Parliament in England were so closely copied, and so gravely presented on a small scale, that it was like looking at Westminster through the wrong end of a telescope....

We lay there seven hours, to deliver and exchange the mails. At length, having collected all our bags and all our passengers (including two or three choice spirits, who, having indulged too freely in oysters and champagne, were found lying insensible on their backs in unfrequented streets), the engines were again put in motion, and we stood off for Boston....

The time of leaving Toronto for Kingston is noon. By eight o'clock next morning, the traveller is at the end of his journey, which is performed by steamboat upon Lake Ontario, calling at Port Hope and Coburg, the latter a cheerful thriving little town. Vast quantities of flour form the chief item in the freight of these vessels. We had no fewer than one thousand and eighty barrels on board, between Coburg and Kingston.

The latter place, which is now the seat of government in Canada, is a very poor town, rendered still poorer in the appearance of its market-place by the ravages of a recent fire. Indeed, it may be said of Kingston, that one half of it appears to be burnt down and the other half not to be built up. The Government House is neither elegant nor commodious, yet it is almost the only house of any importance in the neighbourhood.

There is an admirable jail here, well and wisely governed, and excellently regulated, in every respect. The men were employed as shoemakers, ropemakers, blacksmiths, tailors, carpenters, and stonecutters; and in building a new prison, which was pretty far advanced toward completion. The female prisoners were occupied in needlework. Among them was a beautiful girl of twenty, who had been there nearly three years. She acted as bearer of secret despatches for the self-styled Patriots on Navy Island, during the Canadian Insurrection: sometimes dressing as a girl, and carrying them in her stays; sometimes attiring herself as a boy, and secreting them in the lining of her hat. In the latter character she always rode as a boy would, which was nothing to her, for she could govern any horse that any man could ride, and could drive four-in-hand with the best whip in those parts. Setting forth on one of her patriotic missions, she appropriated to herself the first horse she could lay her hands on; and this offence had brought her where I saw her. She had quite a lovely face, though, as the reader may suppose from this sketch of her history, there was a lurking devil in her bright eye, which looked out pretty sharply from between her prison bars.

There is a bomb-proof fort here of great strength, which occupies a bold position, and is capable, doubtless, of doing good service; though the town is much too close upon the frontier to be long held, I should imagine, for its present purpose in troubled times. There is also a small navy-yard, where a couple of Government steamboats were building, and getting on vigorously.

We left Kingston for Montreal on the tenth of May, at half-past nine in the morning, and proceeded in a steamboat down the St. Lawrence River. The beauty of this noble stream at almost any point, but especially in the commencement of this journey when it winds its way among the Thousand Islands, can hardly be imagined. The number and constant successions of these islands, all green and richly wooded; their fluctuating sizes, some so large that for half an hour together one among them will appear as the opposite bank of the river, and some so small that they are mere dimples on its broad bosom; their infinite variety of shapes; and the numberless combinations of beautiful forms which the trees growing on them present: all form a picture fraught with uncommon interest and pleasure.

In the afternoon we shot down some rapids where the river boiled and bubbled strangely, and where the force and headlong violence of the current were tremendous. At seven o'clock we reached Dickenson's Landing, whence travellers proceed for two or three hours by stage-coach: the navigation of the river being rendered so dangerous and difficult in the interval, by rapids, that steamboats do not make the passage. The number and length of those portages, over which the roads are bad, and the travelling slow, render the way between the towns of Montreal and Kingston, somewhat tedious.

Our course lay over a wide, uninclosed tract of country at a little distance from the river-side, whence the bright warning lights on the dangerous parts of the St. Lawrence shone vividly. The night was dark and raw, and the way dreary enough. It was nearly ten o'clock when we reached the wharf where the next steamboat lay; and went on board, and to bed....

At eight we landed again, and travelled by a stagecoach for four hours through a pleasant and well-cultivated country, perfectly French in every respect: in the appearance of the cottages; the air, language, and dress of the peasantry; the sign-boards on the shops and taverns: and the Virgin's shrines, and crosses, by the wayside. Nearly every common labourer and boy, though he had no shoes to his feet, wore round his waist a sash of some bright colour: generally red: and the women, who were working in the fields and gardens, and doing all kinds of husbandry, wore, one and all, great flat straw hats with most capacious brims. There were Catholic Priests and Sisters of Charity in the village streets; and images of the Saviour at the corners of cross-roads, and in other public places.

At noon we went on board another steamboat, and reached the village of Lachine, nine miles from Montreal, by three o'clock. There, we left the river, and went on by land.

Montreal is pleasantly situated on the margin of the St. Lawrence, and is backed by some bold heights, about which there are charming rides and drives. The streets are generally narrow and irregular, as in most French towns of any age; but in the more modern parts of the city, they are wide and airy. They display a great variety of very good shops; and both in the town and suburbs there are many excellent private dwellings. The granite quays are remarkable for their beauty, solidity, and extent....

The steamboats to Quebec perform the journey in the night; that is to say, they leave Montreal at six in the evening, and arrive at Quebec at six next morning. We made this excursion during our stay in Montreal (which exceeded a fortnight), and were charmed by its interest and beauty.

The impression made upon the visitor by this Gibraltar of America: its giddy heights; its citadel suspended, as it were, in the air; its picturesque steep streets and frowning gateways; and the splendid views which burst upon the eye at every turn: is at once unique and lasting.

It is a place not to be forgotten or mixed up in the mind with other places, or altered for a moment in the crowd of scenes a traveller can recall. Apart from the realities of this most picturesque city, there are associations clustering about it which would make a desert rich in interest. The dangerous precipice along whose rocky front, Wolfe and his brave companions climbed to glory; the Plains of Abraham, where he received his mortal wound; the fortress so chivalrously defended by Montcalm; and his soldier's grave, dug for him while yet alive, by the bursting of a shell; are not the least among them, or among the gallant incidents of history. That is a noble Monument too, and worthy of two great nations, which perpetuates the memory of both brave generals, and on which their names are jointly written.

The city is rich in public institutions and in Catholic churches and charities, but it is mainly in the prospect from the site of the Old Government House, and from the Citadel, that its surpassing beauty lies. The exquisite expanse of country, rich in field and forest, mountain-height and water, which lies stretched out before the view, with miles of Canadian villages, glancing in long white streaks, like veins along the landscape; the motley crowd of gables, roofs, and chimney tops in the old hilly town immediately at hand; the beautiful St. Lawrence sparkling and flashing in the sunlight; and the tiny ships below the rock from which you gaze, whose distant rigging looks like spiders' webs against the light, while casks and barrels on their decks dwindle into toys, and busy mariners become so many puppets; all this, framed by a sunken window in the fortress and looked at from the shadowed room within, forms one of the brightest and most enchanting pictures that the eye can rest upon.

In the spring of the year, vast numbers of emigrants who have newly arrived from England or from Ireland, pass between Quebec and Montreal on their way to the backwoods and new settlements of Canada. If it be an entertaining lounge (as I very often found it) to take a morning stroll upon the quay at Montreal, and see them grouped in hundreds on the public wharfs about their chests and boxes, it is matter of deep interest to be their fellow-passenger on one of these steamboats, and mingling with the concourse, see and hear them unobserved.

The vessel in which we returned from Quebec to Montreal was crowded with them, and at night they spread their beds between decks (those who had beds, at least), and slept so close and thick about our cabin door, that the passage to and fro was quite blocked up. They were nearly all English; from Gloucestershire the greater part; and had had a long winter-passage out; but it was wonderful to see how clean the children had been kept, and how untiring in their love and self-denial all the poor parents were.

Cant as we may, and as we shall to the end of all things, it is very much harder for the poor to be virtuous than it is for the rich; and the good that is in them, shines the brighter for it. In many a noble mansion lives a man, the best of husbands and of fathers, whose private worth in both capacities is justly lauded to the skies. But bring him here, upon this crowded deck. Strip from his fair young wife her silken dress and jewels, unbind her braided hair, stamp early wrinkles on her brow, pinch her pale cheek with care and much privation, array her faded form in coarsely patched attire, let there be nothing but his love to set her forth or deck her out, and you shall put it to the proof indeed. So change his station in the world, that he shall see in those young things who climb about his knee: not records of his wealth and name: but little wrestlers with him for his daily bread; so many poachers on his scanty meal; so many units to divide his every sum of comfort, and farther to reduce its small amount....

Which of us shall say what he would be, if such realities, with small relief or change all through his days, were his! Looking round upon these people: far from home, houseless, indigent, wandering, weary with travel and hard living: and seeing how patiently they nursed and tended their young children: how they consulted ever their wants first, then half supplied their own; what gentle ministers of hope and faith the women were; how the men profited by their example; and how very, very seldom even a moment's petulance or harsh complaint broke out among them: I felt a stronger love and honour of my kind come glowing on my heart, and wished to God there had been many Atheists in the better part of human nature there, to read this simple lesson in the book of Life.

We left Montreal for New York again, on the thirtieth of May; crossing to La Prairie, on the opposite shore of the St. Lawrence, in a steamboat; we then took the railroad to St. John's, which is on the brink of Lake Champlain. Our last greeting in Canada was from the English officers in the pleasant barracks at that place (a class of gentlemen who had made every hour of our visit memorable by their hospitality and friendship); and with "Rule Britannia" sounding in our ears, soon left it far behind.

But Canada has held, and always will retain, a foremost place in my remembrance. Few Englishmen are prepared to find it what it is. Advancing quietly; old differences settling down, and being fast forgotten; public feeling and private enterprise alike in a sound and wholesome state; nothing of flush or fever in its system, but health and vigour throbbing in its steady pulse: it is full of hope and promise. To me—who had been accustomed to think of it as something left behind in the strides of advancing society, as something neglected and forgotten, slumbering and wasting in its sleep—the demand for labour and the rates of wages; the busy quays of Montreal; the vessels taking in their cargoes, and discharging them; the amount of shipping in the different ports; the commerce, roads, and public works, all made to last; the respectability and character of the public journals; and the amount of rational comfort and happiness which honest industry may earn: were very great surprises. The steamboats on the lakes, in their conveniences, cleanliness, and safety; in the gentlemanly character and bearing of their captains; and in the politeness and perfect comfort of their social regulations; are unsurpassed even by the famous Scotch vessels, deservedly so much esteemed at home. The inns are usually bad; because the custom of boarding at hotels is not so general here as in the States, and the British officers, who form a large portion of the society of every town, live chiefly at the regimental messes: but in every other respect, the traveller in Canada will find as good provision for his comfort as in any place I know.

WILKIE COLLINS

T HE ENGLISH NOVELIST Wilkie Collins (1824–1889), sometimes called the founder of the modern mystery story, was one
of the best friends of Charles Dickens, and a frequent contributor to
Dickens' magazine, *Household Words*. Wilkie Collins would later
become famous in his own right for his novels *The Woman in White*
and *The Moonstone*, but his friendship with Dickens was of immense
importance to his early success. The two men first met in 1851, and
their friendship deepened. While both were best known to the public for their fiction, they were drawn to each other by their mutual
affection for drama. And given Dickens' later adulterous involvement with Ellen Ternan, he was further attracted to Collins because
"Wilkie was unique in his ability to be both a relaxed and uncenso-
rious companion and a literary ally and collaborator who could
understand Dickens' aims...." Their joint exploration and probably regular delectation of the naughtier pleasures of London can be
gathered from coy references in their surviving correspondence.
They certainly enjoyed acting together in amateur theatricals and
they collaborated in the writing of plays intended originally for
small but elite audiences, later for audiences measured in the thousands.

One such drama, *The Frozen Deep*, is set, for most of its action, in
Canada. The brief first act, set in England, introduces the principals
and establishes the love interests. The second act is located in "the

Arctic" and the third and final act in a cave in Newfoundland. Dickens himself played Richard Wardour, one of the two leads, and Collins the other at the play's première at Dickens' home, Tavistock House, in London on January 6, 1857. The entire production was supervised by Boz (Dickens' popular nickname), and in it he introduced a level of naturalism never seen before on the British stage. The performances were considered outstanding and Dickens' death scenes made even men, the press noted with shock, weep openly. Drama critics for the daily newspapers and magazines were unanimous in describing the production as the high point of the 1857 theatrical year.

As a benefit for the widow of a suddenly deceased friend, the play was revived for a short summer season at the Gallery of Illustrations on Regent Street in London, where its opening night was a command performance attended by a select audience headed by no less than Queen Victoria, Prince Frederick of Prussia, William Makepeace Thackeray, Prince Leopold of Belgium, and Hans Christian Andersen. Evidently, the Queen was, if not amused, at least pleased by what she termed "the high moral tone." Her equerry further reported to the cast that "her Majesty particularly wishes that her high approval should be conveyed to Mr. Wilkie Collins." Hans Christian Andersen added his voice to the many who found Dickens' performance heart-stopping: "[it was] free from all those mannerisms one finds in England and France just in tragic parts ... the death scene so moving that I burst into tears at it."

Clamourings from other cities, and a desire to raise more money for his friend's widow, led Dickens and Collins to mount the play in late August 1857 in Manchester for three performances, and it was here that Dickens' "Canadian play" was to change his life for ever. Because of the large size and demands on the voice of the Manchester theatre, he asked a theatre manager to hire professional actresses for the female roles rather than employ, as Dickens usually had, women from his own family. The manager complied, and one of the women hired was an eighteen-year-old named Ellen Ternan—with whom Dickens fell achingly in love at the first rehearsal.

His passion was eventually reciprocated, and so began an affair that lasted for the rest of Dickens' time on earth. Her presence reigned over his emotions, dominating (some say damaging) the balance of his personal life. The encounter at the rehearsal for the Canadian play was to be equally life-changing (some say damaging) for Ternan. The relationship resulted in Ternan's disappearance from public view for the duration of the affair, while Dickens—caddishly, notoriously—threw over his wife, assigned care of his children to a relative, and arranged endless secret rendezvous with Ternan while all the time denying any contact with the woman.

Perhaps because of Ternan's galvanizing presence, Dickens acted on stage as never before. Wilkie Collins himself noted that:

> At Manchester this play was twice performed; on the second evening before three thousand people. This was, I think, the finest of all its representations. The extraordinary intelligence and enthusiasm of the great audience stimulated us all to do our best. Dickens surpassed himself. He literally electrified the audience.

Dickens' portrayal also affected Dickens. By his own admission, it was while acting as Richard Wardour, the protagonist of *The Frozen Deep*, that he began to examine the idea of a man being reborn via self-sacrifice, an idea which reached fruition soon after in *A Tale of Two Cities*.

Although Collins and Dickens were never again to act together in the play, the drama would not leave their lives. Dickens induced Collins into accompanying him to Doncaster shortly after the Manchester experience, ostensibly to research articles, but in reality so that he could rendezvous with Ellen Ternan, who was playing at a local theatre. Before the tryst could come to fruition, however, Dickens, apparently subconsciously motivated by a desire to re-enact his heroic role in *The Frozen Deep*, forced Collins to go hill-climbing up a notoriously dangerous mountain in the middle of a storm. The cold, damp, and darkness enshrouded them, and in their wanderings, Collins so sprained an ankle that he was unable to walk. Illness, even death by exposure, became a real possibility. Dickens described what then happened: "How I enacted Wardour over again in carrying him down, and what a business it was to get him down ... now I carry him to bed, and into and out of carriages, exactly like Wardour in private life."

Dickens' involvement with Collins' Canadian play was to change his life gigantically in other ways. The innate ham in Dickens (he had made brief theatrical appearances in his youth but the true ham was born at Montreal in 1842 when he made his first adult appearance on a public stage), given encouragement by the reviews of his Wardour performance, was now shamelessly unshackled by his decision to give several solo public readings of his own writing.

That the public readings were physically and mentally exhausting was part of their attraction to Dickens, for it allowed him to set aside the decomposed state of his marriage, and not examine too closely the nature of his infatuation with Ternan. In March 1858, he wrote to Collins:

> All day yesterday I was pursuing the Reading idea ... the domestic unhappiness remains so strong upon me that I can't write, and (waking) can't rest, one minute. I have never known a moment's peace or content, since the last night of *The Frozen Deep*....

Neither author had ever been to the Arctic or Newfoundland. Both made stops in Canada to see friends and give lectures: Dickens in 1842, Collins not until much later, in 1873. Nevertheless, both men were highly aware of this nation throughout the 1850s (when the play was written), due to a more compelling reason: the mystery of (and concomitant incessant discussions concerning) the disappearance of the Franklin expedition.

Searching for the Northwest Passage in the Canadian Arctic on behalf of the Crown, Franklin and his ships and crew had last been seen in 1845. Since they had provisions sufficient to last three years, a search for them was not started until 1848. Dozens of ships sought

Cast photograph (from The Gallery of Illustration production) of *The Frozen Deep*, 1857. Charles Dickens, seated foreground, in profile, and Wilkie Collins, leaning forward, between first and second rows. Courtesy of the Dickens House Museum, London.

news of the men; no news was found. Six years later, a Hudson's Bay factor encountered Inuit who related descriptions of a camp containing the half-eaten remains of thirty to forty white men; the natives led the factor to other Inuit who possessed items bearing the Franklin crest. The factor, without actually seeing the bodies, hastened to England with the traumatic news. It is a marker of the age that people at all levels responded, not with relief that the mystery of the disappearance had been resolved, but rather with anxiety, became obsessed with the alleged cannibalism, and whether gentlemen of British stock would ever stoop to such a "last resource." Today, it is difficult to appreciate the ferocity of Britain's obsession with the Franklin voyage: England had held its breath for years waiting for word of the expedition; speculation concerning its fate filled the newspapers and periodicals and subsumed party conversation. Now that word of the grisly end had arrived, the nation remained further beguiled by the Franklin voyage, conjecturing wildly about the officers, the ratings, the methods of survival, the time it took them to die.

Dickens was especially vigorous in his feelings about the issue, entering into correspondence with Lady Franklin, publishing articles, and issuing rhetoric, most of it, seen with the wisdom of hindsight, pathetically racist. He discounted, for example, the veracity of the Inuit on the grounds that they were mere savages and thus natural liars. He further maintained that it was inconceivable for British gentlemen to stoop to cannibalism, no matter how extreme the conditions: "In weighing the probabilities and improbabilities of the 'last resource,' the foremost question is—not the nature of the extremity; but, the nature of the men." Ultimately, for Dickens, "the frozen Arctic wastes were demonstrably a force that could cause the suspension of noble sentiments. Franklin was a witness to the faith, however, that a heroic man [could possess] a heart resistant to the pressure of such a force."

Recent scholarship indicates that Charles Dickens probably originated the idea for the play *The Frozen Deep*, although Collins wrote the first draft. Collins, still young and relatively unknown as an author, was staying with the Dickens family in France for a few weeks in March 1856, and it was during this vacation, during the midst of "Franklin fever," that the play was conceived as a thinly veiled speculation upon the behaviour of the Franklin officers. To augment their appearance as Arctic explorers, both writers grew beards, Collins keeping his for the rest of his life. Although Collins penned the first version of the play, Dickens substantially revised the work during rehearsals and following the opening night. The earliest extant edition of the play, the prompt-book, is in Dickens' hand.

Wilkie Collins chose to revise the script for a professional production in October 1866 that did not involve Dickens in any way. The event was a financial and aesthetic fiasco. Discouraged, or possibly embarrassed, Collins would allow no further productions of the play. He did, however, translate the play into prose—twice, and in both cases the tale was much better told. A shortened format permitted the narrative to be read from the stage in under two hours during his lecture tour of North America in 1873–4 and most audiences were left emotionally wrought. The abridged, lecture-tour version of the tale seems to have vanished. Ironically, at his major stopover in Canada, Toronto, he chose not to read *The Frozen Deep*. The final expanded version (reproduced in part below) appeared in book form following the lecture tour.

Toronto marked one of the longest stops of his tour. He arrived in the city from Montreal and, in a letter to a friend, gave a brief description of the common trinity of tourist sites. From other correspondence, we know that Collins spent a genuinely delightful Christmas week with his Canadian publishers, Hunter Rose. Wilkie Collins had become associated with the renowned firm in 1870 in an effort to halt the atrocious piracy of British and American titles by Canadian printers, an intellectual abuse permissible only because of the absence of an international copyright agreement. Hunter Rose issued unique Canadian editions of his work thereafter.

The following excerpts from *The Frozen Deep* are the prose equivalents of acts two and three of the original drama. Most of the tale is set in the Arctic, where the protagonists are ice-bound. Desperate to escape, they select certain men to go in search of rescue. Somehow—Canadians will be disappointed or amused to learn the miracle is never explained—the hero rows a boat to Newfoundland, and salvation. The narrative drive of the melodramatic plot comes from the love two men have for the same woman, Clara. One of the men, Richard Wardour, knows that he has lost his place in Clara's affections to an unknown rival, a rival to whom Clara is now engaged to be married. Enamoured but respectful of Clara's decision, Richard Wardour leaves on an expedition for the Canadian north vowing eternal love for Clara, and, should he ever meet him, death to his anonymous rival: "The time may come when I shall forgive *you*, but the man who has robbed me of you shall rue the day when you and he first met."

from THE FROZEN DEEP

Good-bye to England! Good-bye to inhabited and civilised regions of the earth!

Two years have passed since the voyagers sailed from their native shores. The enterprise has failed—the Arctic Expedition is lost and ice-locked in the Polar wastes. The good ships *Wanderer* and *Sea-Mew*, entombed in ice, will never ride the buoyant waters more. Stripped of their light timbers, both vessels have been used for the construction of huts, erected on the nearest land.

The largest of the two buildings which now shelter the lost men, is occupied by the surviving officers and crew of the *Sea-Mew*. On one side of the principal room are the sleeping-berths and the fire-place. The other side discloses a broad doorway (closed by a canvas screen), which serves as means of communication with an inner apartment, devoted to the superior officers. A hammock is slung to the rough raftered roof of the main room as an extra bed. A man, completely hidden by his bedclothes, is sleeping in the hammock. By the fireside there is a second man—supposed to be on the watch—fast asleep, poor wretch! at the present moment. Behind the sleeper stands an old cask, which serves for a table. The objects at present on the table are a pestle and mortar, and a saucepan full of dry bones of animals. In plain words, the dinner for the day. By way of ornament to the dull brown walls, icicles appear in the crevices of the timber, gleaming at intervals in the red firelight. No wind whistles outside the lonely dwelling—no cry of bird or beast is heard. Indoors and out of doors, the awful silence of the polar desert reigns, for the moment, undisturbed....

The first sound that broke the silence came from the inner apartment. An officer lifted the canvas screen in the hut of the *Sea-Mew*, and entered the main room. Cold and privation had sadly thinned the ranks. The commander of the ship—Captain Ebsworth—was dangerously ill. The first lieutenant was dead. An officer of the *Wanderer* filled their places for the time, with Captain Helding's permission. The officer so employed was—Lieutenant Crayford.

He approached the man at the fireside and awakened him.

"Jump up, Bateson! It's your turn to be relieved."

The relief appeared, rising from a heap of old sails at the back of the hut. Bateson vanished, yawning, to his bed. Lieutenant Crayford walked backwards and forwards briskly, trying what exercise would do towards warming his blood.

The pestle and mortar on the cask attracted his attention. He stopped and looked up at the man in the hammock.

"I must rouse the cook," he said to himself, with a smile. "That fellow little thinks how useful he is in keeping up my spirits. The most inveterate croaker and grumbler in the world—and yet, according to his own account, the only cheerful man in the whole ship's company. "John Want! John Want! Rouse up, there!"

A head rose slowly out of the bedclothes, covered with a red night-cap. A melancholy nose rested itself on the edge of the hammock. A voice, worthy of the nose, expressed its opinion of the Arctic climate in these words:

"Lord! Lord! here's all my breath on my blanket. Icicles, if you please, sir, all round my mouth and all over my blanket. Every time I have snored I've frozen something. When a man gets the cold into him to that extent that he ices his own bed, it can't last much longer. Never mind! *I* don't grumble."

Crayford tapped the saucepan of bones impatiently. John Want lowered himself to the floor—grumbling all the way—by a rope attached to the rafters at his bed head. Instead of approaching his superior officer and his saucepan he hobbled, shivering, to the fireplace, and held his chin as close as he possibly could over the fire. Crayford looked after him.

"Hullo! what are you doing there?"

"Thawing my beard, sir."

"Come here directly, and set to work on these bones."

John Want remained immovably attached to the fireplace, holding something else over the fire. Crayford began to lose his temper,

"What the devil are you about now?"

"Thawing my watch, sir. It's been under my pillow all night, and the cold has stopped it. Cheerful, wholesome, bracing sort of climate to live in, isn't it, sir? Never mind! I don't grumble."

"No; we all know that. Look here! Are these bones pounded small enough?"

John Want suddenly approached the lieutenant, and looked at him with an appearance of the deepest interest.

"You'll excuse me, sir," he said; "how very hollow your voice sounds this morning!"

"Never mind my voice. The bones! the bones!"

"Yes, sir—the bones. They'll take a trifle more pounding. I'll do my best with them, sir, for your sake."

"What do you mean?"

John Want shook his head, and looked at Crayford with a dreary smile.

"I don't think I shall have the honour of making much more bone soup for you, sir. Do you think yourself you'll last long, sir? I don't, saving your presence. I think about another week or ten days will do for us all. Never mind. I don't grumble."

He poured the bones into the mortar and began to pound them—under protest. At the same moment a sailor appeared, entering from the inner hut.

"A message from Captain Ebsworth, sir."

"Well?"

"The Captain is worse than ever with his freezing pains, sir. He wants to see you immediately."

"I will go at once. Rouse the doctor."...

John Want took himself and his saucepan into the kitchen. A moment later Crayford returned to the hut, and astonished Frank Aldersley by an unexpected question.

"Have you anything in your berth, Frank, that you set a value on?"

Frank looked puzzled.

"Nothing, that I set the smallest value on—when I am out of it," he replied. "What does your question mean?"

"We are almost as short of fuel as we are of provisions," Crayford proceeded. "Your berth will make good firing. I have directed Bateson to be here in ten minutes with his axe."

"Very attentive and considerate on your part," said Frank. "What is to become of me, if you please, when Bateson has chopped my bed into firewood?"

"Can't you guess?"

"I suppose the cold has stupefied me. The riddle is beyond my reading. Suppose you give me a hint?"

"Certainly. There will be beds to spare soon—there is to be a change at last in our wretched lives here. Do you see it now?"

Frank's eyes sparkled. He sprang out of his berth and waved his fur cap in triumph.

"See it?" he exclaimed; "of course I do! The exploring party is to start at last. Do I go with the expedition?"

"It is not very long since you were in the doctor's hands, Frank," said Crayford, kindly. "I doubt if you are strong enough yet to make one of the exploring party."

"Strong enough or not," returned Frank, "any risk is better than pining and perishing here. Put me down, Crayford, among those who volunteer to go."

"Volunteers will not be accepted in this case," said Crayford. "Captain Helding and Captain Ebsworth see serious objections, as we are situated, to that method of proceeding."

"Do they mean to keep the appointments in their own hands?" asked Frank. "I, for one, object to that."

"Wait a little," said Crayford. "You were playing backgammon the other day with one of the officers. Does the board belong to him or to you?"

"It belongs to me. I have got it in my locker here. What do you want with it?"

"I want the dice and the box for casting lots. The captains have arranged—most wisely, as I think—that Chance shall decide among us who goes with the expedition, and who stays behind in the huts. The officers and crew of the *Wanderer* will be here in a few minutes to cast the lots. Neither you nor any one can object to that way of settling the question. Officers and men alike take their chance together. Nobody can grumble."

"*I* am quite satisfied," said Frank. "But I know of one man among the officers who is sure to make objections."

"Who is the man?"

"You know him well enough too. The "Bear of the Expedition,"—Richard Wardour."

"Frank! Frank! you have a bad habit of letting your tongue run away with you. Don't repeat that stupid nickname when you talk of my good friend, Richard Wardour."

"Your good friend? Crayford! Your liking for that man amazes me."

Crayford laid his hand kindly on Frank's shoulder. Of all the officers of the *Sea-Mew*, Crayford's favourite was Frank.

"Why should it amaze you?" he asked. "What opportunities have you had of judging? You and Wardour have always belonged to different ships. I have never seen you in Wardour's society for five minutes together. How can you form a fair estimate of his character?"

"I take the general estimate of his character," Frank answered. "He has got his nickname because he is the must unpopular man in his ship. Nobody likes him—there must be some reason for that."

"There is only one reason for it," Crayford rejoined. "Nobody understands Richard Wardour. I am not talking at random. Remember I sailed from England with him in the *Wanderer*, and I was only transferred to the *Sea-Mew* long after we were locked up in the ice. I was Richard Wardour's companion on board ship for months, and I learnt there to do him justice. Under all his outward defects, I tell you there beats a great and generous heart. Suspend your opinion, my lad, until you know my friend as well as I do. No more of this now. Give me the dice and the box."

Frank opened his locker. At the same time, the silence of the snowy waste outside was broken by a shouting of voices hailing the hut—"*Sea-Mew*, a-hoy!" …

The sailor on watch opened the outer door. There, plodding over the ghastly white snow, were the officers of the *Wanderer* approaching the hut. There, scattered under the merciless black sky, were the crew, with the dogs and the sledges, waiting the word which was to start them on their perilous and doubtful journey.

Captain Helding, of the *Wanderer*, accompanied by his officers, entered the hut—in high spirits at the prospect of a change. Behind them, lounging in slowly by himself, was a dark, sullen, heavy-browed man. He neither spoke nor offered his hand to anybody; he was the one person present who seemed to be perfectly indifferent to the fate in store for him. This was the man whom his brother officers had nick-named the Bear of the Expedition. In other words—Richard Wardour.

Crayford advanced to welcome Captain Helding. Frank—remembering the friendly reproof which he had just received—passed over the other officers of the *Wanderer*, and made a special effort to be civil to Crayford's friend.

"Good morning, Mr. Wardour," he said. "We may congratulate each other on the chance of leaving this horrible place."

"*You* may think it horrible," Wardour retorted "I like it."

"Like it? Good heavens! why?"

"Because there are no women here."

Frank turned to his brother officers, without making any further advances in the direction of Richard Wardour. The Bear of the Expedition was more unapproachable than ever.

In the meantime, the hut had become thronged by the able-bodied officers and men of the two ships. Captain Helding, standing in the midst of them, with Crayford by his side, proceeded to explain the purpose of the contemplated expedition to the audience which surrounded him.

He began in these words:—

"Brother officers and men of the *Wanderer* and *Sea-Mew*, it is my duty to tell you, very briefly, the reasons which have decided

Captain Ebsworth and myself on despatching an exploring party in search of help.... It is my duty to remind you that this, the last place in which we have taken refuge, is far beyond the track of any previous expedition, and that consequently our chance of being discovered by any rescuing parties that may be sent to look after us is, to say the least of it, a chance of the most uncertain kind.... The plan proposed is, that a detachment of the able-bodied officers and men among us should set forth this very day, and make another effort to reach the nearest inhabited settlements, from which help and provisions may be despatched to those who remain here. The new direction to be taken and the various precautions to be adopted, are all drawn out ready. The only question now before us is—Who is to stop here, and who is to undertake the journey?"

The officers answered the question with one accord—"Volunteers!"

The men echoed their officers. "Aye, aye, volunteers."

Wardour still preserved his sullen silence. Crayford noticed him, standing apart from the rest, and appealed to him personally.

"Do you say nothing?" he asked.

"Nothing," Wardour answers. "Go or stay, it's all one to me."

"I hope you don't really mean that?" said Crayford.

"I do."

"I am sorry to hear it, Wardour."

Captain Helding answered the general suggestion in favour of volunteering by a question which instantly checked the rising enthusiasm of the meeting.

"Well," he said, "suppose we say volunteers. Who volunteers to stop in the huts?"

There was a dead silence. The officers and men looked at each other confusedly. The Captain continued.

"You see we can't settle it by volunteering. You all want to go. Every man among us who has the use of his limbs naturally wants to go. But what is to become of those who have not got the use of their limbs? Some of us must stay here and take care of the sick."

Everybody admitted that this was true.

"So we get back again," said the Captain, "to the old question—Who among the able-bodied is to go, and who is to stay? Captain Ebsworth says, and I say, let chance decide it. Here are dice. The numbers run as high as twelve—double sixes. All who throw under six, stay; all who throw over six, go. Officers of the *Wanderer* and the *Sea-Mew*, do you agree to that way of meeting the difficulty?"

All the officers agreed—with the one exception of Wardour, who still kept silence.

"Men of the *Wanderer* and *Sea-Mew*, your officers agree to cast lots. Do you agree too?"

The men agreed without a dissentient voice. Crayford handed the box and the dice to Captain Helding.

"You throw first, sir. Under six, 'Stay.' Over six, 'Go.'"

Captain Helding cast the dice; the top of the cask serving for a table. He threw seven.

"Go," said Crayford. "I congratulate you, sir. Now for my own chance." He cast the dice in his turn. Three. "Stay! Ah, well! well! If I can do my duty and be of use to others, what does it matter whether I go or stay? Wardour, you are next, in the absence of your first lieutenant."

Wardour prepared to cast without shaking the dice.

"Shake the box, man!" cried Crayford. "Give yourself a chance of luck!"

Wardour persisted in letting the dice fall out carelessly, just as they lay in the box.

"Not I!" he muttered to himself "I've done with luck." Saying those words, he threw down the empty box, and seated himself on the nearest chest, without looking to see how the dice had fallen.

Crayford examined them. "Six!" he exclaimed. "There! you have a second chance, in spite of yourself you are neither under nor over—you throw again."

"But!" growled the Bear. "It's not worth the trouble of getting up for. Somebody else throw for me." He suddenly looked at Frank. "You! you have got what the women call a lucky face."

Frank appealed to Crayford. "Shall I?"

"Yes, if he wishes it," said Crayford.

Frank cast the dice. "Five! He stays! Wardour, I am sorry I have thrown against you."

"Go or stay," reiterated Wardour, "it's all one to me. You will be luckier, young one, when you cast for yourself."

Frank cast for himself.

"Eight. Hurrah! I go!"

"What did I tell you?" said Wardour. "The chance was yours. You have thriven on my ill luck."

He rose, as he spoke, to leave the hut. Crayford stopped him.

"Have you anything particular to do, Richard?"

"What has anybody to do here?"

"Wait a little, then. I want to speak to you when this business is over."

"Are you going to give me any more good advice?"

"Don't look at me in that sour way, Richard. I am going to ask you a question about something which concerns yourself."

Wardour yielded without a word more. He returned to his chest, and cynically composed himself to slumber. The casting of the lots went on rapidly among the officers and men. In another half hour chance had decided the question of "Go" or "Stay" for all alike. The men left the hut. The officers entered the inner apartment for a last conference with the bed-ridden captain of the *Sea-Mew*. Wardour and Crayford were left together, alone....

Crayford touched his friend on the shoulder to rouse him. Wardour looked up, impatiently, with a frown.

"I was just asleep," he said. "Why do you wake me?"

"Look round you, Richard. We are alone."

"Well—and what of that?"

"I wish to speak to you privately, and this is my opportunity. You have disappointed and surprised me today. Why did you say it was all one to you whether you went or stayed? Why are you the only man among us who seems to be perfectly indifferent whether we are rescued or not?"

"Can a man always give a reason for what is strange in his manner or his words?" Wardour retorted.

"He can try," said Crayford quietly, "when his friend asks him."

Wardour's manner softened.

"That's true," he said. "I *will* try. Do you remember the first night at sea, when we sailed from England in the *Wanderer*?"

"As well as if it was yesterday."

"A calm, still night," the other went on, thoughtfully. "No clouds, no stars. Nothing in the sky but the broad moon, and hardly a ripple to break the path of light she made in the quiet water. Mine was the middle watch that night. You came on deck, and found me alone —"

He stopped. Crayford took his hand, and finished the sentence for him.

"Alone—and in tears."

"The last I shall ever shed," Wardour added bitterly.

"Don't say that. There are times when a man is to be pitied, indeed, if he can shed no tears. Go on, Richard."

Wardour proceeded—still following the old recollections, still preserving his gentler tones.

"I should have quarrelled with any other man who had surprised me at that moment," he said. "There was something, I suppose, in your voice, when you asked my pardon for disturbing me that softened my heart. I told you I had met with a disappointment which had broken me for life. There was no need to explain further. The only hopeless wretchedness in this world is the wretchedness that women cause."

"And the only unalloyed happiness," said Crayford, "the happiness that women bring."

"That may be your experience of them," Wardour answered. "Mine is different. All the devotion, the patience, the humility, the worship that there is in man I laid at the feet of a woman. She accepted the offering as women do—accepted it easily, gracefully, unfeelingly—accepted it as a matter of course. I left England to win a high place in my profession before I dared to win her. I braved danger and faced death. I staked my life in the fever-swamps of

Africa to gain the promotion that I only desired for her sake—and gained it. I came back to give her all, and to ask nothing in return but to rest my weary heart in the sunshine of her smile. And her own lips—the lips I had kissed at parting—told me that another man had robbed me of her. I spoke but few words when I heard that confession, and left her for ever. 'The time may come,' I told her, 'when I shall forgive *you*. But the man who has robbed me of you shall rue the day when you and he first met.' Don't ask me who he was! I have yet to discover him. The treachery had been kept secret; nobody could tell me where to find him; nobody could tell me who he was. What did it matter? When I had lived out the first agony, I could rely on myself—I could be patient and bide my time."

"Your time? What time?"

"The time when I and that man shall meet, face to face. I knew it then; I know it now—it was written on my heart then, it is written on my heart now—we two shall meet and know each other!... Here in the freezing cold, or away in the deadly heat—in battle or in shipwreck—in the face of starvation, under the shadow of pestilence—I, though hundreds are falling round me, I shall live! live for the coming of one day! live for the meeting with one man!"

... Bateson—appointed to chop Frank's bed-place into firing— appeared punctually with his axe. Wardour, without a word of warning, snatched the axe out of the man's hand.

"What was this wanted for?" he asked.

"To cut up Mr. Aldersley's berth there into firing, sir."

"I'll do it for you! I'll have it down in no time!" He turned to Crayford. "You needn't be afraid about me, old friend. I am going to do the right thing. I am going to tire my body and rest my mind."

The evil spirit in him was plainly subdued—for the time at least. Crayford took his hand in silence, and then (followed by Bateson) left him to his work....

Axe in hand, Wardour approached Frank's bed-place.

"If I could only cut the thoughts out of me," he said to himself, "as I am going to cut the billets out of this wood!" He attacked the bed-place with the axe like a man who well knew the use of his instrument....

A long strip of wood fell to his axe—long enough to require cutting, in two. He turned it, and stooped over it. Something caught his eye—letters carved in the wood. He looked closer.

The letters were very faintly and badly cut. He could only make out the first three of them; and, even of those, he was not quite certain. They looked like C.L.A.—if they looked like anything. He threw down the strip of wood irritably.

"Damn the fellow (whoever he is) who cut this! Why should he carve that name, of all the names in the world?"

He paused, considering—then determined to go on again with his self-imposed labour. He was ashamed of his own outburst. He looked eagerly for the axe. "Work, work! Nothing for it but work." He found the axe, and went on again.

He cut out another plank.

He stopped, and looked at it suspiciously.

There was carving again on this plank. The letters F. and A. appeared on it.

He put down the axe. There were vague misgivings in him which he was not able to realise. The state of his own mind was fast becoming a puzzle to him.

"More carving," he said to himself. "That's the way these young idlers employ their long hours. F.A.? Those must be his initials—Frank Aldersley. Who carved the letters on the other plank? Frank Aldersley, too?"

He turned the piece of wood in his hand nearer to the light, and looked lower down it. More carving again, lower down! Under the initials F. A. were two more letters—C.B.

"C.B.?" he repeated to himself. "His sweetheart's initials, I suppose! Of course—at his age—his sweetheart's initials."

He paused once more. A spasm of inner pain showed the shadow of its mysterious passage outwardly on his face.

"*Her* cypher is a C.B.," he said, in low broken tones. "C.B.—Clara Burnham."

He waited, with the plank in his hand; repeating the name over and over again, as if it was a question he was putting, to himself.

"Clara Burnham? Clara Burnham?"

He dropped the plank and turned deadly pale in a moment. His eyes wandered furtively backwards and forwards between the strip of wood on the floor and the half-demolished berth. "O God! what has come to me now?" he said to himself, in a whisper. He snatched up the axe with a strange cry—something between rage and terror. He tried—fiercely, desperately tried—to go on with his work. No! strong as he was, he could not use the axe. His hands were helpless; they trembled incessantly. He went to the fire; he held his hands over it. They still trembled incessantly; they infected the rest of him. He shuddered all over. He knew fear. His own thoughts terrified him.

"Crayford!" he cried out. "Crayford! come here, and let's go hunting."

No friendly voice answered him. No friendly face showed itself at the door. An interval passed, and there came over him another change. He recovered his self-possession almost as suddenly as he had lost it. A smile—a horrid, deforming, unnatural smile—spread slowly, stealthily, devilishly over his face. He left the fire; he put the axe away softly in a corner; he sat down in his old place, deliberately self-abandoned to a frenzy of vindictive joy. He had found the man! There, at the end of the world—there, at the last fight of the Arctic voyagers against starvation and death—he had found the man!

The minutes passed.

He became conscious, on a sudden, of a freezing stream of air pouring into the room.

He turned, and saw Crayford opening the door of the hut. An officer was behind him. Wardour rose eagerly and looked over Crayford's shoulder.

Was it—could it be—the man who had carved the letters on the plank? Yes! Frank Aldersley!... Captain Helding and the officers who were to leave with the exploring party, returned to the main room on their way out. Seeing Crayford, Captain Helding stopped to speak to him.

"I have a casualty to report," said the captain, "which diminishes our numbers by one. My second lieutenant, who was to have joined the exploring party, has had a fall on the ice. Judging by what the quartermaster tells me, I am afraid the poor fellow has broken his leg."

"I will supply his place," cried a voice at the other end of the hut.

Everybody looked round. The man who had spoken was Richard Wardour.

Crayford instantly interfered—so vehemently as to astonish all who heard him.

"No!" he said. "Not you, Richard! not you!"

"Why not?" Wardour asked sternly.

"Why not, indeed?" added Captain Helding. "Wardour is the very man to be useful on a long march. He is in perfect health, and he is the best shot among us. I was on the point of proposing him myself."

Crayford failed to show his customary respect for his superior officer. He openly disputed the Captain's conclusion.

"Wardour has no right to volunteer," he rejoined. "It has been settled, Captain Helding, that chance shall decide who is to go and who is to stay."

"And chance has decided it," cried Wardour. Do you think we are going to cast the dice again, and give an officer of the *Sea-Mew* a chance of replacing an officer of the *Wanderer*? There is a vacancy in our party, not in yours; and we claim the right of filling it as we please. I volunteer, and my captain backs me. Whose authority is to keep me here after that?"

"Gently, Wardour," said Captain Helding. "A man who is in the right can afford to speak with moderation." He turned to Crayford. "You must admit yourself," he continued, "that Wardour is right this time. The missing man belongs to my command, and in common justice one of my officers ought to supply his place."

It was impossible to dispute the matter further. The dullest man present could see that the captain's reply was unanswerable. In sheer despair, Crayford took Frank's arm and led him aside a few steps.

The last chance left of parting the two men was the chance of appealing to Frank.

"My dear boy," he began, "I want to say one friendly word to you on the subject of your health, I have already, if you remember, expressed my doubts whether you are strong enough to make one of an exploring party. I feel those doubts more strongly than ever at this moment. Will you take the advice of a friend who wishes you well?"

Wardour had followed Crayford. Wardour roughly interposed before Frank could reply.

"Let him alone!"

Crayford paid no heed to the interruption. He was too earnestly bent on withdrawing Frank from the Expedition to notice anything that was said or done by the persons about him.

"Don't, pray don't, risk hardships which you are unable to bear!" he went on entreatingly. "Your place can be easily filled. Change your mind, Frank. Stay here with me."

Again Wardour interfered. Again he called out, "Leave him alone!" more roughly than ever. Still deaf and blind to every consideration but one, Crayford pressed his entreaties on Frank.

"You owned yourself just now that you were not well seasoned to fatigue," he persisted. "You feel (you must feel) how weak that last illness has left you? You know (I am sure you know) how unfit you are to brave exposure to cold and long marches over the snow."

Irritated beyond endurance by Crayford's obstinacy—seeing, or thinking he saw, signs of yielding in Frank's face—Wardour so far forgot himself as to seize Crayford by the arm and attempt to drag him away from Frank. Crayford turned and looked at him.

"Richard," he said, very quietly, "you are not yourself. I pity you. Drop your hand."

Wardour relaxed his hold with something of the sullen submission of a wild animal to its keeper. The momentary silence which followed gave Frank an opportunity of speaking at last.

"I am gratefully sensible, Crayford," he began, "of the interest which you take in me —"

"And you will follow my advice?" Crayford interposed eagerly.

"My mind is made up, old friend," Frank answered, firmly and sadly. "Forgive me for disappointing you. I am appointed to the Expedition. With the Expedition I go." He moved nearer to Wardour. In his innocence of all suspicion, he clapped Wardour heartily on the shoulder. "When I feel the fatigue," said poor simple Frank, "you will help me, comrade—won't you? Come along!"

Wardour snatched his gun out of the hands of the sailor who was carrying it for him. His dark face became suddenly irradiated with a terrible joy.... Over the snow and over the ice! "Come! where no human footsteps have ever trodden and where no human trace is ever left...."

Blindly, instinctively, Crayford made an effort to part them. His brother officers, standing near, pulled him back. They looked at each other anxiously. The merciless cold, striking its victims in various ways, had struck in some instances at their reason first. Everybody loved Crayford. Was he, too, going on the dark way that others had taken before him? They forced him to seat himself on one of the lockers. "Steady, old fellow!" they said kindly—"steady!" Crayford yielded, writhing inwardly under the sense of his own helplessness. What in God's name could he do? Could he denounce Wardour to Captain Helding on bare suspicion—without so much as the shadow of a proof to justify what he said? The captain would decline to insult one of his officers by even mentioning the monstrous accusation to him. The captain would conclude, as others had already concluded, that Crayford's mind was giving way under stress of cold and privation. No hope—literally, no hope now but in the numbers of the expedition. Officers and men, they all liked Frank. As long as they could stir hand or foot they would help him out the way—they would see that no harm came to him.

The word of command was given; the door was thrown open; the hut emptied rapidly. Over the merciless white snow—under the merciless black sky—the exploring party began to move. The sick and helpless men, whose last hope of rescue centred in their departing messmates, cheered faintly. Some few whose days were numbered sobbed and cried like women. Frank's voice faltered as he turned back at the door to say his last words to the friend who had been a father to him.

"God bless you, Crayford!"

Crayford broke away from the officers near him, and, hurrying forward, seized Frank by both hands. Crayford held him as if he would never let him go.

"God preserve you, Frank! I would give all I have in the world to be with you. Good-bye! Good-bye!"

Frank waved his hand—dashed away the tears that were gathering in his eyes—and hurried out. Crayford called after him, the last, the only, warning, that he could give:

"While you can stand, keep with the main body, Frank!"

Wardour, waiting till the last—Wardour, following Frank through the snowdrift—stopped, stepped back, and answered Crayford at the door:

"While he can stand he keeps with Me."

Alone! alone on the Frozen Deep!

The Arctic sun is rising dimly in the dreary sky. The beams of the cold northern moon, mingling strangely with the dawning light, clothe the snowy plains in hues of livid grey. An ice-field on the far horizon is moving slowly southward in the spectral light. Nearer, a stream of open water rolls its slow black waves past the edges of the ice. Nearer still, following the drift, an iceberg rears its crags and pinnacles to the sky; here, glittering in the moonbeams; there, looming dim and ghostlike in the ashy light.

Midway on the long sweep of the lower slope of the iceberg, what objects rise and break the desolate monotony of the scene? In this awful solitude can signs appear which tell of human life? Yes! The black outline of a boat just shows itself, hauled up on the berg. In an ice-cavern behind the boat, the last red embers of a dying fire flicker from time to time over the figures of two men. One is seated, resting his back against the side of the cavern. The other lies prostrate with his head on his comrade's knee. The first of these men is awake, and thinking. The second reclines, with his still white face turned up to

the sky—sleeping or dead. Days and days since, these two have
fallen behind on the march of the Expedition of Relief. Days and
days since, these two have been given up by their weary and failing
companions as doomed and lost. He who sits thinking is Richard
Wardour. He who lies sleeping or dead is Frank Aldersley.

The iceberg drifts slowly: over the black water: through the ashy
light. Minute by minute the dying fire sinks. Minute by minute the
deathly cold creeps nearer and nearer to the lost men.

Richard Wardour rouses himself from his thoughts, looks at the
still white face beneath him, and places his hand on Frank's heart. It
still beats feebly. Give him his share of the food and fuel still stored
in the boat, and Frank may live through it. Leave him neglected
where he lies; and his death is a question of hours, perhaps minutes—who knows?

Richard Wardour lifts the sleeper's head and rests it against the
cavern side. He goes to the boat and returns with a billet of wood.
He stoops to place the wood on the fire, and stops. Frank is dreaming, and murmuring in his dream. A woman's name passes his lips.
Frank is in England again—at the ball—whispering to Clara the
confession of his love.

Over Richard Wardour's face there passes the shadow of a deadly
thought. He rises from the fire; he takes the wood back to the boat.
His iron strength is shaken, but it still holds out. They are drifting
nearer and nearer to the open sea. He can launch the boat without
help; he can take the food and the fuel with him. The sleeper on the
iceberg is the man who has robbed him of Clara—who has wrecked
the hope and the happiness of his life. Leave the man in his sleep,
and let him die!

So the Tempter whispers. Richard Wardour tries his strength on
the boat. It moves; he has got it under control. He stops, and looks
round. Beyond him is the open sea. Beneath him is the man who has
robbed him of Clara. The shadow of the deadly thought grows and
darkens over his face. He waits with his hands on the boat—waits
and thinks.

The iceberg drifts slowly: over the black water: through the ashy light. Minute by minute the dying fire sinks. Minute by minute the deathly cold creeps nearer to the sleeping man. And still Richard Wardour waits—waits and thinks....

Once more the open Sea—the sea whose waters break on the shores of Newfoundland! An English steamship lies at anchor in the offing. The vessel is plainly visible through the open doorway of a large boat-house on the shore; one of the buildings attached to a fishing-station on the coast of the island.

The only person in the boat-house at this moment, is a man in the dress of a sailor. He is seated on a chest, with a piece of cord in his hand, looking out idly at the sea. On the rough carpenter's table near him lies a strange object to be left in such a place—a woman's veil.

What is the vessel lying at anchor in the offing?

The vessel is the *Amazon,*—despatched from England to receive the surviving officers and men of the Arctic Expedition. The meeting has been successfully effected, on the shores of North America, three days since. But the homeward voyage has been delayed by a storm which has driven the ship out of her course. Taking advantage, on the third day, of the first returning calm, the commander of the *Amazon* has anchored off the coast of Newfoundland, and has sent ashore to increase his supplies of water before he sails for England. The weary passengers have landed for a few hours, to refresh themselves after the discomforts of the tempest. Among them are the two ladies. The veil left on the table in the boat-house is Clara's veil.

And who is the man sitting on the chest, with the cord in his hand, looking out idly at the sea? The man is the only cheerful person in the ship's company. In other words—John Want.

Still reposing on the chest, our friend who never grumbles, is surprised by the sudden appearance of a sailor at the boat-house door.

"Look sharp with your work, there, John Want!" says the sailor; "Lieutenant Crayford is just coming to look after you."...

"Have you done cording that box?"

This time the voice is a voice of authority—the man at the doorway is Lieutenant Crayford himself. John Want answers his officer in his own cheerful way.

"I've done it as well as I can, sir—but the damp of this place is beginning to tell upon our very ropes. I say nothing about our lungs—I only say our ropes."

Crayford answers sharply. He seems to have lost his former relish for the humour of John Want.

"Pooh! To look at your wry face, one would think that our rescue from the Arctic regions was a downright misfortune. You deserve to be sent back again.".…

Having entered that unanswerable protest, John Want shouldered the box, and drifted drearily out of the boat-house.

Left by himself, Crayford looked at his watch, and called to a sailor outside.

"Where are the ladies?" he asked.

"Mrs. Crayford is coming this way, sir. She was just behind you when you came in."

"Is Miss Burnham with her?"

"No, sir; Miss Burnham is down on the beach with the passengers. I heard the young lady asking after you, sir."

"Asking after me?" Crayford considered with himself, as he repeated the words. He added, in lower and graver tones, "You had better tell Miss Burnham you have seen me here."

The man made his salute and went out. Crayford took a turn in the boat-house.

Rescued from death in the Arctic wastes, and reunited to a beautiful wife, the lieutenant looked, nevertheless, unaccountably anxious and depressed. What could he be thinking of? He was thinking of Clara.

On the first day when the rescued men were received on board the *Amazon*, Clara had embarrassed and distressed, not Crayford only, but the other officers of the Expedition as well, by the manner in which she questioned them on the subject of Frank Aldersley and Richard Wardour. She had shown no signs of dismay or despair when she heard that no news had been received of the two missing men. She had even smiled sadly to herself, when Crayford (out of compassionate regard for her, declared that he and his comrades had not given up the hope of seeing Frank and Wardour yet. It was only when the lieutenant had expressed himself in those terms—and when he had apparently succeeded in dismissing the painful subject—that Clara had startled every one present by announcing that she had something to say in relation to Richard and Frank, which had not been said yet. Though she spoke guardedly, her next words revealed suspicions of foul play lurking in her mind—exactly reflecting similar suspicions lurking in Crayford's mind—which so distressed the lieutenant, and so surprised his comrades, as to render them quite incapable of answering her. The warnings of the storm which shortly afterwards broke over the vessel, were then visible in sea and sky. Crayford made them his excuse for abruptly leaving the cabin in which the conversation had taken place. His brother officers, profiting by his example, pleaded their duties on deck, and followed him out.

On the next day, and the next, the tempest still raged, and the passengers were not able to leave their state-rooms. But now, when the weather had moderated and the ship had anchored—now, when officers and passengers alike were on shore, with leisure time at their disposal—Clara had opportunities of returning to the subject of the lost men, and of asking questions in relation to them, which would make it impossible for Crayford to plead an excuse for not answering her. How was he to meet those questions? How could he still keep her in ignorance of the truth?

These were the reflections which now troubled Crayford, and which presented him, after his rescue, in the strangely inappropriate character of depressed and anxious man. His brother officers, as he well knew, looked to him to take the chief responsibility. If he declined to accept it, he would instantly confirm the horrible suspicion in Clara's mind. The emergency must be met; but how to meet it—at once honourably and mercifully—was more than Crayford could tell. He was still lost in his own gloomy thoughts, when his wife entered the boat-house. Turning to look at her, he saw his own perturbations and anxieties plainly reflected in Mrs. Crayford's face.

"Have you seen anything of Clara?" he asked. "Is she still on the beach?"

"She is following me to this place," Mrs. Crayford replied. "I have been speaking to her this morning. She is just as resolute as ever to insist on your telling her of the circumstances under which Frank is missing. As things are, you have no alternative but to answer her."

"Help me to answer her, Lucy. Tell me, before she comes in, how this horrible suspicion first took possession of her. All she could possibly have known, when we left England, was that the two men were appointed to separate ships. What could have led her to suspect that they had come together?"

"She was firmly persuaded, William, that they would come together, when the Expedition left England. And she had read in books of Arctic travel of men left behind by their comrades on the march, and of men adrift on icebergs. With her mind full of these images and forebodings, she saw Frank and Wardour (or dreamed of them) in one of her attacks of trance. I was by her side—I heard what she said at the time. She warned Frank that Wardour had discovered the truth. She called out to him, 'While you can stand, keep with the other men, Frank!—'"

"Good God!" cried Crayford; "I warned him myself, almost in those very words, the last time I saw him."

"Don't acknowledge it, William! Keep her in ignorance of what you have just told me; she will not take it for what it is—a startling coincidence, and nothing more. She will accept it as positive confirmation of the faith, the miserable superstitious faith, that is in her. So long as you don't actually know that Frank is dead, and that he has died by Wardour's hand, deny what she says—mislead her for her own sake—dispute all her conclusions as I dispute them. Help me to raise her to the better and nobler belief in the mercy of God!" She stopped and looked round nervously at the door way. "Hush!" she whispered; "do as I have told you. Clara is here."...

The man was a sinister and terrible object to look at. His eyes glared like the eyes of a wild animal; his head was bare; his long grey hair was torn and tangled; his miserable garments hung about him in rags. He stood in the doorway, a speechless figure of misery and want, staring at the well spread table like a hungry dog.

Steventon spoke to him.

"Who are you?"

He answered in a hollow voice:

"A starving man."

He advanced a few steps—slowly and painfully, as if he was sinking under fatigue.

"Throw me some bones from the table," he said. "Give me my share along with the dogs."

There was madness as well as hunger in his eyes while he spoke those words. Steventon placed Mrs. Crayford behind him, so that he might be easily able to protect her in case of need, and beckoned to two sailors who were passing the door of the boat-house at the time.

"Give the man some bread and meat," he said, "and wait near him."

The outcast seized on the bread and meat with lean long-nailed hands that looked like claws. After the first mouthful of food he stopped, considered vacantly with himself, and broke the bread and meat into two portions. One portion he put into an old canvas wallet that hung over his shoulder. The other he devoured voraciously. Steventon questioned him.

"Where do you come from?"

"From the sea."

"Wrecked?"

"Yes."

Steventon turned to Mrs. Crayford.

"There may be some truth in the poor wretch's story," he said. "I heard something of a strange boat having been cast on the beach, thirty or forty miles higher up the coast. When were you wrecked my man?"

The starving creature looked up from his food, and made an effort to collect his thoughts—to exert his memory. It was not to be done. He gave up the attempt in despair. His language, when he spoke, was as wild as his looks.

"I can't tell you," he said. "I can't get the wash of the sea out of my ears. I can't get the shining stars all night, and the burning sun all day, out of my brain. When was I wrecked? When was I first adrift in the boat? When did I get the tiller in my hand and fight against hunger and sleep? When did the gnawing, in my breast, and the burning in my head, first begin? I have lost all reckoning of it. I can't think; I can't sleep; I can't get the wash of the sea out of my ears. What are you baiting me with questions for? Let me eat!"

Even the sailors pitied him. The sailors asked leave of their officer to add a little drink to his meal.

"We've got a drop of grog with us, sir, in a bottle. May we give it to him?"

"Certainly!"

He took the bottle fiercely, as he had taken the food—drank a little—stopped—and considered with himself again. He held up the bottle to the light, and, marking how much liquor it contained, carefully drank half of it only. This done, he put the bottle in his wallet along with the food.

"Are you saving it up for another time?" said Steventon.

"I'm saving it up," the man answered. "Never mind what for."

He looked round the boat-house as he made that reply, and noticed Mrs. Crayford for the first time.

"A woman among you!" he said. "Is she English? Is she young? Let me look closer at her."

He advanced a few steps towards the table.

"Don't be afraid, Mrs. Crayford," said Steventon.

"I'm not afraid," Mrs. Crayford replied. "He frightened me at first—he interests me now. Let him speak to me if he wishes it."

He never spoke. He stood, in dead silence, looking long and anxiously at the beautiful Englishwoman.

"Well?" said Steventon.

He shook his head sadly, and drew back again with a heavy sigh.

"No!" he said to himself, "that's not *her* face. No! not found yet."

Mrs. Crayford's interest was strongly excited. She ventured to speak to him.

"Who is it you want to find?" she asked. "Your wife?"

He shook his head again.

"Who then? What is she like?"

He answered that question in words. His hoarse hollow voice softened little by little into sorrowful and gentle tones.

"Young," he said; "with a fair, sad face—with kind, tender eyes—with a soft, clear voice. Young, and loving, and merciful. I keep her face in my mind, though I can keep nothing else. I must wander, wander, wander—restless, sleepless, homeless—till I find her! Over the ice and over the snow; tossing on the sea, tramping over the land; awake all night, awake all day; wander, wander, wander, till I find her!"

He waved his hand with a gesture of farewell, and turned wearily to go out.

At the same moment Crayford opened the yard door.

"I think you had better come to Clara," he began and checked himself, noticing the stranger. "Who is that?"

The shipwrecked man, hearing another voice in the room, looked round slowly over his shoulder. Struck by his appearance, Crayford advanced a little nearer to him. Mrs. Crayford spoke to her husband as he passed her.

"It's only a poor mad creature, William," she whispered, "ship-wrecked and starving."

"Mad?" Crayford repeated, approaching, nearer and nearer to the man. "Am *I* in my right senses?" He suddenly sprang on the outcast, and seized him by the throat. "Richard Wardour!" he cried, in a voice of fury. "Alive! Alive, to answer for Frank!"

The man struggled. Crayford held him.

"Where is Frank?" he said. "You villain, where is Frank?"

The man resisted no longer. He repeated vacantly—

"Villain? and where is Frank?"

As the name escaped his lips, Clara appeared at the open yard door, and hurried into the room.

"I heard Richard's name!" she said. "I heard Frank's name! What does it mean?"

At the sound of her voice the outcast renewed the struggle to free himself, with a sudden frenzy of strength which Crayford was not able to resist. He broke away before the sailors could come to their officer's assistance. Half-way down the length of the room he and Clara met one another face to face. A new light sparkled in the poor wretch's eyes; a cry of recognition burst from his lips. He flung one hand up wildly in the air. "Found!" he shouted, and rushed out to the beach before any of the men present could stop him.

Mrs. Crayford put her arms round Clara and held her up. She had not made a movement; she had not spoken a word. The sight of Wardour's face had petrified her.

The minutes passed, and there rose a sudden burst of cheering from the sailors on the beach, near the spot where the fishermen's boats were drawn up. Every man left his work. Every man waved his cap in the air. The passengers, near at hand, caught the infection of enthusiasm, and joined the crew. A moment more, and Richard Wardour appeared again in the doorway, carrying a man in his arms. He staggered, breathless with the effort that he was making, to the place where Clara stood, held up in Mrs. Crayford's arms.

"Saved, Clara!" he cried. "Saved for *you*!"

He released the man, and placed him in Clara's arms.

Frank! Footsore and weary, but living! Saved—saved for her!

"Now, Clara," cried Mrs. Crayford, "which of us is right? I, who believed in the mercy of God—or you, who believed in a dream?"

She never answered; she clung to Frank in speechless ecstasy. She never even looked at the man who had preserved him—in the first absorbing joy of seeing her lover alive. Step by step, slower and slower, Richard Wardour drew back and left them by themselves.

"I may rest now," he said, faintly. "I may sleep at last. The task is done. The struggle is over."

His last reserves of strength had been given to Frank. He stopped, he staggered, his hands wavered feebly in search of support. But for one faithful friend, he would have fallen. Crayford caught him. Crayford laid his old comrade gently on some sails strewn in a corner, and pillowed Wardour's weary head on his own breast. The tears streamed over his face. "Richard! Dear Richard!" he said. "Remember—and forgive me."

Richard neither heeded nor heard him. His dim eyes still looked across the room at Clara and Frank.

"I have made *her* happy!" he murmured. "I may lay down my weary head now on the mother earth that hushes all her children to rest at last. Sink, heart! sink, sink to rest! Oh, look at them!" he said to Crayford, with a burst of grief. "They have forgotten me already."

It was true! The interest was all with the two lovers. Frank was young, and handsome, and popular. Officers, passengers, and sailors, they all crowded round Frank. They all forgot the martyred man who had saved him—the man who was dying in Crayford's arms.

Crayford tried once more to attract his attention—to win his recognition while there was yet time.

"Richard, speak to me! Speak to your old friend!"

He looked round; he vacantly repeated Crayford's last word.

"Friend?" he said. "My eyes are dim, friend; my mind is dull. I have lost all memories but the memory of her. Dead thoughts—all dead thoughts but that one! And yet, you look at me kindly! Why has your face gone down with the wreck of all the rest?"

He paused. His face changed; his thoughts drifted back from present to past. He looked at Crayford vacantly; lost in the terrible remembrances that were rising in him, as the shadows rise with the coming night.

"Hark ye, friend!" he whispered. "Never let Frank know it. There was a time when the fiend within me hungered for his life. I had my hands on the boat. I heard the voice of the Tempter speaking to me: 'Launch it, and leave him to die!' I waited, with my hands on the boat and my eyes on the place where he slept. 'Leave him! leave him!' the Voice whispered. 'Love him!' the lad's voice answered, moaning and murmuring in his sleep. 'Love him, Clara, for helping *me*!' I heard the morning wind come up in the silence over the great deep. Far and near, I heard the groaning of the floating ice, floating, floating, to the clear water and the balmy air. And the wicked Voice floated away with it—away, away, away for ever! 'Love him! love him, Clara, for helping *me*.' No wind could float that away. 'Love him, Clara'—"

His voice sank into silence; his head dropped on Crayford's breast. Frank saw it. Frank struggled up on his bleeding feet, and parted the friendly throng round him. Frank had not forgotten the man who had saved him.

"Let me go to him!" he cried. "I must, and will go to him! Clara, come with me."

Clara and Steventon supported him between them. He fell on his knees at Wardour's side; he put his hand on Wardour's bosom.

"Richard!"

The weary eyes opened again. The sinking voice was heard feebly once more.

"Ah! poor Frank. I didn't forget you, Frank, when I came here to beg. I remembered you, lying down outside in the shadow of the boats. I saved you your share of the food and drink. Too weak to get at it now! A little rest, Frank! I should soon be strong enough to carry you down to the ship."

The end was near. They all saw it now. The men reverently uncovered their heads in the presence of Death. In an agony of despair, Frank appealed to the friends round him.

"Get something to strengthen him, for God's sake! Oh, men! men! I should never have been here but for him! He has given all his strength to my weakness; and now, see how strong I am, and how weak *he* is! Clara! I held by his arm all over the ice and snow. *He* kept watch when I was senseless in the open boat. *His* hand dragged me out of the waves, when we were wrecked. Speak to him, Clara! speak to him!" His voice failed him, and his head dropped on Wardour's breast.

She spoke, as well as her tears would let her.

"Richard! have you forgotten me?"

He rallied at the sound of that beloved voice. He looked up at her, as she knelt at his head.

"Forgotten you?" Still looking at her, he lifted his hand with an effort, and laid it on Frank. "Should I have been strong enough to save him, if I could have forgotten *you?*" He waited a moment, and turned his face feebly towards Crayford. "Stay!" he said. "Some one was here and spoke to me." A faint light of recognition glimmered in his eyes. "Ah, Crayford! I recollect now. Dear Crayford! Come nearer! My mind clears; but my eyes grow dim. You will remember me kindly for Frank's sake? Poor Frank! why does he hide his face? Is he crying? Nearer, Clara—I want to look my last at *you.* My sister Clara! Kiss me, sister, kiss me before I die!"

She stooped and kissed his forehead. A faint smile trembled on his lips. It passed away; and stillness possessed the face—the stillness of Death.

Crayford's voice was heard in the silence.

"The loss is ours," he said. "The gain is his. He has won the greatest of all conquests—the conquest of himself. And he has died in the moment of victory. Not one of us here but may live to envy *his* glorious death."

The distant report of a gun came from the ship in the offing, and signalled the return to England and to home.

CLIVE SINCLAIR

L ONDON-BORN Clive Sinclair (1948–) has had a steadily rising
literary reputation in England and abroad. In 1982, he was one
of twenty fiction authors chosen as the "Best of Young British Novelists," and shortly thereafter he became the literary editor of the London *Jewish Chronicle*, a position he held until 1987. He has published
two collections of stories, four novels, a book of literary criticism,
and a travel book, all to enviable acclaim. To date, his work has been
translated into ten languages.

While it may be argued that all fiction contains autobiographical
elements, the following story is especially poignant for the author,
because it was during a holiday journey from Toronto to Quebec in
1975 (his first of three brief visits to Canada), trapped in a blizzard,
"certain of freezing to death," that he proposed to the woman who
became his wife. Clive Sinclair describes the event:

> During the course of that journey I collected several images,
> from which the story developed. 1) The thaw was underway so
> that the landscape looked like a half-finished painting. 2) It was
> a false spring, and, midway between Quebec and Montreal, we
> were trapped by a blizzard.... 3) Near the end of a meal in a
> country hotel a fellow diner suddenly howled and ran from the
> room, knocking over his chair. Recalling these incidents in tran-
> quility, I was taken with the idea of white-outs, and the

concomitant implication that Canada was a blank page in world history. I decided to show that fear, like pain, travels well, and recognizes no boundaries. I wanted to explain that man's scream. Hence the conjunction of Canada and the Holocaust.

The author, for aesthetic reasons, has chosen to tell the tale from the point of view of Canadians. Given the brevity of his time in the country, this might seem foolhardy, but it is a measure of his daring—and his skill—that the verisimilitude is so strong. The story was published in his second book, *Hearts of Gold* (1979), winner of the Somerset Maugham Award.

_____

THE CREATURE ON MY BACK

I have a creature on my back. It is invisible. No one knows it is there but me. It clings to my shoulders like an imp and tries to pull me to the ground. Paul Klee has written the line: "To stand despite all possibilities to fall." That about sums up my life. A constant struggle not to fall. In moments of despair I joke about the gravity of my situation. Naturally I can tell no one about the creature, what could I say? I envy hunchbacks, at least everyone can see the burden they carry.

I did not feel the creature climb on to my back. It was not there when I went to see the headhunter. I do not know why she is called a headhunter. She is not a hot-shot with a blow-pipe, a collector of shrunken heads, but just an agent who finds work for creative types in advertising agencies. She had landed me a two-week job writing the new campaign for Aphrodite—you know, the soap that put Aphro into Aphrodisiac. She was feeding chocolate drops to the

Pekinese that was curled like a caddie above her crotch. Her scarlet lips smiled. She flattered me, but I too was insincere. Once when her dog was ill I telephoned to inquire after its health.

Aphrodite is manufactured by a multi-national giant, Player & Gamble. Player & Gamble is run like a holy order; equally concerned with converting the masses and preserving its own mysteries. Before I was allowed to work on their product I was compelled to take certain oaths. I was also handed a document entitled "Player & Gamble Security Requirements." It contained a brief prolegomenon on the necessity of security, followed by a series of commandments. 1. Thou shalt treat all documents from the originator as secret. 2. Thou shalt speak in a mutually understandable code when discussing P&G business over the telephone. 3. Thou shalt not talk of P&G in public places. Etcetera. Then there were the parables, telling of men led astray by "strangers," "reporters," "intruders," "men in dark glasses," "seductresses" and other agents of the Great Competitor. But I was not troubled. The new campaign became a great success.

However, the success did nothing for Sarah. Sarah is my wife. Poor Sarah was having a bad time. Late one night she came into my study.

"Well," she said, "it seems that I have been going through a very real emotional crisis."

I didn't take her seriously, which was a mistake.

"There is no such state as 'very real,'" I said, "something is either real or it isn't."

"Jesus," she said.

"Further," I said, "to whom does 'it seem'? I bet you wouldn't have known a thing about it if good Dr. Eggplant hadn't winkled out this 'emotional crisis.'"

"His name is Dr. Eckhardt," she said. She was grim-faced, white, breathing hard. None of them good signs.

"Well," I said, "it seems to me that these visits to Dr. Eckhardt are doing you no good at all."

I had gone too far.

"JESUS CHRIST!" Sarah screamed. "I walk in and tell you I've practically had a nervous breakdown and all you do is give me literary criticism. All right, my use of language may not satisfy your precious New Critics, but I'm not talking about some book, I'm talking about me. I mean real life. I MEAN, DO I HAVE TO EXPRESS MY FEELINGS IN POETIC FORM BEFORE YOU'LL TAKE ANY NOTICE? Right! I'll tell you exactly what I'm feeling now, as precisely as possible. FUCK YOU!"

She slammed the door. The front door also slammed.

An hour later, when I was becoming frantic with worry, she returned. I apologized. We discussed Dr. Eckhardt's findings seriously.

"Dr. Eckhardt says," she said, "that my mind is stalling on a one-way track. It seems that this is messing up everything; it means that I am only functioning at one-third effectiveness."

Of course I knew what the real problem was. Sarah's shoulder was not wept upon. Too much of my life was hidden, even from Sarah.

This was my fault, but I could not correct it. We had talked it over many times, my self-sufficiency.

"So what remedy does the doctor recommend?" I asked.

"He doesn't know yet," she said. "He wants me to see him more often."

Without warning my heart swelled like a balloon. In truth, I was terrified of losing Sarah. Then the words came into my mind. I forced myself to voice them.

"Sarah," I said, "let's have a baby."

Sarah said she must ask Dr. Eckhardt first.

He advised her to wait, explained that what she required was an egocentric not a concentric solution. He suggested that rather than have a baby she should experiment with infidelity. He said that it would do her more good than having a baby. Why? Because if she slept around she could choose her role, examine her options dispassionately, and control her emotions, letting them flow outward only when she decided. Thus growing emotionally self-sufficient.

"That's what you want, isn't it?" he said.

"I think so," said Sarah.

He told her that she must decide.

Sarah sat in his office, looking glum. She wasn't sure if she was ready to have a baby, but Dr. Eckhardt's alternative was unattractive.

"I'll tell you what," said the doctor, "as a compromise try acting."

By coincidence they were planning the Christmas show at Sarah's school (Sarah being a teacher of history at Edgebrook High, a progressive establishment). After weeks of impassioned discussion, hours of self-analysis, careful examination of how the play would affect the teacher-kid relationship, they threw out the classics and plumped instead for Picasso's *Four Girls*. They were thrilled with the inter-disciplinary nature of this, an opportunity to draw together the art and drama departments. The only serious objection came from some of the more conservative members of staff.

"Do you realize," they said, "that the characters are naked most of the play?"

This was hotly debated, but on a democratic vote the radicals prevailed. A motion by some militant women teachers that two of the girls should be played by boys was also carried.

"To force the kids to re-evaluate their respective roles in society."

Casting did not take long. Sarah got her part by default. No one else wanted it.

"I have to slaughter a goat and drink its blood while I'm starkers," explained Sarah. "Dr. Eckhardt is delighted."

Body-stockings were *de rigueur* during rehearsals. "To make sure you feel really naked on the night," said the director.

Unlike Dr. Eckhardt I had misgivings. "Do you think this is the sort of thing the Head of History should be doing?" I asked. But I needn't have worried.

The press got hold of the story. WOMEN TEACHERS TO APPEAR NAKED WITH BOYS IN PICASSO SEX SHOW. There was a scandal. The production was killed.

"That's a relief," confessed Sarah.

She gets pregnant instead.

Lisa is the first person we tell. We are spending the evening with Lisa and Robin. Cross-legged on their floor watching television. Robin wrote the score for the Aphrodite commercial, a moody moog background to our lathered lady in the shower. So the pair of us sit; he a musician of some standing, having written for the Canadian National Ballet, but wanting to be a rock 'n' roll star; me a novelist with sales below 1,000, wanting to be as famous as Leonard Cohen; getting kudos from a soap commercial. Lisa accuses us both of exploiting women. She shakes her shapely head; her silver earrings shiver. A long man with an erect penis hangs from her left lobe, from her right dangles a woman with a swollen belly. Woman's fate. Lisa's fate.

Then Sarah announces, "I'm pregnant."

There is a knock at the door. Enter Helga and Ron. Helga is Robin's former wife, Ron is his best friend, best-man at their wedding. Ron is carrying a young boy, asleep in his arms; the son of Robin and Helga. He is put quietly into the bedroom which already contains Eve and Mai, Lisa's daughters by Robin and her former husband. A couple of joints are lit up and passed around. Wine is poured. A wind blowing off Lake Ontario rattles the bamboo blinds and rustles the leaves of the avocado plants that stand on the window sills. We get very stoned.

"Do you know," said Lisa to Sarah, "when you said you were pregnant I didn't know whether to congratulate you or tell you the name of a good abortionist."

"Oh," says Sarah, "we definitely want it."

"Abortion is such an ugly word," says Helga, "though termination of pregnancy isn't any better."

"I know a terrible story about an abortionist," says Ron, "do you want to hear it?"

"Oh, yes!"

"Well, up in Catholic Quebec," begins Ron, "where a lot of people are still uptight about women—you know the French—abortions are not so readily available. I had this friend, a real nice lady, who got herself with child. The father didn't want to know about it.

She can't turn to her family. Very upright. So she asks me for help. I find out the name of a woman who does douches, an old French woman who lives on a farm in the middle of nowhere. Batiscan, that's the place. We go there, one beautiful mid-winter day. It doesn't take long. Walking away I notice drops of blood on the snow. Very dark blood. The miscarriage was beginning. Twenty hours too early. Why am I telling you this? It's a horrible story. The girl died. Had a haemorrhage and bled to death. Shit! I wish I'd kept my mouth shut!"

Then the soap commercial reappears on the television. It makes us giggle. Even Ron who is crying and giggling at the same time.

Next morning something odd occurs while I am leafing through the newspaper. I become convinced that someone else is looking at it over my shoulder. I even know what article is being read. A report concerning the burial in Israel of two bars of soap. Made by the Nazis out of human fats. Sarah is being sick in the bathroom, I taste vomit in my mouth too, and feel a sudden spasm of pain between my shoulder blades, an embryonic kick in the back. What a grotesque spectacle that funeral must have been! What a metaphor for the human condition! I thank God I didn't know about this last night. Or I might have blurted it out like Ron's story of the dead girl. We would have invented a commercial for the soap. We would have giggled. In the bathroom I hear Sarah rinsing her mouth and washing her hands. If the Nazis had had their way she could be washing her hands with the mortal remains of Sigmund Freud.

When my pay from Player & Gamble arrives we decide to take a trip. To spend Easter in Quebec. We take the Turbo to Montreal. The woman in the seat behind starts to smoke a cigarette just as the train pulls out of the station. I turn around and tell her she's in a no-smoking section. The woman looks amazed. Without a word she gets up and walks away. Only the smoke remains, hovering like a ghost over her empty seat. We pick up speed as we skim through the townships of Oshawa and Napanee. We flit through forests of pine and silver birch. Everywhere the snow is melting, so that the landscape looks like a half-finished painting. After Kingston we follow the St. Lawrence north-east on its course to Montreal.

Vieux Montreal is deserted in the icy drizzle of early Saturday morning. There are many antique shops full of objects from the back-country; especially expertly carved duck decoys. The fashion stores fill their windows with lady decoys. Sarah is finally attracted by one displaying a bright red dress. Inside the couturière has lifeless blonde hair and a lopsided face. She is enormously tall. Sarah asks the price of the dress and when she exclaims it's way too much the lady drops the price by twenty dollars. Still too expensive, but Sarah decides to try it on. I watch her legs grow naked beneath the wooden door of the cubicle; and I am reminded of the shower scene in the soap commercial. Unexpectedly I feel a sudden fear of separation from Sarah.

I am beckoned. I see that Sarah has on a clinging dress made of some velvety material. Its main feature is the way it is cut in the front to show off the greater part of her tits. If she leaned forward you could see her nipples. The neckline is not a traditional V but open-ended so that the whole of her belly is also on show as though prepared for surgery. The woman is smiling horribly at me.

"It's a bit revealing, isn't it?" asks Sarah.

"There's a modesty flap you can sew on the front," says the lady, "most people do."

"I don't think so," says Sarah, "it's not for me."

"It fits you like a glove," says the woman. "I'll let you have it for thirty-five dollars."

I am no longer rational. I will be upset if Sarah buys the dress.

"No," she says.

"You are making a mistake," says the lady. She is annoyed. "I don't know why she won't buy it," the woman says to me. "I made her a perfectly good offer."

I sense hostility between the shop-owner and myself, as though she blamed me for Sarah's refusal to buy.

"You didn't like that dress, did you?" says Sarah, when we are outside again.

"I hated it."

"I can't explain, but there was something creepy about that shop," says Sarah, "that woman, she reminded me of a witch from Grimms' fairy-tales."

Or a wardress from a concentration camp.

We rent a car and drive out into the country for dinner. A note outside the restaurant reads: "After 6:00 pm we appreciate gentlemen wearing jackets and ties." That sort of place. We are seated beside a picture window. Beyond Lake Massawippi is frozen and floodlit, a sea of glass. It is a big dining room, but there are no other diners. Loudspeakers hang from the wooden beams.

"What is the music?" I ask the waitress.

"Strauss waltzes," she says, "my favourite composer."

We order escargots to start; they come fat and juicy; they drip butter and taste of garlic. A man enters the dining-room, distinguished, wearing a jacket and tie; white-haired, ruddy-faced, blind drunk. He lurches across the room to the strains of "The Blue Danube," bumping into tables, attempting to stay on course with the aid of chair backs. The waitress sees him, rushes over, helps him to a seat. It is clear that the waitress is fond of him.

"Would you like something to eat, doctor?" she asks.

"I'm not hungry," he says, "just bring me a drink."

"Come on, Doc, you've got to eat something," the waitress says.

"Just bring me a drink!"

She goes to the bar.

"Terrible, terrible," mutters the doctor. "I've had a terrible day." He begins to moan.

We continue eating, but in the deserted dining room the doctor is impossible to ignore. "Dr. Eckhardt's ghost," jokes Sarah.

"Terrible, terrible," he repeats, again and again. Suddenly he pushes himself to his feet. His chair topples backwards but does not fall. "I don't want to live any more!" he cries. He weaves a way around the wooden tables and walks sobbing out of the room. Before he vanishes I glimpse, fleetingly, the form of a homunculus clinging to his back.

We look like Lisa's earrings. Sarah's naked, belly swelling. I'm ur bodies have silver linings, outlined by light from the ke. Sarah gasps as I enter her, feeling an expansion of flesh in nes... Her breath comes in pants. HHH, HHH. Like a train. Our rhythms gather speed. Up and down. Like a train. My body concentrates, my thoughts freewheel. No smoking on this train. Verboten. You must have a shower. The doctor will give you a bar of soap. It's the woman from the dress shop. Aphrodite, the soap that put Aphro into Aphrodisiac. The doctor will turn you into a bar of soap. Herr Doktor. What if he is a Nazi doctor tormented by his past? GO AWAY!

"I'm coming! I'm coming!" screams Sarah.

She jerks, shudders to a halt. Then all thoughts are mercifully sucked from my mind. Swelling. Swelling. Swell.... They say that the blood-soaked ground in Germany and Poland still cries out *in memoriam*. Here in Canada our only echoes from the past are visual, immediate, reflections. My favourite building in Toronto stands on the corner of York Street, a skyscraper that's like a giant mirror; looking as though a lake had been taken, poured into a rectangular receptacle, squared off, then placed in a vertical plane. Usually it is full of blue sky and puffs of cloud. Canada seems to have absorbed nothing; all thoughts, all feelings bounce off frozen surfaces and vanish in the unpolluted air.

On a back-country road heading north to Quebec. Driving through a peaceful valley. The dark pines on the hilltops give the sky a ragged edge. The air is luminous, the snow tinted rose-red by the sun, all dramatized by the fathomless cobalt sky. The bellies of the drifting clouds shine as their shadows cross the fields of snow. We are looking forward to our dinner in Quebec. Sarah says something, but I have no chance to reply. My head is suddenly jerked back, my fingers loosen their grip on the steering-wheel, and the car runs out of control. It swerves left across the road. I react instinctively; I pull the car back towards the right. For an instant I think I've got it under control. But the car hits black ice and I can't hold it.

"We're going!" I yell. I'm not thinking any more. I put my arm around Sarah, shielding her. The other hand's still on the wheel but I can't do anything now. We shoot off the road at some crazy angle and for a second we're in the air. We tilt towards Sarah's side, but I've got her tight. Then there's a thump and we hit the ground and stop.

Dead silence.

Sarah? No reply. SARAH?

"I'm okay," she whispers. I put my hand on her belly. "That's all right, too," she says.

We blame the ice. The hook from the tow-truck bites into the car and heaves us back on to the road. No damage, not even a scratch. I do not tell Sarah that the creature on my back has tried to kill us. We dine in Quebec.

We breakfast at a café called Le Gaulois, among intellectual Quebecois. The man at the next table eats his fried egg in an ostentatious manner; he balances the unbroken yolk on his fork and takes it in one mouthful. Tiny yellow bubbles appear on his lips. We must hurry. The fast-flowing St. Lawrence is filled with ice floes. It has been snowing all morning. Already there have been many accidents; cars colliding, unable to stop at crossroads. On the outskirts of Quebec I must make a decision: whether to stay north and go down to Montreal on Route 138, or to take the Trans-Canada Highway, south of the river.

"We'll start off on 138," I say, "but if the snow gets worse we'll cross to the Trans-Canada at Trois Rivières."

It gets much worse. The snow is no longer coming down in flakes, but rather in thin pencil lines, drawn horizontal by the wind, as though it were trying to fill in all the space around us with white. We are travelling in convoy now, a line of cars trying to follow the curve of the road (which, in turn, must be following the indentations of the river, lost in white) going slower and slower with each mile. We tick off the miles we do this way; the signposts to Trois Rivières are regular; they appear every two miles: 30 to go, 28, 26, 24. We're passing them every ten minutes or so. All we have to do is keep this up.

But the weather isn't getting any better. "The blizzard, which came in last night from the Great Lakes states has already dumped a

foot of snow on Montreal, and as yet shows no sign of abating," says
the man on the car radio. So we've been driving into the blizzard all
day! "Watch out for 'white-outs,'" warns the man. What? On an
exposed flank of a curve in the road, with the wind blowing directly
at us from across the river a "white-out" is defined; the car is suddenly immersed in snow, swept over by a wave of white nothingness
which hits the windshield with a splat. At about four in the afternoon we pass the 22-mile marker. The weather continues to worsen;
even without "white-outs" the visibility is practically nil. Sarah is
very tense. We cross the Petite Rivière Batiscan. There are huge
drifts on either side of the road. Snow is blowing wildly off the tops.
Not only must I keep the car going down this narrow alley between
the banks of snow avoiding abandoned trucks, without thinking
about oncoming traffic, but now I've got to do it blindfold. It is as if
the creature on my back has expanded to fill the whole world, and it
is this shrieking banshee of a world that I am fighting as I wrestle
with the steering-wheel. Finally, blinded, I drive straight into a drift.
We're stuck.

"What shall we do?" says Sarah.

I haven't a clue.

Between gusts of wind I can make out a house about one hundred yards to our right, and I think I can see someone moving about
in there. We remain where we are until it begins to get dark, expecting rescue; but no one comes, nor any snow ploughs. The car is
almost buried, we must leave. We can just open my door wide
enough for us to squeeze out. We have decided to make for the
house. Beyond the door is bedlam. The wind is so loud we cannot
speak; it rushes at us like an animal, clawing us with snow. Given the
chance it would rip our clothes and our bodies too. We clamber to
the top of the drift so that we are on a level with the car roof, and we
begin to walk in the direction of the house. We see it as a flickering
light. In seconds we're soaked. Already we're panting. Snow is hurled
non-stop against us, icy air flies up our nostrils. It is difficult to
breathe.

The light has almost gone from the day. More, the known world has been obliterated as utterly as at Pompeii. Through the gloom we can see the house glimmering, the only certain fixture in the landscape. I hold Sarah tight. Twice the creature tries to take her from me as she is sucked into the soft snow; twice I pull her back. The snow is deepest here, the high drifts around the house, but now we're past them too, slipping down towards the back door of the place. Sanctuary.

We can smell wood smoke, a wonderful smell.

An old man opens the door. Dressed in a faded blue French peasant smock. He fusses around us, concerned to see that we don't drip on the linoleum. A fat woman (about the right age to be his daughter) takes our coats and hats and hangs them near the stove. She has a few words of English.

"Welcome," she says. "Please sit down with the others." She beckons us through the cheerful kitchen with its great wood-burning stove into the L-shaped living-room.

The ancient has already returned, sitting in his rocking-chair, listening to the radio. We are introduced to the woman's husband, a Gallic type; his shoulders poised permanently on the point of a shrug. At the table half a dozen other refugees from the storm sit drinking gin. I tick off the characters: the smooth travelling salesman, the joker with the goatee beard, his silent resentful wife, a pretty girl with a diamond engagement ring, an unrelated moody youth who clenches his fists in response to some inner tension, the old lady with the lap dog. Eight strangers trapped by the raging blizzard. A favourite movie plot.

Actually there is an old movie on the television in the other part of the room which no one is watching, a Randolph Scott yarn dubbed into French. Above the set, pinned to the wall, is Christ crucified. A bookcase is filled with religious texts, mainly on Catholicism. At the end of the L stands a piano upon which rests a coloured photograph of a young girl in nurse's uniform; I assume it is of the woman's daughter, but upon closer inspection it seems altogether too old-fashioned. We find the bathroom, a doorless cubicle in the couple's bedroom, containing both toilet and sink. The bedroom is gloomy; there is another cross on the wall and plastic flowers in vases on the dressing-table, alongside many pills for the symptoms of old age. Conversation continues at the table. Only the boy has departed, gone around the corner to watch the cowboy film.

"We did not expect the snow," says the farmer in French, "we were planning to tap our maple trees today. But now the sap has frozen again."

I wander back to the television. The commercials are on; would you believe it, it's Aphrodite again! The kid seems to fancy the girl in the shower. I do not like the look of him, those clenched fists; I fear that later, in the night, he will try to rape Sarah.

We sleep fully clothed on the sofa. We are not disturbed. But at dawn Sarah rises and rushes to the cubicle in the bedroom where she is sick several times. Later the farmer's wife looks carefully into her pale face and says, "Are you sure you came here by accident, my dear, you weren't looking for me, were you?" She stares at me and says, "Are you the father?"

I am speechless. Where are we? Then I remember. BATISCAN. Is it possible? Have we landed up with the abortionist who killed Ron's friend? I calm down, no need to be over-dramatic. This woman is not evil; most probably she thinks she is doing us a kindness, thinks we need coaxing before we'll admit why we have come. But how can she be an abortionist? She is Catholic.

"It is very clean here," says the woman, opening the bedroom door for our inspection, showing us the cubicle with its spotless sink and the two bars of soap. "There is no danger, I used to be a nurse."

I am helpless, the creature on my back has its hands firmly clasped over my mouth.

"Come into the cubicle, my dear," she says to Sarah, "and let me examine you.

I cry out, "Don't go!" but the words are soundless. I cannot help Sarah.

"You're mistaken," says Sarah. "I want the baby."

As Sarah's belly grows so do my struggles with the creature on my back. I wrestle with it constantly. In the mornings it attempts to hold me to the bed. During the day it tries to throw me to the ground. Even at nights I am not free. I dream that I am pinned to the floor and must watch helpless while a bloody embryo is torn from Sarah's open belly. The thing is made of soap. At last I confide in Sarah. But the confession does not lift the weight from my shoulders. So Sarah suggests that I see her shrink. Next I tell Dr. Eckhardt about the creature on my back. He walks around me.

"I can see nothing," he says.

"It is there, none the less," I say.

"Well, you are a *mensch,* you know life is a struggle," says Dr. Eckhardt, "there is a Yiddish saying: 'Shoulders are from God, and burdens too.'"

"Why my shoulders?" I ask.

"Listen," says Dr. Eckhardt, "you are lucky. You have a creature on your back. Such things are not common in Canada. It may yet go away. As for myself, I have a number on my arm. A souvenir of Europe."

JULES VERNE

H E SPENT less than one day in Canada, yet Canada is the setting for a scarcely credible seven of his novels. His Canadian
visit was limited to a dash to the Horseshoe Falls, but the bulk of his
Canadian fictional settings are places he never saw: our Far North,
and Quebec.

Because Jules Verne (1828–1905) was human he was a paradox.
Singular, then, must have been his joy at discovering in Canada certain situations, fictional or historical, which allowed him to recon-
cile many of his apparent contradictions.

Deeply conservative and a devout Catholic, Verne was thrilled to
discover from his reading—seduced might be more accurate—that the
Quebecois seemed to maintain fealty to the revered values of royalist
France. He believed they held supreme the unappealable rights of the
seigneur, adored the *habitants'* love of the land, and assumed as natural the preponderant authority of the Church. Verne came to believe,
in other words, that Quebec preserved (lived!) the good old days.

Canada, as opposed to France, held other allures. Tory by nature,
Verne was loath to endorse the rebellions that had recently rocked
France (earlier he had supported the Royalist insurrection). Yet
Verne was galvanized by the French-Canadian fight against English
domination, particularly the Rebellion of 1837, seeing it, ironically,
as model behaviour. As Verne scholar Edward Baxter notes, Jules
Verne applauded the vigour of the Quebecois struggle:

348

He saw the 1837 Rebellion, with its initial sacrifices and eventual vindication, as a source of inspiration to his fellow countrymen. The humiliation of the Franco-Prussian War still rankled in his memory. He himself had suffered a loss of income when the occupation of Paris had put his publisher temporarily out of business. His country had lost the two provinces of Alsace and Lorraine. If French-Canadians could take up arms in an attempt to free themselves from subservience to a foreign power, he reasoned, could not the citizens of Alsace and Lorraine do the same?

The charisma, even beguilement, of Quebec for Verne resulted in a long novel set almost entirely in the province: *Family Without a Name* (1889).

Rightly assuming that his audience would be unfamiliar with the leading characters and origins of the 1837 Rebellion, Verne prefaced *Family Without A Name* with a capsule history of Canada which might be called, to be generous, peculiarly distorted. A venomous screech at the British, the introduction fails to see the Rebellion in any terms other than racial. Verne uses an almost Marxist vocabulary to describe the pitiless oppressors and the noble, suffering *patriotes*. For a man who never visited the province, his patrician, even hortatory tone is absurd. Charmingly naïve, perhaps, from our vantage, but still absurd.

When the full title of Verne's most famous book is given, the reader begins to comprehend the seriousness of the influence of Canada on his writing: *Twenty Thousand Leagues under the Sea, or The Marvellous and Exciting Adventures of Pierre Aronnax, Conseil, his Servant, and Ned Land, a Canadian Harpooner.* Just as the Canadian is the decent, down-to-earth figure in the opera *La Cambiale di Matrimonio* by Rossini, the democratic demeanour of Ned Land and his salt-of-the-earth speech are foil to the paternalistic European erudition of Pierre Aronnax, Professor of Natural History at the Museum of Paris, and leader of the nautical expedition. Listen to the ingenuous reverence of the Professor for the rugged honesty, and near noble savagery of his chief mate:

Ned Land was a Canadian, with an uncommon quickness of hand, and who knew no equal in his dangerous occupation. Skill, coolness, audacity and cunning he possessed in a superior degree, and it must be a cunning whale or a singularly "cute" cachalot to escape the stroke of his harpoon.

Ned Land was about forty years of age; he was a tall man (more than six feet high), strongly built, grave and taciturn, occasionally violent, and very passionate when contradicted. His person attracted attention, but above all, the boldness of his look, which gave a singular expression to his face.

Who calls himself Canadian calls himself French; and little communicative as Ned Land was, I must admit that he took a certain liking for me. My nationality drew him to me, no doubt. It was an opportunity for him to talk, and for me to hear, that old language of Rabelais, which is still in use in some Canadian provinces. The harpooner's family was originally from Quebec, and was already a tribe of hardy fishermen when this town belonged to France.

Little by little, Ned Land acquired a taste for chatting, and I loved to hear the recital of his adventures in the polar seas. He related his fishing, and his combats, with natural poetry of expression; his recital took the form of an epic poem, and I seemed to be listening to a Canadian Homer singing the Iliad of the regions of the north.

Four of Verne's novels are set in these romantically perceived polar seas. *The English at The North Pole* (1864) and *The Ice Desert* (1866) are occasionally cited as one novel titled *The Adventures of Captain Hatteras* (1886). Canadians concerned about current American insensitivity to our territorial claims in the Arctic would find much that is tragicomic in *The Purchase of the North Pole* (1891). *The Golden Volcano* (1906) is a morality tale of greed and virtue, with moments of piquancy and moments of unintended humour.

Apart from maps and guidebooks, and a diurnal visit, how did Jules Verne nourish his perception of Canada? Clearly, for his books set in our North, he relied on commercial popular novelists for much of his colour. For native lore, scenes of hunting, a sense of the breadth of the land, he owed much more to James Fenimore Cooper, whose novels were widely available in France. Significantly, neither of these American writers dealt much with the implications for Canada of the Plains of Abraham, and so the virulence of Verne's lopsided view of our history can only be attributed, apart from his native antipathy to things British, to his extensive reading of nationalist francophone historians, particularly François-Xavier Garneau. While Verne never met Garneau, their views of literature and national struggle were as close and parallel as canal banks. Garneau's heroic view of Quebec history and his emotional appeal to glorious days gone by permeate Verne's Canadian books so profoundly, they obscure his vision and render his overall sight of Canada astigmatic. But like all paramours, though his vision might be askew, he relished the perception with confidence, and passionately extolled to all comers the unblemished merits of his beloved.

The following excerpt from *The Fur Country or Seventy Degrees North Latitude* epitomizes Verne's fascination with the idea of Canada—and his head-shaking ignorance of the place. The principal characters are a Canadian Lieutenant Hobson (a soldier unexplainably working for the Hudson's Bay Company), and the Briton's Mrs. Barnett (a world traveller and ur-feminist), and Thomas Black (an astronomer seeking the perfect vantage point for a solar eclipse). The party sets out from Fort Reliance for the Arctic Ocean, and after a variety of perils worthy of Pauline, establishes an outpost at Cape Bathurst. Unbeknownst to the group, their end of the peninsula has been cut adrift by an earthquake, and they wander the Ocean and Bering Sea on their floating island until it eventually melts to nothing. Predictably, the principals are saved, ironically by the same Inuit they had earlier despised.

In the novel, Verne seems to believe that dogsleds can speed over grass, dry land, and ocean beach, even in summer, that ten-foot pits can be easily dug into permafrost, that Arctic shores are lacking in stones, that forests abound north of the treeline—despite all of these imbecilic caricatures, his portrayal of our land and people resonates with enthralment—often even affection—for the singular otherness of Canada, for that which, no matter how seemingly horrible, distinguishes our land and people from the rest of the world.

Verne is blunt in declaiming that it takes a special breed to survive in the North. If the breed is Caucasian, then Verne's description is laudatory. If the breed is aboriginal, his vocabulary can, on occasion, be appalling. Before jumping to conclusions about the unilateral severity of his racism, however, the reader is advised to digest the entire novel to garner the full range of his feelings about the natives of Canada. That Verne, later in *The Fur Country*, has the Inuit play a role conveying much heroism and nobility may be insufficient for some readers to forgive him. Generously considered, the native generosity to the whites could be seen as decency personified. Less generously considered, it could be imperialism, disguised adroitly as fair trade, that may even have been hidden from the consciousness of the author: you give me all of your land, and I'll give you some beads in exchange. Reading the novel, one fears that Verne assumed paternalistically that the natives should instinctively play servant to the "superior" intruding peoples. As with Arthur Conan Doyle, Verne's lexicon again forces the debate: are we right to try to retrofit today's morality onto the statements or assessments of those who lived a century ago, and if so, to what degree? Regardless, one recoils at many of Verne's descriptions of the natives, not only because they are inherently offensive, but because one intuits they were typical of the age. Because they hailed from the pen of Jules Verne, they obtained a currency so wide as to make them commonplace.

This excerpt from *The Fur Country* recounts the protagonists' first encounter with the large mammals of the region.

from THE FUR COUNTRY

The only one of the four windows through which it was possible to look into the court of the fort was that opening at the end of the entrance passage. The outside shutters had not been closed; but before it could be seen through it had to be washed with boiling water, as the panes were covered with a thick coating of ice. This was done several times a day by the Lieutenant's orders, when the districts surrounding the fort were carefully examined, and the state of the sky, and of the alcohol thermometer placed outside, were accurately noted.

On the 6th January, towards eleven o'clock in the morning, Kellet, whose turn it was to look out, suddenly called the Sergeant, and pointed to some moving masses indistinctly visible in the gloom. Long, approaching the window observed quietly.

"They are bears!"

In fact half-a-dozen of these formidable animals had succeeded in getting over the palisades, and, attracted by the smoke from the chimneys, were advancing upon the house.

On hearing of the approach of the bears, Hobson at once ordered the window of the passage to be barricaded inside; it was the only unprotected opening in the house, and when it was secured it appeared impossible for the bears to effect an entrance. The window was, therefore, quickly closed up with bars, which the carpenter Mac-Nab wedged firmly in, leaving a narrow slit through which to watch the movements of the unwelcome visitors.

"Now," observed the head carpenter, "these gentlemen can't get in without our permission, and we have time to hold a council of war."

"Well, Lieutenant," exclaimed Mrs. Barnett, "nothing has been wanting to our northern winter! After the cold come the bears."

"Not after," replied the Lieutenant, "but, which is a serious matter, *with* the cold, and a cold so intense that we cannot venture outside! I really don't know how we shall get rid of these tiresome brutes."

"I suppose they will soon get tired of prowling about," said the lady, "and return as they came."

Hobson shook his head as if he had his doubts.

"You don't know these animals, madam. They are famished with hunger, and will not go until we make them!"

"Are you anxious, then?"

"Yes and no," replied the Lieutenant. "I don't think the bears will get in; but neither do I see how we can get out, should it become necessary for us to do so."

With these words Hobson turned to the window, and Mrs. Barnett joined the other women, who had gathered round the Sergeant, and were listening to what he had to say about the bears. He spoke like a man well up in his subject, for he had had many an encounter with these formidable carnivorous creatures, which are often met with even towards the south, where, however, they can be safely attacked, whilst here the siege would be a regular blockade, for the cold would quite prevent any attempt at a sortie.

Throughout the whole day the movements of the bears were attentively watched. Every now and then one of them would lay his great head against the window pane and an ominous growl was heard.

The Lieutenant and the Sergeant took counsel together, and it was agreed that if their enemies showed no sign of beating a retreat, they would drill a few loopholes in the walls of the house, and fire at them. But it was decided to put off this desperate measure for a day or two, as it was desirable to avoid giving access to the outer air, the inside temperature being already far too low. The walrus-oil to be burnt was frozen so hard that it had to be broken up with hatchets.

The day passed without any incident. The bears went and came, prowling round the house, but attempting no direct attack. Watch was kept all night, and at four o'clock in the morning they seemed to have left the court—at any rate, they were nowhere to be seen.

But about seven o'clock Marbre went up to the loft to fetch some provisions, and on his return announced that the bears were walking about on the roof.

Hobson, the Sergeant, Mac-Nab, and two or three soldiers seized their arms, and rushed to the ladder in the passage, which communicated with the loft by a trap-door. The cold was, however, so intense in the loft that the men could not hold the barrels of their guns, and their breath froze as it left their lips and floated about them as snow.

Marbre was right; the bears were all on the roof, and the sound of their feet and their growls could be distinctly heard. Their great claws caught in the laths of the roof beneath the ice, and there was some danger that they might have sufficient strength to tear away the woodwork.

The Lieutenant and his men, becoming giddy and faint from the intense cold, were soon obliged to go down, and Hobson announced the state of affairs in as hopeful a tone as he could assume.

"The bears," he said, "are now upon the roof. We ourselves have nothing to fear, as they can't get into our rooms; but they may force an entrance to the loft, and devour the furs stowed away there. Now these furs belong to the Company, and it is our duty to preserve them from injury. I ask you then, my friends, to aid me in removing them to a place of safety."

All eagerly volunteered, and relieving each other in parties of two or three, for none could have supported the intense severity of the cold for long at a time, they managed to carry all the furs into the large room in about an hour.

Whilst the work was proceeding, the bears continued their efforts to get in, and tried to lift up the rafters of the roof. In some places the laths became broken by their weight, and poor Mac-Nab was in despair; he had not reckoned upon such a contingency when he constructed the roof, and expected to see it give way every moment.

The day passed, however, without any change in the situation. The bears did not get in; but a no less formidable enemy, the cold, gradually penetrated into every room. The fires in the stoves burnt low; the fuel in reserve was almost exhausted; and before twelve o'clock, the last piece of wood would be burnt, and the genial warmth of the stove would no longer cheer the unhappy colonists.

Death would then await them—death in its most fearful form, from cold. The poor creatures, huddled together round the stove, felt that their own vital heat must soon become exhausted, but not a word of complaint passed their lips. The women bore their sufferings with the greatest heroism, and Mrs. Mac-Nab pressed her baby convulsively to her ice-cold breast. Some of the soldiers slept, or rather were wrapped in a heavy torpor, which could scarcely be called sleep. At three o'clock in the morning, Hobson consulted the thermometer hanging in the large room, about ten feet from the stove.

It marked 4° Fahrenheit below zero.

The Lieutenant pressed his hand to his forehead, and looked mournfully at his silent companions without a word. His half-condensed breath shrouded his face in a white cloud, and he was standing rooted to the spot when a hand was laid upon his shoulder. He started, and looked round to see Mrs. Barnett beside him.

"Something must be done, Lieutenant Hobson!" exclaimed the energetic woman; "we cannot die like this without an effort to save ourselves!"

"Yes," replied the Lieutenant, feeling revived by the moral courage of his companion—"yes, something must be done!" and he called together Long, Mac-Nab, and Rae the blacksmith, as the bravest men in his party. All, together with Mrs. Barnett, hastened to the window, and having washed the panes with boiling water, they consulted the thermometer outside.

"Seventy-two degrees!" cried Hobson. "My friends, two courses only are open to us, we can risk our lives to get a fresh supply of fuel, or we can burn the benches, beds, partition walls, and everything in the house to feed our stoves for a few days longer. A desperate alternative, for the cold may last for some time yet; there is no sign of a change in the weather."

"Let us risk our lives to get fuel!" said Sergeant Long.

All agreed that it would be the best course, and without another word each one set to work to prepare for the emergency.

The following were the precautions taken to save the lives of those who were about to risk themselves for the sake of the general good:

The shed in which the wood was stored was about fifty steps on the left, behind the principal house. It was decided that one of the men should try and run to the shed. He was to take one rope wound round his body, and to carry another in his hand, one end of which was to be held by one of his comrades. Once at the shed, he was to load one of the sledges there with fuel, and tie one rope to the front, and the other to the back of the vehicle, so that it could be dragged backwards and forwards between the house and the shed without much danger. A tug violently shaking one or the other cord would be the signal that the sledge was filled with fuel at the shed, or unloaded at the house.

A very clever plan, certainly; but two things might defeat it. The door of the shed might be so blocked up with ice that it would be very difficult to open it, or the bears might come down from the roof and prowl about the court. Two risks to be run!

Long, Mac-Nab, and Rae, all three volunteered for the perilous service; but the Sergeant reminded the other two that they were married, and insisted upon being the first to venture.

When the Lieutenant expressed a wish to go himself, Mrs. Barnett said earnestly, "You are our chief; you have no right to expose yourself. Let Sergeant Long go."

Hobson could not but realise that his office imposed caution, and being called upon to decide which of his companions should go, he chose the Sergeant. Mrs. Barnett pressed the brave man's hand with ill-concealed emotion; and the rest of the colonists, asleep or stupefied, knew nothing of the attempt about to be made to save their lives.

Two long ropes were got ready. The Sergeant wound one round his body above the warm furs, worth some thousand pounds sterling, in which he was encased, and tied the other to his belt, on which he hung a tinder-box and a loaded revolver. Just before starting he swallowed down half a glass of rum, as he said, "to insure a good load of wood."

Hobson, Rae, and Mac-Nab accompanied the brave fellow through the kitchen, where the fire had just gone out, and into the passage. Rae climbed up to the trap-door of the loft, and peeping through it, made sure that the bears were still on the roof. The moment for action had arrived.

One door of the passage was open, and in spite of the thick furs in which they were wrapped, all felt chilled to the very marrow of their bones; and when the second door was pushed open, they recoiled for an instant, panting for breath, whilst the moisture held in suspension in the air of the passage covered the walls and the floor with fine snow.

The weather outside was extremely dry, and the stars shone with extraordinary brilliancy. Sergeant Long rushed out without a moment's hesitation, dragging the cord behind him, one end of which was held by his companions; the outer door was pushed to, and Hobson, Mac-Nab, and Rae went back to the passage and closed the second door, behind which they waited. If Long did not return in a few minutes, they might conclude that his enterprise had succeeded, and that, safe in the shed, he was loading the first train with fuel. Ten minutes at the most ought to suffice for this operation, if he had been able to get the door open.

When the Sergeant was fairly off, Hobson and Mac-Nab walked together towards the end of the passage.

Meanwhile Rae had been watching the bears and the loft. It was so dark that all hoped Long's movements would escape the notice of the hungry animals.

Ten minutes elapsed, and the three watchers went back to the narrow space between the two doors, waiting for the signal to be given to drag in the sledge.

Five minutes more. The cord remained motionless in their hands! Their anxiety can be imagined. It was a quarter of an hour since the Sergeant had started, plenty of time for all he had to do, and he had given no signal.

Hobson waited a few minutes longer, and then tightening his hold on the end of the rope, he made a sign to his companions to pull with him. If the load of wood were not quite ready, the Sergeant could easily stop it from being dragged away.

The rope was pulled vigorously. A heavy object seemed to slide along the snow. In a few moments it reached the outer door.

It was the body of the Sergeant, with the rope round his waist. Poor Long had never reached the shed. He had fallen fainting to the ground, and after twenty minutes' exposure to such a temperature there was little hope that he would revive.

A cry of grief and despair burst from the lips of Mac-Nab and Rae. They lifted their unhappy comrade from the ground, and carried him into the passage; but as the Lieutenant was closing the outer door, something pushed violently against it, and a horrible growl was heard.

"Help!" cried Hobson.

Mac-Nab and Rae rushed to their officer's assistance; but Mrs. Barnett had been beforehand with them, and was struggling with all her strength to help Hobson to close the door. In vain; the monstrous brute, throwing the whole weight of its body against it, would force its way into the passage in another moment.

Mrs. Barnett, whose presence of mind did not forsake her now, seized one of the pistols in the Lieutenant's belt, and waiting quietly until the animal shoved its head between the door and the wall, discharged the contents into its open mouth.

The bear fell backwards, mortally wounded no doubt, and the door was shut and securely fastened.

The body of the Sergeant was then carried into the large room. But, alas! the fire was dying out. How was it possible to restore the vital heat with no means of obtaining warmth?

"I will go—I will go and fetch some wood!" cried the blacksmith Rae.

"Yes, Rae, we will go together!" exclaimed Mrs. Barnett, whose courage was unabated.

"No, my friends, no!" cried Hobson; "you would fall victims to the cold, or the bears, or both. Let us burn all there is to burn in the house, and leave the rest to God!"

And the poor half-frozen settlers rose and laid about them with their hatchets like madmen. Benches, tables, and partition walls were thrown down, broken up, crushed to pieces, and piled up in the stove of the large room and kitchen furnace. Very soon good fires were burning, on which a few drops of walrus-oil were poured, so that the temperature of the rooms quickly rose a dozen degrees.

Every effort was made to restore the Sergeant. He was rubbed with warm rum, and gradually the circulation of his blood was restored. The white blotches with which parts of his body were covered began to disappear; but he had suffered dreadfully, and several hours elapsed before he could articulate a word. He was laid in a warm bed, and Mrs. Barnett and Madge watched by him until the next morning.

Meanwhile Hobson, Mac-Nab, and Rae consulted how best to escape from their terrible situation. It was impossible to shut their eyes to the fact that in two days this fresh supply of fuel would be exhausted, and then, if the cold continued, what would become of them all? The new moon had risen forty-eight hours ago, and there was no sign of a change in the weather! The north wind still swept the face of the country with its icy breath; the barometer remained at "fine dry weather;" and there was not a vapour to be seen above the endless succession of ice-fields. There was reason to fear that the intense cold would last a long time yet, but what was to be done? Would it do to try once more to get to the wood-shed, when the bears had been roused by the shot, and rendered doubly dangerous? Would it be possible to attack these dreadful creatures in the open air? No, it would be madness, and certain death for all!

Fortunately the temperature of the rooms had now become more bearable, and in the morning Mrs. Joliffe served up a breakfast of hot meat and tea. Hot grog was served out, and the brave Sergeant was able to take his share. The heat from the stoves warmed the bodies and reanimated the drooping courage of the poor colonists, who were now ready to attack the bears at a word from Hobson. But the

Lieutenant, thinking the forces unequally matched, would not risk the attempt; and it appeared likely that the day would pass without any incident worthy of note, when at about three o'clock in the afternoon a great noise was heard on the top of the house.

"There they are!" cried two or three soldiers, hastily arming themselves with hatchets and pistols.

It was evident that the bears had torn away one of the rafters of the roof, and got into the loft.

"Let every one remain where he is!" cried the Lieutenant. "Rae, the trap!"

The blacksmith rushed into the passage, scaled the ladder, and shut and securely fastened the trap-door.

A dreadful noise was now heard—growling, stamping of feet, and tearing of claws. It was doubtful whether the danger of the anxious listeners was increased, or the reverse. Some were of opinion that if all the bears were in the loft, it would be easier to attack them. They would be less formidable in a narrow space, and there would not be the same risk of suffocation from cold. Of course a conflict with such fierce creatures must still be very perilous, but it no longer appeared so desperate as before.

It was now debated whether it would be better to go and attack the besiegers, or to remain on the defensive. Only one soldier could get through the narrow trap-door at a time, and this made Hobson hesitate, and finally resolve to wait. The Sergeant and others, whose bravery none could doubt, agreed that he was in the right, and it might be possible that some new incident would occur to modify the situation. It was almost impossible for the bears to break through the beams of the ceiling, as they had the rafters of the roof, so that there was little fear that they would get on to the ground-floor.

The day passed by in anxious expectation, and at night no one could sleep for the uproar made by the furious beasts. The next day, about nine o'clock, a fresh complication compelled Hobson to take active steps.

He knew that the pipes of the stove and kitchen furnace ran all along the loft, and being made of lime-bricks but imperfectly cemented together, they could not resist great pressure for any length of time. Now some of the bears scratched at the masonry, whilst others leant against the pipes for the sake of the warmth from the stove; so that the bricks began to give way, and soon the stoves and furnace ceased to draw.

This really was an irreparable misfortune, which would have disheartened less energetic men. But things were not yet at their worst. Whilst the fire became lower and lower, a thick, nauseous, acrid smoke filled the house; the pipes were broken, and the smoke soon became so thick that the lamps went out. Hobson now saw that he must leave the house if he wished to escape suffocation, but to leave the house would be to perish with cold. At this fresh misfortune some of the women screamed; and Hobson, seizing a hatchet, shouted in a loud voice—

"To the bears! to the bears, my friends!"

It was the forlorn-hope. These terrible creatures must be destroyed. All rushed into the passage and made for the ladder, Hobson leading the way. The trap-door was opened, and a few shots were fired into the black whirlpool of smoke. Mingled howls and screams were heard, and blood began to flow on both sides; but the fearful conflict was waged in profound darkness.

In the midst of the *mêlée* a terrible rumbling sound suddenly drowned the tumult, the ground became violently agitated, and the house rocked as if it were being torn up from its foundations. The beams of the walls separated, and through the openings Hobson and his companions saw the terrified bears rushing away into the darkness, howling with rage and fright.

HARRIET
BEECHER STOWE

H ARRIET BEECHER STOWE (1811–1896) did not permit her
ignorance of Canada to stop her from using the country as a
setting for the dramatic conclusions to two of her best known works.
Like Jules Verne, she had at first but a brief view of Canada from the
perch of Niagara Falls (made during a tour of the area in 1834) and it
is even possible that she did not cross the border but only looked
over to the Canadian shore from the American side. In a letter to a
friend, she writes in a style tinged with a strict religious fervour:

> I have seen it (Niagara) and yet live. Oh where is your soul? Never
> mind, though. Let me tell, if I can, what is unutterable. Elisa-
> beth, it is not *like* anything; it did not look like anything I
> expected; it did not look like a waterfall. I did not once think
> whether it was high or low; whether it roared or didn't roar;
> whether it equalled my expectations or not. My mind whirled
> off, it seemed to me, in a new, strange world. It seemed unearthly,
> like the strange, dim images in the Revelation. I thought of the
> great white throne; the rainbow around it; the throne in sight like
> unto an emerald; and oh! that beautiful water rising like moon-
> light, falling as the soul sinks when it dies, to rise refined, spiritu-
> alized, and pure.

As descriptions of Niagara go, this is hardly memorable, except for the tantalizing fact that it hints at a vision of Canada more ethereal, more benign, than is encountered elsewhere in foreign descriptions of the Falls. The religious envelope to her depiction suggests that, in her novels, subconsciously at least, Stowe regarded Canada as a place of blissful refuge because it was entered by such divine gates. She used adjectives more normally associated with the celestial: free, noble, equitable, pure. This is not to say that she thought of Canadians as angels. She just didn't think of them much at all. Canadians were certainly human to her; but she thought of Canada holistically, as an ideal nation (one of singular beneficence), rather than as a place where real individuals resided. In her mind, and certainly in *Uncle Tom's Cabin*, and in her second novel, *Dred*, the further one travels north, the more benign, the more Christian, is the treatment of blacks.

By contrast, in Louisiana—as far from Canada as it was then possible for an American slave to live—the treatment of blacks is far from angelic: the slaveowner Simon Legree whips Uncle Tom to death. But, even in Stowe's deepest south, empathetic characters do exist, although it is no coincidence that Stowe gives such characters Canadian connections: the most sympathetic of the southern slave owners, Augustine St. Clare, is a descendant of Acadians, and his daughter is named Evangeline, after the Longfellow heroine who pined for a happiness she had known uniquely in Canada.

Harriet Beecher was born and raised in Connecticut, but moved as a young woman with her father to Cincinnati, Ohio where he was to head the Theological Seminary. While there, she married one of her father's students, later a professor in his own right, Calvin Stowe. Debates about slavery were increasing in vehemence in mid-century and in middle America, but the passage of the Fugitive Slave Act in 1850 helped to galvanize many, including Harriet Beecher Stowe, into political action.

Around this time, she met Reverend Josiah Henson, the liberated slave whose life, more than any other, was to be the basis of Uncle Tom. When he was an adolescent, Henson's shoulders had been broken during a whipping, permanently restricting the motion of his arms. Yet he forgave his master. Another owner promoted him to overseer, and entrusted him with the transfer of an entire plantation of slaves. In her book *A Key To Uncle Tom's Cabin*, Stowe describes the subsequent actions of Henson which have made the appellation "Uncle Tom" pejorative to so many blacks today:

> Henson was to take them alone, without any other attendant, from Maryland to Kentucky, a distance of some thousands of miles, giving only his promise as a Christian that he would faithfully perform this undertaking. On the way thither they passed through a portion of Ohio, and there Henson was informed that he could now secure his own freedom and that of all his fellows, and he was strongly urged to do it. He was exceedingly tempted and tried, but his Christian principle was invulnerable. No inducements could lead him to feel that it was right for a Christian to violate a pledge solemnly given, and his influence over the whole band was so great that he took them all with him into Kentucky.

Such was his gratitude to Henson for this selflessness, the slaveowner cruelly ordered his son to sell Henson in New Orleans. On the trip down the Mississippi River, the son became deathly ill, and survived solely because of the ministrations doled by Henson. For saving the life of the slaveowner's son, Henson was rewarded with cursory compliments, and the knowledge that he was still going to be sold. Finally, sufficiently fed up, Henson set off with his family for Canada, by foot, by night, resting by day: fugitive slaves.

Reaching Lake Erie, they encountered the sympathetic skipper of a lake boat, who transported the Hensons to Fort Erie. Years later, with the aid of an amanuensis, he wrote his autobiography, and described his arrival:

> It was the 28th of October 1830, in the morning when my feet first touched the Canada shore. I threw myself on the ground,

rolled in the sand, seized handfuls of it and kissed them, and danced around till, in the eyes of several who were present, I passed for a madman.

After some years working as a hired hand in the Niagara Peninsula, Henson began a collective farm near Dresden, Ontario, with others who had arrived on the underground railway. The site has been designated by the Government of Ontario as the Uncle Tom's Cabin Historic Site.

Some sense of Stowe's reverential fascination with Henson's life story can be gleaned from her description of his settlement in Canada: "With a degree of prudence, courage and address which can scarcely find a parallel in any history, he managed, with his wife and two children, to escape into Canada. Here he learned to read, and by his superior talent and capacity for management, laid the foundation for the fugitive settlement of Dawn, which is understood to be one of the most flourishing in Canada."

Taking elements of Henson's life as her starting point, Stowe created her first novel, a long work distinguished by the then relatively unknown fictional device of parallel principal plots. While Uncle Tom descends into a maelstrom of barbarity, culminating with his death under the whipcord of Legree, his friends George and Eliza Harris escape, via various machinations, to Canada, freedom, and a new life.

Uncle Tom's Cabin was published in book form in 1852 and quickly became one of the bestselling novels of nineteenth-century America. It was translated into several languages, and its author welcomed the international celebrity so occasioned. She was probably less happy with the stage adaptations of the story, each subsequent version more ludicrous in its distortions than the last. One French version has the fugitive George and Eliza Harris canoeing east on Lake Erie, pursued by a slave-catcher. In desperation, they paddle down the Niagara River and somehow (alas, the playwright has omitted the mechanism from the stage directions) they plunge over the gorge, land upright in their canoe, and continue to paddle to safety on Canada's shores while leaving their pursuer drowned in the cataract's fury. In many of the productions, several of the characters who die in the novel, including Uncle Tom, were allowed to live. Perhaps the most preposterous of the British productions was the one which featured the unusual arrival of George Harris in Canada: as he stepped, finally a free man, onto Canadian soil:

> he took out of one of his coattails a large cotton pocket handker-chief which displayed the British emblem, and spread it under his chin like porous-plaster. This was the cue for the orchestra, which struck up "God Save the Queen."

While it is a relief to dismiss such foolish work with a smile, it is also sobering to recall that, in the absence of any stage productions at the time which accurately portrayed Canada or Canadians, many foreigners would have formed their image of this country on the basis of such nonsense. Anyone who doubts this need only witness today the pervasiveness with which Hollywood has propagated parodies, for example, of Arabic culture. Let no one doubt the popularity of Harriet Beecher Stowe's story: as late as 1878, more than a quarter of a century after the first publication, London saw five different productions of *Uncle Tom's Cabin*—all running concurrently.

Many people regard Stowe as an abolitionist, but they are wrong. While she was opposed to slavery, she did not align herself with abolitionists. Rather, initially at least, she hoped that the argument of her novel and intellectual rigour would win the slaveowners over to her point of view. Doubt still exists regarding her views on race and on whether blacks untouched by white ancestors were even capable of self-administration. In 1854, for instance, she reported, without irony, on a conversation she had in England with the Duke of Argyll:

> I told him my impression was, that Canada would be a much better place to develop the energies of the [black] race. First, on the account of its cold and bracing climate; second, because never having been a slave state, the white population there are more thrifty and industrious and of course the influence of such

a community was better adapted to form thrift and industry in the negro.

In this one remark, Harriet Beecher Stowe epitomizes much of the ignorance, arrogance, and generosity with which so many Americans regard Canada. Ignorance because she was unaware that Canada did not ban slavery until 1834 (posters for slave sales in Toronto, for example, can be seen in museums); arrogance because it did not even cross her mind to consult Canadians in advance about her plans for their country (for her, Canada was but a *tabula rasa* where the failed experiments of Americans could be recast and reworked successfully by presumably wiser, chastened Americans; if Canadians happened to be present, they would presumably either mind their own business or come to see the superiority of the American experiments); and generosity because nonetheless she continued to regard the country as a kinder, gentler, superior America, the land where the fresh start was still possible, the final frontier where all races, red, white, and black, might live in harmony—this vision of a reborn America, of course, being an assuredly left-handed compliment from the Canadian perspective. Notably, when she made the above remark, she still had not seen the country with her own eyes in any meaningful way.

By the time she came to write *Dred*, her second novel, Stowe's attitude to blacks, the south, slaveowners, the harmony of the races, everything which earlier had been marked by optimism, was now transmogrified by pessimism and despair—all, that is, except for her vision of Canada. Her despondency can be sensed from the subtitle of her book: *A Tale of the Great Dismal Swamp*. From this cheery beginning, things get worse: well-intentioned slaveowner Edward Clayton conspires to do all he can to educate and elevate his charges, usually with disappointing results. The lugubrious tale proceeds until, after hundreds of dolorous and perplexing pages, Edward Clayton decides where real contentment lies: Canada. The principals of the novel move to this nation and live happily ever after in arcadian harmony.

Like her neighbour Mark Twain, Stowe suffered from Canadian

book pirates, and hoping to curtail their theft of her copyright of an upcoming book, *Oldtown Folks*, she chose to reside in Montreal from May 11-19, 1869, in order to be "resident" on soil of the British Empire on the day when her book was published.

Given the Olympian image she had projected onto the country in the 1850s, her reports on its actual existence make it seem merely human. Only one letter seems to survive from this Montreal visit: a note to her daughter describing the extreme variances in the weather, her room on rue Notre Dame, and the fact that she was invited to evening parties with pleasant, hospitable people. This letter, then, is hardly the shout of "Eureka!" one might have expected from an author arriving in what she had presented as the black person's Shangri-la.

Stowe was far more loquacious, however, in her epistles written for *Hearth & Home*, a weekly periodical of which she was one of two editors. Over three weeks, she described her preparations for, arrival in, visit to, and departure from Montreal (without alluding to her copyright problems) in terms which any Montrealer—any Canadian—today will find peculiar: for distraction, for example, she attends three different church services within a single day. More oddly, one would scarcely know from her commentary that she has spent a week in the largest French-speaking city on the continent; her ears and gaze are almost entirely reserved for English-speaking culture and persons.

The following pacific commentary, however, was penned against a tempestuous background: as reading material for her voyage, Stowe had purchased a book only recently published in the United States, *My Recollections of Lord Byron* by Countess Guiccioli, the last acknowledged mistress of the legendary poet. During her week in Canada, with each turn of the page, Stowe became more and more enraged at what she regarded as an Italian harlot's calumny of Lady Byron. Before her return to the U.S.A., Stowe was determined to write the work which she had hitherto never dared to contemplate, a lengthy composition that would expose Lord Byron's incestuous involvement with his half-sister. The article appeared in *The Atlantic*, and was later published as *Lady Byron Vindicated* (1870).

Harriet Beecher Stowe in Montreal, May 1869. By this date, Notman of Montreal was the most celebrated portrait photographer on the continent, and like many visitors to Canada, Stowe availed herself of the chance for a formal portrait. Courtesy of the McCord Museum of Canadian History, Notman Photographic Archives.

Immediately, the English press and public, until now among her grandest champions, violently turned against her, vilifying her writing as nothing more than slander of a great Briton. Her reputation never recovered.

Of the three articles touching on Canada in *Hearth & Home*, the first deals mainly with her preparations for the voyage and her departure from her home in Florida near the St. John's River. The following excerpt is from the second and third articles, dated June 5 and 12, 1869.

June 5, 1869

On the St. John's, north, we find only the first chilly buddings of spring. In the public square of Montreal, where the city authorities collect and deposit the street-cleanings of winter snows, there still remain cold unmelted snow-banks and now and then, in passing through the streets, one looks down an alley, or through into a yard, to see still a snow-bank. Nevertheless, even in Canada, spring has come. We were invited last evening to a friendly tea in the outskirts of the city, high up on the sides of a mountain. There a Canadian brother editor hath built him a fair tabernacle which overlooks all Montreal—the wide course of the St. Lawrence far and near. From an elevated terrace in his grounds, we could look on a wide panorama, and count the distant mountain-peaks around. In a clear day, we were told that Mount Mansfield, in Vermont, was to be seen in the tableau. The grounds were blooming with beds of hyacinths, and with hundreds of thousands of tulips just in bud, and ready to pour forth their blossoms in a few weeks.

Our friend is a wonderful tulip-fancier, and such an array, such a number of ranges of tulip-beds, we never saw before. In a week or two, that mountain dwelling will be like an army with banners. Then we went into a greenhouse, and saw such a wonderful show of blossoming pelargoniums; florists' flowers of every shade, from most brilliant white to darkest crimson, with every kind of fleck, and streak, and mottle, and stain, and mark in which these florist wonders disport themselves. We saw oleanders, such as we left growing wild and free on the banks of the St. John's River, looking down on us over the shelves of the greenhouse. These cold regions seem to stimulate men to fling down the gauntlet at the feet of Nature. They heap up glass houses and kindle fires, and make to themselves an artificial tropics among their snow-banks, and insist on disputing with reluctant Nature, inch by inch, her fruits and her flowers.

The spring hue, when once declared, comes by leaps and bounds. Leaves long delaying seem to be full born in a day. The short three months of vegetation are almost all full hot summer, with very little spring. And for six months of the year there is one deep, un-broken snow—then bid good-by to their fences, and ride four feet above them over a wide solid snow-plain.

Our friend took us to a young mountain-ash tree which had been maimed and mutilated by its weight of snow, and showed us how, standing under a wall, it had been buried under fifteen feet of the winter covering; and yet there it was, good as new, with its young shoots fresh upon it.

In the yard, nicer than all these, were a lot of blooming young girls, whom it might do one's heart good to look at. They were as bright-cheeked and glowing as if they had been flowers of the tropics. There was no trace of the snow-bird in their complexions but rather the brightness of the Florida pomegranate. We have remarked this wholesome brilliancy of complexion and roundness of outline in the girls of Canada as a sign that the climate, though severe, is not unhealthy.

"Tell me, girls," I said to a group of them, among whom I was sitting in the evening, "now, which do you like best—winter or summer?"

All said: "Winter."

"Why, what do you do in winter?"

"Oh! we skate, and we walk on snow-shoes, and we have sleigh-rides, and the air is so splendid and so clear!"

The home life in Canada has much of the warm, hospitable richness of the English stock. In the circle where we have principally visited during our sojourn here, the blood and lineage of England and Scotland are plainly to be distinguished. It is almost like being in the old countries again to be with them. Scotland, in particular, has done a great work toward the making up of Canada. One recognizes the good old traditional Scotch names on the signs in the streets, and one sees marks of the blood in the high cheek-bones, the keen, bright, thoughtful eyes, the warm natures, the shrewd practical sense, and the intense yet repressed enthusiasm which characterize the Scotch people. Canada is a sturdy country to have to do with, and largely from this admixture of Scotch element.

During the whole time since we have been here in Montreal, and for days before, the Episcopal Synod have been trying to choose a metropolitan Bishop of Montreal, and have remained fixed in a dead lock, the clergy voting for one man and the laity for another with untiring pertinacity. Last autumn, after a long season of such fruitless balloting, the Synod adjourned over to spring, without making any choice, and it really seemed for a time as if a similar result must take place this spring. We wondered at the thing till we went into the Synod and saw the unmistakable Scotch faces of the laity. One could see that the Campbells, and the Frazers, and the Macs of every ilk and name were there, staunch as so many shepherd-dogs, and as determined. Time is no sort of account to a Scotchman; when once he has got his foot down, you might as well try to move Loch Lomond.

It was a stormy sort of session, for the House of Bishops did the nominating; but Sandie had his hand in at the voting, and Sandie had his opinion as to what he ought to have in his bishop, and meant to keep to it.

There is no doubt about it that Scotchmen are but indifferently adapted to the Episcopal Church. There were many scenes in this

convention flavored with an unmistakable spice of Jenny Geddes'
three-legged stool, that played such a part in times of old.

The candidate of the laity was the Bishop of Huron, or, as they
call him here in Canada, the *Lord* Bishop of Huron, who is, we are
informed, decidedly Low Church in his sentiments, who preaches
and prays and tends the sheep at all hours in the way that it seems to
these Canadians a bishop ought to do.

But as the Bishop of Montreal is a metropolitan, aud his authority extends over every other bishop it was deemed desirable by the
Bishop and clergy that he should be a man of no one party; but a
man of wide culture, broad views, genial and tolerant piety, who
could understand and wisely guide men of all differing shades of
opinion.

Their candidates were men selected from the flower of the
English Church, men with a marked record as writers and laborers
for good; but the mere fact of their being from across the water, laid
them all open to suspicion. Sandie was jealous of his rights, and
prompt to smell popery and Puseyism in every English name; and,
besides all that, Sandie has a great passion for having his own way,
because it is his own way, which is quite constitutional with him; and
so, for day after day the dead lock continued. Finally, however, the
two parties came to an agreement upon Dr. Oxenden, of England, a
moderate man with evangelical tendencies, the author of many popular works of practical piety and well reputed for piety and learning.

A Scotch lay delegate, who gave forth his sentiments quite freely
in the public room of the Ottawa House, seemed not particularly
pleased with the result.

"Here we've been staying all this time in Montreal at our own
charge, paying our own way, and we ought to have got the victory on
our side," he said, "but the Montreal folk deserted us."

"And pray who have you got at last?"

"Oh! I don't know; it's either Oxygen or Hydrogen—I don't just
remember which."

Montreal is a most religious city. It was founded as a Romish missionary station, and when ceded by the French to the English it was

with the express stipulation of reserving to the Church all the grants of land and money: all the privileges and immunities that they enjoyed under France.

The land, far as the eye can reach, around Montreal is the property of different religious orders who, by its rise in value, have become immensely rich. Hospitals, convents, and churches on the grandest scale, and with the most ample accommodations, are the result.

The English Church and the Scotch Presbyterian, and the Congregationalists from the United States, have not been behindhand with their religious buildings, and, in consequence, Montreal is a mountain of churches. Every shade and form of faith is here well represented in wood or stone, and the gospel feast set forth in every form and shape to suit the spiritual appetite of all inquirers.

A long list of newspaper advertisements in the Saturday evening paper sets forth such an amount of preaching and praying in various places on Sunday, that the stranger is puzzled with the variety.

At daybreak on Sunday morning a loud chorus of bells announced to the world that it was Whit-Sunday, or, as our Catholic brethren call it, Pentecost.

We had choice of many churches, but on the principle of seeking out the sect that is everywhere spoken against, we chose a small Ritualistic church on a narrow, obscure street, which is repudiated by the Church and ridiculed by the world, who give it the designation of "Wood's Minstrels." Here we found, however, a crowded congregation of serious, earnest people, who *sung* the ordinary English service of the Book of Common Prayer, instead of saying it. Now, as the Rubric expressly provides that it shall be said or sung, it is hard to see what departure from order there is in that.

The music used was the Gregorian tunes, and everyman, woman, and child in the house stood up and joined heartily and with one accord, and looked so serious and earnest that we could not but ask whether it would be any better or more acceptable to God if they had sat in dozing quietude while a quartette choir in a distant part of the church performed their praises and prayers for them in the most select opera airs of the season. Such are the practices that we remember in many churches where the praises of God are entirely given over into the hands of three or four paid artists. The sermon was very short, very earnest, very simple and scriptural, and although entirely without any ambition or effort at rhetorical or logical power, had much that might edify a simple Christian. There were one or two expressions which we could have wished different, which struck us as unwise, but, on the whole, the spirit of the whole was refreshingly earnest and devout.

Would it not be better if those who spend their breath in scolding about ritualistic movements would, in place of this, imitate certain points in their service—their energy, their whole-hearted devotion? If each party, instead of abusing the other, would study and endeavor to adopt each other's really useful and strong points, would not the Church and the world both be improved?

In the afternoon, the Rev. Mr. Frazer preached in the Scotch Presbyterian church. Here too was a crowded, serious, earnest congregation, and here too was congregational singing from the old Scotch version, the whole congregation standing up and singing the good old tunes of Lennox with a loud voice, in a refreshing manner. Mr. Frazer is a zealous preacher, of the style that we should call Revivalist in the States, and is, we perceive, very widely known and appreciated here. In the evening, that we might go to the extreme end of the pole, we went to a private hall to hear Lord A.P. Cecil, the son of the Marquis of Exeter, a Plymouth brother, who threw up his commission as officer in the British army that he might devote himself to the work of a missionary in the wilds of Canada.

At the appointed hour, we saw upon the platform a tall, slender young man, of about five and twenty, well formed, lithe and elastic in his figure, with a finely turned head, rather delicate and classical features, with small white hands, and an appearance betokening breeding and refinement. He was dressed in a simple gray suit, and had a small testament and hymn-book.

He began by reading the first verse of a revival hymn, which he then sung, and was joined in it by the whole audience. He then knelt down and prayed with an impassioned, earnest simplicity that was quite touching. After this he opened his testament and began an exposition of Luke 15. His audience seemed to be mostly composed of plain earnest people of the middle and working classes, who had come with testaments provided, which they also opened and followed him.

The principal characteristic of his preaching was a fervent, earnest simplicity and an undoubting faith. Faith—simple, literal faith in the words of Jesus, seemed to be the whole of his message. It was a pointing to the personal present Jesus, and a plea with every soul to embrace him as a saviour.

When we returned late in the evening to our hotel, our waiter appeared to suppose that of course we had been attending the preaching of the Church of the Jesuits, and seemed so sincerely to lament that we had missed it, and gave such glowing accounts of what we should have heard, that we were quite obliged to him. Thus earnestly, in so many ways in this cold, intense, earnest Canada, is the One Great Concern pressed upon our attention.

For ourselves, we listened to one and all with no desire to criticize, and with the hope that in all we heard Christ preached that therein we may rejoice—and will rejoice.

In our very neighborhood the wondrous sound of the great bells of Notre Dame tell us of services going on there, which doubtless bring peace to many pious souls who have been led by the ancient pathways of Rome.

The services there are not to us intelligible, but we do not the less appreciate what they may be to those differently educated. The schools, hospitals, works of charity of the Romish Church here, are something *immense*, and we should not envy the heart of that person who could pass through them all without a thrill of sympathy and a wishing of Godspeed to those workers for human good.

We are yet undecided whether to go Quebec or not. The weather is cold, sour, and forbidding, and from the St. John's, Florida, to the St. John's, Canada, is a freezing exchange. We can well understand how it comes to pass that animals hibernate in winter. We are in a torpid and sleepy state, and but half alive, and a little more of the same sort of sensation would dispose us to roll up in a ball like a squirrel, and lie down to a six month's nap, and not wake till summer is fully declared.

Meanwhile, we are most fortunate in having found most comfortable quarters. The Ottawa House has nice, cosy rooms, finely furnished and nicely cared for, and we sit by "our ain fireside" and enjoy warmth and comfort, though the skies scowl without. If one wants a home-like, quiet, well-kept rest in Montreal, we can cheerfully recommend the Ottawa House....

June 12, 1869

We fancy the St. John's South, calling to the St. John's North: "What are the girls doing up where you are?"

One always wants, you know, to find out what *the girls* are doing.

"Skating and having parties on snow shoes, and sliding down hill," says St. John's North. "What are your girls doing?"

"Fanning themselves, and gathering jessamine-blossoms and orange-buds, and eating the perfected oranges off the bough."

The Montreal young people have a way of sliding down hill, to which they give a peculiar name, with an Indian sound, that sounded like "To-ba-gan-ing." We beg pardon of the belles of Montreal, but though many lovely lips pronounced this sound to us with the assurance that it was something splendid, we could not get nearer the sound than that.

It consists in sliding down hill, as near as we can make it out, upon a series of lithe, elastic sleds, made of strips of bark; the whole set being tied together, and ladies and gentlemen interchangeably sitting together.

We observed that the mammas spoke the thing doubtfully. But the young men and maidens with enthusiasm. There is a spice of danger in it, now and then an upset of a train, and maybe a sprain, or the breaking of a limb—something verging on the heroic, you see; something in the way of adventure gives spice to an affair.

We saw a great many pretty girls in Montreal; they made quite a deep impression upon us. They are blooming, spicy, spirited, and understand the arts and crafts of womanhood to quite good purpose, and it really made one long to know more of them, to be there a day or two.

We take this occasion to send our love to half a dozen of them, who will know what we mean when they read this; for, dear *Hearth and Home*, you must know that we were quite flattered to find *you* in brisk circulation among some of them, and to hear that you were quite worn out with being read there.

Which do we like the best, the St. John's, South, or St. John's, North? Don't ask us. Every latitude and soil and region has its flowers. We remember once being at the Great St. Bernard in the middle of August. The lake was half frozen over, and our mule sank to his middle in a snow-drift, and we said: "This is the region of utter desolation." Nevertheless, walking out, we found four or five kinds of flowers growing low and close to the ground, whose imperishable and peculiar beauty has haunted our mind ever since.

There was a green velvet moss with a feathery pink blossom; there was a low, starry blue gentian, the blue of which was like illuminated *Lapis lazuli*; and there was still another fringed gentian that actually stood and blossomed in snow-drifts, each stalk with its little ring of space around it, where the snow had melted by the plants vitality. Yes, there were flowers even there, and flowers whose rare beauty was peculiar to that cold latitude. And so it is with social life in colder regions. Nevertheless, for our individual self, we could not bear it. The air of Canada weighed on us like a mountain. The nerves that had been all smoothed out and softened to dreamy rest in the sunny regions of Florida became tense, and knotted, and twisted, and cramp and rheumatism and a strange feeling of utter oppression came over us. Our limbs seemed heavy; we could scarcely mount the stairs, and we were all the time wishing we were asleep. We were, in fact, approaching the first stages of hibernation such as puts the white bears to rest for six months in the polar regions.

SAMUEL BUTLER

S AMUEL BUTLER (1835–1902), the English author of *Erewhon* and *The Way of All Flesh,* had made a small fortune raising sheep in New Zealand. Upon returning to Great Britain, he received and followed bad financial counsel, and invested most of his life savings in the fetchingly named Canada Tanning Extract Company. The company had been founded by a Lindsay, Ontario, man who believed his process for extracting tannin from tree bark would revolutionize the leather tanning business. While the extraction process was indeed impressive, regrettably for future sales, it hideously and permanently coloured the leather.

As a major investor in the firm, Butler had been appointed one of the company's directors. Concerned about its investment, the Board sent him to Montreal in June 1874 to investigate the enterprise's development problems at nearby village production sites. Still believing that the company's fortunes could be turned around, he arrived in Canada, full of expectation. In a letter to his sister May he wrote:

> We are now well in the St. Lawrence only about 300 miles from Quebec.... I have six clear weeks of holiday or what is just as good, and am already in very good condition. We saw some fine ice bergs: they are quite equal to their reputation for beauty: we are now passing close to the coast—a lovely cloudless day and I

grudge every minute that I am not on deck ... the South Coast of New Foundland is very bleak: mountains ranging up to I shd think 1,800 or 2,000 feet, but with large fields of snow, and sometimes gullies with snow filling them not 200 or 300 ft. above the sea....

Shortly after this he wrote to a woman friend, May Savage, with some wonderment at the customs of the French Canadians:

I am to stay with a "habitant" to-morrow in order that I may go to mass on Sunday and inspire the village with confidence in the company. Madame Vigneau has had so many lodgers since we started, that she has become quite rich, and out of gratitude has had a four-dollar mass said for the company. This is the best mass that money can buy in these parts; the cheapest is 25 cents or one shilling; the average is about half a dollar. I have instructed our agent to have an occasional mass said on our account, about 6 two-dollar masses a year for each set of weeks. This I am told will be about the right thing. There are bears and wolves and great cariboo deer in our woods—as big as oxen, but I have not seen any.

Butler returned to London to give his report, demanding severe changes in the on-site management of the company. Endowed by the Board with broader corporate powers, he returned to Montreal in August 1874, staying much longer than originally planned—staying, in fact, until the end of 1875. His Canadian experience resulted in his financial ruin. More than his naïve fellow directors, he could see, despite his impressive manoeuvres as a business executive, that the firm was doomed.

The Canadian experience, however, was a catalyst in his maturing. By mail, he improved his troubled relationship with his father. And when the affairs of business allowed him time, he sketched out ideas for future books, especially *Life and Habit*.

Given his financial losses and frustrations, it is not surprising that though he was cheered by the scenery, Butler found Montreal and environs an insult to the spirit. He also found the food wanting: "When the Canadians have a decent restaurant, they will be nicer people, and when they are nicer people they will have a decent restaurant."

He even found Canadian humour painful: "When I was there I found their jokes like their roads—very long, and not very good, leading to a little tin point of a spire which has been remorselessly obvious for miles without seeming to get any nearer." It was in this frame of mind, believing the culture as banal as the cuisine, that he wrote his notorious castigation of Montreal, a poem whose regard has outlasted that of the Rev. Charles Spurgeon, a Baptist preacher in Victorian England legendary for his fiery delivery and prudish severity.

A PSALM OF MONTREAL

The City of Montreal is one of the most rising and, in many respects, most agreeable on the American continent, but its inhabitants are as yet too busy with commerce to care greatly about the masterpieces of old Greek Art. In the Montreal Museum of Natural History I came upon two plaster casts, one of the Antinous and the other of the Discobolus—not the good one, but in my poem, of course, I intend the good one—banished from public view to a room where were all manner of skins, plants, snakes, insects, etc., and, in the middle of these, an old man stuffing an owl.

"Ah," said I, "so you have some antiques here; why don't you put them where people can see them?"

"Well, sir," answered the custodian, "you see they are rather vulgar."

He then talked a great deal and said his brother did all Mr. Spurgeon's printing.

The dialogue—perhaps true, perhaps imaginary, perhaps a little of the one and a little of the other—between the writer and this old man gave rise to the lines that follow:

Stowed away in a Montreal lumber room
The Discobolus standeth and turneth his face to the wall;
Dusty, cobweb-covered, maimed and set at naught,
Beauty crieth in an attic and no man regardeth:
          O God! O Montreal!

Beautiful by night and day, beautiful in summer and winter,
Whole or maimed, always and alike beautiful —
He preacheth gospel of grace to the skin of owls
And to one who seasoneth the skins of Canadian owls:
          O God! O Montreal!

When I saw him I was wroth and I said, "O Discobolus!
Beautiful Discobolus, a Prince both among gods and men!
What doest thou here, how camest thou hither, Discobolus,
Preaching gospel in vain to the skins of owls?"
          O God! O Montreal!

And I turned to the man of skins and said unto him, "O thou
    man of skins,
Wherefore hast thou done thus to shame the beauty of the Discobolus?"
But the Lord had hardened the heart of the man of skins
And he answered, "My brother-in-law is haberdasher to Mr.
    Spurgeon."
          O God! O Montreal!

"The Discobolus is put here because he is vulgar —
He has neither vest nor pants with which to cover his limbs;

I, Sir, am a person of most respectable connections —
My brother-in-law is haberdasher to Mr. Spurgeon."
                    O God! O Montreal!

Then I said, "O brother-in-law to Mr. Spurgeon's haberdasher,
Who seasonest also the skins of Canadian owls,
Thou callest trousers 'pants,' whereas I call them 'trousers,'
Therefore thou art in hell-fire and may the Lord pity thee !"
                    O God! O Montreal!

"Preferest thou the gospel of Montreal to the gospel of Hellas,
The gospel of thy connection with Mr. Spurgeon's haberdashery
    to the gospel of the Discobolus?"
Yet none the less blasphemed the beauty saying, "The Discobo-
    lus hath no gospel,
But my brother-in-law is haberdasher to Mr. Spurgeon."
                    O God! O Montreal!

GIOACCHINO ROSSINI

O NE OF THE GREATEST STORYTELLERS in music who ever lived began his operatic career with a farce featuring a Canadian. Gioacchino Rossini (1792–1868), the son of musical parents, while not himself a child prodigy, did give hints at an early age that he was destined for a career in music. Indeed, when he was a boy his singing voice was so fine (one is cut to the quick to discover) that consideration was given to castrating him in order to husband his soprano range. Fortunately for posterity, he was allowed to grow normally, studying music in Bologna while working part-time (to supplement the family income) as a singer and harpsichord player in itinerant provincial opera companies. From such humble beginnings he was to rise to become so famous that, as Stendhal exclaimed, "the fame of this hero knows no bounds except that of civilization itself."

During one of his part-time assignments, Rossini met the Morandis, a husband and wife team of musicians who were much impressed by the young man's musical knowledge and uncanny photographic memory for music. In 1810, the Morandis were scheduled to play at the Teatro San Moisè in Venice.

At that time, opera in the major cities of Italy was attended by the wealthy night after night for reasons more social than musical, a situation demanding an incessant flow of new operas to feed the demand for diversion. The impresario at the San Moisè, the Marchese

Cavalli, had scheduled five operas for a single season (Italian opera traditionally had three seasons per year), four of the operas to be pre-mières. A composer commissioned to write one of the new operas reneged at the eleventh hour on his commitment. The Marchese Cavalli, anxious to find a quick solution, happily welcomed the Morandis' suggestion that Rossini—though only eighteen years of age—should be called upon to create an opera, metaphorically overnight. *Carpe diem.* Rossini, like a young lion lusty with the smell of first prey in the air, raced to Venice and seized this chance by the nape.

Accounts vary regarding how long he actually took to compose the music for the one-act farce *La Cambiale di Matrimonio.* At most, he took a fortnight. The libretto, as was standard, had been written first, in this case by Gaetano Rossi after a popular comedy by Camillo Federici. Given the circumstances, Rossini probably had little opportunity to suggest changes. Constraints on the time available for musical composition were not his only challenge: the egos of the singers made the rehearsals painful:

> It is amusing to observe that, even on this very early occasion, the actors protested, not only that the music Rossini had written for them was too difficult and must be modified, but that the noisiness of the orchestra (how often will this reproach be made!) must be diminished. Rossini went home and burst into tears; but he ended by allowing Morandi to make the necessary changes, and, on November 3rd, 1810 ... before eight hundred spectators, his first opera was given.... Rosa Morandi took the principal part; the *primo buffo* Raffanelli was a good actor; there was a competent and agreeable trio, an air for soprano which was a foretaste of Rosina's [in *The Barber of Seville*] and a love-duet—"*Tornami a dir che m'ami*"—which was positively Belli-nesque in its rippling tenderness.... The proof of the operetta's relative success lies in its twelve performances of that season.

Musically, the opera, which premièred on November 3, 1810, has attracted high praise. One of Rossini's major biographers, Francis Toye, says of Rossini's first work for the stage:

> There are at least two attractive arias, a first-class trio with musical subjects, and characters admirably contrasted, and a duel scene which for comic martial swagger could not well be bettered. The most remarkable features of the score as a whole are its gaiety and high spirits. Indeed, it may be doubted whether any previous opera, Mozart's *Entführung* and Cimarosa's *Matrimonio Segreto* not excepted, had ever before been characterised by such sparkle, such a wholly irresponsible sense of fun. These, of course, were precisely the new attributes brought by Rossini into music.

The opera was remounted in Spain in 1816, and in German in Vienna in 1837 as *Der Bräutigam aus Canada*. The earliest Canadian performance would appear to have been a student production at the University of British Columbia in 1959. In our time, the opera has been recorded with no less a figure than Renata Scotto, and a compact disc and a video featuring other major performers have recently been issued.

From a Canadian point of view, the story of *La Cambiale di Matrimonio* is a most attractive one, for the central character, a Canadian, has, in comparison with the buffoonery of the Europeans, a personality nuanced, sensible, and morally decent. The meaning of the title of the opera is difficult to convey in English, for it is more than just a marriage contract. Inherent in the title is the sense of a purchase order, or even more accurately, an I.O.U.

The plot begins with the pompous English merchant Sir Toby Mill at his home in London, bemoaning his inability to comprehend a globe, a compass, and the magnetic north. In other words, from the very beginning of the opera, a subtle contrast is established: whereas Slook, the wealthy Canadian merchant, can travel with ease halfway round the globe, Sir Toby Mill, the European, cannot find his way across a simple map.

Mill's struggles with geography are interrupted by the arrival of a letter indicating Slook's imminent advent. Among other business matters, Slook asks for help in finding a wife to take back with him to Canada. Mill is eager to welcome the Canadian to his home, not only because he hopes to conclude much business with the man "from the Colonies" but because he sees a chance to offer his own daughter, Fanny, to Slook in marriage. Unfortunately for Fanny, Mill is such a boor that he speaks of his daughter as he does his merchandise, and even proposes to wed her to Slook by means of a promissory note, a bill of exchange, an I.O.U., a *"cambiale di matrimonio."* Perhaps wilfully, Sir Toby Mill seems unaware that Fanny is deeply in love with a poor bookkeeper, Edward Milfort. That amorous relationship, however, will never come to fruition under normal circumstances. Sir Toby will paternally forbid Fanny connubial bliss with someone so beneath her wealth and station.

Slook's arrival derives its comic appeal from the clash of cultures: the stage directions dictate that he should be costumed outrageously, which most directors interpret as part voyageur, part Indian brave. He is fiercely taken aback by the fawning of the servants and their attempts to relieve him of his outer clothes and to kiss his hand—the audience, then, is initially intended to believe that Slook is a bumpkin unfamiliar with even the elementary customs and manners of sophisticated cities.

Fanny, until she later realizes she is to be sold to Slook, immediately finds him charming; Slook, still unaware of the father's intentions, finds Fanny attractive; Sir Toby, because the customer is always right, finds Slook's Canadian, therefore uncommon, forthrightness of speech delightful.

Left alone, Fanny and Slook come to realize the purport of *la cambiale.* While acknowledging the barbarity of her father's method of transaction, Slook would like to have Fanny as his wife, and tries to woo her. But no fool, he soon garners the reason for her stiff reluctance, deduces her love for Edward, and settles on a noble course of action.

Wanting to please Fanny, and also to teach her father a lesson, Slook decides to make Edward Milfort his heir, and countersigns *la cambiale* over to Edward. Because Edward will now be rich, and because he has a document giving him conjugal rights to Fanny, Sir Toby has no choice but to accede. The opera ends with Edward and Fanny happy in the knowledge they will soon be married; the father happy because his daughter will wed a rich man; and Slook, returning to Canada, happy because he has done the right thing. The following are scenes appearing early in the opera.

---

from LA CAMBIALE DI MATRIMONIO

[*The Promissory Note of Marriage*]

Cast

TOBY MILL	Merchant
FANNY	His daughter
EDWARD MILFORT	Bookkeeper
SLOOK	Canadian merchant
NORTON	Mill's Cashier
CLARINA	Fanny's maid
	Various servants and employees of Toby Mill

TOBY Norton, my friend has arrived: he will be disembarking momentarily. From the boat he writes that he wants to close the deal, personally inspect the merchandise.

NORTON But what...

TOBY Quickly, Clarina, go and air the rooms overlooking the garden, and be quick about it.... Listen, tell my daughter to put on her Sunday best. Go! (*Clarina exits. Toby calls his servants by name, giving orders to each of them who come, and once they have received their orders, they leave.*)

Isachetto! My best carriage...

Salomone! My finest suit...

Lorenzo! One, possibly two more for dinner.

Set three extra places. We must go all out

to honour a man so special, grand, loyal:

Isn't that so, Norton?

NORTON (*trenchantly*) Yes, they broke the mold...

TOBY And his letter that came the other day!

Oh, such ingenuity! What sentiments!

Such trust! A true and rare voice

from the Golden Age, that in this Age of Iron,

seems even more surprising, more sublime.

NORTON Well, that depends on how one views the matter.

TOBY You have doubts, but listen:

(*he finds the previous letter*) I have read it a thousand times, and it has a style so rare it seems as new as when I read it first.

(*he reads aloud*) "Sir, etc. etc. etc., I have resolved to form a matrimonial agency. Over here, there is nothing of the sort. Thus, by the first ship to depart for these Colonies, kindly send me a wife matching the following measurements and qualities." Ah, what brilliant prose!

NORTON (*ironically*) Breathtaking!

TOBY And the best is yet to come.

(*continuing to read*) "No dowry is required, provided she comes from an honest family, not more than thirty years of age: docile, no freckles or blemishes, and a reputation absolutely untarnished: She should have a healthy and robust temperament, in order to stand up to the sea-crossing and the hardness of our weather, because, having just got her, I would hate to lose her, and be forced to bring in new supplies."

NORTON (*aside*) That's the worst nonsense I've ever heard!

TOBY Ah, such exactitude! Note the precision!
But the best is yet to come.
(*continuing to read*) "Upon receipt in good condition, as per the above, upon presentation of this letter as identification, or notarized copy of same, to avoid misunderstanding, I hereby declare that I will honour the signature and wed the bearer within two days of arrival, or upon first sight, whichever is more convenient, and I send you my best wishes. Yours sincerely. Slook of Canada." (*he inserts the letter into a book on a desk*)

NORTON And what were you contemplating?

TOBY Of fulfilling the order. As a matter of fact, I already have, and as soon as he arrives, he will be presented with the promissory note by my own daughter.

NORTON By Miss Fanny?

TOBY Of course. Why so surprised?

NORTON And if she doesn't like him?

TOBY Oh, but she must. Oh, yes indeed.

NORTON But what if she had…

TOBY What could she have?

NORTON But…

TOBY But! You annoy me, always contradicting!

NORTON But…

TOBY Enough! Leave!
(*Norton beginning his exit*) And the new bookkeeper?

NORTON I still haven't hired one.

TOBY Better hurry. We have much to do over the next little while. Ah, I can't wait for the hour when I can hug my dear North American! Oh, what a perfect husband for my daughter! Oh, what pleasure. What jolly good luck! (*exits*)

NORTON Poor Miss Fanny! But I still hope that our dear North American has come to Europe in vain!

Scene Three

(*Fanny and Edward, amorously arm in arm, enter*)

EDWARD Tell me again that you love me.
  That you'll always be mine.
FANNY I'll be whatever you desire,
  I'll be the one who adores you.
  You fill my soul with love,
  and it returns your love.
EDWARD And will you be mine?
FANNY I hope so.
EDWARD We are going to be so contented.
FANNY Oh, how happy!
EDWARD and FANNY (*together*) What delightful enchantment
  Is this requited love!
  Our love is propitious
  And by it we swear,
  And may it bring happiness
  To my tender heart.
EDWARD Yes, my dearest, let us hope. In just a few days my uncle
  will arrive. I place all of my trust in his affection for me.
FANNY But what about this man my father is expecting today!
  Lately, his words have been unnerving!
EDWARD However, when the two of us come to an agreement!…

Scene Four

(*Norton enters*)

NORTON Have you seen Mr. Mill?
TOBY Not as yet. What's the matter? Why are you so upset?
NORTON Terrible news: but not to worry. You're going to be married.

FANNY Oh my God!

EDWARD What are you talking about?

FANNY But how?

EDWARD And to whom?

NORTON There is a … look, why don't you read the marriage contract yourself, and then you can laugh. (*Fanny and Edward read, displaying hints of anger and temper.*)

FANNY Oh Edward!

NORTON Ah! What do you say?

EDWARD I'm shaking with rage: and is this any way to do things?

NORTON As if he were a proper businessman and Miss Fanny nothing more than merchandise.

EDWARD But this time his deal is just speculation.

FANNY It's impossible to believe my own father would sink so low as to forfeit me.

Scene Five

TOBY (*off stage*) Hurry! Quickly!

FANNY Ah, it's him! If he sees you!

TOBY (*off stage*) Everyone, ready!

EDWARD What can I do?

FANNY Poor us!

TOBY (*enters*) Norton … Fanny … Good, everyone is here … (*he sees Edward, and says suspiciously and impetuously*) Who are you? What do you want in this house? Why are you here? What's on your mind?

FANNY He is…

EDWARD (*confused*) Sir…

NORTON He is the new bookkeeper.

TOBY (*inspects*) Too young … and too *à la mode*.

NORTON That's his loss.

EDWARD I'm ready to dress according to your wishes.

TOBY Bravo! He's not so bad after all. Norton will tell you what I want.

FANNY [Sighs in relief]

TOBY Steady on, my child, and listen: a foreign chap is due to arrive presently, and you will be good to him, and give him these letters ... (*He removes the letter from the book, folds it, brings forth another letter, and gives both letters to Fanny.*)

FANNY And who is he? But I ... But...

TOBY Your future is secured...

(*Carriage bells are heard*)

Ah! The carriage ... he's here:

I'm going to greet him: Servants,

gather here ... here ... and here ... there.

Ah, you will see ... Fanny, cheer up!

(*Exits in high spirits with servants*)

FANNY Ah, woe is me...

NORTON Be watchful!

EDWARD Leave this to me.

FANNY What are you going to do?

EDWARD Have faith in him who loves you, and you will see.

Scene Six

(*A variety of servants precede Slook who is dressed so whimsically as to be a caricature, nonetheless grave: he enters baffled, protecting himself bodily from servants who are anxious to take his hat, carry his cane and kiss his hands.*)

SLOOK Thank you... Thank you...

Have patience ... not so fast, I said;

Slow down, will you?... what a compliment!

You good people confuse me:

Whoa! I said ... easy does it ... Hey! Enough!

I can't go forward I'm so mixed up...

Thank you... Thank you ... I'm confused...

I *do* know how you do things in Europe.

Just slow down, and let me start
to deliver my greetings as *I* want to.
(Slook escapes to the door, dons his hat, re-enters while removing his hat, and bows like a courtier.)

FANNY, CLARINA, EDWARD, NORTON *(aside)* Such a figure! And what manners!
I want to laugh but cry too!

TOBY *(aside)* Such ingenuousness! And what manners!
I'm going to love him even more!

SLOOK Firstly, I salute, kiss and hug
the lord and master of the house.
Then I do the same, with cordiality
of course, to the ladies.
(He approaches them, but they hurriedly retreat.)
What's the matter? Isn't it the custom here
To give a big hug to every woman?
Oh dear! What a pain!
What a primitive way to meet and chat!
We in Canada are blessed
with innocent freedom!
We're able to show, *sans façons*,
open hearts, friendly faces.
Of course we kiss, sure we hug,
but no one is offended.
Beautiful ladies, dearest ladies,
please show a little pity.
Don't force me to return
sour-faced to Canada.
So, then, please teach me: I don't want to cut a poor figure: but I must tell you, from my point of view, Europe seems all affectation.

FANNY *(aside)* Dear North American!

TOBY Hear! Hear! Long live the beautiful simplicity of North America.

SLOOK *(indicates Fanny)* Who is that zesty maiden?

TOBY Your type, eh? She has a letter of recommendation for you.

SLOOK I'll take it from her with all my heart.

EDWARD (*aside*) I am enraged!

FANNY (*aside*) Calm down!

SLOOK Have you managed to fulfill that purchase order I sent?

TOBY It's my hope that as soon as you've inspected the goods, you'll want to seal the deal.

SLOOK Even better! A good merchant wastes no time.

TOBY Cast your eye over there at that young woman: Norton, accompany the bookkeeper to his office. (*again, to Slook*) Make yourself at home, I beg you.

SLOOK OK.

TOBY Up there are your rooms.

SLOOK Thanks. (*Toby exits*)

EDWARD (*aside*) Oh Fanny! I'm so distraught!

NORTON (*to Edward*) Come on.

EDWARD (*shakes Slook strongly by the hand while gritting his teeth*) Goodbye, Mr. North America. (*exits with Norton*)

Scene Seven

(*Slook and Fanny*)

SLOOK "Servant!" (*behind Edward's back*) Boy, in Europe they definitely have strange and innovative compliments.

FANNY (*aside*) Behold the decisive moment.

SLOOK Meanwhile, let's have a look at the young lady ... there is a certain *je ne sais quoi* ... definitely ... statuesque and beautiful.

FANNY (*aside*) I'm certainly not going to utter the first word!

SLOOK So quiet! Such modesty! I'll begin. (*He approaches and bows.*) At your service, dear young lady!

FANNY But I am your servant! (*Respectfully, she lowers her gaze.*)

SLOOK Who are you, then? What do you want?

FANNY Read, and then you will know. (*hands him the letters*)

SLOOK (*reads*) Concise. I like that. (*continues to read with manifest pleasure*)

FANNY (*aside*) I'm going to have a fit.

SLOOK (*after reading, with enthusiasm*) Very good, Sir Toby! Very well done! (*with gallantry*) Would you please me by coming a little closer?

FANNY Right where I am is fine.

SLOOK But "there" is not so fine for me. And why do you keep your little eyes lowered?

FANNY Modesty…

SLOOK (*quickly*) I want to tell you … that is to say … do you have any idea what is in these letters?

FANNY No.

SLOOK No? (*aside*) I can only pull one word at a time. (*to Fanny*) Then pay attention, because there is something about you.

FANNY Hurry up, then.

SLOOK (*reads*) "Dear Mr. Slook. We have supplied you with a wife of the age, quality, and condition you requested, with all papers in order. She is our only daughter, Fanny, who will give you this letter along with the one you sent. Therefore, pay to the bearer on sight, or within two days (whichever is more convenient) the debts and obligations you have contracted with the undersigned. Yours in faith. Toby Mill."

FANNY (*aside*) What humiliation!

SLOOK So, what do you say about that?

FANNY (*aside*) Courage is needed here. (*to Slook*) So what do you think of it?

SLOOK I'm going to honour my signature.

FANNY (*with conviction*) Ah, don't do it; I beg you, renounce your promissory note!

SLOOK Why?

FANNY Because I am not merchandise for you, and it will do you no honour.

SLOOK Seems to me it's the best contract I've ever seen. For such wonderful goods,

I'd give all my worldly possessions.
I'd turn over every penny,
and invest all of my capital
to realize a dividend in pleasure
of at least one hundred per cent.

FANNY Look for other goods,
Bargains cover the globe!
But I am not for you,
No, this will bankrupt you.
Leave me in liberty
I beg you with all my heart.

SLOOK But why? Explain.

FANNY I would like to tell you … but…

SLOOK You're opposed to marriage?

FANNY Quite the opposite … but…

SLOOK Do I seem to be a demon?

FANNY That's not what I said … but!

SLOOK (*impetuously*) For God's sake, Madame,
Let's have no more "buts."

FANNY You still don't know
what I mean by "but."

SLOOK Marry me and that will be enough.
What will be will be.

FANNY If my prayers are not enough
I have other tricks up my sleeve.

SLOOK Then, I must be a devil.

FANNY That's not what I said … but…

Scene Eight

(*Edward enters in a suppressed rage, and speaks with full sarcasm.*)

EDWARD That precious little face,
Those eyes brimming with love,

That perfect mix of
Grace and singular beauty
Were made for another love.
My good man, they are not for you.
I advise you, from the bottom of my heart,
Return to Canada.
(*takes Slook's hand and shakes it forcefully*)

SLOOK But sir, why should you care at all
   About my personal matters?

FANNY He does it out of compassion
   solely for his friends.

EDWARD Because this is a large matter,
   Yours, mine and hers.

SLOOK (*upset*) But this is a piece of merchandise
   Which is totally my property.
   I'm going to speak to Sir Toby
   and he'll vouch for what I say.

EDWARD (*proudly*) Woe to you if you speak to him!

FANNY (*to Edward*) Steady on. Play along.

SLOOK But this is farcical!

EDWARD One day you'll thank me.

SLOOK Who are you anyway?

EDWARD You'll soon know.

SLOOK (*asks Fanny*) You tell me…

FANNY I suspect you've already guessed.

SLOOK The promissory note is straightforward.

EDWARD My good man, tear it up.

SLOOK (*passionately*) Tear it up! Me? Slook? But what then…?

EDWARD (*proudly*) Shut up, I'm warning you.

SLOOK (*upset*) Are you threatening me?

EDWARD and FANNY Yes, tremble with fear.

SLOOK But why? What have I done?

FANNY (*excitedly*) I don't like you.
   I cannot love you.
   I'm ready to torment you.

And with this hand, if you take it in marriage,
I will scratch out your ugly eyes.
A real hell will flare before you.

EDWARD I know how to slice open your veins,
and send you by mail back to Canada.

SLOOK Oh my! Oh my!
Poor Slook!
Thank you Sir.
Such a kind heart.
Scratch out my eyes.
Mercy!
Oh, these guys
are really tough.

FANNY I will scratch out
your ugly eyes.
I don't like you.
I cannot love you.
If you take this hand in marriage,
I will scratch out your ugly eyes.
A real hell will flare before you.

EDWARD You're in trouble
if you squeal, believe me.
You'll be sorry,
You're in trouble
if you talk.
If you don't renounce
the promissory note,
I'll send you by mail
back to Canada!
I know to slice open your veins.
If you delay your departure
I'll send you by mail
back to Canada.

JORGE LUIS BORGES

THE GREAT Argentinian author Jorge Luis Borges (1878–1986) made at least three separate trips to Canada, but there seem to be no published documents detailing his impressions of the Canadians he met or the places he visited. Sadly, the CBC, given the chance to record Borges' talk at the University of Toronto in 1968, refused to do so on the grounds that "he's a bad broadcaster."

References to this country are few and fleeting in Borges' imaginative writing. In *The Book of Sand* ("Utopia of a Man Who Is Tired") for example, there is this line: "The planet is populated by collective spectres: Canada, Brazil, the Swiss Congo and the Common Market." And in *Dr. Brodie's Report* ("The Duel"), Borges writes "Clara liked Ottawa's climate—after all, she was of Scottish descent."

In fact, the only serious comment made by Borges about Canada appeared in his book *Atlas*, where the presence of a major native-Canadian artifact in Argentina gave him pause.

THE TOTEM

Plotinus of Alexandria refused to allow a portrait to be made of himself, we are told by Porphyry, alleging that he was merely a shadow of the Platonic prototype and that a portrait would be the shadow of a shadow. Pascal rediscovered this argument against the art of painting. The image we see here is a photograph of a facsimile of an idol in Canada, that is: the shadow of a shadow of a shadow. Its original, so to say, stands, elevated but without a cult following, behind the last of the three rail stations in Retiro. It is an official gift of the Canadian government. That country does not mind being identified with a barbarous image. No South American government would run the risk of being represented by the effigy of a crude anonymous divinity.

We know all these things and yet our imagination is taken with the notion of an exiled totem, a totem darkly demanding mythologies, tribes, incantations and even perhaps sacrifices. We know nothing of its cult following: one more reason to dream it in the equivocal twilight.

BLAISE CENDRARS

B LAISE CENDRARS (1887–1961), French art critic, poet, novelist, and filmmaker, was fond of deliberately confounding others
by mixing fact with fiction in his biography. So, pending further
scholarly research, it is impossible to know when—or even
whether—he visited Canada, although in a letter to the eminent
American biographer Stanley Kunitz he maintained he really had
been to this country. Inference from his writing allows us to conclude that he probably stopped over in Vancouver early in his life. At
that time he was an inveterate world traveller. Limited (if any) contact with Canada, however, was no impediment to his actually writing about the country, although the detail in the following poems
suggest tantalizingly that he was an eye-witness.

As an author, particularly in his poetry, he was adamant that language, no matter its source, was but the raw material of literature.
Admittedly, this is a truism granted by most authors. Other authors,
though, did not regard the copyrighted arrangements of words by
fellow writers to be an ethically correct ore to mine. In the age of
cubism and surrealism, such taboos against plagiarism struck Cendrars as silly niceties. So, partly to tweak the nose of the Establishment, and partly to make an aesthetic point, Cendrars created forty
poems (published as *Documentaires* in France) primarily using
phrases found in a commercial science fiction novel, *Le mystérieux
Docteur Cornelius* by Gustave Le Rouge, an author forgotten by

both time and today's critics. The poems are written in what became known as his postcard style, that is, as spare phrasings—unadorned observations—to appear as the impressions of an astute traveller in foreign lands.

Cendrars admitted freely that he had used Le Rouge's novel as his source; indeed, disingenuously he maintained he had done so in part to demonstrate to Le Rouge himself that Le Rouge was a natural poet. More accurately, he was creating with the poems the literary equivalents of Marcel Duchamp's "ready-mades," those everyday objects such as urinals or bicycle wheels which, by putting them in an artistic milieu, Duchamp then classified *objets d'art*. The *Documentaires*, though, are not so much "found poems" (the literary equivalent of "ready-mades") as collages of phrasings found here and there throughout the original novel, artfully modified or mixed with his own poetic sentences.

Regardless of the motivation behind their creation, the fact remains that Blaise Cendrars created three compelling poems in his renowned "postcard style"—about three very different places in Canada.

THOUSAND ISLANDS

Here the landscape is one of the most beautiful in North America
The immense sheet of the lake is of an almost white blue shade
Hundreds and hundreds of small green islands float on the calm
    surface of the limpid waters
The delightful cottages built in brightly colored bricks make that
    landscape look like an enchanted kingdom
Luxurious maple or mahogany boats dressed with elegant signal

flags and bunting and covered with multicolored canopies ply
between the islands
All idea of strain toil and poverty is alien to this graceful setting for
multimillionaires

The sun disappears on the horizon of Lake Ontario
The clouds dip their folds into vats in dyes of violet-purple scarlet
and orange
What a beautiful evening whisper Andrée and Frédérique sitting on
the terrace of a medieval castle
And the drone of ten thousand motorboats answers their ecstasy

VANCOUVER

Ten p.m. has just struck barely heard through the thick fog that
muffles the docks and the ships in the harbor
The wharfs are deserted and the town is wrapped in sleep
You stroll along a low sandy shore swept by an icy wind and the
long billows of the Pacific
That lurid spot in the dank darkness is the station of the Canadian
Grand Trunk
And those bluish patches in the wind are the liners bound for the
Klondike Japan and the West Indies
It is so dark that I can hardly make out the signs in the streets where
lugging a heavy suitcase I am looking for a cheap hotel

Everyone is on board
The oarsmen are bent on their oars and the heavy craft loaded to
the brim plows through the high waves
A small hunchback at the helm checks the tiller now and then
Adjusting his steering through the fog to the calls of a foghorn
We bump against the dark bulk of the ship and on the starboard

quarter Samoyed dogs are climbing up
Flaxen in the gray-white-yellow
As if fog was being taken in freight

NORTH

I. Spring

There is vigor and strength in the Canadian spring as in no other
    country in the world
Under the thick layer of snow and ice
Suddenly
Bountiful nature
Tufts of violets white blue and pink
Orchids sunflowers tiger lilies
In the venerable avenues lined with maple trees black ash trees and
    birches
Birds fly and sing
In the thickets covered with buds and young and tender shoots
The cheerful sun is the color of licorice

Alongside the road woods and cultivated lands stretch for more
    than five thousand miles
It is one of the largest estates in the district of Winnipeg
In the middle stands a farmhouse solidly built of squared stones and
    looking like a manor
That is where my good friend Coulon lives
Up before dawn he rides a tall light-bay mare from farm to farm
The flaps of his hareskin cap dangle on his shoulders
Black eye and bushy eyebrows
In high spirits
A pipe hugging his chin

The night is misty and cold
A wild western wind moans through the elastic fir trees and larches
A small gleam of light widens
A fire crackles
The smoldering conflagration bums up bushes and brushwood
The tumultuous wind blows about clusters of resinous trees
Huge torches flare up one after the other
The conflagration spreads around the horizon with an imposing
    slowness
White trunks and black trunks turn blood red
Dome of chocolate smoke from which millions of sparks flakes of
    fire fly off high up and low down
Behind the curtain of flames you can see tall shadows writhe and
    drop down
Felling axes bang in the air
An acrid fog spreads over the blazing forest circled by the team of
    woodsmen

II. Countryside

Magnificent landscape
Verdant forests of fir trees beech trees chestnut trees interrupted by
    flourishing fields of wheat oats buckwheat hemp
This is a land of plenty
Besides the area is totally deserted
Only occasionally will you meet a peasant driving a haycart
In the distance the birches stand like silver pillars

III. Fishing and Hunting

Wild ducks pintails teals geese plovers bustards
Grouse thrushes
Arctic hares ptarmigans

Salmon rainbow trout eels
Gigantic pike and crayfish with a particularly delicate flavor

Rifle slung on the shoulder
A bowie knife hanging from the belt
The sportsman and the Red Indian bend under their load of game
Wood pigeons red-legged partridges strung on slings
Wild peacocks
Prairie gobblers
And even a large white and russet eagle that swooped down from
     the clouds

IV. Harvest

A six-cylinder car and two Fords in the middle of the fields
In every direction as far as the horizon the slightly slanting
swaths crisscross into a wavering diamond-shaped checkerboard
     pattern
Not a tree
From the North comes down the rumble and rattle of the automo-
     tive thrasher and forage wagon
And from the South come twelve empty trains to pick up the wheat

MARK HELPRIN

ONE OF AMERICA'S pre-eminent novelists and short-story writers, Mark Helprin (1947–) currently resides in Seattle, Washington. He grew up on the other side of the country, however, residing at various points in New England. Although he has never lived in Canada, for several decades he has been a frequent visitor to its metropolitan centres. As the following story admirably illustrates, his senses have been keenly alert during these Canadian encounters, for he has been a perceptive witness of our people and our geography. He has described the story, which appeared originally in *The New Yorker* on October 18, 1982, as "100% Canadian."

PASSCHENDAELE

Cameron preferred to keep away from the eastern border of his land, because it ran the entire length of a ridgeline on high meadows that dropped away into the alluring darkness of Sanderson's pine-filled woods. The terrain was little different on one side of the ridge or the other. Soft clearings floated among the dark evergreens; long meadows on mountainsides stretched for benevolent mile after benevolent mile, covered with wild flowers in spring and deep snow in winter; and mountain streams, which Cameron knew some people called freshets or torrents (and which he called water), cut through everything, tumbling down, roaring through small gorges, until they became the calm black water of the larger rivers. And if not quite pacified, they were saddened, for the mountains were behind them and there would be no more white falls or breathlessly cold channels but just slow water that had run its course through air once blue.

The presence of a fence in such a place was hard to understand, as the land on either side was much the same, except that one side was Cameron's and the other Sanderson's. But, for Cameron, Sanderson's tranquil clearings, meadows, and woods were magically animate and electrified, because he was in love with Sanderson's wife.

The near and distant forest across the wire was much like Mrs. Sanderson herself—beyond reach, oblivious of what he thought or felt, and extraordinarily, painfully, beautiful. The chance that he would see her on the fence line was remote: he never had, and expected that he never would. There were too many open miles, and the scale of things in that country, British Columbia, in the Stanford Range, did not encourage incidental meetings, though it would have harbored easily a hundred million well-protected trysts. It was only that the meadows led to her, the clearings and woods surrounded her, she had ridden through them, and they were hers. Even though he was in his middle age and she not far behind, he loved her without control or dignity, the way he would have loved her had he been nineteen.

Several times a year, Cameron had to repair the fences on the eastern side because much of the wire was not new, and would rust to powder if left in place. Some of the posts were set in wet ground and tended to rot, staggering like the wounded, tilting the fence and tangling its wires. Sometimes a steer broke through, possessed, perhaps, with madness or fear. And bears tore up the lines, like raiders attacking a railway, so purposefully that their work would have been easy to confuse with that of a man, had they not always left behind their unmistakable tracks.

The eastern side was the higher side. That portion of Cameron's land rose in the direction of Mt. King George and Mt. Joffre, mountains on which there were glaciers and perpetual snowfields. It was the difficult and slow side as well, because it was so inaccessible and high. He had to ride in on horseback and bring the wire along in a coil wrapped in rawhide. Any posts needed for replacement had to be cut on the spot, with an axe. If a hole had to be sunk, he had to do it with a folding shovel, since the gasoline-powered auger he carried in his truck was far too heavy to bring up onto the eastern ridge. All in all, the eastern side was difficult in many ways.

For three days in June, Cameron had ridden the fence, leaving before the sun came up, returning home at dusk, and he had been lucky. There were only a few posts to be pounded in with the heel of the axe; a few dozen slipped wires, fixed with a bent double-edged nail and some hammer blows; and some partial breaks, mostly of the top wire, which was stressed more than the others by temperature contractions or drifting snow.

The fourth day, he judged, would be his last up there, and he might get home late in the afternoon instead of at eight or nine, knowing that he would not have to go out east again until the fall (to bring in the steers), when he was likely to see Sanderson on the other side of the fence, doing the same thing that he was doing.

By one in the afternoon, he had risen to the higher meadows, where there were not many trees and he could see just about everything, including the valley that led eventually to Sanderson's house, and faint trails of smoke from the Sandersons' fire. Or perhaps they were branding, curing meat, or burning deadwood. Ahead for six miles or so was the rest of the fence. It ended in the northeast, flat up against a vertical rock wall half a thousand feet high.

No mountain goat, much less a steer, could have bent his neck to see the top of that wall. Though they had no one to tell them about the danger of falling rocks, or lightning that slithered down the face, and though presumably they had no historical memory and could not conclude by either logic or deduction that it was dangerous, the steers kept clear of the foot of the wall, wisely, even though the grass there was richer and greener than it was anywhere else. And, for some unknown reason, perhaps because bears in high meadows are happier than bears in the woods, at this altitude they were content to use the baffles, and seldom tore at the wire. The last six had always been the easiest of the miles, and they were surely the most beautiful.

When Cameron was young, when it was still his father's place, and he had yet to marry, he had loved to finish riding fences at the sheer wall in the northeast corner. At that time, the adjoining ranch was owned by the Reeds, whose son, several years older than Cameron, was killed at Passchendaele.

"You know what?" young Reed had once said to the even younger Cameron. "Everyone's talking about how dangerous it will be in the war. But I'm not worried about that at all. I'm worried about the fact that a certain number of years after I come back I'll be so old that I'll be supposed to die. I don't like that idea, so I've decided that I'm not going to die."

"Ever?" Cameron had asked, wondering what the older boy was up to.

"Ever." was Reed's answer. "Or should I say never." And then he had smiled in such a way as to make young Cameron think that, even if his friend were excessively foolish, he was excessively brave.

Cameron himself had longed to go, but was too young; and, much later, discovered that he had become a man only when he stopped envying Charles S. R. Reed for having been killed in battle. During the First War, and for the many years thereafter until the Sandersons came from Scotland, the eastern side had been for Cameron a lovely isolated place with a life of its own. He would spend days in the forests there, or on the high meadows, and, if the weather was good, would be taken up entirely by nature.

Fiercely in its grip, in the trance of youth, in the sunshine at eight thousand feet, he could go for days like an animal—not ever thinking, but riding, leaping, plunging into the ice-cold pools and glacier melts, stalking birds and game—with the same eyes and heart as a bear, an elk, or a horse. But only until the weather turned, for when it was gray and rainy, or sleeting in June, and when the awesome thunderheads stopped their artillery in the distance and passed overhead to drench and freeze him, he thought and calculated with a city dweller's devotion to thinking and calculation. Nothing was what it was, simply, but became instead the symbol or the part of something else. Time forced its own consideration. Ambition reigned, as did disharmony. But when he was sixteen, eighteen, or twenty, the disturbances, like the storms, were dispelled and forgotten in one blue morning.

That was before Reed sold out to the Sandersons, in the middle of the Depression; not because he was hard pressed but because he had never stopped grieving for his son. "There's nothing wrong with war," the senior Reed had said to Cameron, when young Charles S.R. Reed had been five months gone toward Passchendaele, "except that it destroys the ones you love. I fought against the Boer in South Africa—I volunteered to go because I was madly in love and I wanted to be worthy. I shouldn't have spoken of it to my son. But if I hadn't, he would have gone anyway, for he, too, was in love. I just hope that he comes back to me alive."

It was said, on no specific authority, that the elder Reed disappeared to some city, where he was bitter and alone; that the Sandersons had paid him a good price; and that Mrs. Sanderson's family was wealthy enough to have given the young couple a wedding present of a thousand acres of the most beautiful land in the world. However, their wealth could not have matched the gossip, since Reed sold off the best three-quarters of his herd, and the Sandersons lived until the end of the Second War in a painful frugality that elsewhere might have been called poverty.

But on those thousand acres there was in Cameron's eyes no such thing as poverty, even if the lady of the house possessed only a single dress for summer, and a worn one at that. There was no poverty for them, even if they had few luxuries, no telephone, no electricity. And to wash they had had to take water from a stream, heat it over a wood fire, and pour it into a huge gold-rimmed porcelain bowl that, before it was chipped, had probably been a salad bowl in a hotel or railroad buffet, since on it in ornate gilt lettering were the initials CPR.

That bowl had come to mean something to Cameron, the way material objects do to people in bad weather or big cities, or to people in love. He remembered it because she had been standing by it, with her hand touching the rim, the first time he had ever seen her—on a cold mountain-summer morning in 1935.

Sanderson had been in the mountains for a year or more before Cameron had encountered him on the ridge, mending the fence. Cameron rode up, dismounted, and watched in silence. No matter that for ten miles in any direction they were the only two beings that could talk. Neither spoke.

Every now and then, the recently arrived Scotsman looked up at the man on the other side of the fence, who stared at him in unexplained amusement. But he would be damned before he would speak first to an uncivil Canadian who had lived in the wilderness since birth and probably had little more in his head than had a bear or a wild ram.

For half an hour, Cameron watched his new neighbor diligently mend the fence. Either someone had shown Sanderson how, or he had thought it out himself, but his splices would last as long as the steel. Cameron thought that if he would be forgiven for not speaking, he had found a friend.

Just as Sanderson finished and was about to mount his horse, Cameron said, "Will you send me a bill, then? Or are you a monk from some religious order, doing the Lord's work in mufti?"

"I beg your pardon?" the Scotsman asked in such a heavy accent that Cameron immediately realized how he had known about mending fences: he, too, was a countryman.

"I was just wondering if you were a travelling monk."

"And why would you wonder that?" Sanderson replied coldly.

"It's either something like that or you're uncommonly generous. Anyway, you have my thanks."

Sanderson looked at the fence.

"Right," said Cameron. "It's mine."

"I've been working on the bastard for four days now," Sanderson said bitterly. "Why isn't it marked?"

"It's not the custom here. You should have asked."

"Reed told me that I had to keep up the southern and western fences."

"No," Cameron said, shaking his head. "South and east, hereabouts, most of the time. When you get into Alberta, it changes. There are people straddling the provincial border who don't have to worry about any fences. They're on the line where ways of doing things meet, and they reap the benefits. Of course, it could have been just the reverse, too, and I'm sure that in some places there are those who have to tend their wire in all directions. We're both lucky, though, in our way. We share the north wall. I've got a lot of river on my property as well, and there's no fence like a fast deep river."

"Now I know," Sanderson said. "You can take over from here. Maybe I'll send you a bill."

"You can send it if you'd like. Doesn't mean that I'll pay it though."

"Don't worry about it," Sanderson said as he got on his horse. Although Sanderson appeared to be in no mood to talk, Cameron suspected that Sanderson regarded him as a gentle adversary, and Cameron believed that there was never a better means for a man to make a friend than in a fight of little consequence.

"Our eastern fence is mended, all but the last easy six," Cameron announced to his wife at dinner that night.

"How so?" she asked.

"Sanderson did it. He thought it was his."

"Did he put in much wire?"

"Plenty. I haven't seen it all, but he replaced it, just as I do—not only where it's broken but where you can tell it's going to break."

"You ought to give him back what we've gained."

"He didn't have to put it there."

"I've heard that they're having a hard time," his wife said. "Why don't you bring him some wire, and some beef, since they probably can't afford to slaughter one of their own animals."

"I suppose I could do that. He seems like a nice fellow. There's probably a lot he can learn from me."

"He may not think of it in quite that way." Mrs. Cameron said.

"I don't see why he shouldn't. Our family has been here more than half a century—he arrived a few months ago. It shows. He spent four days fixing a fence that didn't belong to him. But all right. When I go there," he asked, "do you want to come with me?"

"No. But tell me about Sanderson's wife. If she seems nice, then I'll ride over, too."

The next day, Cameron found himself in front of Sanderson's house, screaming "Hallo!" to no avail. Though a rich volume of smoke issued from the chimney, no one answered. They were away and had left far too big a fire burning unattended, or they wanted nothing to do with him. And he had ridden twenty miles, carrying heavy coils of wire and another big package, and to go visiting had put on his best riding boots and a new Black Watch shirt.

He decided to leave the wire on the porch and the meat just inside, away from raccoons and bears. He wanted to write a note, and thought that they might have a pen or pencil somewhere near the door. He wouldn't have to go all the way in.

He took the leather off the coils of wire and carried them up onto the porch. When he stepped into the shade, he realized that on his way over he had been pleasantly sunburned by the June sun and the snowfields. "Hallo!" he said, rapping at the door. When there was no answer, he opened the latch and looked in.

The fire was blazing. A large iron kettle hung over the flames, and was just beginning to steam. There must be someone here, he thought. And then, as his eyes fully adjusted to the light and he looked about the room, he saw that there was.

Sanderson's wife, her left hand clasped against her chest in fright, stared at him from across a wooden table. She was wearing only a slip, of a gray metallic sheen and of a pearly salmon color. To have been polite, Cameron should have turned away. To have been wise, he might have left for good.

But he couldn't take his eyes off her. "I called and called," he said. "Didn't you hear me?"

Then, as if to establish his credentials, he pointed at the coils of wire on the porch and held up the large package of steak. "I'm your neighbor. I've brought your husband some wire and some beef. I wanted to leave a note, but I didn't have a pen, so I just stepped inside."

As he waited for an answer, he was free to look at her. She remained motionless, her right hand gripping the side of the bowl with the golden rim. Just her arms, hands, and fingers were enough to mark her as a beauty. Her eyes were lucid and green, and the thick soft hair that was piled atop her head and fell about her face in long wisps and exquisitely curling locks was a matte red so rich and subdued that it made him giddy. And her complexion, which showed, too, on her shoulders and chest, was a cross between mottled red and ivory. Cameron's paralysis was not lessened by her gorgeous expression of surprise, by her silver and gold rings, and by a light gold neck chain splayed across the lace trim of the slip.

She motioned for him to go outside. He moved back and looked at the bowl, trying to remember its smallest detail, down to the curl of the letters, for he wanted to be able to recall the scene with the power to renew it. Then he went out onto the porch, shut the door behind him, and stepped into the sunlight.

He wished that when she joined him in the daylight she would be ugly, and that the way she had struck him as so beautiful would prove to have been an illusion of the soft dim light—this for the sake of his lovely wife, whom he loved and did not want to wish to abandon, and because he knew that he was not suitable for Mrs. Sanderson. He imagined that a man suited to her would have to be many ranks above him, though Sanderson, it seemed, was not.

Since he could never have her, he would have to hate her for it. Even had she and he been unmarried, having her would have been out of the question. But, then, what about Sanderson? He was not a god. Perhaps she was as beautiful as she appeared to be only to Cameron. Perhaps, given time, she would leave her husband. Or, given more time, he would die. Perhaps, Cameron thought, on the ride over the snowfields in the strong sun he had been too rapturous. Then he remembered her face.

Having lost this debate with himself, he stamped his foot against the boards, sorry that he had ever seen her, bitter about the imbalance that the sight of her made clear to him, and angry that he now felt low when just that morning he had ridden across the high meadows, in sight of a snowy line of peaks to the north, feeling that there was no place higher that he or anyone else would want to go. As he was turning to leave, she walked onto the porch, in an old-fashioned flowered dress, and made Cameron wish for Sanderson to come galloping in and distract him from the lacerating and untouchable beauty that was even finer in the daylight than it had been in the dim interior of the house, for in the house there had not been any of the blue glacial light that seemed to lift her off the earth and make her smile something not of this world.

She carried pencils and paper. "I don't need that," Cameron said. "I was going to leave a message if no one was in. But you're in, you see."

She shook her head to say no, smiled, and pointed to herself. She's crazy, he thought.

Then she raised a hand perfectly adorned in rings, and tapped her left ear. When next she put her index finger across her lips twice in succession, he understood.

"You can't hear," he said, already moving his lips more deliberately, so that she might understand. She nodded. "You can't talk."

She sat down on the step in the sunlight and made room for him to follow. "I can talk," she wrote on the pad, in a firm but delicate hand, "but they say it doesn't come out very well, so I prefer to write."

"Do you talk to your husband?" he asked.

"Yes," she wrote. "Only to him and to my parents, who are in Scotland. I also talk to the animals, since I am told they sound even worse than I do." She smiled. "Please," she continued, as he drank in every movement of her hands and eyes, "don't mention this to anyone. In all of Canada, you are the only one who knows."

"Why?" he asked.

"I am ashamed," she wrote. She indicated emphasis and nuance with the pen (by writing very fast or very slow; bearing down hard; by returning to underline or circle; and by drawing the letters one way or another, to look shaky, flat, tired, or animated) and with her facial expressions.

"There's nothing to be ashamed of," he told her.

"That may be so," she wrote quickly, "but long experience has shown me that it's best this way. I have always preferred to keep to myself."

"But what if you have to go into Invermere? They'll know then."

"I've been there only once. If we have to, we go to Calgary to shop. It's bigger, and no one knows us there."

"Calgary is a long way off," he said.

"Invermere is small," she wrote back.

"Well, I won't dispute that," he answered.

"Are you married?" she wrote.

"Yes."

"Then," she put down, "please don't tell even your wife. If I could hear and talk like everyone else, I would talk no end to other women, and I suspect that I'm not unusual in that desire, except that I don't get to realize it."

"She wanted to visit," Cameron said. "When the pass is open, it's not that far on a good horse. Would you enjoy that?"

"No" was the written answer. "Or, rather, yes. But, again, *my* experience tells me that it would not be a good idea."

Cameron took a chance. "Because of me?" he asked bluntly, wondering if she knew the effect of her beauty.

Evidently, she did, for she nodded, and then, as if for emphasis, wrote, "Yes."

"Isn't that a lot to presume?" He was bluffing. It wasn't anything at all to presume, but he thought she might become interested in him if she imagined that he, of all men, could not see or did not care about her beauty. "Experience," she wrote.

Because Cameron looked dejected, she added, "If you feel distraught, don't worry. It will pass."

"I don't think it will."

"Don't be silly." Her hand flew across the pad. "A man doesn't have his head turned forever. After all, you don't know me."

"And if I did?"

"I won't demean myself. But I do tend to draw men to me very strongly at first, only to see them drop away much relieved and delighted to go."

He wished that he had been more circumspect. But to have been so might have been a far greater fault. It was not the first time he had been defeated by great desire, and he felt completely inadequate, dismissed, and rejected. He left abruptly, because he was sure that she wanted him to go, because he wanted so much to stay, because, quite simply, he loved her.

He never remembered much about the feverish and unhappy ride home, or how many times he had dismounted to pace back and forth in agony and puzzlement. He did, of course, resolve never to see her again. And he was a man of strong and tenacious resolution.

Late in the afternoon, Cameron came to the meadows that led to the high wall. The meadows stretched for a mile, and were dotted with stands of small pine that grew sheltered from the wind in depressions and hollows. At almost nine thousand feet, the horse moved slowly and breathed hard, and his rider found himself in a trance of sparkling altitude. The sky was flawless and still as Cameron inspected the last portion of his fence. Progressing slowly upward, he was sure that there would be no breaks. Where the final meadow began to rise steeply to the wall, he was going to check the fence from a distance, and turn around without actually making a ceremonial finish at the cliff itself—in touching it the way a swimmer touches the wall of a pool before he will credit himself with a lap. But he saw from the base of the meadow that a long portion of the fence was down. The wire was shining in the sunlight, spread in every direction on the field. The posts had been pushed over, snapped at the base, and scattered. With luck, if he had enough wire, and could salvage enough, and work fast enough, he might repair it by dark, and then ride home by starlight on trails that he could take blind.

He cantered over to the damage. He knew from the tracks that a grizzly bear had done it—or perhaps two, while the cubs watched. Either they had been too big to get through the baffles, which were untouched, or they had just wanted the high meadow to be completely open. Because the splinters were moist and the leaves of the moss compressed, he knew that it had happened while he was just a few miles away thinking placidly about his good luck. The bears themselves might be gone, or they might be taking a nap somewhere amidst the sunny boulders. Removing his rifle from its scabbard, he worked the bolt to put a bullet in the chamber, and leaned the weapon against a rock. It was not that he expected the bears to lie in ambush for him but, rather, that in working hard he might not notice them until his horse panicked.

They had pulled down sixteen stakes and broken eleven at the base, rendering them unusable. The wire was severed in two dozen places. Only a bear could have done that, even with the low-grade light steel that he had always used on the high meadows. His coil of wire was greatly diminished after the repairs he had made on the way up. If he had enough, it would be just enough, and still it would be hard to do it right. The splicing would be weak—no tripled windings—and he would have to use fewer posts, spacing them farther apart than usual. But the fence might hold, especially if the bears were on their way to some distant, higher paradise in the north. He set to work.

First, he rode a mile and a half back into the timber. Although he could have used the meadow's little pines for posts, at that altitude they took forever to grow, and destroying them might have turned the upper pasture into a rutted and barren hillside when the rains washed the thin layer of soil off its base of rock and scree. In the timber, hidden from the world by distance, height, and the perfect maze and soft green baffling of a thousand thick pines, he used his axe to cut and trim half a dozen small trees. He was a very strong man, he had used an axe nearly every day of his life from the time he was a small child, and the axe he used was the best available, sharpened with a soft stone and oil, and kept, like some kind of strange one-legged falcon, in a leather hood. The trees went down in a stroke: they might as well have been celery. And he trimmed them of their branches with several sweeps close to the trunk. After a series of hatchetlike blows at the narrowing end, he had a sharp fence post soaked with its own resin as if it had been designed for placement in wet ground.

He tied the posts up in two bundles and dragged them out of the woods. Then he slung them over his saddle and walked the horse back to the break. If the break had occurred sooner, steers might have passed through, though it was early in the season for steers to have reached the high pastures. But even then it would hardly have mattered. Sanderson would have pushed them back over, and he would have done the same for Sanderson's animals, with nothing said between them. In the twelve years since he thought one day that he had found a friend in Sanderson, he had seen him only half a dozen times along the fence or in Invermere, where Mrs. Sanderson had been forgotten and it was generally assumed that Sanderson lived alone.

Mrs. Cameron's warm invitation, a week in the mail even though the lands adjoined, was never answered. Now that his children were old enough to ride by themselves wherever they wanted, Cameron feared that they might ride east on some adventure and discover the great secret of his life. But, being young, they would not have been able to see her in the way that he had seen her. Perhaps no one did, although she had implied that at least some had; and she had known immediately that, as she put it, his head had been turned. Perhaps she had had children, had aged, and lost her beauty. He wished that she had, but knew that no such thing could ever happen to her. That her features had, accidentally, been fine and unusual had little bearing on the woman herself. If she had lost the accidental beauty of her form, it would only have served to accentuate the substance that form had been privileged to convey.

One of the things that hurt him most in his speculations east was the possibility that she had died or gone away, and that, without his knowledge, his life had been rendered meaningless. And he didn't know her name, which was difficult to bear in light of the way that he loved her.

After several years, he did not think of her very often. By the time England was again at war (this time he was too old), it seemed almost as if he had forgotten her. After all, his wife, too, was a beauty, with a softness that Mrs. Sanderson did not have, and the luck of a pretty face and a graceful body. But she was not as deeply faulted as Mrs. Sanderson, or quite as radiant. Anyway, it had been the fault—the deafness and the mistaken, unnecessary shame—that had driven deep into Cameron's heart.

As the years went by, he put her more and more out of his mind. But in the end time was immaterial. Suddenly, in the midst of a false peace, he would dream of her, and for weeks thereafter be wounded by intense desire. Then the desire would slowly fade, and he would continue getting older, waiting for the next potent and surprising reawakening. Were it not for this, he would have been a happy man. Perhaps he was a happy man even so.

The posts had to be placed in rocky soil, and it was not easy to sink them. He was like the soldier he had never been, breathing hard and evenly, sweating, taken up by his love of the work, for only work could conduct away his unfortunate passion. Because of the new spacing, four or five new holes had to be made, and a similar number of broken pieces extracted from the ground. Some were easy, some not easy at all. How fine the task, though, of building back this fence, with all his strength, discipline, and experience. It was for the sake of the lovely woman he had married, for the children they had had, for Sanderson, for Mrs. Sanderson, and for himself—though he couldn't see exactly how it was to his benefit unless it were purely a matter of honor.

He pounded in the posts, until they flattened against the under-lying sheet of rock. His strokes with the heel of the axe were perfect. Each downward blow married solidly with the posthead; and the timing, too, was perfect.

The second and last time he had seen her had been in Vancouver during the war. The disarray of the cattle market had brought him to the coast seeking a better price for his beef. He never got it, and he never found out what she had been doing there, apart from bowling on the green, in a formal white suit, in the company of a lot of pretty old ladies who took the game very seriously.

He was resting in Stanley Park, on the peninsula, at midday, watching the old ladies at their game, when she appeared and took her turn. A full ten minutes passed before he was able to believe that it was actually she, and then to summon the courage to rise. But when he did approach her, it was easy. He almost floated across the bowling green, hypnotized, pushing the carefully placed shots all to hell with his feet and making a flock of enemies.

She recognized him immediately, and when she turned to face him her expression was reminiscent of those days when strong sunshine and deep shadow alternate in silent breathtaking contrast, and the joy and sadness that swept across her face told him that he was not the only one to have spent the years in longing and perplexity.

They stood in the center of the green, oblivious of a growing stream of reprimands—she because she could not hear them, and he because he was enthralled. The old ladies were incensed: not only had their game been spoiled but they had been ignored. So they returned the fire and resumed play, paying no attention to the two wickets who stood, apparently insensate, staring at one another in the middle of the contest. Balls began to whiz about like shrapnel.

They didn't notice; they could not look away. With no words spoken, all custom was shattered as he put his hands on either side of her white waistband, touching her gently. She extended her arms, and they found themselves in a subdued embrace, still apart, an embrace suitable for a crowded Vancouver bowling green. But everything was said, at last, and in the silence that she had always known.

A ship full of men who looked at the city hard, knowing that they might not ever be back, began a series of powerful whistle blasts as it coasted through the inlet on its way to the war at sea. This, the deep steam whistle, was the one thing she could hear, or, rather, feel—a symphony for her, the one precious rumbling sound of the world. It pushed through her chest and took her by surprise, moving her by its suddenness and beauty. She held up one of her hands and spread her fingers to see them vibrate, as the air itself was shaken from its sleep. He had told her that he loved her, and admitted it finally and forever to himself. At least he had done that. And though she hardly knew him, she knew him enough, standing on the Vancouver bowling green, to cry.

After the posts were up, Cameron began to string the wire. Not only had it been broken but he himself was obliged to cut it in the stringing, and to replace rusted lengths that likely would not stand being stretched onto a new arrangement of posts and baffles. The skill with which be wielded the splicing tool was something of which he did not think to be proud. But he had the sure facility of a fisherman mending his nets, or a woman years at the loom, and there was no tentativeness in his movements, which seemed to pull his hands forward as quickly as they would follow.

As he worked, his thoughts turned to Mrs. Sanderson. There were undoubtedly things in the mountains to make up for a love that was unfulfilled. When his tongue was tied, when he could not act, or in the punishment of forever parting, he had discovered flawless compensation. And if the discipline that kept him from her had not been so sweet in itself he would long ago have jumped his horse over the fence and ridden down to the house at the base of the thin column of smoke. But having what he desired was not important, for the mountains would remember, and, once, in Vancouver, he had been lucky.

When he finished, the sun was red and gold, sitting on a sharp and distant ridge. The new wire looked like lines of silver and platinum, and the pine posts were solid and black. A pool of melted water had formed in the middle of a patch of snow about a hundred feet from the fence. Cameron took off his clothes, walked across the snow, and threw himself in. The water was even colder than be had expected, but, wanting to get clean, he thrust his head under and rolled himself over. The pain of doing such a thing was pleasant, for, afterward, when he rose slick and sparkling from the ice water, he was warm and relaxed, and he could reflect pleasurably upon the half a minute or so of breathless cold when his discipline had kept him under and served him well. After he had dressed, he threw the saddle on his horse, cinched it up, and put back the bit. When his tools were gathered and tied on, and the rifle chamber emptied, he mounted. The wind was clean and cool.

He walked the horse from the first splice to the last, and swept his eyes over each new post and each component twisting of the wire, up to the rock wall itself. Then he veered across the meadow and wound down through patches of snow now blood-red with sunset. Several hundred yards east of the fence, he reined the horse around to face what he had done. It was a good piece of work, and undoubtedly it would hold. The wires now glowed like molten metal.

He was not a stupid man. He knew what he was about to do, he knew very well, and he finally felt a deep brotherhood with young Charles S.R. Reed, who had gone to Passchendaele of his own accord, and who, in his lack of wisdom, had perhaps been wise.

Cameron realized that the horse would want to canter, and that he would have to kick him into a gallop. As they crossed the quilt-work of snow and grass, the horse would begin to tense for the jump, and his rider would have to let out the reins. They would take the fence quite easily.

Whatever he did, his heart would be half broken. But to be alive, perhaps, was to have a heart half broken and half newborn. That was what Reed had risked at Passchendaele, for he had not gone to war except to come back to love.

Like the soldier he had never been, Cameron spurred his horse toward the ranks of glowing wire. They took the fence. They cleared it by at least two feet, and left it behind in the sunset, a very sad thing.

UMBERTO ECO

THROUGHOUT the 1950s and 1960s, Umberto Eco (1932–) gained increasing fame in Italy for the quality of his research in James Joyce studies, and in semiotics (the cross-cultural study of signs), and for his labours as a producer of quality radio and television programs. Despite these modest and gratifying successes, no one, including the author himself, was prepared for the response to his first novel, *The Name of the Rose*, an intellectual whodunit set in a monastic library, first published in Italian in 1980. The book, quickly translated into dozens of languages, sold millions of copies in hardback, millions more in paperback, and gave many readers their first insight into scriptoria as well as the delights and tribulations of semiotics—a branch of learning renowned for its recondite vocabulary and abstruse texts. *The Name of the Rose* was followed by *Foucault's Pendulum*, which sold nearly as well as its antecedent: both books are famous for confounding general readers, such has been Eco's joy in filling his mystery novels with asides on the hermetic, mediaeval worlds with which he is obviously intimate. Both novels have, perhaps uniquely, been beneficiaries of the author's decision to write and publish commentaries on his own creative writing: in other words, books he has penned about books he has penned.

The author's alacrity with books and their repositories has led him to be perceived, almost against his wishes, as an expert on libraries. As such, he was invited in 1983 to give the keynote address at festivities marking a major anniversary of the Biblioteca Comunale in Milan. Part of his speech was devoted to citing an alphabet of horrors for library users. But much of the talk (excerpted below) was devoted to giving his Italian audience a description of an ideal, or nearly ideal, library, and one can only imagine the surprise of Eco's more chauvinist listeners when they were told that one of these libraries was in Canada.

Umberto Eco first came to this country in 1977, thanks to the Italian Cultural Institute, to give an academic lecture at the University of Toronto. While here, he discovered that the city was then the leading centre in the world for semiotics studies. He returned to Toronto in 1979 and 1981 to take appropriate courses in his field. It was during these visits in particular that he explored the city (which he likens to "a marvellous cocktail between New York and London, at a human size. To me Toronto is the city in which to walk.") and in Toronto he became acquainted with Robarts Library, here so affectionately described. In subsequent years, he has returned frequently to Toronto, not as a student, but as a lecturer in his own right, and as a novelist, to read at Harbourfront.

Apart from his hometown of Bologna, he has lived in Toronto longer than he has lived in any other city.

———————

Now I tell you the story of two libraries of human scale, two libraries I love, visit, and when I can, frequently patronize. I do not mean that they are the best in the world or that there are not others similar to these two: but these are the ones that I have gone to regularly: they are the Sterling Library of Yale, and the new library of the University of Toronto (Robarts), the former for one month, the latter for three months. They are different from each other, at least in the same way that the Pirelli skyscraper in Milan is different from the Church of Saint Ambrose, especially from the architectural point of view. The Sterling Library is a neo-Gothic monastery; that of Toronto is a masterpiece of contemporary architecture. There are differences between them, but I put the two together in order to show that they are the two libraries I really love.

They are open until midnight, and also on Sunday. Toronto has good indexes, with a series of computers that are user-friendly and technologically up-to-date.... The Toronto library also contains information on what is available in neighbourhood libraries. However the most beautiful thing about these two libraries is that a research reader can gain access to the stacks, i.e., you do not ask a librarian for a book; with a card you merely go past an electronic Cerberus, take the elevator, and then you are in the stacks.... The library of the University of Toronto is brightly lit. The student or scholar can wander around, burrow among the books on the shelves, and there are very comfortable armchairs where he can sit and read. At Yale, less so. Then he can pick up the book and make photocopies. Photocopying machines abound; in Toronto there is even an office that changes the one-dollar bills into coins, so that everybody who has enough coins can photocopy a book of even 700-800 pages. The patience of the Canadians is infinite: they wait until I reach the 700th page before complaining. Naturally, you can also take the book out on loan; the rules are very simple and the procedure is expedient. After you have wandered around the twelve or thirteen floors of stacks and have picked up the books you want to read, you write on a card the title of the book you want to borrow, you deliver it to the counter and you leave. Who has access to the stacks? Whoever has a card, which is very easy to obtain (in an hour or so, and by telephone)....

In Toronto, everything is magnetic: the young student who is registering the borrowed book slides the book on a small machine, removing the magnetic contact, and then you go through an electronic door (similar to those at airports) and if you happen to have hidden in your pocket Volume 108 of *Patrologia Latina* a bell starts ringing and the theft is immediately discovered. Naturally, there is a problem in such a library: that is, the extremely high traffic in books; so there is always the difficulty of finding a volume you are specifically seeking, or of finding one that was consulted the previous day. Instead of rooms for general reading, there are carrels or reading booths. The scholar can ask for a special carrel where he can keep his volumes and he can go there to work whenever he likes.

However, when you cannot find the volume you want, you can find out in a few minutes who borrowed the book by tracking it down by telephone. As a consequence, this kind of library has very few watchdogs but lots of clerks....

This library in Toronto suits me. I can spend a whole day there in a state of holy serenity: I read the newspapers, I take the books I choose down to the cafeteria, then I go and look for others if I make any discoveries. I enter the library with the intention of getting involved with English Empiricism, but I end up reading the commentators on Aristotle, I miss the next floor, enter an area where I did not think I would end up (the medical section) and then I find the works of Galen with all the philosophical references. The library, in this way, becomes an adventure.

But what might be the drawbacks to this type of library?...

[One] nuisance is that it allows, encourages, the so-called xerocivilization. The xerocivilization, which is the civilization of the photocopier, carries within itself, together with all the obvious comforts, a series of negative aspects for the editorial world and also for the legal world. Xerocivilization implies the breakdown of the idea of copyright. It is true however that in these libraries (in which there are dozens and dozens of copiers), if someone goes to the reference counter and asks to copy a whole book, the librarian will say that it is impossible because it is against the copyright law. But if you have enough coins, and you copy the book yourself, nobody says anything....

If the library is, as Borges maintains, a model of the universe, let's try to transform it into a human universe ... such as the library of the University of Toronto.

JOHN BURROUGHS

A LTHOUGH he did publish a book of poems, American author
John Burroughs (1837–1921) was—and is—regarded as a literary essayist. Indeed, he was one of the first "nature writers" in the
sense that we use the term today, and in his lifetime was esteemed to
be among America's finest prose stylists.

He was also an influential literary critic. With his book *Walt
Whitman: Poet and Person* he became one of the earliest commentators to signal Whitman's paramount place in American letters. Vari-
ously a journalist, civil servant, and fruit farmer, he spent most of
the latter half of his life in the Catskills writing belles lettres: essays
on science, philosophy, travel, conservation, and, of course, nature
in all its manifestations.

In July 1877, with his wife away for medical treatment, Burroughs and a friend departed for a fishing trip to the Lac St. Jean
region of Quebec. His initial appraisal of his only Canadian sally
was negative: "August 6 [1877] Aaron and I returned from our Canadian trip the 4th, having been gone since July 16th, a long hard trip
of 2,300 miles and not very agreeable or satisfying, except the week
spent in the woods, on Jacques Cartier's river, 65 miles north of Quebec." Such crabbiness is partly explained by the chaotic haste in
which he set out. His departure for a fishing vacation was so dishev-
elled, he actually forgot to take his fishing rod. Yet, with time to
reflect, the nuances of the trip mellowed his response. And by

November of 1877 he had written "The Halcyon in Canada," an essay long and peripatetic like a Canadian creek, an essay as mellifluous as its title. Originally published in *Scribner's Monthly*, it was later printed in his 1879 collection *Locusts and Wild Honey*, a text fundamental to the history of the environmental movement.

---

from THE HALCYON IN CANADA

The halcyon or kingfisher is a good guide when you go to the woods. He will not insure smooth water or fair weather, but he knows every stream and lake like a book, and will take you to the wildest and most unfrequented places. Follow his rattle and you shall see the source of every trout and salmon stream on the continent. You shall see the Lake of the Woods, and far-off Athabaska and Abbitibbe, and the unknown streams that flow into Hudson's Bay, and many others. His time is the time of the trout, too, namely, from April to September. He makes his subterranean nest in the bank of some favorite stream, and then goes on long excursions up and down and over woods and mountains to all the waters within reach, always fishing alone, the true angler that he is, his fellow keeping far ahead or behind, or taking the other branch. He loves the sound of a waterfall, and will sit a long time on a dry limb overhanging the pool below it, and, forgetting his occupation, brood upon his own memories and fancies.

The past season my friend and I took a hint from him, and, when the dog-star began to blaze, set out for Canada, making a big detour to touch at salt water and to take New York and Boston on our way....

The first peculiarity one notices about the farms in this northern country is the close proximity of the house and barn, in most cases the two buildings touching at some point,—an arrangement doubt-less prompted by the deep snows and severe cold of this latitude. The typical Canadian dwellinghouse is also presently met with on entering the Dominion,—a low, modest structure of hewn spruce logs, with a steep roof (containing two or more dormer windows) that ends in a smart curve, a hint taken from the Chinese pagoda....

As we neared Point Levi, opposite Quebec, we got our first view of the St. Lawrence. "Iliad of rivers!" exclaimed my friend. "Yet unsung!"

The Hudson must take a back seat now, and a good way back. One of the two or three great water-courses of the globe is before you. No other river, I imagine, carries such a volume of pure cold water to the sea. Nearly all its feeders are trout and salmon streams, and what an airing and what a bleaching it gets on its course! Its history, its antecedents, are unparalleled. The great lakes are its camping grounds; here its hosts repose under the sun and stars in areas like that of states and kingdoms, and it is its waters that shake the earth at Niagara. Where it receives the Saguenay it is twenty miles wide, and when it debouches into the Gulf it is a hundred. Indeed, it is a chain of Homeric sublimities from beginning to end. The great cataract is a fit sequel to the great lakes; the spirit that is born in vast and tempestuous Superior takes its full glut of power in that fearful chasm. If paradise is hinted in the Thousand Islands, hell is unveiled in that pit of terrors.

Its last escapade is the great rapids above Montreal, down which the steamer shoots with its breathless passengers, after which, inhaling and exhaling its mighty tides, it flows calmly to the sea.

The St. Lawrence is the type of nearly all the Canadian rivers, which are strung with lakes and rapids and cataracts, and are full of peril and adventure.

Here we reach the oldest part of the continent, geologists tell us; and here we encounter a fragment of the Old World civilization. Quebec presents the anomaly of a medieval European city in the midst of the American landscape. This air, this sky, these clouds, these trees, the look of these fields, are what we have always known;

but these houses, and streets, and vehicles, and language, and physiognomy are strange. As I walked upon the grand terrace I saw the robin and kingbird and song sparrow, and there in the tree, by the Wolfe Monument, our summer warbler was at home. I presently saw, also, that our republican crow was a British subject, and that he behaved here more like his European brother than he does in the States, being less wild and suspicious. On the Plains of Abraham excellent timothy grass was growing and cattle were grazing. We found a path through the meadow, and, with the exception of a very abundant weed with a blue flower, saw nothing new or strange,— nothing but the steep tin roofs of the city and its frowning wall and citadel. Sweeping around the far southern horizon, we could catch glimpses of mountains that were evidently in Maine or New Hampshire; while twelve or fifteen miles to the north the Laurentian ranges, dark and formidable, arrested the eye....

To the north and northeast of Quebec, and in full view from the upper parts of the city, lies a rich belt of agricultural country, sloping gently toward the river, and running parallel with it for many miles, called the Beauport slopes. The division of the land into uniform parallelograms, as in France, was a marked feature, and is so throughout the Dominion. A road ran through the midst of it lined with trees, and leading to the falls of the Montmorenci. I imagine that this section is the garden of Quebec. Beyond it rose the mountains. Our eyes looked wistfully toward them, for we had decided to penetrate the Canadian woods in that direction.

One hundred and twenty-five miles from Quebec as the loon flies, almost due north over unbroken spruce forests, lies Lake St. John, the cradle of the terrible Saguenay. On the map it looks like a great cuttlefish with its numerous arms and tentacles reaching out in all directions into the wilds. It is a large oval body of water thirty miles in its greatest diameter. The season here, owing to a sharp northern sweep of the isothermal lines, is two or three weeks earlier than at Quebec. The soil is warm and fertile, and there is a thrifty growing settlement here with valuable agricultural produce, but no market nearer than Quebec, two hundred and fifty miles distant by water, with a hard, tedious land journey besides. In winter the settlement can have little or no communication with the outside world.

To relieve this isolated colony and encourage further development of the St. John region, the Canadian government is building a wagon-road through the wilderness from Quebec directly to the lake, thus economizing half the distance, as the road when completed will form, with the old route, the Saguenay and St. Lawrence, one side of an equilateral triangle. A railroad was projected a few years ago over nearly the same ground, and the contract to build it given to an enterprising Yankee, who pocketed a part of the money and has never been heard of since. The road runs for one hundred miles through an unbroken wilderness, and opens up scores of streams and lakes abounding with trout, into which, until the road-makers fished them, no white man had ever cast a hook.

It was a good prospect, and we resolved to commit ourselves to the St. John road. The services of a young fellow whom, by reason of his impracticable French name, we called Joe, was secured, and after a delay of twenty-four hours we were packed upon a Canadian buckboard with hard-tack in one bag and oats in another, and the journey began. It was Sunday, and we held up our heads more confidently when we got beyond the throng of well-dressed church-goers. For ten miles we had a good stone road and rattled along it at a lively pace. In about half that distance we came to a large brick church, where we began to see the rural population or *habitants*. They came mostly in two-wheeled vehicles, some of the carts quite fancy, in which the young fellows rode complacently beside their girls. The two-wheeler predominates in Canada, and is of all styles and sizes. After we left the stone road, we began to encounter the hills that are preliminary to the mountains. The farms looked like the wilder and poorer parts of Maine or New Hampshire. While Joe was getting a supply of hay of a farmer to take into the woods for his horse, I walked through a field in quest of wild strawberries. The season for them was past, it being the 20th of July, and I found barely enough to make me think that the strawberry here is far less pungent and high-flavored than with us.

The cattle in the fields and by the roadside looked very small and delicate, the effect, no doubt, of the severe climate. We saw many rude implements of agriculture, such as wooden plows shod with iron.

We passed several parties of men, women, and children from Quebec picnicking in the "bush." Here it was little more than a "bush;" but while in Canada we never heard the woods designated by any other term. I noticed, also, that when a distance of a few miles or of a fraction of a mile is to be designated, the French Canadian does not use the term "miles," but says it's so many acres through or to the next place.

This fondness for the "bush" at this season seems quite a marked feature in the social life of the average Quebecker, and is one of the original French traits that holds its own among them. Parties leave the city in carts and wagons by midnight, or earlier, and drive out as far as they can the remainder of the night, in order to pass the whole Sunday in the woods, despite the mosquitoes and black flies. Those we saw seemed a decent, harmless set, whose idea of a good time was to be in the open air, and as far into the "bush" as possible.

The post-road, as the new St. John's road is also called, begins twenty miles from Quebec at Stoneham, the farthest settlement. Five miles into the forest upon the new road is the hamlet of La Chance (pronounced La Shaunce), the last house till you reach the lake, one hundred and twenty miles distant. Our destination the first night was La Chance's; this would enable us to reach the Jacques Cartier River, forty miles farther, where we proposed to encamp, in the afternoon of the next day.

We were now fairly among the mountains, and the sun was well down behind the trees when we entered upon the post-road. It proved to be a wide, well-built highway, grass-grown, but in good condition. After an hour's travel we began to see signs of a clearing, and about six o'clock drew up in front of the long, low, log habitation of La Chance. Their hearthstone was outdoor at this season, and its smoke rose through the still atmosphere in a frail column toward the sky. The family was gathered here and welcomed us cordially as we drew up, the master shaking us by the hand as if we were old friends. His English was very poor, and our French was poorer, but, with Joe as a bridge between us, communication on a pinch was kept up. His wife could speak no English; but her true French politeness and graciousness was a language we could readily understand. Our supper was got ready from our own supplies, while we sat or stood in the open air about the fire. The clearing comprised fifty or sixty acres of rough land in the bottom of a narrow valley, and bore indifferent crops of oats, barley, potatoes, and timothy grass. The latter was just in bloom, being a month or more later than with us. The primitive woods, mostly of birch with a sprinkling of spruce, put a high cavernous wall about the scene. How sweetly the birds sang their notes seeming to have unusual strength and volume in this forest-bound opening! The principal singer was the white-throated sparrow, which we heard and saw everywhere on the route. He is called here *la siffleur* (the whistler), and very delightful his whistle was. From the forest came the evening hymn of a thrush, the olive-backed perhaps, like, but less clear and full than, the veery's.

In the evening we sat about the fire in rude home-made chairs, and had such broken and disjointed talk as we could manage. Our host had lived in Quebec and been a school-teacher there; he had wielded the birch until he lost his health, when he came here and the birches gave it back to him. He was now hearty and well, and had a family of six or seven children about him.

We were given a good bed that night, and fared better than we expected. About one o'clock I was awakened by suppressed voices outside the window. Who could it be? Had a band of brigands surrounded the house? As our outfit and supplies had not been removed from the wagon in front of the door I got up, and, lifting one corner of the window paper, peeped out: I saw in the dim moonlight four or five men standing about engaged in low conversation. Presently one of the men advanced to the door and began to rap and call the name of our host. Then I knew their errand was not hostile; but the weird effect of that regular alternate rapping and calling ran through my dream all the rest of the night. Rat-tat, tat,

tat,—La Chance; rat-tat, tat,—La Chance, five or six times repeated before La Chance heard and responded. Then the door opened and they came in, when it was jabber, jabber, jabber in the next room till I fell asleep.

In the morning, to my inquiry as to who the travelers were and what they wanted, La Chance said they were old acquaintances going a-fishing, and had stopped to have a little talk.

Breakfast was served early, and we were upon the road before the sun. Then began a forty-mile ride through a dense Canadian spruce forest over the drift and boulders of the Paleozoic age. Up to this point the scenery had been quite familiar,—not much unlike that of the Catskills,—but now there was a change; the birches disappeared, except now and then a slender white or paper birch, and spruce everywhere prevailed. A narrow belt on each side of the road had been blasted by fire, and the dry, white stems of the trees stood stark and stiff. The road ran pretty straight, skirting the mountains and threading the valleys, and hour after hour the dark, silent woods wheeled past us. Swarms of black flies—those insect wolves—way-laid us and hung to us till a smart spurt of the horse, where the road favored, left them behind. But a species of large horse-fly, black and vicious, it was not so easy to get rid of. When they alighted upon the horse we would demolish them with the whip or with our felt hats, a proceeding the horse soon came to understand and appreciate. The white and gray Laurentian boulders lay along the roadside. The soil seemed as if made up of decayed and pulverized rock, and doubtless contained very little vegetable matter. It is so barren that it will never repay clearing and cultivating.

Our course was an up-grade toward the highlands that separates the watershed of St. John Lake from that of the St. Lawrence, and as we proceeded the spruce became smaller and smaller till the trees were seldom more than eight or ten inches in diameter. Nearly all of them terminated in a dense tuft at the top, beneath which the stem would be bare for several feet, giving them the appearance, my friend said, as they stood sharply defined along the crests of the mountains, of cannon swabs. Endless, interminable successions of these cannon swabs, each just like its fellow, came and went, came and went, all day. Sometimes we could see the road a mile or two ahead, and it was as lonely and solitary as a path in the desert. Periods of talk and song and jollity were succeeded by long stretches of silence. A buckboard upon such a road does not conduce to a continuous flow of animal spirits. A good brace for the foot and a good hold for the hand is one's main lookout much of the time. We walked up the steeper hills, one of them nearly a mile long, then clung grimly to the board during the rapid descent of the other side.

We occasionally saw a solitary pigeon—in every instance a cock—leading a forlorn life in the wood, a hermit of his kind, or more probably a rejected and superfluous male. We came upon two or three broods of spruce grouse in the road, so tame that one could have knocked them over with poles. We passed many beautiful lakes; among others, the Two Sisters, one on each side of the road. At noon we paused at a lake in a deep valley, and fed the horse and had lunch. I was not long in getting ready my fishing tackle, and, upon a raft made of two logs pinned together, floated out upon the lake and quickly took all the trout we wanted.

Early in the afternoon we entered upon what is called *La Grande Brûlure*, or Great Burning, and to the desolation of living woods succeeded the greater desolation of a blighted forest. All the mountains and valleys, as far as the eye could see, had been swept by the fire, and the bleached and ghostly skeletons of the trees alone met the gaze. The fire had come over from the Saguenay, a hundred or more miles to the east, seven or eight years before, and had consumed or blasted everything in its way. We saw the skull of a moose said to have perished in the fire. For three hours we rode through this valley and shadow of death. In the midst of it, where the trees had nearly all disappeared, and where the ground was covered with coarse wild grass, we came upon the Morancy River, a placid yellow stream twenty or twenty-five yards wide, abounding with trout. We walked a short distance along its banks and peered curiously into its waters. The mountains on either hand had been burned by the fire until in places their great granite bones were bare and white.

At another point we were within ear-shot, for a mile or more, of a brawling stream in the valley below us and now and then caught a glimpse of foaming rapids or cascades through the dense spruce,—a trout stream that probably no man had ever fished, as it would be quite impossible to do so in such a maze and tangle of woods.

We neither met, nor passed, nor saw any travelers till late in the afternoon, when we descried far ahead a man on horseback. It was a welcome relief. It was like a sail at sea. When he saw us he drew rein and awaited our approach. He, too, had probably tired of the solitude and desolation of the road. He proved to be a young Canadian going to join the gang of workmen at the farther end of the road.

About four o'clock we passed another small lake, and in a few moments more drew up at the bridge over the Jacques Cartier River, and our forty-mile ride was finished. There was a stable here that had been used by the road-builders, and was now used by the teams that hauled in their supplies. This would do for the horse; a snug log shanty built by an old trapper and hunter for use in the winter, a hundred yards below the bridge, amid the spruces on the bank of the river, when rebedded and refurnished, would do for us. The river at this point was a swift, black stream from thirty to forty feet wide, with a strength and a bound like a moose. It was not shrunken and emaciated, like similar streams in a cleared country, but full, copious, and strong. Indeed, one can hardly realize how the lesser watercourses have suffered by the denuding of the land of its forest covering, until he goes into the primitive woods and sees how bounding and athletic they are there. They are literally well fed and their measure of life is full. In fact, a trout brook is as much a thing of the woods as a moose or deer, and will not thrive well in the open country.

Three miles above our camp was Great Lake Jacques Cartier, the source of the river, a sheet of water nine miles long and from one to three wide; fifty rods below was Little Lake Jacques Cartier, an irregular body about two miles across. Stretching away on every hand, bristling on the mountains and darkling in the valleys, was the illimitable spruce woods. The moss in them covered the ground nearly knee-deep, and lay like newly fallen snow, hiding rocks and logs, filling depressions, and muffling the foot. When it was dry, one could find a most delightful couch anywhere.

The spruce seems to have colored the water, which is a dark amber color, but entirely sweet and pure. There needed no better proof of the latter fact than the trout with which it abounded, and their clear and vivid tints. In its lower portions near the St. Lawrence, the Jacques Cartier River is a salmon stream, but these fish have never been found as near its source as we were, though there is no apparent reason why they should not be....

I had been told in Quebec that I would not see a bird in the woods, not a feather of any kind. But I knew I should, though they were not numerous. I saw and heard a bird nearly every day, on the tops of the trees about, that I think was one of the crossbills. The kingfisher was there ahead of us with his loud clicking reel. The osprey was there, too, and I saw him abusing the bald eagle, who had probably just robbed him of a fish. The yellow-rumped warbler I saw, and one of the kinglets was leading its lisping brood about through the spruces. In every opening the white-throated sparrow abounded, striking up his clear sweet whistle, at times so loud and sudden that one's momentary impression was that some farm boy was approaching, or was secreted there behind the logs. Many times, amid those primitive solitudes, I was quite startled by the human tone and quality of this whistle. It is little more than a beginning; the bird never seems to finish the strain suggested. The Canada jay was there also, very busy about some important private matter.

One lowery morning, as I was standing in camp, I saw a lot of ducks borne swiftly down by the current around the bend in the river a few rods above. They saw me at the same instant and turned toward the shore. On hastening up there, I found the old bird rapidly leading her nearly grown brood through the woods, as if to go around our camp. As I pursued them they ran squawking with outstretched stubby wings, scattering right and left, and seeking a hiding place under the logs and debris. I captured one and carried it into camp. It was just what Joe wanted; it would make a valuable decoy. So he kept it in a box, fed it upon oats, and took it out of the woods with him.

We found the camp we had appropriated was a favorite stopping-place of the carmen who hauled in supplies for the gang of two hundred road-builders. One rainy day near nightfall no less than eight carts drew up at the old stable, and the rain-soaked drivers, after picketing and feeding their horses, came down to our fire. We were away, and Joe met us on our return with the unwelcome news. We kept open house so far as the fire was concerned; but our roof was a narrow one at the best, and one or two leaky spots made it still narrower.

"We shall probably sleep out-of-doors to-night," said my companion, "unless we are a match for this posse of rough teamsters."

But the men proved to be much more peaceably disposed than the same class at home; they apologized for intruding, pleading the inclemency of the weather, and were quite willing, with our permission, to take up with pot-luck about the fire and leave us the shanty. They dried their clothes upon poles and logs, and had their fun and their bantering amid it all. An Irishman among them did about the only growling; he invited himself into our quarters, and before morning had Joe's blanket about him in addition to his own.

On Friday we made an excursion to Great Lake Jacques Cartier, paddling and poling up the river in the rude box-boat. It was a bright, still morning after the rain, and everything had a new, fresh appearance. Expectation was ever on tiptoe as each turn in the river opened a new prospect before us. How wild, and shaggy, and silent it was! What fascinating pools, what tempting stretches of trout-haunted water! Now and then we would catch a glimpse of long black shadows starting away from the boat and shooting through the sunlit depths. But no sound or motion on shore was heard or seen. Near the lake we came to a long, shallow rapid, when we pulled off our shoes and stockings, and, with our trousers rolled above our knees, towed the boat up it, wincing and cringing amid the sharp, slippery stones. With benumbed feet and legs we reached the still water that forms the stem of the lake, and presently saw the arms of the wilderness open and the long deep blue expanse in their embrace. We rested and bathed, and gladdened our eyes with the singularly beautiful prospect. The shadows of summer clouds were slowly creeping up and down the side of the mountains that hemmed it in. On the far eastern shore, near the head, banks of what was doubtless white sand shone dimly in the sun, and the illusion that there was a town nestled there haunted my mind constantly. It was like a section of the Hudson below the Highlands, except that these waters were bluer and colder, and these shores darker, than even those Sir Hendrik first looked upon; but surely, one felt, a steamer will round that point presently, or a sail drift into view! We paddled a mile or more up the east shore, then across to the west, and found such pleasure in simply gazing upon the scene that our rods were quite neglected. We did some casting after a while, but raised no fish of any consequence till we were in the outlet again, when they responded so freely that the "disgust of trout" was soon upon us....

Caribou abound in these woods, but we saw only their tracks; and of bears, which are said to be plentiful, we saw no signs.

Saturday morning we packed up our traps and started on our return, and found that the other side of the spruce-trees and the vista of the lonely road going south were about the same as coming north. But we understood the road better and the buckboard better, and our load was lighter, hence the distance was more easily accomplished.

I saw a solitary robin by the roadside, and wondered what could have brought this social and half-domesticated bird so far into these wilds. In *La Grande Brûlure*, a hermit thrush perched upon a dry tree in a swampy place and sang most divinely. We paused to listen to his clear, silvery strain poured out without stint upon that unlistening solitude. I was half persuaded I had heard him before on first entering the woods....

We arrived at La Chance betimes, but found the "spare bed" assigned to other guests; so we were comfortably lodged upon the haymow. One of the boys lighted us up with a candle and made level places for us upon the hay.

La Chance was one of the game wardens, or constables appointed by the government to see the game laws enforced. Joe had not felt entirely at his ease about the duck he was surreptitiously taking to town, and when, by its "quack, quack," it called upon La Chance for protection, he responded at once. Joe was obliged to liberate it then and there, and to hear the law read and expounded, and be threatened till he turned pale beside. It was evident that they follow the home government in the absurd practice of enforcing their laws in Canada. La Chance said he was under oath not to wink at or permit any violation of the law, and seemed to think that made a difference.

We were off early in the morning, and before we had gone two miles met a party from Quebec who must have been driving nearly all night to give the black flies an early breakfast. Before long a slow rain set in; we saw another party who had taken refuge in a house in a grove. When the rain had become so brisk that we began to think of seeking shelter ourselves, we passed a party of young men and boys—sixteen of them—in a cart turning back to town, water-soaked and heavy (for the poor horse had all it could pull), but merry and good-natured. We paused a while at the farmhouse where we had got our hay on going out, were treated to a drink of milk and some wild red cherries, and when the rain slackened drove on, and by ten o'clock saw the city eight miles distant, with the sun shining upon its steep tinned roofs.

The next morning we set out per steamer for the Saguenay, and entered upon the second phase of our travels, but with less relish than we could have wished. Scenery hunting is the least satisfying pursuit I have ever engaged in. What one sees in his necessary travels, or doing his work, or going a-fishing, seems worth while, but the famous view you go out in cold blood to admire is quite apt to elude you. Nature loves to enter a door another hand has opened; a mountain view, or a waterfall, I have noticed, never looks better than when one has just been warmed up by the capture of a big trout. If we had been bound for some salmon stream up the Saguenay, we should perhaps have possessed that generous and receptive frame of mind—that open house of the heart—which makes one "eligible to any good fortune," and the grand scenery would have come in as fit sauce to the salmon. An adventure, a bit of experience of some kind, is what one wants when he goes forth to admire woods and waters,—something to create a draught and make the embers of thought and feeling brighten. Nature, like certain wary game, is best taken by seeming to pass by her intent on other matters.

But without any such errand, or occupation, or indirection, we managed to extract considerable satisfaction from the view of the lower St. Lawrence and the Saguenay....

It was very sultry when we left Quebec, but about noon we struck much clearer and cooler air, and soon after ran into an immense wave or puff of fog that came drifting up the river and set all the fog-guns booming along shore. We were soon through it into clear, crisp space, with room enough for any eye to range in. On the south the shores of the great river appear low and uninteresting, but on the north they are bold and striking enough to make it up,—high, scarred, unpeopled mountain ranges the whole way. The points of interest to the eye in the broad expanse of water were the white porpoises that kept rolling, rolling in the distance, all day. They came up like the perimeter of a great wheel that turns slowly and then disappears. From mid-forenoon we could see far ahead an immense column of yellow smoke rising up and flattening out upon the sky and stretching away beyond the horizon. Its form was that of some aquatic plant that shoots a stem up through the water, and spreads its broad leaf upon the surface. This smoky lily-pad must have reached nearly to Maine. It proved to be in the Indian country in the mountains beyond the mouth of the Saguenay, and must have represented an immense destruction of forest timber.

The steamer is two hours crossing the St. Lawrence from Rivière du Loup to Tadousac. The Saguenay pushes a broad sweep of dark blue water down into its mightier brother that is sharply defined from the deck of the steamer. The two rivers seem to touch, but not to blend, so proud and haughty is this chieftain from the north. On the mountains above Tadousac one could see banks of sand left by the ancient seas. Naked rock and sterile sand are all the Tadousacker has to make his garden of, as far as I observed. Indeed, there is no soil along the Saguenay until you get to Ha-ha Bay, and then there is not much, and poor quality at that.

What the ancient fires did not burn the ancient seas have washed away. I overheard an English resident say to a Yankee tourist, "You will think you are approaching the end of the world up here." It certainly did suggest something apocryphal or antemundane,—a segment of the moon or of a cleft asteroid, matter dead or wrecked. The world-builders must have had their foundry up in this neighborhood, and the bed of this river was doubtless the channel through which the molten granite flowed. Some mischief-loving god has let in the sea while things were yet red-hot, and there has been a time here. But the channel still seems filled with water from the mid-Atlantic, cold and blue-black, and in places between seven and eight thousand feet deep (one and a half miles). In fact the enormous depth of the Saguenay is one of the wonders of physical geography. It is as great a marvel in its way as Niagara.

The ascent of the river is made by night, and the traveler finds himself in Ha-ha Bay in the morning. The steamer lies here several hours before starting on her return trip, and takes in large quantities of white birch wood, as she does also at Tadousac. The chief product of the country seemed to be huckleberries, of which large quantities are shipped to Quebec in rude board boxes holding about a peck each. Little girls came aboard or lingered about the landing with cornucopias of birch-bark filled with red raspberries; five cents for about half a pint was the usual price. The village of St. Alphonse, where the steamer tarries, is a cluster of small, humble dwellings dominated, like all Canadian villages, by an immense church. Usually the church will hold all the houses in the village; pile them all up and they would hardly equal it in size; it is the one conspicuous object, and is seen afar; and on the various lines of travel one sees many more priests than laymen. They appear to be about the only class that stir about and have a good time. Many of the houses were covered with birch-bark, the canoe birch,—held to its place by perpendicular strips of board or split poles.

A man with a horse and a buckboard persuaded us to give him twenty-five cents each to take us two miles up the St. Alphonse River to see the salmon jump. There is a high saw-mill dam there which every salmon in his upward journey tries his hand at leaping. A raceway has been constructed around the dam for their benefit, which it seems they do not use till they have repeatedly tried to scale the dam. The day before our visit three dead fish were found in the pool below, killed by too much jumping. Those we saw had the jump about all taken out of them; several did not get more than half their length out of the water, and occasionally only an impotent nose would protrude from the foam. One fish made a leap of three or four feet and landed on an apron of the dam and tumbled helplessly back; he shot up like a bird and rolled back like a clod. This was the only view of salmon, the buck of the rivers, we had on our journey.

It was a bright and flawless midsummer day that we sailed down the Saguenay, and nothing was wanting but a good excuse for being there. The river was as lonely as the St. John's road; not a sail or a smokestack the whole sixty-five miles. The scenery culminates at Cape Trinity, where the rocks rise sheer from the water to a height of eighteen hundred feet. This view dwarfed anything I had ever before seen. There is perhaps nothing this side the Yosemite chasm that equals it, and, emptied of its water, this chasm would far surpass that famous canyon, as the river here is a mile and a quarter deep. The bald eagle nests in the niches in the precipice secure from any intrusion. Immense blocks of the rock had fallen out, leaving areas of shadow and clinging overhanging masses that were a terror and fascination to the eye. There was a great fall a few years ago, just as the steamer had passed from under and blown her whistle to awake the echoes. The echo came back, and with it a part of the mountain that astonished more than it delighted the lookers-on. The pilot took us close around the base of the precipice that we might fully inspect it. And here my eyes played me a trick the like of which they had never done before. One of the boys of the steamer brought to the forward deck his hands full of stones, that the curious ones among the passengers might try how easy it was to throw one ashore. "Any girl ought to do it," I said to myself, after a man had tried and had failed to clear half the distance. Seizing a stone, I cast it with vigor and confidence, and as much expected to see it smite the rock as I expected to live. "It is a good while getting there," I mused, as I watched its course: down, down it went; there, it will ring upon the granite in half a breath; no, down—into the water, a little more than half way! "Has my arm lost its cunning?" I said, and tried again and again, but with like result. The eye was completely at fault. There was a new standard of size before it to which it failed to adjust itself. The rock is so enormous and towers so above you that you get the impression it is much nearer than it actually is. When the eye is full it says, "Here we are," and the hand is ready to prove the fact; but in this case there is an astonishing discrepancy between what the eye reports and what the hand finds out.

Cape Eternity, the wife of this colossus, stands across a chasm through which flows a small tributary of the Saguenay, and is a head or two shorter, as becomes a wife, and less rugged and broken in outline.

From Rivière du Loup, where we passed the night and ate our first "Tommy-cods," our thread of travel makes a big loop around New Brunswick to St. John, thence out and down through Maine to Boston,—a thread upon which many delightful excursions and reminiscences might be strung. We traversed the whole of the valley of the Metapedia, and passed the doors of many famous salmon streams and rivers, and heard everywhere the talk they inspire; one could not take a nap in the car for the excitement of the big fish stories he was obliged to overhear.

The Metapedia is a most enticing-looking stream; its waters are as colorless as melted snow; I could easily have seen the salmon in it as we shot along, if they had come out from their hiding-places. It was the first white-water stream we had seen since leaving the Catskills; for all the Canadian streams are black or brown, either from the iron in the soil or from the leechings of the spruce swamps. But in New Brunswick we saw only these clear, silvershod streams; I imagined they had a different ring or tone also. The Metapedia is deficient in good pools in its lower portions; its limpid waters flowing with a tranquil murmur over its wide, evenly paved bed for miles at a stretch. The salmon pass over these shallows by night and rest in the pools by day. The Restigouche, which it joins, and which is a famous salmon stream and the father of famous salmon streams, is of the same complexion and a delight to look upon. There is a noted pool where the two join, and one can sit upon the railroad bridge and count the noble fish in the lucid depth below. The valley here is fertile, and has a cultivated, well-kept look.

We passed the Jacquet, the Belledune, the Nepissisquit, the Miramichi ("happy retreat") in the night, and have only their bird-call names to report.

NOTES

2 "he planned his attack on the RAF recruiters": See, for example, Frederick-Karl, *William Faulkner, American Writer,* pp. 111-2, and Joseph Blotner, *Faulkner: A Biography*, pp.206-7. Given Faulkner's friendship in New Haven with Lieutenant Todd, a Canadian recruiter, it seems unlikely that Faulkner and Stone could have been so badly informed. However, given the youth of the applicants and their probable nervousness, and in the absence of evidence to the contrary, the legend of the English vicar and the English accent must stand.

4 "when it begins to turn crimson, it is very pretty": William Faulkner, *Thinking of Home: William Faulkner's Letters to His Mother and Father 1918-1925,* ed. James G. Watson, pp. 72-3.

5 "Scotch in kilts, French, Canadians, English": Faulkner, *Thinking of Home,* pp. 80-1.

5 "They are very unselfish and good natured": Faulkner, *Thinking of Home,* p. 83.

5 "I couldn't sleep at all the first night.": Faulkner, *Thinking of Home,* pp. 84-5.

6 "I'll look like a pair of fashionable shoes soon": Faulkner, *Thinking of Home,* p. 88

7 "flat end of the earth at the pole": Faulkner, *Thinking of Home,* p. 93.

7 "it lasts so much longer": Faulkner, *Thinking of Home,* p. 110.

7 "with whom he shared rooms at Wycliffe College": Michael Millgate has treated Faulkner's stay in Toronto with admirable clarity in two articles published in the *University of Toronto Quarterly* (Vol. XXXV, No. 2, Jan. 1966, and Vol. XXXVII, No. 2, Jan. 1968). In the early 1980s, Professor Millgate and I explored Wycliffe College hoping to find Faulkner's domicile, using as

our guide a map showing the room layout in 1917 (supplied to Professor
Millgate in the mid-1960s by one of Faulkner's classmates and fellow cadets).
Alas, the interior of the building had been radically rebuilt over the years,
and we could only approximate where he slept. The outside of the building
(at least the façade facing onto Hoskin Avenue) appears to be unchanged
from Faulkner's time. I am grateful to Michael Millgate for his generosity in
sharing his data with me, and for taking the time to explore Wycliffe College.

7   "think that I am French, from Montreal, for some reason": Faulkner, *Thinking of Home*, p. 102

7   "it's great sport while it lasts": Faulkner, *Thinking of Home*, pp. 116-7

8   "a pilot's licence which I can do quite easily now": Faulkner, *Thinking of
Home*, p. 129.

8   "the nation's finest military tailor, William Scully of Montreal": Joseph Blotner, *Faulkner: A Biography* pp. 229-230.

10   "and ended up hanging on the rafters": Murry C. Falkner, *The Falkners of
Mississippi*, pp. 90-1.

11   "a fictional method which held for much of his career": Karl, *William
Faulkner*, p. 117.

11   "what time and the Armistice had denied": A friend of Faulkner's, William
Evans Stone, recalled seeing Faulkner wearing these coats as late as 1960: "It
was a cold, misty night. He was wearing his trench coat, a favourite garment
since his Royal Canadian Air Force days." This quotation also displays a
common confusion between the RAF and the RCAF (the Canadians did not
have their own nominal air force until after the First World War). Faulkner
appears not to have minded the affiliation with the RCAF, as he never cor-
rected anyone (and there were many) who made the understandable error.
See William Evans Stone, "Our Cotehouse", in *William Faulkner of Oxford*,
ed. James W. Webb and A. Wigfall Green, pp. 76-8.

11   "in order to join the Air Force of the United States": See especially Malcolm
Cowley, *The Faulkner-Cowley File*, pp. 71-84 for a blatant example of
Faulkner's equivocating over the falsehoods of his war record. In a letter to a
nephew (April 3, 1943) who had just enlisted in the USAF, Faulkner, although
generously sending the nephew one of his shoulder pips, stretched the truth
to new lengths: "Enclosed is a luck piece. I wore it on the shoulder strap of
my overcoat. A stripe, light blue, on a khaki band, went with it to show rank:
like Navy rank: one stripe, Pilot Flying Officer (Lieut.), two stripes, Flight
Lieut. (Captain), two and a half, Squadron Leader, three, Wing Commander, four, Group Captain. I don't think you can wear it on your uniform, but
you might ask permission from your Station Commander, tell him where it
came from, your godfather, perhaps you can wear it. If not, you might have it
welded onto a belt buckle, or onto your dog-tag, or clamped onto something

to carry in your pocket. Anyway, keep it with you. You will probably find something else while you are flying that you will believe in, but keep them both. I would have liked for you to have had my dog-tag, RAF, but I lost it in Europe, in Germany. I think the Gestapo has it; I am very likely on their records right now as a dead British flying officer-spy.

"You will find something else as you get along, which you will consider your luck. Flying men always do. I had one. I never found it again after my crack-up in '18. But it worked all right, as I am still alive." See Joseph Blotner, *Selected Letters of William Faulkner*, p. 170. The account of the "crash" which Faulkner gave to *The New Yorker* in the Nov. 28, 1931 issue is almost identical to the depiction of a crash in "Love," an unpublished and unusual short story abandoned by Faulkner after approximately 50 pages. Faulkner wrote three drafts of "Love" as prose, and a film treatment survives. The *New Yorker* crash account has parallels, of course, with the rough touchdown of "Landing in Luck."

12 "half-credible claim to the *élan* of being an aviator": Blotner, *William Faulkner*, p. 427.

12 "which may have been the decisive turnabout of his life.": Karl, *William Faulkner*, p. 111.

13 "it is likely that he would have returned to Canada to do his duty": Letter from WF to Robert Haas, October 5, 1940. See Blotner, *Selected Letters of William Faulkner*, p. 136.

13 "Am proud to have belonged to RAF even obscurely": Blotner, *Selected Letters of William Faulkner*, p. 297.

30 "(the First had been held in 1909 in England)": Robert Donald, *The Imperial Press Conference in Canada*, pp. 1-5.

30 "we leap out of the train at little stopping places and take hurried, busy exercise": Anna Sebba, *Enid Bagnold: A Biography*, p. 77

30 "They hoick us from banquet to banquet and take us over steel plants and round the towns": Sebba, p. 78.

37 "But I have been there—and I admit that I loathe it": John Dos Passos, *The Fourteenth Chronicle: Letters and Diaries of John Dos Passos*, ed. Townsend Ludington, pp. 100-1.

41 "the entire pattern of his apprenticeship would have been seriously altered and damaged": Charles Fenton, *The Apprenticeship of Ernest Hemingway*, p. 75.

43 "Hadley became pregnant": James R. Mellow, *Hemingway: A Life Without Consequences*, pp. 233-4.

44 "the arch-criminal, Ernest Hemingway": Sylvia Beach, *Shakespeare and Company*, pp. 86-8.

44 "from this city": Quoted in James R. Mellow, *Hemingway: A Life Without Consequences*, p. 241.

45 "to beat Hindmarsh": Charles Fenton, *The Apprenticeship of Ernest Hemingway*, pp. 256-7.

45 " 'That saves me killing him,' said Hemingway": Tom Williams, letter to the editor, *Frank Magazine*, May 14, 1992, p. 29

45 "the fistulated asshole of the father of seven among Nations": Quoted by Kenneth S. Lynn, in *Hemingway*, p. 219.

47 "I like them": Ernest Hemingway, *Dateline: Toronto*, pp. 415-6.

47 "where he had been able to write well": Hemingway, Introduction to *The Short Stories of Ernest Hemingway*, p.v.

48 "Toronto had destroyed ten years of his literary life": Both remarks are found in Carlos Baker, *Ernest Hemingway*, pp. 153-4.

48 "It was why I was sad to quit newspaper work": Quoted in Charles Fenton, *The Apprenticeship of Ernest Hemingway*, p. 257.

49 "a story of all the tough guys": Quoted in Carlos Baker, *Ernest Hemingway*, p. 208.

52 "the inverted r's of my mother's family.": Elizabeth Bishop, "The Country Mouse" in *Elizabeth Bishop: The Collected Prose* p. 17.

53 "the suburbs of Boston where I lived later": Elizabeth Bishop, in an interview with Ashley Brown, originally printed in *Shenandoah* 17, No.2 (Winter 1966), pp. 3-19, reprinted in *Elizabeth Bishop and Her Art*, p. 291.

54 "that this was not true": From "Primer Class" in *Elizabeth Bishop: The Collected Prose*, pp. 10-11.

54 "the smoothness of yard-goods": "The Map" in Elizabeth Bishop, *The Complete Poems 1927-1979*, p. 3.

54 "poetry and music than religion": Robert Giroux, Introduction to *Elizabeth Bishop: The Collected Prose*, p.xiii.

54 "So I'm full of hymns": Quoted by Robert Giroux, Introduction to *Elizabeth Bishop: The Collected Prose*, p.xiii.

76 "I was unequivocally happy": Mark Strand in a letter dated Sept. 1, 1992, to Greg Gatenby.

80 "Douglas Hyde was as well-known as James Joyce": John Montague to Greg Gatenby, personal communication, Jan. 1992.

81 "a profound effect on Yeats": *Dictionary of Irish Literature*, p. 303.

81 "one of the most memorable trips of his life": J.E. and G.W. Dunleavy, *Douglas Hyde: A Maker of Modern Ireland*, p. 144.

83 "behind a caribou skin": J.E. and G.W. Dunleavy, *Douglas Hyde: A Maker of Modern Ireland*, p. 146.

84 "think only of themselves": J.E. and G.W. Dunleavy, *Douglas Hyde: A Maker of Modern Ireland*, p. 150.

84 "than in six months in Dublin": J.E. and G.W. Dunleavy, *Douglas Hyde: A Maker of Modern Ireland*, p. 148.

84 "refreshing to be among them": J.E. and G.W. Dunleavy, *Douglas Hyde: A Maker of Modern Ireland*, p. 150-1.

84 "a myriad of Canadian newspapers": The poem was first published in *The University Monthly* in Fredericton in January 1892.

To Canada

Oh beautiful northern maiden
    When the ice-god unbendeth his bow
What a robe have I seen thee arrayed in
    When thou doffest thy garland of snow!
What a robe have I seen thee arrayed in
    Where the wild rivers jubilant flow,
And the maple with buds over-laden
    Exults over Winter her foe,
        And nestles a greeting to me.

The singers of summer are coming
    To hide in thy tremulous hair,
I hear the gold woodpecker drumming
    In the depth of the forest in there,
And the little bird-fairy that humming
    Shoots by where the flowers are fair,
From the south with the sun they are coming
    To joy in thy odorous air,
        And taste of the wonderful North.

The ravaging winter is over,
    The Wizard of Silence is fled,
And violets peep from their cover,
    And daisies are raising their head.
Earth blushes to life like a lover,
    And wakes in her emerald bed,
And she and the heavens above her
    In torrents of sunshine are wed,
        Forgetting the swoon of the snow.

By the pole slope that Canada faces
    The ice giants hurtle and reel,
For her seven months winter she cases

> Her land in a casket of steel.
> Yet I pine for her mighty embraces
>   In the home of the moose and the seal,
> And I pine for her beautiful places
>   And sad is the feeling I feel
>   When snow flakes remind me of her.

85 "organized in six bands" For an historical overview of Malecite history and customs see the booklet (currently available from the Canadian Ministry of Indian and Northern Affairs) by Wilson D. Wallis and Ruth Sawtell Wallis, *The Malecite Indians of New Brunswick* (Ottawa, Ministry of Northern Affairs and National Resources, 1957).

94 "into the sixties": Personal communication with Caroline Greene and Louise Dennys, August 1, 1993.

103 "I still like it": Personal correspondence with Greg Gatenby, Aug. 9, 1992.

110 "horrible delays and *déceptions*": Henry James, *The Complete Notebooks of Henry James*, ed. Leon Edel, pp. 318-9.

111 "better than anything in England": From a letter generously sent to me by Leon Edel, July 21, 1991.

130 "in its embryonic development": Most of my description of Twain's relations with Canadian publishers is based upon the remarkably well-documented essay by Gordon Roper, "Mark Twain and his Canadian Publishers: A Second Look," published in the *Papers of the Bibliographical Society of Canada*, v.5 (Toronto, Bibliographical Society of Canada, 1966). Roper's emphasis, of course, is on Twain, but he does refer in passing to similar problems faced by some other prominent American writers. Despite the excellence of Roper's article, book piracy by Canadians in the Victorian era is an area of our literary history deserving of far deeper and wider study; there seems to be no book-length study of the issue, and I was unable to locate any doctoral theses dealing with the matter.

131 "think it would hold water": Hamlin Hill, *Mark Twain's Letters to his Publishers, 1876-1894*, p. 67. Quoted in Gordon Roper, "Mark Twain and His Canadian Publishers: A Second Look," p. 38.

132 "if the thing can be done": Quoted in Gordon Roper, "Mark Twain and His Canadian Publishers: A Second Look," p. 48.

132 "in every village in the Union": Quoted in Gordon Roper, "Mark Twain and His Canadian Publishers: A Second Look," pp. 48-9.

133 "you would enjoy your birthday, I think": Mark Twain, *Mark Twain's Letters*, Albert Bigelow Paine, ed., v.1, pp. 407-9.

134 "so I break off my sermon": letter, dated Montreal, Nov.29/81, courtesy of Mark Twain Project. The letter also appears in *The Love Letters of*

Mark Twain, Dixon Wechter, ed., pp. 205-6.

135 "thoroughly worn out": Unpublished letter dated Quebec, Midnight, Dec. 2 [1881].

135 "or enjoy the food": Mark Twain, *Mark Twain's Letters*, Albert Bigelow Paine, ed., v.I, pp. 409-10.

137 "I was all right, again": Letter dated May 24, 1883, courtesy of the Mark Twain Project. The letter also appears in Dixon Wechter, ed., *The Love Letters of Mark Twain*, pp. 215-6.

139 "Nova Scotia and New Brunswick coasts": This yachting trip is the least well-documented of Twain's visits to Canada. Paine (in *Mark Twain: A Biography*, p.1139) refers briefly to the trip, and tantalizingly mentions a log of the journey kept by Twain. The log has not been published in its entirety. See also brief references in Paine's *Mark Twain's Letters*, v.2, p. 712.

144 "the periodical *Grip*": The influential periodical (1883-1896) which Smith had founded but two months previously. A young Maritimer, Charles G.D. Roberts, recently arrived in Toronto, was the journal's first editor. In her authorized biography of Roberts (who went on to become one of the most famous poets in Canada) Elsie Pomeroy relates an anecdote the details of which could only have come from Roberts himself: "During that winter, Roberts had the great pleasure of meeting Matthew Arnold.... Arnold, tall, not unlike Dr. Pelham Edgar in appearance ... was most gracious and cordial to the young poet. When Goldwin Smith presented Roberts, Arnold put his arm around him, saying "This is the boy I wanted to meet," and then kept Roberts beside him. He remembered *Orion* [Roberts' first book of poems] and also remembered having written Roberts a most encouraging and helpful letter at the time of its publication." See Elsie Pomeroy, *Sir Charles G.D. Roberts*, p.50.

145 "better than nothing": Goldwin Smith, *A Selection from Goldwin Smith's Correspondence*, ed. Arnold Haultain, pp. 155-6.

145 "furs for you in Canada": Matthew Arnold, *Letters of Matthew Arnold 1848-1888*, ed. George W.E. Russell, v.2, p. 254.

145 "a goose to prefer it to Canada": Arnold, *Letters*, v.2, pp. 257-8.

145 "following his visit": Holograph letter, Art Gallery of Ontario Archives, Toronto.

149 "politically formative year of his life": John Sutherland, note in his edition of Jack London's *John Barleycorn*, p. 225.

150 "sat down and wept": Jack London, *The Road*, pp. 60-2.

150 "my success as a storywriter": Earle Labor, "Jack London" entry in *Dictionary of Literary Biography*, v. 78, p. 250.

154 "my married sister in San Francisco": Jack London, *The Road*, pp. 142-6.

155 "it out pretty well": letter to Elwyn Hoffman, June 17, 1900, in *The Letters of Jack London*, ed. Earle Labor *et al.*, v. 1, p. 194.

156 "the protection of life and property": Pierre Berton, *Klondike*, p.xxiii.

157 "the White Horse River": By far the finest treatment of Jack London and the Klondike is, appropriately, *Jack London and the Klondike* by Franklin Walker. No discussion of London in the North is possible without reference to this impressive volume.

158 "I mean a year from now": Letter to Cornelius Gepfert, Nov. 5, 1900, in *The Letters of Jack London*, v. 1, p. 217. See his letters (July 12, 1901, and Sept. 22, 1901) to the same correspondent for similar wishful thinking.

158 "a tithe as well": Letter to Hellier Denselow, July 28, 1914, *in The Letters of Jack London*, v. 3, p. 1358

158 "in both Canada and the United States.": Arthur Stringer, "The Canada Fakers," *Canada West Magazine*, Oct. 1908. See also the issues of Dec. 1908, March 1909 and April 1909, for follow-up articles and responses. For Jack London's vigorous response, see his letter (Aug. 2, 1909) in King Hendricks and Irving Shepard, *Letters from Jack London*, pp. 282-4, also published in Earle Labor *et al.*, *The Letters of Jack London*, v.2, p. 822-3. Any Canadian will note immediately the near-total absence of the word "Canada" from critical discussions of Jack London by foreign, especially American, scholars. Even today, U.S.A. savants seem unable to bring themselves to use the word in their descriptions of London's Klondike writing. Capitalized words such as Northland, Far North, North, and Arctic endlessly pepper their texts, as if, no doubt subconsciously but nevertheless grudgingly, they cannot quite bring themselves to believe that such a great adventure story did *not* happen in the United States.

177 "two very different places": Considering the wide currency of the Voltaire remark, it is surprising to me that it seems to have escaped lengthy analysis by the academic world. For an interesting semi-scholarly discussion of Voltaire's views of Canada, see "L'opinion de Voltaire sur le Canada", a discussion among savants recorded in *Séances et Travaux de L'Académie des Sciences Morales et Politiques: Compte Rendu* (Paris, 1900), where an argument is made that Voltaire was referring to the Ohio Territory when speaking of the acres of snow "near Canada."

177 "moved, even distressed": The following excerpts from his sometimes punning, sometimes ambiguous correspondence, while far from comprehensive, give a sense of the range of his remarks. Reading these and other references to Canada, I believe it is obvious that when Voltaire expresses rage about Canada, it is not about the land itself so much as the incompetence of the French government and Paris administration in their decisions regarding Canada.

Aug. 19, 1745: "So we gain Flanders in order to regain Canada one day.

Meanwhile, beavers become expensive; I am tempted to propose bigwigs instead of [beaver] hats. So please find under your high hat, your bigwig, some means of giving us peace."

May 5, 1758: "I wish Canada were at the bottom of the frozen sea, even if it is with the holy Jesuit fathers of Quebec, and I would that we were busy in Louisiana planting cocoa, indigo, tobacco and fruit, instead of paying four million in order to save face before our enemy, the English, who understand far better than the gentlemen of Paris the nature of the sea and the world of business."

Nov. 21, 1759: "Canada is only an eternal topic for unhappy wars, and I am fed up and fuming."

Oct. 13, 1759: "We French had the bright idea of establishing ourselves in Canada, on top of the snow between the bears and the beavers, of course only after the English had settled their flourishing colonies four hundred leagues from the most beautiful place on earth, and yet they still chase us out of our Canada."

May 8, 1763: "Will the Government never pardon me for having said the English have taken Canada? (and in parentheses had offered four years ago to sell to the English, which would have solved the matter once and for all, as the brother of Mr. Pitt had proposed to me)? But let us put Canada aside and talk about the Iroquois who would have me burned at the stake for having cast an ironic glance on these most ridiculous matters."

178   "more true to life": Letter to Gabriel Cramer. See *The Complete Works of Voltaire*, ed. Theodore Besterman, Correspondence, D 14279.

178   "the critical attention that it deserves": By far the best and most comprehensive evaluation in English is John S. Clouston, *Voltaire's Binary Masterpiece L'Ingénu Reconsidered*. But see also the lucid introduction by Roger Pearson to his 1990 translation of *L'Ingénu*, and the fine introduction to the 1960 translation by J.H. Brumfitt and M.I.G. Davis.

198   "called *Letters from America*": See Martin and Hall, *Rupert Brooke in Canada*, for an excellent and comprehensive treatment of Brooke's opinions of and association with Canada.

216   "thrilling accounts of them all": Edith Lewis, *Willa Cather Living* (New York, Knopf, 1953) pp. 153-4.

217   "which is so striking": Benjamin George, "Willa Cather as a Canadian Writer," in *Western American Literature*, Vol. XI, No.3, (Nov. 1976), pp. 259-60.

217   "fragments of her soul": Sergeant, *Willa Cather: A Memoir*, p. 243.

244   "The shock was so great that it killed her likewise": The text is quoted in the editor's introduction to "Evangeline" in *The Complete Poetical Works of Henry Wadsworth Longfellow*, p. 71.

245 "heard of or read": Manning Hawthorne and H.W.L. Dana, *The Origin and Development of Longfellow's "Evangeline,"* p. 12.

245 "Acadia for the subject of my song": Hawthorne and Dana, *The Origin and Development of Longfellow's "Evangeline,"* p. 14.

245 "not Evangeline but rather 'Gabrielle'": In his *Journal*, Longfellow wrote: "[Nov.] 28th [1845]. Set about 'Gabrielle,' my idyl in hexameters, in earnest. I do not mean to let a day go by without adding something to it, if it be but a single line." On December 7th he continued, "I know not what name to give to,—not my new baby, but my new poem. Shall it be 'Gabrielle,' or 'Celestine,' or 'Evangeline'?" See *Life of Henry Wadsworth Longfellow With Extracts from his Journals and Correspondence*, ed. Samuel Longfellow (Boston, Houghton Mifflin, 1891), p. 26.

245 "I wrote the last lines this morning": Hawthorne and Dana, *The Origin and Development of Longfellow's "Evangeline,"* p. 36.

246 *"Essais poétiques"*: Including a translation of the work of a well-known poet may have been simple homage—or a canny career move. Lemay proudly sent a copy to Longfellow upon publication. Longfellow, a Classics professor, fluent in French, replied tactfully on October 27, 1865:

> More especially, let me thank you for that portion of your work which is devoted to "Evangeline." I feel under great obligations to you for this mark of your regard; not only that you have chosen this poem for translation, but you have performed the always difficult task with so much ability and success.
>
> There is only one thing that I demur at; namely your making my Evangeline die; "Elle avait terminé sa malheureuse vie." However, I shall not quarrel about that. My object is not to criticize, but to thank you...

(The Letters of Henry Wadsworth Longfellow, ed. Andrew Hilen, v. 4, p. 514.) Five years later, Lemay published a revised translation, upon which Longfellow commented, "In looking over your version of Evangeline" I am struck again by its many beauties, and my former impression is confirmed. I am glad to see that you have made the slight change at the close, thus following more faithfully the original." *(The Letters of Henry Wadsworth Longfellow*, ed. Andrew Hilen, v. 5, p. 390).

246 "ecclesiastical, historical, or poetical": Quoted in W. Sloane Kennedy, *Henry W. Longfellow*, p. 279.

247 "the icebergs, the frozen seas, Labrador": Samuel Longfellow, *Life of Henry Wadsworth Longfellow With Extracts from his Journals and Correspondence*, p. 81.

247 "Down East: The Missionary of Acadie": Hawthorne and Dana, *The Origin and Development of Longfellow's "Evangeline,"* p. 10.

247 "the south shore of Lake Superior": See Chase S. Osborn and Stellanova Osborn, *"Hiawatha" With Its Original Indian Legends*, p. 61. Various myths

and incidents used in Hiawatha had wide currency among the Ojibway and cannot be said to be purely American or Canadian. One Indian maiden's hymn adapted by Longfellow had clear origins in Canada. For discussion of this see C. and S. Osborn, *Schoolcraft-Longfellow-Hiawatha*, pp. 210 ff.

247 "the American side is preferable": [June] 10th…. Leave Niagara for Toronto after dinner today. After supper, took a stroll through the main street of Toronto with E.; then to bed in our gloomy Castle of Otranto, called the Rossin House.

[June] 12th. From Kingston, down the St. Lawrence in the steamboat; first, among the "Thousand Islands," then down the rapids, which is exciting. But in the afternoon we ran aground in Lake St. Francis, where we remained fast, till two steam-tugs got us off in the evening and conveyed us to the shore. We passed the night snugly at the landing-place.

[June] 13th. Started early, and passed through the lake, and down the Coteau, Cedar, and Cascade Rapids, and across Lake St. Louis. At a wretched little Indian village of huts, with moss-covered roofs, Caughnawaga, the Indian pilot Baptiste came on board and steered us down the last and most dangerous of the rapids, the Lachine. We reached Montreal for breakfast, at the St. Lawrence hotel. A day in Montreal is not much time for so nice a place. We all like it. Pass the forenoon in rambling through the streets, and the afternoon in a drive round the mountain.

[July 10th] I can make no record of these days. Better leave them wrapped in silence. Perhaps some day God will give me peace. (Samuel Longfellow, *Life of Henry Wadsworth Longfellow; With Extracts from his Journals and Correspondence*, pp. 384-5.)

259 "aspiration towards independence": Arthur Conan Doyle, *Memories and Adventures*, pp. 309-10.

260 "'Try Canadian Pacific Railway,' said Holmes": Arthur Conan Doyle, "The Adventure of Black Peter," in *The Strand*, v. 27 (March 1904), p. 84.

260 "precipitously to their deaths": Christopher Redmond, *Welcome to America, Mr. Sherlock Holmes*, p. 134.

262 "the conditions which they loved": Arthur Conan Doyle, "Western Wanderings," in *The Cornhill Magazine*, March 1915, pp. 290-1.

262 "his memoir of the period": , Arthur Conan Doyle, *Our Second American Adventure*.

263 "the psychic possibilities of the place": Doyle, *Our Second American Adventure*, p. 201.

263 "on British soil": Doyle, *Our Second American Adventure*, p. 198.

263 "no more pleasant waiting place": Doyle, *Our Second American Adventure*, p. 198.

264 "baseball is the better game": Doyle, *Our Second American Adventure*, p. 224.

266 "its psychic possibilities": Doyle, *Our Second American Adventure*, pp. 228-23.

266 "the main streets of the Lakehead": "Sherlock Holmes' Lakehead Link," article in *Lakehead Living*, July 15, 1986, p. 25.

267 "a European standard": Doyle, *Our Second American Adventure*, p. 233.

267 "free thought and free institutions": Doyle, *Our Second American Adventure*, p. 234.

268 "by others are diabolical": Doyle, *Our Second American Adventure*, p. 237.

268 "but always interesting": Address to the Canadian Club, Ottawa, July 2, 1914. Near the end of his address, Doyle then must have abashed his audience, given that he was known as a prose writer, not a poet. Certainly he asked for its forbearance. His conclusion, it was noted at the time, was met with "prolonged cheers":

> Before I sit down I will read a verse or two in which I was able, perhaps, to compress a little more of that feeling which Canada has awakened, than can be done in prose. Poetry is like the pemmican of literature: it is compressed thought, and one can mingle emotion with it, which one cannot always do in prosaic speech. I will read you, if I may, these few lines before I take my seat. I call it "The Athabasca Trail" since Athabasca is the place where we have for some time been living an open air life.

The Athabasca Trail

My life is gliding downwards; it speeds swifter to the day
When it shoots the last dark canon to the Plains of Far-away,
But while its stream is running through the years that are to be,
The mighty voice of Canada will ever call to me.
I shall hear the roar of rivers where the rapids foam and tear,
I shall smell the virgin upland with its balsam-laden air,
And shall dream that I am riding down the winding woody vale,
With the packer and the packhorse on the Athabasca Trail.

I have passed the warden cities at the eastern water-gate,
Where the hero and the martyr laid the corner stone of State,
The *habitant, coureurs de bois*, and hardy *voyageur*,
Where lives a breed more strong at need to venture or endure?
I have seen the gorge of Erie where the roaring waters run,
I have crossed the Inland Ocean, lying golden in the sun,
But the last and best and sweetest is the ride by hill and dale,
With the packer and the packhorse on the Athabasca Trail.

I'll dream again of fields of grain that stretch from sky to sky,
And the little prairie hamlets, where the cars go roaring by,
Wooden hamlets as I saw them—noble cities still to be

To girdle stately Canada with gems from sea to sea;
Mother of a mighty manhood, land of glamour and of hope,
From the eastward sea-swept Islands to the sunny western slope,
Ever more my heart is with you, ever more till life shall fail,
I'll be out with pack and packer on the Athabasca Trail.

275 "slain in duels": Richard Aldington, "Introduction" to Cyrano de Bergerac's *Voyages to the Moon and the Sun*, p. 17.

276 "the beginning of the eighteenth century": Aldington, Introduction to Cyrano de Bergerac's *Voyages to the Moon and the Sun*, p. 4.

276 "Richard Aldington": Aldington, Introduction to Cyrano de Bergerac's *Voyages to the Moon and the Sun*, p. 4.

277 "persecution and punishment": Aldington, Introduction to de Bergerac's *Voyages to the Moon and the Sun*, p. 38.

277 "Gulliver in Brobdingnag": William A. Eddy, *Gulliver's Travels: A Critical Study*, pp. 22 and 61.

285 "the <u>English</u>": Underlined ten times in the original.

286 "the creation of the world": Charles Dickens, *The Pilgrim Edition: The Letters of Charles Dickens*, ed. Madeline House *et al.*, v. 3, pp. 210-11.

286 "nothing but Beauty and Peace": *Letters of Charles Dickens*, v.3, p. 216.

287 "since leaving home": *Letters of Charles Dickens*, v. 3, p. 226.

287 "*The Frozen Deep*": See the entry for Wilkie Collins in this volume.

287 "surrounded by English": *Letters of Charles Dickens*, v. 6, pp. 67-9.

297 "who could understand Dickens' aims": Catherine Peters, *The King of Inventors*, p. 99.

298 "I burst into tears at it": Queen Victoria and Hans Christian Andersen both quoted in Catherine Peters, *The King of Inventors*, p. 174.

299 "life-changing (some say damaging) for Ternan": See Claire Tomalin's wonderful *The Invisible Woman: The Story of Nelly Ternan and Charles Dickens* for a full description of the evolution of the affair.

299 "He literally electrified the audience": Kenneth Robinson, *Wilkie Collins*, p. 114.

299 "*A Tale of Two Cities*": Robinson, *Wilkie Collins*, p.108.

300 "like Wardour in private life": Quoted in Peters, *The King of Inventors*, p. 179.

300 "the last night of the Frozen Deep": Quoted in Peters, *The King of Inventors*, p. 188.

302 "the pressure of such a force": Robert Louis Brannan, *Under the Management of Mr. Charles Dickens*, p. 19.

302 "Recent scholarship": Brannan, *Under the Management of Mr. Charles Dickens*, pp. 1-2 ff.

302 "the rest of his life": Robinson, *Wilkie Collins*, p. 102. Peters also notes in her biography (*The King of Inventors*, p. 21) that Collins discovered the beard "helped to balance his face, compensating for the bulging forehead and disguising a slight weakness about the chin."

303 "the common trinity of tourist sites": Letter to Sebastien Schlesinger, December 25, 1873 (fMS Am 1363, Houghton Library, Harvard University).

349 "citizens of Alsace and Lorraine do the same?": Edward Baxter, Introduction to Verne's *Family Without A Name*, pp. i-ii.

363 "refined, spiritualized, and pure": Quoted in Charles Edward Stowe, *The Life of Harriet Beecher Stowe Compiled from Her Letters and Journals* p. 75.

365 "with him into Kentucky": H.B. Stowe, *A Key to Uncle Tom's Cabin*, p. 26.

366 "I passed for a madman": *An Autobiography of Rev. Josiah Henson 1789-1876*, p. 95.

366 "one of the most flourishing in Canada": Stowe, *Key To Uncle Tom's Cabin*, p. 27.

367 "the cataract's fury": Described in Thomas F. Gossett's *Uncle Tom's Cabin and American Culture*, pp. 282-3.

367 "God Save the Queen": Quoted in Gossett, *Uncle Tom's Cabin and American Culture*, p. 370.

367 "all running concurrently": Cited in Gossett, *Uncle Tom's Cabin and American Culture*, p. 369.

381 "I have not seen any": Quoted in Peter Raby, *Samuel Butler: A Biography*, pp. 147-8.

382 "a decent restaurant": Hans-Peter Breuer, *The Note-Books of Samuel Butler*, v. 1, p. 78.

382 "without seeming to get any nearer": Breuer, v. 1, p. 61.

386 "its twelve performances of that season": Lord Derwent, *Rossini and Some Forgotten Nightingales*, pp. 61-2.

387 "the new attributes brought by Rossini into music": Francis Toye, *Rossini: A Study in Tragi-Comedy*, p. 21.

387 "recently been issued": A Mercury Records LP (SR 2-9009). The compact disc recording features Bruno Praticò, Alessandra Rossi, Bruno de Simone, and the English Chamber Orchestra (Claves CD 50-9101). The video (Teldec Video 9031-71479-3) records a live performance of 1989 featuring John del Carlo, Janice Hall, David Quebler, Alberto Rinaldi, and the Stuttgart Radio Symphony Orchestra.

401 "three separate trips to Canada": Borges' most important encounter with

Canada happened in 1968. In that year, he spoke at the National Library in Ottawa, at the Sidney Smith Building at the University of Toronto, and at Sir George Williams (now Concordia) University in Montreal. The Toronto visit is perceptively and amusingly reported by John Robert Colombo in *Canadian Forum*, v. 48 (1968), pp. 6-9. Borges made at least one other trip to Canada: Prime Minister Pierre Trudeau, in the early 1980s, arranged for him to fly directly to Ottawa from Argentina for a private meeting.

401 "he's a bad broadcaster": Quoted by Colombo. See note immediately above.

403 "he really had been to this country": Stanley J. Kunitz and Howard Haycraft, *Twentieth Century Authors*, p. 260.

404 "that Le Rouge was a natural poet": Blaise Cendrars, *Complete Postcards from the Americas/Poems of Road and Sea*, trans. Monique Chefdor, p. 56.

409 "'100% Canadian'": Mark Helprin in a letter dated August 15, 1991, to Greg Gatenby.

428 "the city in which to walk": Umberto Eco to Greg Gatenby, personal letter, Jan. 13, 1989.

431 "65 miles north of Quebec": Quoted in Barrus, Clara Barrus, *The Life and Letters of John Burroughs*, p. 197.

431 "forgot to take his fishing rod": Barrus, *The Life and Letters of John Burroughs*, p. 196.

EXCERPT SOURCES

Adcock, Fleur. "Coast to Coast." *The Honest Ulsterman.* No. 75 (May 1984), pages 30-34. Reprinted by permission of the author.

Arnold, Matthew. Letter to Goldwin Smith, 2 May 1884. Reprinted by permission of the Art Gallery of Ontario, Edward P. Taylor Research Library and Archives, Toronto.

Bagnold, Enid. *Enid Bagnold's Autobiography.* London: Heinemann, 1969. © 1969 Timothy Angus Jones, Laurian Comtesse D'Harcourt, Richard Bagnold Jones, and Dominic Jones. Reprinted by permission of Reed Book Services.

Bishop, Elizabeth. "In the Village." From *The Collected Prose.* Edited by Robert Giroux. New York: Farrar, Straus, & Giroux, 1984. Copyright © 1984 by Alice Methfessel. Reprinted by permission of Farrar, Straus, & Giroux, Inc.

Bishop, Elizabeth. "The Map." *The Complete Poems 1927-1979.* New York: Farrar, Straus, & Giroux, 1983. Copyright © 1979, 1983 by Alice Methfessel. Reprinted by permission of Farrar, Straus, & Giroux, Inc.

Blackwood, Algernon. *Episodes before Thirty.* Toronto: Cassell and Company, Ltd., 1923. Reprinted by permission of A.P. Watt Ltd.

Borges, Jorge Luis, with Kodama, Maria. "The Totem." *Atlas.* Translated by Anthony Kerrigan. New York: E.P. Dutton, 1985. Copyright © 1984 by Editorial Sudamericana S.A. English translation Copyright © 1985 by Anthony Kerrigan. Used by permission of Dutton Signet, a division of Penguin Books USA Inc.

Breton, André. *Arcane 17.* Translated by Zack Rogow. © Zack Rogow, reprinted from *Arcanum 17* (Los Angeles: Sun & Moon Press, 1994). Published originally in

France as *Arcane 17* (Jean-Jacques Pauvert). Reprinted by permission of Sun & Moon Press. Also published in Canada by Coach House Press.

Brooke, Rupert. *The Letters of Rupert Brooke*. Edited by Geoffrey Keynes. New York: Harcourt, Brace, and World, 1968. Reprinted by permission of Faber and Faber Ltd.

Burroughs, John. "The Halcyon in Canada." *The Complete Writings of John Burroughs*. Volume 3, *Locusts and Wild Honey*. New York: William Wise, 1924.

Butler, Samuel. "A Psalm of Montreal." *The Essential Samuel Butler*. Edited by G.D.H. Cole. London: Jonathan Cape, 1950.

Cable, George Washington. *George W. Cable: His Life and Letters*. Edited by Lucy Leffingwell Cable Bikle. New York: Charles Scribner's Sons, 1928.

Camus, Albert. *American Journals*. Translated by Hugh Levick. New York: Paragon House Publishers, 1987. Reprinted by permission of Paragon House.

Cather, Willa. "Before Breakfast." *The Old Beauty and Others*. New York: Alfred A. Knopf, 1948. Copyright 1948 by Alfred A. Knopf, Inc. Reprinted by permission of the publisher.

Cendrars, Blaise. "Thousand Islands", "Vancouver", and "North." *Complete Postcards from the Americas/Poems of Road and Sea*. Translated by Monique Chefdor. Berkeley: University of California Press, 1976. Copyright © 1976 The Regents of the University of California. Reprinted by permission of University of California Press.

Collins, Wilkie. *The Frozen Deep and Other Tales*. London: Chatto & Windus, 1874.

Cyrano de Bergerac, Savinien. *Voyages to the Moon and the Sun*. Translated by Richard Aldington. New York: E.P. Dutton & Co., 1923. Reprinted by permission of George Routledge & Sons, Ltd.

Dickens, Charles. *American Notes*. 2 vols. London: Chapman and Hall, 1842.

Dos Passos, John. *The Fourteenth Chronicle*. Edited by Townsend Ludington. Boston: Gambit Incorporated, 1973. Reprinted by permission of Townsend Ludington.

Doyle, Arthur Conan. "To the Rocky Mountains in 1914." *Memories and Adventures*. London: Hodder and Stoughton Limited, 1924.

Eco, Umberto."De Biblioteca." *Sette anni di desideri*. Milan: Bompiani, 1983. Original translation by Francesca Valente and Greg Gatenby. Reprinted by permission of the author.

Faulkner, William. "Landing in Luck." In *William Faulkner: Early Prose and Poetry*. Edited by Carvel Collins. Toronto: Little, Brown and Company, 1962.

——*Thinking of Home: William Faulkner's Letters to His Mother and Father 1918-1925*. Edited by James G. Watson. New York: W.W. Norton & Company, 1992. Letters Copyright © 1992 by W.W. Norton. Reprinted by permission of W. W. Norton.

Greene, Graham. "Dear Dr. Falkenheim." *Collected Stories*. London: The Bodley Head and William Heinemann, 1972. © Verdant S.A. 1972.

Helprin, Mark. "Passchendaele." *The New Yorker*. 18 October 1982, 50-58. Reprinted by permission of The Wendy Weil Literary Agency, Inc. Copyright © 1982 by Mark Helprin.

Hemingway, Ernest. "Canadians: Wild/Tame." and "I Like Canadians." *Dateline: Toronto*. Edited by William White. New York: Charles Scribner's Sons, 1985. Reprinted with permission of Charles Scribner's Sons, an imprint of Macmillan Publishing Company, from *Ernest Hemingway: Dateline Toronto*, edited by William White. Copyright © 1985 Mary Hemingway, John Hemingway, Patrick Hemingway, and Gregory Hemingway.

Hyde, Douglas. "On Some Indian Folk-lore" *Language, Lore, and Lyrics*. Kill Lane, Blackrock: Irish Academic Press, 1986. Reprinted by permission of Douglas Sealy.

James, Henry. *Portraits of Places*. London: Macmillan and Co., 1883.

London, Jack. "In a Far Country." *The Son of the Wolf*. New York: Houghton, Mifflin, and Company, 1900.

Longfellow, Henry Wadsworth. *The Complete Poetical Works of Henry Wadsworth Longfellow*. New York: Houghton Mifflin Company, 1922.

[Rossini, Gioacchino]. Rossi, Gaetano. *La Cambiale di Matrimonio*. Music by Gioacchino Rossini. Original translation by Francesca Valente and Greg Gatenby.

Rossi, Gaetano. *La Cambiale di Matrimonio*. Music by Gioacchino Rossini. Original translation by Francesca Valente and Greg Gatenby.

Sinclair, Clive. "The Creature on My Back." *Hearts of Gold*. London: Allison & Busby, 1979. Reprinted by permission of the author.

Stowe, Harriet Beecher. "From the St. John's, South, to the St. John's, North." *Hearth & Home*, June 5, 1869, 376-77, and June 12, 1869, 392-93.

Strand, Mark. "The House in French Village." *Selected Poems*. Atheneum: New York: 1980. Copyright 1979, 1980 by Mark Strand. Reprinted by permission of Alfred A. Knopf, Inc.

Tournier, Michel. *Gemini.* Translated by Anne Carter. London: Collins, 1981. Originally published as *Les Météores* by Michel Tournier. Copyright © Gallimard, 1975. Reprinted by permission of Editions Gallimard.

Twain, Mark. "Dinner Speech." In *Mark Twain Speaking.* Edited by Paul Fatout. Iowa City: University of Iowa Press, 1976.

——Letter to Olivia Clemens, 2 December 1881. Mark Twain's previously unpublished words quoted here are copyright 1993 by Manufacturers Hanover Trust Company as Trustee of the Mark Twain Foundation, which reserves all reproduction or dramatization rights in every medium. Quotation is made with the permission of the University of California Press and Robert H. Hirst, General Editor, Mark Twain Project.

Verne, Jules. *The Fur Country.* Translated by N. D'Anvers. Boston: J.R. Osgood, 1874.

Voltaire, François Marie Arouet de. "The Ingenu." *Candide and Other Stories.* Translated by Roger Pearson. Oxford: Oxford University Press, 1990. © Roger Pearson 1990. Reprinted from *Candide and Oher Stories* by Voltaire, translated by Roger Pearson (World's Classics, 1990) by permission of Oxford University Press.

Every effort has been made to contact copyright holders; in the event of an inadvertent omission, please notify the publisher.

BIBLIOGRAPHY

Adcock, Fleur. Letter to author, 9 August 1992.

Arnold, Matthew. Letter to Goldwin Smith, 2 May 1884. Art Gallery of Ontario Archives, Toronto.

[Arnold, Matthew.] *Letters of Matthew Arnold. Volume II: 1848-1888.* Edited by George W.E. Russell. New York: Macmillan and Co., 1895.

Baker, Carlos. *Ernest Hemingway.* New York: Scribner, 1969.

Barrus, Clara. *The Life and Letters of John Burroughs.* Boston: Houghton Mifflin, 1925.

Beach, Sylvia. *Shakespeare and Company.* Lincoln, Nebraska: University of Nebraska Press, 1980.

Berton, Pierre. *Klondike.* (Revised Edition.) Markham, Ontario: Penguin Books, 1972.

Bishop, Elizabeth. *The Collected Prose.* Edited by Robert Giroux. New York: Farrar, Straus, & Giroux, 1984.

——. *The Complete Poems 1927–1979.* New York: Farrar, Straus, & Giroux, 1983.

Blain, Virginia; Grundy, Isobel; and Clements, Patricia, Editors. *The Feminist Companion to Literature in English.* New Haven: Yale University Press, 1990.

Blotner, Joseph. *Faulkner: A Biography.* 2 Vols. New York: Random House, 1974.

Brown, Ashley. "An Interview with Elizabeth Bishop." *Elizabeth Bishop and her Art.* Edited by Lloyd Schwartz and Sybil P. Estes. Ann Arbor: University of Michigan Press, 1983.

Breuer, Hans-Peter. *The Note-Books of Samuel Butler.* Lanham, Maryland: University Press of America, 1984.

Brown, E. K. "Homage to Willa Cather." *Yale Review* 36 (September 1946): 77-92.

[Butler, Samuel]. *The Notebooks of Samuel Butler.* Edited by Hans-Peter Breuer.

Lanham, Maryland: University Press of America, 1984.

Cendrars, Blaise. *Complete Postcards from the Americas/Poems of Road and Sea.* Translated by Monique Chefdor. Berkeley: University of California Press, 1976.

Chefdor, Monique. *Blaise Cendrars.* Boston: Twayne, 1980.

Clouston, John S. *Voltaire's Binary Masterpiece* L'Ingénue *Reconsidered.* New York: Peter Lang, 1986.

Collins, Wilkie. *The Frozen Deep and Other Tales.* London: Chatto & Windus, 1874.

———. Letter to Sebastian Schlesinger, 25 December 1873. fMS Am 1363 Houghton Library, Harvard University, Cambridge, Massachusetts.

Collins, Wilkie, and Dickens, Charles. *Under the Management of Mr. Charles Dickens.* Edited by Robert Louis Brannan. New York: Cornell University Press, 1966.

Colombo, John Robert. "On Meeting Jorge Luis Borges." *Canadian Forum* 48 (April 1968): 6-9.

Cowley, Malcolm. *The Faulkner-Cowley File.* New York: The Viking Press, 1966.

Cyrano de Bergerac, Savinien. *Voyages to the Moon and the Sun.* Translated by Richard Aldington. New York: E.P. Dutton & Co., 1923.

Derwent, Lord. *Rossini and Some Forgotten Nightingales.* London: Duckworth, 1934.

[Dickens, Charles.] *The Letters of Charles Dickens.* Edited by Mamie Dickens and Georgina Hogarth. New York: Macmillan and Co.,1893.

———. *The Pilgrim Edition: The Letters of Charles Dickens.* Edited by Madeline House *et al.* Oxford: Clarendon Press, 1974.

Dictionary of American Biography.

Dictionary of Irish Literature

Dictionary of Literary Biography

Dictionnaire de Biographie Française.

Donald, Robert. *The Imperial Press Conference in Canada.* London: [n.d., 1922?].

[Dos Passos, John.] *The Fourteenth Chronicle: Letters and Diaries of John Dos Passos.* Edited by Townsend Ludington. Boston: Gambit Incorporated, 1973.

Doyle, Arthur Conan. "The Adventure of Black Peter." *The Strand Magazine* 27 (March 1904): 243-255.

———. *Memories and Adventures.* London: Hodder and Stoughton Limited, 1924.

———. *Our Second American Adventure.* London: Hodder and Stoughton Limited, 1924

——— "Some Impressions." In *Addresses Delivered Before the Canadian Club of Ottawa*

1914-1915. Edited by F.A. Acland. Ottawa: Rolla L. Crain Co., Limited, 1915.

——. "Western Wanderings." *The Cornhill Magazine* 38 (February, March, and April 1915): 145-152, 289-297, 433-43.

Doyle, James. *North of America: Images of Canada in the Literature of the United States 1775-1900.* Toronto: ECW Press, 1983.

——. *Yankees in Canada.* Downsview, Ontario: ECW Press, 1980.

Dunleavy, Janet Egleson and Gareth W. *Douglas Hyde: A Maker of Modern Ireland.* Berkeley: University of California Press, 1991.

Eddy, William A. *Gulliver's Travels: A Critical Study.* Gloucester, Mass.: Peter Smith, 1963.

Falkner, Murry C. *The Falkners of Mississippi.* Baton Rouge: Louisiana State University Press, 1967.

Faulkner, William. "Interview in *The New Yorker.*" In *Lion in the Garden: Interviews with William Faulkner, 1926-1962.* Edited by James B. Meriwether and Michael Millgate. New York: Random House, 1968.

——. "Landing in Luck." In *William Faulkner: Early Prose and Poetry.* Edited by Carvel Collins. Toronto: Little, Brown and Company, 1962.

——. "Love." Manuscripts Department, University of Virginia Library, Charlottesville, Virginia.

——. "Manservant." In *Faulkner's MGM Screenplays.* Edited by Bruce F. Kawin. Knoxville: University of Tennessee Press, 1982.

[Faulkner, William.] *Selected Letters of William Faulkner.* Edited by Joseph Blotner. New York: Random House, 1977.

——. *Thinking of Home: William Faulkner's Letters to His Mother and Father 1918-1925.* Edited by James G. Watson. New York: W.W. Norton & Company, 1992.

Fenton, Charles. *The Apprenticeship of Ernest Hemingway.* New York: Farrar, Straus, & Young, 1954.

George, Benjamin. "Willa Cather as a Canadian Writer." *Western American Literature* 11 (November 1976): 249-61.

Gossett, Thomas F. *Uncle Tom's Cabin and American Culture.* Dallas: Southern Methodist University Press, 1985.

Hawthorne, Manning, and Henry Wadsworth Longfellow Dana. *The Origin and Development of Longfellow's "Evangeline."* Portland, Maine: The Anthoensen Press, 1947.

Hemingway, Ernest. *Dateline: Toronto.* Edited by William White. New York: Charles Scribner's Sons, 1985.

——. *The Short Stories of Ernest Hemingway.* New York: Charles Scribner's Sons, 1955.

[Hemingway, Ernest.] *Selected Letters.* Edited by Carlos Baker. New York: Scribner, 1981.

Henson, Josiah. *An Autobiography of the Rev. Josiah Henson, 1789-1876.* London: Frank Cass and Company Limited, 1971.

Howells, W.D., and Mark Twain. *The Niagara Book.* New York: Doubleday, Page & Co., 1901.

Hyde, Douglas. "To Canada." *The University Monthly* 11 (January 1892): 1.

Institut de France. "L'opinion de Voltaire sur le Canada." *Séances et Travaux de L'Académie des Sciences Morales et Politiques.* (1900): 412-19.

James, Henry. *The Complete Notebooks of Henry James.* Edited by Leon Edel and Lyall H. Powers. New York: Oxford University Press, 1987.

Karl, Frederick. *William Faulkner, American Writer.* New York: Weidenfeld & Nicolson, 1989.

Kennedy, W. Sloane. *Henry W. Longfellow.* Boston: D. Lothrop & Company, 1882.

Kunitz, Stanley. *American Authors 1600-1900.* New York: The H.W. Wilson Company, 1938.

———. [Dilly Tante, pseud.] *Living Authors: A Book of Biographies.* New York: The H. W. Wilson Company, 1931.

Kunitz, Stanley J., and Howard Haycraft. *Twentieth Century Authors.* New York: The H.W. Wilson Company, 1961.

Leacock, Stephen. "Mark Twain and Canada." *Queen's Quarterly* 42 (Spring 1935): 68-81.

Lewis, Edith. *Willa Cather Living.* New York: Alfred A. Knopf, 1953.

London, Charmian. *The Book of Jack London.* New York: The Century Co., 1921.

London, Jack. *John Barleycorn.* Edited by John Sutherland. Oxford University Press, 1984.

———. *The Road.* Edited by I.O. Evans. London: Arco Publications, 1967.

[London, Jack.] *Letters from Jack London.* Edited by King Hendricks and Irving Shepard. New York: Odyssey Press, 1965.

———. *The Letters of Jack London.* Edited by Earle Labor *et al.* Stanford, California: Stanford University Press, 1988.

Longfellow, Henry Wadsworth. *The Complete Poetical Works of Henry Wadsworth Longfellow.* New York: Houghton Mifflin Company, 1922.

[Longfellow, Henry Wadsworth.] *The Letters of Henry Wadsworth Longfellow.* Volumes 4-5. Edited by Andrew Hilen. Cambridge, Massachusetts: The Belknap Press of Harvard University Press, 1972, 1982.

———. *Life of Henry Wadsworth Longfellow with Extracts from his Journals and Correspondence.* Volume 2. Edited by Samuel Longfellow. New York: Houghton Mifflin and Company, 1891.

Lorch, F.W. *The Trouble Begins at Eight: Mark Twain's Lecture Tours.* Ames, Iowa: Iowa State University Press, 1968.

Lynn, Kenneth S. *Hemingway.* London: Simon and Schuster, 1989.

Martin, Sandra, and Roger Hall. *Rupert Brooke in Canada.* Toronto: Peter Martin Associates, 1978.

McCullough, David. "Elizabeth Bishop." In *People, Books, and Book People,* 20-22. New York: Harmony Books, 1981.

Mellow, James R. *Hemingway: A Life Without Consequences.* New York: Houghton Mifflin Company, 1992.

Millgate, Michael. "Faulkner in Toronto: A Further Note." *University of Toronto Quarterly* 37:2 (January 1968): 197-202.

———. "William Faulkner, Cadet." *University of Toronto Quarterly.* 35:2 (January 1966), 117-32.

National Cyclopedia of American Biography

Osborn, Chase S. and Stellanova. *"Hiawatha" With Its Original Indian Legends.* Lancaster, Pennsylvania: The Jaques Cattell Press, 1944.

———. *Schoolcraft-Longfellow-Hiawatha.* Lancaster, Pennsylvania: The Jaques Cattell Press, 1942.

Paine, Albert Bigelow. *Mark Twain: A Biography.* New York: Harper and Brothers, 1912.

Peters, Catherine. *The King of Inventors: A Life of Wilkie Collins.* London: Secker and Warburg, 1991.

Pomeroy, Elsie. *Sir Charles G. D. Roberts.* Toronto: The Ryerson Press, 1943.

Raby, Peter. *Samuel Butler: A Biography.* London: The Hogarth Press, 1991.

The Reader's Encyclopedia of American Literature.

Redmond, Christopher. *Welcome to America, Mr. Sherlock Holmes.* Toronto: Simon & Pierre, 1987.

Robinson, Kenneth. *Wilkie Collins.* London: The Bodley Head, 1951.

Roper, Gordon. "Mark Twain and his Canadian Publishers: A Second Look." *Papers of the Bibliographical Society of Canada.* Volume 5 (1966), 30-89.

Rossi, Gaetano. *La Cambiale di Matrimonio.* Music by Gioacchino Rossini. [Sound Recording, CD.] Featuring Bruno Praticò, Alessandra Rossi, Bruno de Simone, and the English Chamber Orchestra (Claves CD 50-9101), 1991.

———. *La Cambiale di Matrimonio.* Music by Gioacchino Rossini. [Sound Recording, LP.] Mercury Records (SR 2-9009).

[Rossini, Gioacchino]. Rossi, Gaetano. *La Cambiale di Matrimonio.* Music by Gioacchino Rossini. [Sound Recording, CD.] Featuring Bruno Praticò, Alessandra Rossi, Bruno de Simone, and the English Chamber Orchestra (Claves CD 50-9101), 1991.

——. Rossi, Gaetano. *La Cambiale di Matrimonio*. Music by Gioacchino Rossini. [Sound Recording, LP.] Mercury Records (SR 2-9009).

Sebba, Anna. *Enid Bagnold: A Biography*. London: Weidenfeld & Nicolson, 1986.

Sergeant, Elizabeth Shepley. *Willa Cather: A Memoir*. New York: J.B. Lippincott, 1953.

[Smith, Goldwin.] *A Selection from Goldwin Smith's Correspondence*. Edited by Arnold Haultain. Toronto: McClelland and Goodchild, 1913.

Stone, Williams Evans. "Our Cotehouse." In *William Faulkner of Oxford*. Edited by James W. Webb and A. Wigfall Green. Nashville, Tennessee: Louisiana State University Press, 1965.

Stowe, Charles Edward. *Life of Harriet Beecher Stowe Compiled from Her Letters and Journals*. New York: Houghton, Mifflin and Company, 1889.

Stowe, Harriet Beecher. *Dred; A Tale of the Great Dismal Swamp*. London: Andrews and Company, 1856.

——. *A Key to Uncle Tom's Cabin*. Boston: John P. Jewett & Co., 1853.

——. *Uncle Tom's Cabin*. New York: Houghton, Mifflin and Company, 1894.

Strand, Mark. Letter to Greg Gatenby, 1 September 1992.

Stringer, Arthur. "The Canada Fakers." *Canada West* 4 (October 1908): 1137-1147.

Tomalin, Claire. *The Invisible Woman: The Story of Nelly Ternan and Charles Dickens*. London: Viking, 1990.

Toye, Francis. *Rossini: A Study in Tragi-Comedy*. London: William Heinemann Ltd., 1934.

Twain, Mark [Samuel Langhorne Clemens]. *Following the Equator*. Hartford, Connecticut: The American Publishing Company, 1897.

——. Letters to Olivia Clemens, 29 November 1881, 2 December 1881, 24 May 1883. Mark Twain Papers, The Bancroft Library, University of California, Berkeley, California.

——. *The Man That Corrupted Hadleyburg*. New York: P.F. Collier & Son Co., 1901.

——. *Mark Twain Speaking*. Edited by Paul Fatout. Iowa City: University of Iowa Press, 1976.

[Twain, Mark.] *Mark Twain's Letters*. Edited by Albert Bigelow Paine. New York: Harper & Bros., 1917.

——. *Mark Twain's Letters to his Publishers, 1876-1894*. Edited by Hamlin Hill. Berkeley and Los Angeles: University of California, 1967.

——. *The Love Letters of Mark Twain*. Edited by Dixon Wechter. New York: Harper & Brothers, 1947.

Verne, Jules. *The Claim on Forty-Mile Creek: Part One of the Golden Volcano*. Translated by I.O. Evans. London: Arco Publications, 1962.

———. *Family Without a Name.* Translated by Edward Baxter. Toronto: N.C. Press Limited, 1982.

———. *The Fur Country.* Translated by N. D'Anvers. Boston: J.R. Osgood, 1874.

———. *The Works of Jules Verne.* Volume 13. Edited by Charles F. Horne. New York: Vincent Parke and Company, 1911.

Voltaire, François Marie Arouet de. *Candide and other stories.* Translated by Roger Pearson. Oxford: Oxford University Press, 1990.

———. *The Complete Works of Voltaire.* Volume 116. Edited by Theodore Besterman. Banbury, Oxfordshire: The Voltaire Foundation, Thorpe Mandeville House, 1974.

———. *L'Ingénu and Histoire de Jenni.* Edited by J.H. Brumfitt and M.I. Gerard Davis. Oxford: Basil Blackwell, 1960.

[Voltaire, François Marie Arouet de.] *Voltaire's Correspondence.* Edited by Theodore Besterman. Geneva: Institut et Musée Voltaire, 1958-65.

Walker, Franklin. *Jack London and the Klondike.* San Marino, California: The Huntington Library, 1966.

Wallis, Wilson D. and Ruth Sawell. *The Malecite Indians of New Brunswick.* Ottawa: Ministry of Northern Affairs and Natural Resources, 1957.

Newspapers and Periodicals

The Atlantic Monthly

The Evening Telegram (Toronto)

Frank Magazine

The Gazette (Montreal)

The Globe (Toronto)

The Globe and Mail (Toronto)

Lakehead Living

The Mail (Toronto)

The Mail & Empire (Toronto)

The Political Register

The Star Weekly

The Toronto Daily Star

ACKNOWLEDGEMENTS

During an interview with Earle Birney at his apartment on Balliol Street in Toronto in 1978, he regaled me with stories of many authors, but his detailed descriptions of Emma Goldman lecturing at the Labour Temple on Gerrard Street widened my eyes and my horizons: this book is one result of that first experience of a larger world.

Special accolades are owed to Francesca Valente, Director of the Italian Cultural Institute, Toronto. Her indefatigable generosity in helping with translations was humbling to behold. She and her husband, Professor Branko Gorjup, as friends, have been as oaks when foul winds were blowing heavy.

Ann Beattie, while trying to enjoy a holiday, found a waif manuscript of Faulkner for me in Charlottesville. I owe her much, including at least two days of vacation.

Martine Charron was an insightful translator, and helped me to see how Voltaire saw Canada.

Marian Fowler, contemplating a book similar to mine, on learning that my work was well underway, magnanimously withdrew from the field and was wonderfully openhanded with her research notes. For this behaviour, she is a model and is to be commended.

Steven Temple and David Mason are two of the many Canadian antiquarian book dealers who have been unstinting in sharing their inimitable knowledge of authors with me. Thanks also to William Hoffer, Deborah Dearlove and Janet Inksetter for helping with particular writers.

Among librarians, Richard Landon, Chief of the Thomas Fisher Rare Book Library, University of Toronto, has been exemplary. I have always found his contributions of fact or opinion exciting and relevant, and his comments and suggestions perennially poignant. His staff have consistently endured my last-minute or unusual requests with grace and forbearance. The staff at the Perkins Library, Duke University, Durham, North Carolina showed this northener what must have been extraordinary southern hospitality during my three months in their stacks; I continue to marvel at the generosity of their assistance. Bruce Whiteman, Head Librarian at McGill University, was ever willing to drop more important matters to handle my questions about souls in Montreal; for that relief, much thanks.

No writer could want a more dedicated, conscientious, and hard-working assistant than Peter LaRocca. His uncomplaining labours over what were too often inordinate hours were much above the call of duty. The accuracy of his research saved me hundreds of hours—and much anxiety. I hope he finds a university department worthy of his dedication to scholarship and hard work.

While not a Luddite, I am no expert with computers, so a gigabyte of gratitude to Ningsheng Tao, and to George Rodaro for more than once saving my bacon as well as my files. My fulltime staff at the Reading Series make any boss proud and my writing tasks less haggard: special thanks to Geoffrey Taylor, Laura Comello, Carla Lucchetta, Alexandra Montgomery, Iain Newbigin, Christine Rassias and Claudia Li.

The following also deserve special thanks for the help they offered: Debra Adams, Regional Communications Officer, Indian and Inuit Affairs, Amherst, Nova Scotia. Lynda Anthony. Margaret Atwood. Denison Beach. Andrew Bean, Deputy Curator, Dickens House Museum, London, England. Claire Bourassa. Janice Braun, Editorial Assistant, Mark Twain Papers, Bancroft Library, University of California. Helen Burkes, Special Collections, Howard-Tilton Memorial Library, Tulane University, New Orleans. Barry Callaghan. Dr. C.A. Christie, Directorate of History, National Defence Headquarters, Ottawa. George Elliot Clarke. Adrienne Clarkson. Philip Collins, Professor of English, University of Leicester. John Robert Colombo. Michael Coren. Bob Crewe, *Toronto Star.* Wendy Dathan, Curator, Grand Manan Museum, Grand Harbour, Grand Manan, N.B. Robertson Davies. Janet Egleson Dunleavy and Gareth W. Dunleavy. Professor James Doyle, Wilfrid Laurier University. Leon Edel. Laura A. Endicott, Public Service Assistant, Special Collections, University of Virginia Library. Ezra T. Ernst, Permissions Coordinator, Little, Brown and Company. Anne Ferdinands, Ministry of the Environment, Lands & Parks, Victoria, B.C. Mary Flagg, Manager and Research Officer, The Harriet Irving Library, University of New Brunswick. Shawna L. Fleming, Editorial Associate, Mark Twain Papers, Bancroft Library, University of California. Goldwin S. French, Editor-in-Chief, Ontario Historical Study Series. Roy and Margaret Gatenby. Graeme Gibson. Alain Giroux, The Archives, Art Gallery of Ontario. Norah Hague, McCord Museum of Canadian History, Notman Photographic Archives, Montreal. Simon Hernandez, Mark Twain Project, Bancroft Library, University of California. Sara S. Hodson, Curator of Literary Manuscripts, and Catharine Powell, Huntington Gallery and Library. Cameron Hollyer and Victoria Gill, Arthur Conan Doyle Room, Metropolitan Toronto Reference Library. Staff of Houghton Library, Harvard University. William Howarth, Professor of English, Princeton University. Dr.

M. Kapches, Royal Ontario Museum, Toronto. Michael Kenneally. E. Bruce Kirkham, Professor of English, Ball State University, Muncie, Indiana. Hermione Lee. John Lindahl, Curator, Willa Cather Historical Center, Red Cloud, Nebraska. Janice O'Connor, Museum Technician, Longfellow National Historic Site, Cambridge, Massachusetts. Townsend Ludington, American Studies Dept., University of North Carolina. Gary A. Lundell, Reference Specialist, University of Washington Libraries. Margaret Maloney, Toronto Public Libraries. Alberto Manguel. Margaret I. McBurney. Robert McGhee, Archaeological Survey of Canada. Gary L. Menges, Head, Special Collections, University of Washington Libraries. Bruce Meyer. Robert Michel, University Archivist, McGill University. Michael Millgate, Professor of English, University of Toronto. Brett Millier. Staff, Mississippi Department of Archives and History. Paul Monlezun, Research Assistant, Directorate of History, National Defence Headquarters, Ottawa. John Montague. Albert Moritz. New York Historical Society. Richard Ogar, Bancroft Library, University of California, Berkeley. Linda Oliver, Patricia Goldman, and the Staff of Pratt Library, Victoria University. Paragon House Publishers. Catharine Peters. Chris Petter, University Archives, University of Victoria, B.C. L.R. Pfaff, Deputy Librarian/Reference Librarian, Art Gallery of Toronto. Peter Raby. Susan Ravdin, Special Collections, Bowdoin College Library, Brunswick, Maine. Christopher Redmond. Christopher Reid, Faber & Faber, London. Stewart Renfrew, Archivist, Queen's University Archives, Kingston. Staff of the Interlibrary Loan Department, Robarts Library, University of Toronto. Micheline Robert, Reference Consultant, Public Archives of Canada. Diana Royce, Librarian, Stowe-Day Foundation. John Ralston Saul. Douglas Sealy. Margaret Cather Shannon. A.J. Shortt, Curator, National Aviation Museum. Arthur Smith, Opera America, Washington, D.C. Janet Adam Smith. Helen C. Southwick. Bernard L. Stein, The Riverside Press. Phyllis Sutherland. Edward P. Taylor Research Library and Archives. Freda Taylor, National Library, Ottawa. Thomas A. Tenney, English Dept., College of Charleston, Charleston, S.C. Wendy Thomas, Public Service Librarian, Schlesinger Library, Radcliffe College. Michel Tournier. Lord Tweedsmuir. Isabel Vincent. Barbara Wilson, Research Center Manager, Archives of American Art, Smithsonian Institution. James Woodress, Professor of English, University of California.

After fifteen years of research in this field, I am in the embarrassing position of knowing that there are many people I have forgotten to include in this list. For their omission from the acknowledgements, I beg their forgiveness.

INDEX